SONG OF THE FORGOTTEN

SARA A. LATIMER

Oakhaven
Thornley
Highthorn Castle
Guardians Watch
Gyldmare
Haverford
Ashbourne
Ashbourne Mount
Granger House
Oaken Channel

Whiterok
North Elder Sea
N
W
E
S
ountry of Gaultaine

To my mother, her mother, her mother, and hers. I carry you all within my hooting laughter, toothy grin, and love of reading.

Content Advisory

This story is intended for adult readers. It includes mature themes such as sexuality and death. It is not suitable for younger audiences.

PROLOGUE

"You are a princess," Mother said into my shoulder, her words a warm breath against my cheek, "and royals do not cry."

She pulled away to inspect me, her forced smile failing to reach her eyes, which appeared more blue because of the red that edged them. Clearly, royals cried, just not in front of others.

"Be a good girl for Vega at Granger House." She narrowed her gaze. "Learn as much as you can. Study hard, read lots of books, become a strong rider. Learn all the things needed to become a proper lady for when you return to court."

I looked down, knowing it was goodbye.

Mother lifted my chin. "I'll come and visit you with the new baby. How does that sound, my love? Papa, your little brother, and me."

I nodded in obedience. Then, horses trotted up, a carriage in tow. Mother noted them and struggled to her feet. Lady's maids rushed to her side. Papa was not there to help her up.

"I am *fine*," she said as she made it to her usual stance, maneuvering her swollen belly under layers of fur and gown. Gingerly, she fixed the crown atop her head, Highthorn Castle a shadow looming behind her.

The frigid wind whipped her hair into a fury as fat snowflakes stuck to her raven locks. This vision of Mother would remain forever frozen in that moment, like the snow-covered ground on that frostbitten day.

"Come now, Princess Elowyn," said Vega with an outstretched hand. She led me to the waiting carriage.

I was too little to climb up myself. Vega scooped me up with ease and placed me safely inside before returning to Mother.

"Take care of her, Vey."

"Of course, Your Majesty." Vega bowed, but Mother pulled her into a long embrace. The pair clung to one another as if the moment they let go, the whole world would shatter.

Then, without another word, Vega turned and walked to the carriage. She held her chin high despite the frown tugging on her lips. She boarded, horses huffed, and we lurched forward.

I jumped to the window for one last look at Mother, hoping a wave goodbye would stop her from forcing a smile or crying in secret. I watched as she grew smaller and smaller and smaller.

No one ever came to visit me at Granger House. No Mother, no Papa, and no baby.

Chapter 1

"We're late, Elowyn," Vega said through spent breath, over the clipped sounds of our heels.

"I wouldn't be late if I didn't have to dress up in this ridiculous garb," I muttered, pulling at the maroon brocade bodice that bit into my ribs.

Laughter shrilled down the wide hall. The scent of mulled wine and crackling pork skin followed it.

Twenty years had passed since I'd last walked Highthorn Castle. I hardly remembered it, having been barely a child when I left. Yet its memory haunted me every day I was away. My father's deafening silence had only deepened that dread.

Until his letter arrived.

Elowyn,

I welcome you to Highthorn Castle for the Yule Day feast. We expect your arrival tomorrow morning.

Great be the Guardians,

King Eadric Blackthorn

It was the first letter he had ever sent me directly, and I wasn't sure if I should be hopeful or afraid. At least I knew he wouldn't easily welcome me back into the fold, no matter how hard Vega had tried to convince us both of the contrary. But if I was clever, maybe I could gain a foothold within his court.

At the threshold, the feast roared inside, waiting to swallow me whole. Hundreds of unfamiliar faces reveled in laughter, libations, and dance. Jesters, their bells tinkling, somersaulted to luscious music. The sharp scent of evergreen cut through the air. Garlands wrapped every railing, adorned with red bows as large as my head. They must have cut down a forest to drown this place in Yule. It was sensational.

If only I could have enjoyed it.

Fear slammed into my diaphragm, making each breath a struggle. Or was it the damned dress? I tried to calm my mind. I could do this. I *had* to do this.

Earn his admiration. Join his court. Then do *something* other than sit around and wait, like patronize an artist or musician. Maybe utilize a courtier's stipend to support an almshouse for the sick and destitute. Finally, use the blood that ran through my veins to make a mark on this world.

With a nod, I acknowledged the man stationed near the entrance and clad in the king's colors. Black and bloodred.

"Lady Elowyn Blackthorn!" he bellowed.

The show had begun.

Faces, whitened like mine as if we were all sickly, turned in unison like heads on pikes. *Finally*, they would get a good look at the king's discarded daughter, the child of the Whore of Oakhaven, whom he had executed. The daughter he had stripped of titles when he proclaimed his marriage invalid. A cautionary tale in the flesh. Guilty of the most unforgivable crime known to man: being female. Especially reprehensible in the absence of a male heir.

I could practically hear Vega's thoughts as she side-eyed me: *Smile, Elowyn. You are a lady.*

Years of banishment from court to a rural mountainside property of the crown made me forget that fact often.

"First, greet the king and queen. Remember to curtsy," Vega advised. "Do not rise or speak until the king acknowledges you and be sure to *smile*."

There it was. I wanted to roll my eyes but kept my face in check. I knew all of this; it was practically carved into my skull at this point. But my governess was only trying to help. She knew just how badly I needed this to go well.

Quickly, I tipped my chin in understanding. Vega faded from my side without a word and I was on my own.

Wearing my practiced grin like armor, I walked across the room. I felt the weight of every guest's eyes on me, compounded by the heaviness of the ridiculous, ornate gown Father had gifted me—likely meant to silence any rumors that I was unkempt. Even though I absolutely had been for the better part of my exile.

Vega had written to my father many times before about my need for proper financial support, but the letters were ignored. Like my existence. So we used what little stipend I received to pay for tutors. Not on clothes befitting my status.

Now, I could speak five languages, debate the intricacies of politics with finesse, knew all the great wars and the reasons they happened, dance the popular steps, and play an array of instruments, the virginal being my favorite.

Men bowed at my presence and women quickly curtsied in my wake. My heart beat in triple time. Their eyes on me felt so peculiar, yet even stranger, *good*.

I was a true lady, raised in a crumbling country house, and now these people couldn't take their bloody eyes off me.

A hearty laugh boomed through the great hall, rumbling through me and seeming to quake my very world. The laughter of a king. He held a large tankard that sloshed as he toasted the man to his left. His face was full and ruddy, the same freckles that marked my cheeks speckling his, but his hair was a faded reddish-gray, lacking my fire.

For one brief second, he almost looked human. Less legendary in the flesh. His belly, fat and soft. His amber eyes that I'd inherited underscored with tired, sagging bags.

The queen at his side rested a hand on her swollen belly.

She was pregnant.

The sight sent a feeling like a small blade between my ribs.

Her lips were pressed into a thin, tight line as she nodded curtly to a short, portly man whispering beside her. Her yellow hawk's eyes sliced across the crowd in my direction.

I mustered my strength, tucking away the feelings that cut and burned. I had prepared for this moment my entire life and I wouldn't ruin it with feelings. Now was the time to show my father I was fit to be within his court. Because that was the only way I could secure any semblance of even minute power. The only way a bastard could make any impact in this country.

Make the king like you. Or die trying.

But another part of me, which I despised, secretly hoped he would also accept me.

Maybe even love me. If I was worthy.

I stepped closer, into his atmosphere, and the room silenced.

I curtsied deeply before the king and his queen, who sat above all. The weight of their gaze was heavy and judging. My muscles cramped and my soul ached in bitter embarrassment as I waited for him to acknowledge my existence.

The king finally spoke. "Who be this lady before me?" He was loud, his words not just for me but for all.

My heart clanged in my chest. I took a deep breath and commanded it to slow.

"It is I, Your Majesty, Lady Elowyn Blackthorn," I said, still holding my pose perfectly.

"My daughter? There is no way *you* are *my* daughter. She is but a wee thing." His bravado reverberated through me, threatening to knock me down.

But I rose, tall and straight, to meet the king's gaze.

He tapped his fingers on the arm of his throne, waiting.

I had read every chronicle about my father I could get my hands on. Questioned tutors viciously for hours on every account of his actions and intentions. The circumstances of his life from childhood to the present day. I even interrogated Vega, for the millionth time, on the carriage ride to Guardian's Watch about what she remembered of him when she served my mother long ago.

There were three absolutes I gathered about the king. He was a proud man. He was a violent man. But most importantly, he *greatly* admired wit.

"Of course it is I, if you are the distinguished King Eadric, protector of glorious Oakhaven." I looked around for show. "Or do I have the wrong great castle?"

Then he did the most frightening thing of all. He smiled. A belly laugh followed, booming from his barrel chest.

Our audience, the court, exchanged uneasy glances as they laughed apprehensively along.

"My *good* daughter." The king stood from his throne and stalked in my direction. His stature was intimidating, but I had earned my height from him. Together, we stood tall over his courtiers.

"It is good to see you." His large arms engulfed me in an unexpected hug that was too tight. Air rushed out of my lungs as his arms constricted around me and lifted me from the ground.

The acrid scent of ale and cardamom seeping off him nearly choked me. He dropped me and a big paw fell onto my shoulder.

"Look at you, a Blackthorn you be! I could spot those fiery tresses from atop Highthorn's ramparts." He tugged on the long plait that swung over my shoulder, woven with ruby and pearl hairpins he had given me. It was a wonder Vega had tamed my wild curls at all. "Let us hope you can drink like a Blackthorn too, because Yule is a time to celebrate and be merry!" he said to the crowd, who cheered in response.

A man appeared with a platter of tankards. The king took one and pushed it into my palms without even a second glance, spilling some on my dress in his carelessness. Then he stalked back to his throne. Dismissing me.

That was it.

The eyes of his court followed his lead, falling from me in disinterest. Taking shreds of my pride with them.

Song filled the room, conversation overtook the silence, and Vega appeared back at my side.

"That went *very* well," she said with a grin.

It did? Gulping the mead, I tried to quell my dry mouth. My hands trembled as a whirlwind of thoughts spun round.

I knew I'd have to play the part. Smile, curtsy, and deliver my lines. I rehearsed every step, every word, and the performance was flawless. Every mark met. Then why did the entire interaction feel completely *wrong*?

Vega ushered me to rows of long tables set with candles twinkling among rivers of evergreen and holly garlands. We sat as servers with platters of meats and sweetbreads filled the plates before us. But I wasn't hungry. I only craved mead.

The sweet-sour taste went down with ease, promising to rinse away the bad taste left in my mouth. Maybe the ill-tasting thoughts and feelings could be washed away with drink too.

Twenty years. He sent me away for twenty fucking years. Killed my mother. Annulled their marriage. Called me a bastard. Banished me. Never wrote or visited. And he pretended all was fine. He didn't even look sorry.

He called me good daughter. Yet treated me like a stranger.

Flames sizzled in my chest, turning my heart to ash and crumpling it. Leaving only a hole in its place, begging to be filled with more drink and rage.

"Ever since the queen's wretched son built that damned city on the sea, it keeps happening," a graying courtier sitting next to me said to another, his words pulling me from my firestorm. "Two ships down just this week."

The queen's son?

"The ship last month had ten of my horses on it. Then poof, gone," his conspirator added with a snap of his finger. "Six hundred gold and my best crew, vanished without a trace."

The first hushed to a treasonous whisper. "We all know what it be, even if the king denies it. Nymphaea calls her children to stop the abomination built in her domain." The man scowled. "*Sirens.*"

"Lady Elowyn. *Elowyn.*" Vega pinched my arm swiftly to get my attention. "Elowyn!"

"What?"

The pair noticed me, and with wide eyes, stood and left.

Dammit.

"Be sure to eat some food. It isn't good to drink on an empty stomach," Vega said through a counterfeit smile. She took the nearly-empty tankard from my hands, placing it on the table, only to have a diligent servant girl refill it.

"Those men were speaking of sirens."

"It's not polite to eavesdrop," Vega dismissed swiftly, picking at her plate.

"They were speaking of them as if they were real." I knew people believed in the mythical creatures, but surely not educated men at court. "They said they took ships and men because the queen's son created some city on the sea. What does that even mean?"

"Some are more zealous than others and blame the Guardians and their children for everyday tragedies. And they speak of Sir Cedric Gyldford's city on the sea, which is a very impressive feat. He spearheaded the creation of a rather large port off the coast of Gyldmare they call Whiterok." Her soft green eyes widened in excitement. "Might I add, he's here this evening, unwed, and reportedly very handsome, but a bit rakish."

I didn't even bother to ask how she already knew he was unwed.

"Why have I never heard of this place before?" I asked. It was an oddity that surely would have captured my attention: a man-made port out on open water. How did the ocean not eat it away?

"You mean why haven't I kept you up on the latest ship and harbor news? Likely because you won't take your head out of a book long enough to even discuss what dress you'll wear for the day, Elowyn." She gave me an impish smile. "Now, enough maritime talk. Let us discuss instead how *well* that went. How are you feeling?"

Worthless. Invisible. Angry.

"Did you know the queen was with child?" I asked, prodding the wound that the queen's pregnant swell had cut.

"No. But they say that is why the king married her," Vega said softly, her eyes looking me over compassionately, gauging my hurt as if I was a wounded dove that had flown into a glass window. "She has four sons from her previous husband, the Duke of Gyldmare."

Soon she'd have a fifth. The king's long-awaited heir. Rendering me even less than the nothing I already was.

"I wish to dance," I exclaimed, shooting to my feet.

"What? You hate to dance."

It was true. But if I sat there a moment longer watching Vega look sorry for me, I would go mad. So, I strode to the center of the feasting hall, weaving through the people who shuffled in and out of the crowded space.

I would dance, be happy, and pretend that my life was wonderful.

I would smile just as Vega said.

Even when it hurt.

Chapter 2

The music swelled, cuing the dance.

The women joined in the middle, our fingertips brushing each other as we spun opposite the men, our dresses rippling with the motion.

Eyes caught on my figure, the men smiling broadly while their counterparts sized me up. Laughter shot from my chest, gaining me a few dagger-sharp looks. But I didn't care. This. This was what I needed. Whatever it was, the glances, the regard, it filled me with so much *pleasure*.

The song slowed as we reached toward the outer circle for our fated matches. The tempo shifted and two men gripped my hand at once.

Confused by the fumble, I looked between them. One had grasped me, the other clenching my partner's grip. The man who caught me first scowled back at the other, who reluctantly retreated and found another to dance with.

My partner's hand fell firmly on my hip as we twirled. He was handsome with blond hair neatly tied behind his neck, but when he smiled he revealed uneven rows of rot-black teeth.

"My lady, I hope it is not inappropriate for me to say that you are the most beautiful woman here," he said a little too close to my face, the words putrid from soured breath.

I tried not to inhale the scent. "Thank you, sir."

Around and around we went as the music sped along, his strong hand too tight on me. Thankfully, we parted.

I moved outside the circle again with the other women, the men now spinning in the middle. I watched as they twirled and twirled, their heads swiveling on their necks, jerking to get a better sight of … me? What in the Guardians' names was going on?

The music slowed as a stout redhead hip-checked the man beside him and snatched me up, pulling me to his front, his whole body plastered against mine.

"Y-y-you look marvelous this evening, Elowyn," he stammered informally between gasps, sweat beading on the scraggly red hairs above his upper lip.

"Do I know you?" I questioned.

"Of course, I am your cousin, Sir Flad." My *cousin* ground his hips and other parts of himself distastefully deeper into me. I tried to wedge my hands between us, but struggled against his strength. Finally, the music sped up again. Sir Flad was not eager to let go of me, but with a solid shove I helped him on his way.

This game was losing its charm.

Round and round we went, the men all shoving one another like lunatics. Someone tripped my *dear* cousin—disgusting—sending him hurtling into a lady, and the music was now at its peak.

Spectators gawped. The king's sonorous laugh crashed through the room as he caught the show. Great. This was not the attention I wanted. This was mortifying.

I prayed to the Guardians that the floor would cave in and swallow me whole.

The music slowed and the sharks circled, ready to feast on my flesh.

Then a dark-haired figure cut through the chaos and stood before me.

He was the most gorgeous man I'd ever seen. Emerald-green eyes narrowed at me through midnight-black waves tossed carelessly back. His broad, full mouth rested above a strong, rounded jaw set with a dimple at its center. His large, almost-hooked nose would have looked awful on any other face, but on him it was perfect.

Without even a trace of a smile, he held out a hand to me. The way one was *supposed* to perform this step.

Fate may have brought us together, but it was always the woman's choice to accept her partner's hand. Not to have hers seized greedily.

I smiled and accepted.

Dressed impeccably well, he wore tight-fitting pants that followed the fashion, showcasing muscular, long legs. His blue-and-gold tunic was belted at his slim waist and hugged his broad shoulders. He nearly matched my height, only a perfect spare inch or two taller. Entirely my equal.

"No fair!" spat Sir Flad as he and his partner swirled by us.

But he earned no reaction from my partner, just a flat, direct look that sent a chill down my spine. A look that could kill.

"I fear he will survive the humiliation, *unfortunately*," I sneered.

"Not if I had my say." His voice was low and grating, sending a thrill through me. *Interesting*.

"That almost sounded like a threat, Sir ...?"

"You will know my name in good time." With a steady palm resting on the small of my back, he guided me across the floor. Each step we took was in sync, our bodies already accustomed to one another, as if he and I fit wholly together.

"Why not simply tell me your name now?"

"Because then this dance will no longer be enjoyable for either of us."

What did that mean?

"Do you not find this dance agreeable?" I asked, offended.

He looked down at me, face hard and pensive.

"I find it *quite* agreeable," he said, as if it pained him to admit it.

"Are you always this mysterious to dance with?" I asked.

"*Always.*"

I quirked a brow at him. "And why is that?"

I was officially fascinated.

Our hands met above my head as he spun me perfectly, twice. Then his body returned closer, his lips a breath away from my cheek.

"Because I am the eyes and ears of this *dreadful* place."

Was he trying to frighten me? Unnerve me? Awaken ... desire? It wouldn't work. Well, perhaps the latter might, but intimidation tactics would not.

Copying him, I lifted my mouth and said in a rasping rush, "Shall I call you Sir Eyes then? Or Sir Ears?" Two could play at this game.

He laughed warmly, the sensation winding down my spine. "If you say it like that, you may call me whatever you like."

Heat rushed into my cheeks and settled in my belly.

Damn. He was certainly the victor, in this round at least.

The song ended and he pulled away, bowed, and brushed past me, vanishing into the crowd. The eyes and ears of the castle. Gone in an instant.

CHAPTER 3

The king's laughter slammed me back into reality. "My daughter has caught the attention of every male at this feast! Even the queen's son Sir Gyldford cannot resist!"

That was the queen's son? The creator of Whiterok? But he was so young. Only a few years older than me. Vega was right, he was most definitely rakish. The way he'd held me was telling. He knew the topography of the female form too well.

"Blackthorns do burn the brightest in a room," the king cackled for all to hear. "Now, daughter, your governess has informed us you have a gift to share. Is this true?"

Right. My composition. The performance was the key to winning over my father.

"Yes, I'd like to play a musical piece for you and the queen as a Yule gift." This was my time to shine. My chance to show the king what a well-rounded and put-together lady I had become. Talented and brilliant. All the things I *knew* I was at my very core. Titles or not, I had my mind and skill. If the king could only see it, then I'd easily win him over.

"Let's hear it then," he said, then drank from his tankard.

The crowd parted to reveal an elaborate virginal waiting for me. I sank onto the marble bench, its cold seeping into me. I wanted to gape in awe at the instrument; it was the most beautiful thing I'd ever seen. Far more impressive than the simple one I possessed at Granger House.

My fingers savored the ivory keys laid over sumptuous black velvet. The entire body of the instrument was painted with near-perfect images of all four Guardians, which looked real enough to float out of the instrument and perch on my shoulder.

With a steadying breath, I reached into my pocket for the musical piece I had composed. But it only yielded a bit of … lint.

Fuck.

My hands frantically explored every corner, checking the other side, but the music I had written for this exact moment wasn't there.

Fuck, fuck, *fuck*. How did it go? My thoughts swam through a current of mead swirled by dancing, anxiety churning it all faster. All the court's eyes were on me. Holy Guardians above, the king's eyes were on me. I looked to Vega, pleading. But she simply smiled back, unable to read my mind for the first time in my entire life.

"Let us hear you play, daughter," the king said, annoyed.

My hands floated to the keys and my fingers moved as demanded. But it was not my perfectly crafted composition, the impeccable blend of humility and skill that took me hours to prepare. It was stupid hymns.

Around me the crowd chattered, already bored. My stomach clenched.

No one wanted church music. We were not here to worship the Guardians. We were here to worship the night, the glory, to feast and indulge, and be merry.

The eyes fading from me made my heart surge. This was not going well. I needed them to see me. Hear me. I had to impress my father.

My fingers picked up the tempo, recalling the warm-up I often did. It was fast and fearsome. The playing of a master. My fingers twiddled the keys, teasing them quickly. And to my astonishment, the gaze of the court hastily returned to me. Good. But greedily, I wanted more.

Each note began blurring into the next as the virginal sang beneath my touch. Familiar, sharp notes cut through the air. Faster and faster I played, unleashing a frenzied torrent.

A bird thrashing in its cage, finally freed.

Was it too much? Did I care?

It felt so bloody good being completely and totally within my element. All eyes were on me now and it was intoxicating.

Finally, I yielded. My fingers slowed and the pace dwindled until the last note struck, then tapered off, and I rested my hands upon my lap.

Vega and I locked eyes. She was holding her breath. The entire room was. Only the wind's cry through the frigid night dared to sound.

My father drank deeply from his tankard, then stood to his feet and looked at me hard.

Then he clapped.

He clapped loud and slow, thundering through the silent feasting hall. His drunk gaze panned around the room, demanding his court do the same. Or else.

Obliging their king, the crowd broke into applause that roiled through the room. With an uneasy smile, I stood up and curtsied to the king and his court.

"My daughter is of great *talent*. She is beautiful, as all can see, and she is a Blackthorn." But he held no joy in the words. No pride. Every ounce of my body knew it was a lie. This was all a lie. "So, hear me now," the king shouted.

The clapping halted in a heartbeat. The room fell silent as the dead, waiting for the words that could take or spare life.

"My daughter is the greatest prize of Oakhaven, a rare red rose among many thorns. That is why I announce that my daughter, the Rose of Oakhaven, is now accepting proposals of marriage." My stomach sank. "Only the most noble of men will be worthy of my daughter's hand in marriage. All suitors will come forth to *me* with offers and only the most deserving and fruitful partnerships will earn her hand and dowry." The crowd rippled again with applause. "Now. Let us feast on this Guardian's blessed Yule." The king lumbered back to his throne. Music erupted. Laughter exploded.

Too loud, it was all too loud. I needed air.

"Elowyn, are you alright?" Vega caught me as I lost my footing briefly. The room was spinning. Hot, I was so bloody hot in this Guardians-damned gown. And ... fuck, I was going to be sick. My feet moved without warning. I pushed through the crowd of false, smiling fools staring at me, watching me, wanting me but in all the wrong ways.

I needed to get out of here.

I dashed through an open archway, the cold winter hitting me hard, stealing my breath.

Marriage. Marriage? I knew he'd called me here for something. But this. Was this it? Infernum, I should have fucking known. Hot nausea waved through me. I knew it could happen one day, Vega had prepared me, but at five and twenty I was past the normal age to wed by years. I'd assumed being an illegitimate daughter meant being too worthless to sell off to the highest bidder. That no one would want me.

The world tilted on its axis. What if he forced me to marry an old man? Or a disgusting fool like those cretins who'd grabbed and pulled at me.

Or a man like him.

The ladies in my literature married to bring peace across Oakhaven. Forced to spend nights in strangers' beds to prevent wars. To spread their legs, lie back, and think of country. Birth an heir or face being beheaded on the Guardians-damned steps of Highthorn Castle like my mother. Anxiety fully took over as my hands found my neck. I couldn't breathe.

Falling to my knees, I crumpled, gasping for air as snow pinpricked my face and the cold, bitter wind whistled in my ears.

"Are you okay?" a solemn voice questioned. Shooting to my feet, I dusted off my gown. No one could see me like this.

"Yes, yes, I'm fine—I just was a little hot in there and—" My eyes met the man I had danced with. Sir Cedric Gyldford. "Oh, it's you."

He said nothing. Just looked at me with those verdant eyes that I could tell held secrets and sadness.

"I'm quite fine, thank you, Sir Gyldford," I said with a curtsy meant to dismiss him. Turning to the door, I faced the feast inside that seemed to mock me, jeering uproariously. My legs refused to budge.

"Please, call me Cedric."

"That would be *highly* inappropriate." It was already bad enough that I had shamelessly flirted with him before. Men were one of the few vices I indulged, in the safety of Granger House's distance. Inexperienced cooks' sons, a tutor or two. Men who would never dare say they'd bedded the king's daughter because they would face being hanged. But here, of all places, I knew the chaste charade was a necessity. No matter how handsome he was.

I turned back to him, unable to rejoin the feast.

"You didn't know he was to make that announcement, did you?" Cedric asked.

"No, I didn't."

I breathed in the cold air to steady my mind. How did I not know? It was the only answer that made any sense. I was such an *idiot* for being surprised at all. My father would never have called me here to stay.

"Your playing was—"

"Wild and noisy. I know. I'm surprised my governess didn't faint."

"*Liberating*."

I nodded my thanks, unsure if it was a compliment or not. His expression softened for one moment as his glade-green eyes measured me. The wind cried, and I wished to be back home at Granger House, riding a good horse at the base of my mountains in a place as green as the forests in his eyes.

A crisp chill touched my ankle. "Guardians be damned!" flew from me as I kneeled and fingered my torn skirt hem.

"It must have happened when those imbeciles were fighting over you," Cedric said, and kneeled with me.

I wanted to scream. *Nothing* was going to plan.

"My servant could retrieve a needle and thread to mend this," he said, then looked up at me.

Holy Infernum. He was mesmerizing. Severe, dark-haired, and pale-faced, like he needed sunshine and laughter, but set in such exquisite contrast that it made my heart dance.

I could look at him for eternity.

"After, you could return to the feast." His long, dark lashes fluttered as his eyes traced my skirt's hem. Was he inviting me to his private chambers?

A clamor of voices and laughter broke through the night in the distance. It was the stout man who had been whispering at the queen's side earlier with three ladies dressed in blaring colors.

"Oh, hello Lady Elowyn and ... *Sir Gyldford*. What a surprise to see you out here," he bubbled, then let out a hiccup. I hopped to my feet, and Cedric slowly rose at my side.

The ladies fell into hushed whispers.

Sir Gyldford bowed, and in two swift steps disappeared into the night, leaving me to the wolves.

"Hello," I said with a tip of my head, waiting for the trio to curtsy and bow, as per my ranking. But none did.

"What has happened to your skirt, my lady?" the man drawled.

The women beside him chortled.

"I tore it while dancing," I admitted.

"When you were dancing with Sir Gyldford?" the blond woman cackled.

"Were you reliving your *salacious* steps out here together?" the other woman cawed, sending them all erupting into laughter.

Vega hurried out of the feast.

"There you are, my lady," she said in a sigh of relief. "Oh my, what has happened to your skirt?"

More laughter ensued as the small party glided past us.

"You should better monitor your ward, Vega."

How did he know Vega's name?

"She should not be out here dancing with men unaccompanied; it may look improper," he said, smiling like a cat with a mouse in its paws. Then he vanished into the feast with the garish ladies.

Vega's features hardened. "What is he talking about?"

"Sir Gyldford followed me when I left the feast and—"

"He what?" she thundered.

"He followed me out here and we noticed my dress was torn. He was just helping me, but then that repugnant man saw us and—"

"That man is the queen's advisor. And he is a complete snake. Sir Gyldford knows not to be alone with a lady unaccompanied, especially the king's daughter, and *especially* not when her marriageability was just announced." Vega scowled. "Guardians be, Elowyn, you still act like a child. First that ridiculous playing. Now this. I thought you wanted to earn your place at court—gain your father's favor, secure your standing in society, and *prove* you're ready to take your rightful place at Highthorn. What were you thinking?"

"I, I ..." But I had nothing to say. No explanation. I had failed. And worse, I never could have succeeded.

CHAPTER 4

A pillow thumped my face. "Get up, we're going to pray in the chapel," Vega said.

"What time is it?" I groaned through the angry throbbing in my temples from too much drink.

Vega quick stepped to the window and threw open the thick, black velvet curtains to gray, breaking morning.

"We must show the court you're devoted to your prayers." Devoted to my prayers? Since when? We didn't even have a chapel at Granger House besides the small shrines Vega set up in the rose garden. When I was young, I'd kneel beside her. But mostly, I spent my time practicing the virginal, reading, or riding. Anything besides … praying.

Vega perched on my bed and placed a hand on my forehead. I struggled through soft mountains of down and quilts to meet her stare and embrace that cool hand, which eased my splitting headache.

"I know last night did not go as you planned. But I believe there is still hope for you to do as you set out to."

Father's announcement the night before rolled over me again, turning my stomach.

"What do I always tell you?" Vega asked with a quirked brow.

I sighed, burying my head in the blankets.

"Come on now," Vega coaxed.

"There are two versions of oneself in this world. One the courtiers see and one that you are," I said into the goose-feather mattress.

"*Precisely*. We must paint your picture for the court."

She was right. Maybe I could make the most of the betrothal situation. Surely it would take time to find me a suitor. There could be other opportunities to win over the king. To form some sort of relationship with my father.

I sat up, swung my feet over the haven of my bed.

"You're right. I am a noble lady. Witty, smart, well read, talented—"

"But *tame*," Vega added.

The word made me want to wretch at her feet. But we both knew it needed to at least appear to be the truth here.

"Yes, the type of lady who wakes up early and takes to her prayers. I *suppose*," I sighed.

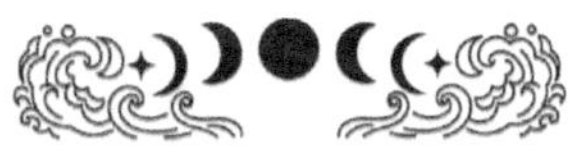

Vega suggested we pray at the chapel nearest the royal quarters on the other side of the castle. After all, what was the point if no one important was there to witness my virtue? The royal wing was where I had hoped to stay instead of the Onyx Chambers where we remained, the rooms set aside for royal guests.

Vega dressed me in a plain wool frock that was deliciously warm against the cold that seeped into the castle walls. Together, hurriedly, we walked to our prayers.

Each window we passed gave us a glimpse into a blinding, white world. Guardian's Watch sleeping in the distance, almost beautiful from such great heights. A hard snow had fallen through the night; a reminder to pray for the poor people in rags I had encountered on the carriage ride here. The stench had been dreadful in the city but not as horrendous as the sight of bodies slumped in alleyways among the snow.

"Why are these people staying out in the cold? They should be inside to keep warm," I had said to Vega in the carriage, a handkerchief drenched with too-sweet perfume pressed to my nose.

"They have no home, or if they do, it is not much warmer than outdoors," Vega answered.

My heart cracked when I saw child-sized bodies.

"Why do they have no home?"

"Because they're too poor."

Yet the gown I wore to the feast could have clothed ten of them.

I shook away the memory. We reached a long hall marked with arches crossing high overhead. At the end, atop towering columns, stood carved figures of the four Guardians. Aeretha, Guardian of sky with her soaring wings was next to Helionyx, Guardian of fire, with his hotheaded scowl. The large, crosshatched stone he was always depicted with was in one of his hands. On the other side of the hall stood Terragos, Guardian of earth, dressed as always in his simple robes beside Nymphaea, Guardian of sea with her fishlike tail.

They stood tall before us. Each Guardian held one palm up to support the ceiling of the chapel, and our world, above our heads. A great sculptor must have chipped away at their bodies for decades.

The scent of burning sage stung my nose as we entered the quiet space. Two long rows of pews waited. We were the first and only visitors to pay homage this early in the morning.

My governess pulled the black velvet kneeler down for us. She reached into her pocket and took out a small string of gems and pearls carved into blue stones and handed it to me.

I knew the bracelet well: mother's prayer beads for her chosen Guardian, Nymphaea. I hadn't held it in years. Vega had kept it safe. It was the last thing in this world that had belonged to my mother. A gift for me, given to my governess, before mother's execution at this very castle.

Now it had returned.

I shifted on my knees to look each Guardian in the eyes. They each had their own stories of jealousy, treachery, and mortal flaws. Likely because they were human-crafted. A blasphemous thought. Maybe it was because of the despair that troubled my life, but I had no faith in the Guardians. I did not believe they were real. There was no magic in this world, no true wielders of fate. There was only the hand you were dealt, fair or poor, that decided whether you became a child out in the snow or a king seated on a throne. Or a bastard in between. But maybe you could make the best of those cards if you were cunning enough.

I was unsure if I was, in fact, cunning enough. Maybe my hand was too shit to win. The night before had been a disaster. If anything, I believed my father loathed me more than ever.

I ran a thumb over the prayer bracelet. My mother likely prayed in this very chapel years ago with these very beads.

Now history repeated itself.

Vega's whispers to her preferred Guardian, Aeretha, beside me filled the room, softly rebounding off the stone-paved walls. We were to recite each prayer eight times. A complete waste of time. But at least the stories were interesting. I looked around the chapel, reciting the words from rote memory while my hands idly thumbed each bead.

"Guardian of the sea, mother of the ocean, master of water. I pray now to Nymphaea." My thumb found the next bead. "Your greatness is to be told until the four Guardians unite again."

Next: "Your story is how you created the sea to hide from Terragos and his wrath, even against his warnings, for he wanted only his world to rule. But he was a callous ruler, and his land hard and cruel."

The next bead was a pearl carved into a fish. Circling my thumb against its grainy texture, I continued, "From the water, you created the sirens in your image, giving them your gift of song and the command to guard your body, to love and protect the sea as you do, from Terragos."

Next: "Terragos was angry, for his people of the land were first. He was jealous because you were wise and created beings who could live on both land and sea." Next: "In his anger, Terragos banished you only to the ocean, cursing your legs into one tail like the fish, like the dolphins, like the great sea serpent Nyraguard. Now you hide in your depths, as do your children."

I reached the final bead. "To take revenge on Terragos each night, you guide the tide to take his land, but he fights back with might in the morning and sends your tide back. Do not take revenge on us, Holy Mother, although we are his children. Grant us safe passage across your body, the sea. Allow us bounty and nourishment from your shores. Make us fluid and forgiving as you are, great Nymphaea, for I honor you. Guardians be."

"Lady Elowyn," a man's voice called, ringing through the chapel.

Vega's head whipped around quickly. "We are at prayer, Sir Guard-win!"

The man who witnessed Cedric and I the night before stood at the threshold of the chapel, hands neatly tucked behind his round body. A devious smile spread across his face.

"My deepest apologies, but the king has asked for Lady Elowyn's audience *immediately*." Vega stood up with a puff to direct me as she angrily shifted her skirts and marched onward. I trailed behind her.

The walk up to the king's private room was long and full of stairs that spent my breath. How the stout man before me managed them with ease was a wonder, but Sir Guardwin did not speak, only maintaining a knowing grin as he followed behind Vega.

I'd never seen her so perturbed. Or was that worry creasing her brow?

We approached the embellished wooden doors. Two guards posted on each side stood unflinching.

"The king has commanded the Lady Elowyn's presence," Vega said.

Each guard took one stiff step forward, and in practiced unison, opened the doors.

I tried not to contort my face in confusion when I saw my father, Cedric, and the queen waiting inside. Why were they all here and what did my father want? Warmth from the fire in the man-tall hearth met us, but no warmth exuded from my father's expression. No. He was as cold as the snow that froze his people outside.

Cedric stood stock-still at his side, and the queen looked out the window a few paces from my father, a loose hand on her pregnant swell.

"Shut the doors," the king shouted, throwing out a hand with his demand. He looked at his wife with no love. Did he look at my mother that way too? Like she was a vessel and not a human.

The doors slammed and shook my spine.

Alone in the lion's den.

The king's eyes narrowed. "Is it true you were alone with Sir Gyldford last night in the courtyard by the feasting hall?"

Vega made to speak but the king's hand halted her. "I wish to hear what she has to say, not your excuses, Vega."

She. Not Elowyn. Not daughter. Only my crime. My sex.

An ember sparked in my gut. With a calming breath, I tried to put it out.

"I left after your announcement of my marriageability to get some fresh air, and Sir Gyldford followed me."

The king sighed. "Guardwin and three ladies saw Sir Gyldford fumbling with your skirts. It was the talk of the evening once *both* you and he disappeared for the rest of the night."

"My skirt tore while dancing. Sir Gyldford offered to mend it." Searching Sir Gyldford for a defense, I found nothing. Only stone as he avoided my gaze.

"Sir, please tell the king what happened."

But he said nothing.

"How could you be so foolish, girl?" The king ground out.

"Nothing happened between us, I swea—"

"Guardians damn it all to bloody Infernum!" He pounded his fist in rage. "I meant your marriage for alliance! Protection for what lies past Oakhaven's borders. You stupid. Foolish. *Girl*." He pounded each syllable into the desk beside him. "A whore just like your mother." The final insult punched me in the gut. "You are to be sent to Gyldmare tomorrow. There you will marry Cedric quietly. Afterward, I never wish to see you again."

My hands trembled. No. This couldn't be.

"We will marry at Whiterok," Sir Gyldford cut in swiftly. The queen turned at that, a strange look flashing through her sharp countenance.

"We do not even know one another, and nothing happened between us." The words snarled from my lips.

Cedric cleared his throat. "After our evening last night I wish to right the wrongs of my transgressions."

Anger flushed my face hot.

"What are you implying, Sir?"

He met my stare, a look of pained disgust on his face. "Because I took your maidenhood, we should marry to right our wrongdoings."

"You *fucking* liar!" I roared, and lunged forward, ready to beat him into a gory pulp.

Vega caught my shoulder, holding me back.

Cedric only watched me with that look of revulsion.

The king sent a goblet flying with the back of his hand, the metal cup clanging on stone flooring.

We all froze.

"Whiterok, Gyldmare, I do not *fucking* care! I just want her out of my court and sight as soon as possible. She is your problem now, Cedric." His eyes narrowed at my governess. "Vega, help her prepare for her journey and tomorrow, you will leave to Aeretha Abbey to await new employment."

My body surged in protest. There had to be something that could be done. Something I could say. I would marry whoever the king ordered me to, but I couldn't lose Vega. I could not bear the thought of being far from her. I'd slept with her close, if not in my bed, my entire life. I needed her. She was all I had.

"Please, don't do thi—"

"All of you out!" the king yelled.

Vega grabbed my wrist and pulled me out the door.

Everything in me wished to fight but Vega dragged me as I begged incoherently.

But no one answered.

No one cared.

Cedric, the queen, and Sir Guardwin followed us out, and the large doors my father hid behind slammed shut.

My ugly, gnarled anger turned on Cedric, now standing in the hall. "You bastard!" Shoving hard into his chest, I screamed, "You fucking bastard!" But he did not move, his muscles tense. The big, repulsive aberration. "You Guardians-damned liar! You think I will marry you? You pathetic excuse for a man!" I shoved him again and again, slamming into hard, muscled flesh.

The queen and Sir Guardwin walked down the hall, unfazed at my show.

"Lady Elowyn ... *Elowyn*! Stop this!" Vega said.

Cedric swiftly snatched my wrists.

"You are *this* repulsed by the thought of being married to me," he practically hissed.

"You implied I had sex with you to my father." My voice cracked under the weight of the pain. *A whore just like your mother.* My mother was no whore, and neither was I. Fuck the king. And fuck this place.

"Did you think I would willingly marry a man who lied about my honor to claim me?" I fought his hold, but it was useless. Defeated, I panted before him. "My mother was executed for less."

Cedric flinched. "He will *never* hurt you." His voice sank low and coarse. "And your honor has nothing to do with what people say in this place. This is a castle filled with illusions and lies. But you should have learned the rules before you ever attempted to play this ridiculous game, especially if you did not wish to be *claimed*." He dropped my wrists and walked past me.

A fire burned within me, inflaming my heart as it surged in my chest, desperate to escape the fate of my flesh.

"Why are you doing this?"

He turned and looked back at me, shaking his head as if in disbelief. "You truly do not understand?"

"Understand what?" I practically yelled, tears blurring my vision.

"I knew you were naive, but I never thought you were foolish enough to not know your worth."

"My worth? Is that why you're doing this? You find some worth in a bastard daughter of the king? A daughter he cannot stand to look at. You think a marriage to me will raise your status so you can get closer to kissing the ring." I let out a joyless laugh. "If I am foolish, then you, Sir, are a complete and utter imbecile about to marry no one of importance. If it wasn't clear enough, let me tell you now: my father hates me and I am worthless."

Those green eyes turned dark as a forest at midnight. "He doesn't hate you. He fears you. They all do."

Then Cedric Gyldford, my betrothed, turned and left me.

Chapter 5

The following morning was disgustingly sunny. The light shimmered on the snow that fell throughout the night.

I ignored the whispers and stares as we walked to my doom.

"They will not see us waver," Vega said at my side through tight lips. She was always right there, with quick advice and a comforting smile, since the day I was first banished from this wretched place. Soon we would be apart.

Rain. I wanted rain. Sopping sheets of rain that hammered the ground and drowned us all. Highthorn, the king, his queen, Cedric, and anyone else who insisted I was not a human but a burden to be shifted from prison to prison.

We stood before the waiting carriage. There always seemed to be one to take me away.

Vega clasped my hands. "We will be together again, I feel it in my bones. Guardians willing."

Fuck the Guardians.

She continued, "I'm proud to have been your governess."

Words caught in my throat, refusing to form. I had nothing to say to the woman who raised me in my mother's absence. Because I was not ready for goodbyes. Not now. Not like this.

Vega dipped before me in farewell, but I—just as Mother had all those years ago—pulled her into a long embrace.

"I love you, Vega," I said in a small voice. The truest thing to my heart I could utter.

Her hand slipped into my pocket in a smooth motion, leaving a weight behind. "I love you too, *Princess* Elowyn."

My heart shattered.

Snowmelt dripped from Highthorn Castle like tears, shimmering in the sunlight that shined on as if my life was not falling apart. I trailed my gaze over the castle's towering walls that hid the king and his court. Someone needed to burn the whole damned place to the ground.

I boarded the carriage; it lurched forward, taking me with it. I couldn't make myself watch Vega shrink with the distance, as I had my mother. That was the last I saw her, and this would not be the last I saw Vega. It couldn't be.

The carriage wound through a stretch of beautiful hills quilted in snow. The cobblestone path was cleared by the work of diligent groundskeepers. A loud groan of wood and metal sounded as the gate relinquished me from the castle grounds. Spitting me out like the rubbish my father deemed me.

Eventually, the wheels of the carriage lost their tempo as the horses dragged them through frozen muck and rot on the road. Buildings rose around us. I didn't miss the dilapidated shacks at the end of narrow alleys, hidden behind grand houses off the main road. They leaned against one another, their sagging shutters closed in an attempt to keep out the cold. That was where those cast aside by my father lived, overlooked.

I had read about Guardian's Watch with wonder my whole life. The pride of my country, once one of the wealthiest cities in the world, at least when my grandsire was king. It was a place where people from all over came to trade and barter. Now it was nothing more than a rat-infested shithole.

My father taxed everyone, except his wealthy companions, into Infernum to fund his fleet of great warships and supply his armies, all for unwinnable wars across the sea. He hoped to claim some foreign title our family possessed long ago. Yet he couldn't even care for his own people here in Oakhaven. But to say any of that, despite all knowing it, would be treason. So instead, the books lied, claiming Guardian's Watch still glorious and my father a great king.

This is a castle filled with illusions and lies. Cedric's words snaked through my mind. That may have been the only truth he spoke at all. That deception seeped from the castle into the streets, slopping into the heart of Oakhaven.

I worked out a hairpin from my thick braid, an unruly curl springing with it. I stared at the gem top, marking its flat planes that winked in the sunlight. I was so easily enamored with the riches I did not even see the trap set before me. I drew open the blind and dropped the gem-laden pin onto the street. They made me sick; they were far too ornate when others starved or froze. I would no longer be a part of the lie. Maybe someone in need could pick it up and sell it.

I pulled out another one, then another, dropping each out the window until none remained and my braid unraveled.

Bubbles of giggles rippled, and footsteps loped with the pace of the carriage's horses past the wood and velvet of the carriage window. I peeked out and smiled at the swarm of children who raced alongside. I mirrored their smiles.

Eager to give them more, I tore off my hood, plucking each pearl and garnet sewn into it, throwing them to the children. They raised up their little dirty hands, reaching. Some caught them; others snapped up the ones that skipped on the ground.

Plucking more gems off the neckline of my gown, I threw another handful, drunk on the feeling of giving to them. Like a madwoman, I unraveled the lacing at my front and shrugged off the dark-crimson velvet overdress, the sleeves lined with black fur. I threw the wad of red and black out the window, reveling at the sight of it being snapped up by a boy.

I could do nothing for this city. For this country. This was all I had: the clothes on my back, given to me by a father who did not love me. So, I gave it to them. My shoes, stockings, more layers of kirtle and gown, until I stripped down to my burnt-yellow petticoat and underdress. It was improper and indecent. Surely people would know it was I who did it, but I didn't care. My honor was already tarnished. I was born with it damaged. Let Highthorn's courtiers talk. At least I tried to dress the people of Oakhaven.

Suddenly, the carriage halted. The children ran off. That last semblance of joy vanished in an instant.

The carriage door swung open.

"My la—oh, *Guardians* above!" The coachman shielded his eyes from my loose, wild hair and state of undress. "My lady, you must stop. The sumptuary laws forbid anyone not of noble birth from owning such finery. The children could face hanging for possessing property of the crown."

Ice settled into my spine.

It was a law I'd never given much thought to because of my privileged blood.

Guilt washed over me as I realized this act wasn't to ease their discomfort. It was to ease mine.

Swallowing my remorse, I snapped, "I do not take lectures from coachmen. Shut the door and ride on."

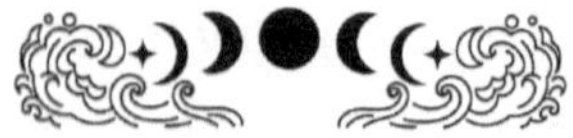

The first hour of silence was painful. The absence of Vega, of anyone, settled into my bones, threatening to splinter them.

My hand wandered to the sewn-in pockets of my petticoat and found its way around mother's prayer beads to Nymphaea. A bitter smile crossed my lips. Sneaky Vega must have slipped it into my pocket. Clasping it on, I ran a thumb over the beads and considered praying to Nymphaea for protection or for guidance from my mother. But didn't. Neither would hear me.

The air shifted warmer as we neared Gyldmare, known for its ports and fishing towns. The scent of salt and sea tried its best to lift my spirits. The children's rhyme of its bounty bobbed through my mind: *Gyldmare by the sea, Nymphaea Guardian be, grant us your gifts, mother of all waters.*

Each region had its own silly tune, sung by mothers—or by governesses, in my case. I'd seen little of Oakhaven through my own eyes, but through books I'd visited every corner. Explored each mountain's peak in Ashbourne, watched over by the Guardian Aeretha, flying through the clouds. Walked the soft, rolling hills of Haverford, through miles of farmlands, laughing with its good country folk who kept us fed, drenched in the sunlight carried across the sky by Helionyx and his dragon.

I'd meandered through Thornley's thick wooded forests where woodsmen worked in the summers felling trees with the permission of Terragos. Through books, I learned to love my country's history. To take pride in its kings and their feats, to honor the Guardians even if I did not have faith in them, because I had faith in tradition. Or so I thought. What good had tradition ever done for me?

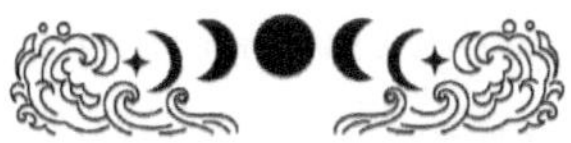

The sky was still dastardly blue as gulls dove at the sea, cawing their song. I stepped out of the carriage. A shelf of land surrounded the port, rocky and dire, capped in clusters of graying snow that clung to its sides like the last of my hopes. Fated to fall into the sea and cease existing at all. Where the land met the waves. This was the end of Oakhaven.

A cool air wafted off the ocean, snapping my hair with its strength. Before me was docked a great ship adorned with a gilded bear with a fish's tail, snarling on the front of its hull. The Gyldfords' heraldic beast. Bile rose in my throat. Soon to be mine.

Then I saw a man on the dock in the distance, tall and broad, stalking in demanding strides. At his side, a pathetic figure draped in black tried to keep pace until they both stood before me.

He looked me up and down, unblushing. Unlike his counterpart, whose gray, protruding eyes widened at my attire. They peered from layers of black silk that wrapped her head to toe, a veil drawn tight across her mouth, stifling any further expression. She was unmistakably a drucia.

"I'm Captain Arlo Fynn," he said with a terse nod. "And you must be the lady I'm to escort to Whiterok?"

He was barely older than myself, young for a captain, but looked quite fine in his leather captain's coat. He was tall, towering over me, sun-kissed and handsome in a worn way. It was like the sea had chiseled his features into dull but dire angles over millennia, like the cliffs that hung around us here.

But handsome or not, I clung to my anger. Because without it, reality threatened to take hold.

"No, sorry, wrong lady. But I saw her run that way. If you hurry, you may catch her." I jerked a thumb over my shoulder.

A smile tugged at the corner of his lips and those damned eyes shone on me, honey-warm like the sun just before setting, encircled in amber, with golden rays beaming from the center, straight into my soul. At that look, absolutely against my will, a gust of air seemed to blow, extinguishing the ire I desperately needed.

He swallowed that smile down the thick column of his throat. I was desperate to have it return. "This drucia shall be your chaperone."

She shrugged off the shawl around her shoulders and wrapped it over mine. I wanted to fight her, but realized how uncomfortable the voyage would be, undressed as I was.

The captain turned abruptly, stalking back to the dock.

The woman finished tying the wrap, then gave a small, silent dip. Great. A babysitter. Drucias were overly religious members of a sect of The Guarded. They honored only Terragos with their muteness in temples built near sacred sites. They were staunch believers that only the one Guardian was the true ruler of all. Which went against everything our religion stood for. This earth belonged to four Guardians, equally and in balance. They lived a miserable existence of heavy, *judgmental* silence. I sighed. Not exactly the most riveting ship companion.

"Where am I to go?" I called to the captain.

"Aboard," he said, not turning to me, and then he swung a solid arm to the ship.

The mute drucia led me to a room below the ship's deck and pointed to a simple wood door with a large metal lock. A stool sat beside it.

"Are you going to lock me in there?" I exclaimed.

Her eyes were sympathetic as she nodded a small yes.

Pure, hot vexation overtook my body. "Guardians fucking be!" Red, searing indignation burned my cheeks.

Yet the drucia pulled out a silver key from deep within the folds of her drapery and unlocked the door.

"I absolutely *refuse* to be locked in there," I roared defiantly.

"What's that noise?" the Captain's voice boomed from the deck above in forced authoritarianism that threatened to make my eyes roll out of their sockets. He leaned on the stair's railing.

The drucia glanced at him, silently pleading for help.

"I refuse to be locked away like a prisoner," I answered for her.

He descended the stairs swiftly, boots echoing on the wooden planks. "These were my direct orders for escorting you. We must voyage on with you under lock and key."

"Absolutely *fucking* not," I spat.

He blinked away the curse and laughed. "Well, you're not what I anticipated."

"Let me guess, you were picturing some meek, polite little woman who would listen to whatever order you sent her way, *Captain*?"

In a heartbeat those eyes were on me again. Devouring me head to toe as he tongued something in his mouth. Then he smiled. The bastard. Broad and beaming.

I bit down the bliss it sent racing through my body.

He shook his head to himself with a scoff, rubbing the bridge of his nose. "Fine then." He stepped forward, and with little effort, grasped my upper arms and moved me into the room. His touch sent an unexpected sensation through me.

We both looked at his grip on my shoulders.

Damn it, were even his hands beautiful? Those long, slender fingers, dotted by one dark beauty mark on his ring finger like a little secret. Hands that would play the virginal like a Guardian. That would play me like a—I cleared my throat, and my mind.

He dropped his hands.

"Listen, I was paid to ensure your safe passage under lock and key, to Whiterok." He released my shoulder. "Those were the terms of the contract I signed, and I am a man of my word."

Then he turned on his heel and carelessly threw over his shoulder, "Dinner is at sunset. You will be let out then." The door slammed behind him and with a turn of a key and a click, they sealed me in.

The ship lurched forward, and for the first time in my life, I left Oakhaven.

CHAPTER 6

I sat on the rickety cot in the room. Was this to be the rest of my existence? Locked doors, orders, and endless waiting. I was always so certain it would be more. I wanted to cry, scream, fight. But for what? To who? My thoughts were driving me mad. I'd be nothing. No one. Forever.

As soon as the sky shaded pink, my fist collided with wood. "The captain said dinner was at sunset!"

Keys rattled and the door swung open, the small drucia waiting on the other side in silence.

I swept past her, ascending the staircase with purpose.

On the deck, the vast sea expanded in every direction, as flat as glass. The fading sun inflamed the world in hues of orange and gold, while the rhythmic sound of sailors at work and the gentle waves against the ship's hull filled the salted air.

It was calm this far from land.

Scanning the deck, I spotted him and his broad figure against the sunset sky.

"Do you at least feed your prisoners around here?" I shouted across the ship.

He turned slowly, expression steadfast despite the curious looks from wide-eyed sailors flitting my way.

With deliberate steps, he approached me.

"I was told you were a lady." He looped his arm into the crook of my elbow firmly, spinning me around. His touch was warm. "Not a barking dog."

I smiled prettily. "If you wish to call me a *bitch*," I said emphasizing the curse loudly, "then come out with it, Captain. Do not hide behind some terrible attempt at wit."

More glances fell in our direction as the captain forced a false smile and firmly navigated us across the bustling ship's deck. Despite the scowl etched into my face, for some sick reason, I savored every moment we touched. He felt real. Corporeal. Like an anchor when the rest of my world was thrown into the air, sent flying, uncertain of its landing.

"Ladies aren't supposed to speak in such a manner," he said in a sharpened whisper that raised gooseflesh down my neck.

I let my stare bore into his features, however handsome.

"Ladies are not supposed to be locked away either," I said.

"I must manage my cargo as I am instructed to," he said, anxiously tonguing his cheek. "Although, I assumed you had been made aware of those arrangements."

"That's what I am then? Cargo." I held his gaze, refusing to back down.

He winced.

The crew moved with practiced ease, acknowledging the captain with nods before returning to their tasks.

"No, and I apologize for the way the situation was managed. I believe the measures were for your safety and in that attempt your dignity was overlooked. I'm sorry for my hand in that." His words were thoughtful and measured.

A savory smell drifted from the direction of the dining hall we were nearing. My mouth watered. I had refused to eat that morning, too grief-stricken to take a bite. But I was never one to miss meals.

"Hungry then?" He smiled, noting the hunger in my eyes. "We'll get you a good meal and return you to your quarters," the captain said in a smooth directive. He was used to giving orders.

"Where will you dine?" I asked.

"With my crew. As I always do."

"Is that not a little beneath a captain?" I mocked, pushing against the strange feelings this man inflicted upon me.

"Some may say so, and few captains do. But it's time well spent eating and speaking with the men who keep my ship afloat."

A good answer that I unfortunately respected.

I slipped out of his grip and marched into a dining room bathed in half-light, where two young men in aprons were setting a long table with care.

"Then I shall dine with them too."

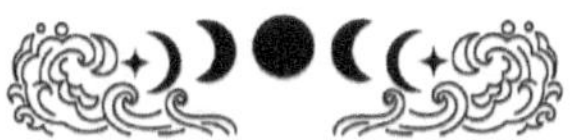

The captain never refused me. Either he didn't want me to cause another scene or attempted to call my bluff, thinking I'd never *actually* want to dine with sailors.

He was rigid and on guard as the room filled with men, each serving one another and eyeing the head of the table where the captain and I sat.

As did my mute chaperone, the drucia, from her quiet corner on the other side of the room.

But eventually the captain settled into his chair as the sun nestled into the waves. The conversation hummed over our empty bowls of stew, the dripping candles gilding the sailors' faces.

A toothless man, Chumly, the captain's right hand, slipped two full tankards of ale into our palms.

"The captain's a good man, me lady, kindest captain I know. One time he paid to have this tooth pulled." Chumly reached into his mouth and pointed to his glistening gums. "Cost two whole gold and he didn't bat an eye."

The captain reached across the table and pulled his sailor's hand from his mouth.

"It's not polite to speak with your mouth full, Chumly. Especially not in front of ladies," the captain said with a chuckle that warmed me through.

"Sorry captain." Chumly answered shyly. "Will you finally tell us, Lady, why are you on this ship?" He leaned in. "We have a runnin' bet."

"I said you're a merchant's wife," the young man next to Chumly shouted, bits of stew flying with the words.

"I said a mayor's betrothed," Chumly offered.

I looked to the captain.

"You haven't told them?"

"I don't know either." He shrugged his heavy shoulders.

"Tell us, Lady," a man cheered, then another bellowed, "Yes, tell us!"

Shaking my head no, I answered, "Better to keep you on your toes, otherwise the ale may stop flowing." That was easier than the truth. That I was headed to marry a man who looked at me with disgust. A man who lied, staining my name, because he wanted to use me.

I smiled and raised my cup, an uproar of cheers following.

"I'm surprised you've lasted this long," the captain said, those ardent eyes peering over his tankard.

"And why is that?" I asked in a murmur.

"It's a rough crowd. They're on their best behavior, but surely a far cry from the nobles you must dine with."

How little he knew. I had played cards with cooks and laughed with gardeners over meals my whole life. Here, I felt far more comfortable than the court of misery I was just banished from, *again*.

"And you believe nobles are more pleasant company?" I asked.

His features flattened.

"No. But you ..." His eyes crosshatched my face, searching. Wanting to ask *something*, "You seem—"

"Captain!" A small boy called as he needled through the crowded room to the captain's side. No older than ten, his little fingers mindlessly latched onto the captain's chair in familiarity.

"How was your watch, Alistar?" the captain questioned as he clapped the boy on the shoulder, shaking the boy's sandy cherub's curls.

"Not a sea beast in sight, sir!" the boy exclaimed.

"Very good. Now go wash up and get yourself something warm to eat, sailor," the captain instructed with authority, despite the ale reddening his cheeks.

"Yes, Captain," the boy answered with a large smile, then scurried off.

"He's quite young," I remarked to the captain, leaning back in my chair as he did.

"Picked him up in Haverford. His father was a farmer, but when he died, the lands went to his brother who didn't want another mouth to feed."

"That's awful," I said softly.

"That is the world," he said, turning to Chumly, who was going on with two other men about a time when he fed seagulls off the bow.

"The food splat right on me face, and the beasts dove and chased me! One even bit me arse!" The room rippled with laughter and so did the captain, his deep, cheerful laugh rumbling through my soul. This was nice. Good people eating, drinking, and being truly happy.

"Captain," I asked, wanting those brilliant, sun-soaked eyes back on me.

"Yes," he answered, half-listening.

"Alistar was on the lookout for beasts, is that what you said?" I asked.

"Yes, I give the shift to younger sailors," he answered, his voice resonating richer than the deepest notes my left hand played on the virginal. I wish I could wield that sound, command it with the mere movement of a little finger.

"Personally, I feel far safer with Alistar on the lookout," I joked in a murmur.

The captain smiled, leaned in, and whispered, "Between you and me, there are no beasts, at least not in these waters."

The gentle, deep octave of his voice sank into my belly.

"*Ah*." I savored him. His tone, those eyes. Both radiant and mild. Like a summer day. "Not a siren in sight then?"

The room instantly silenced.

The captain faced his crew, but their eyes were all turned to me.

"What did she say?" Chumly asked in a scared rasp. All welcome was leaving his face, replaced with guarded terror.

"Wish you *hadn't* said that," The captain said through clenched teeth, then stood from his chair and addressed his crew. "Let's call it a night, men. We have an early start tomorrow."

"But the *woman,* she spoke of the monsters that haunt the seas, desiring the flesh of sailors and—" The word "woman" was on his lips like a swear.

"To bed with all not on night shift. That is an order," the captain demanded.

The men reluctantly obeyed, the shuffle of their chairs and whispers overtaking the sound of the ocean's rush.

The captain looked down at me, still in my chair. "You as well, Lady." He nodded to the drucia standing by the door waiting for me. "Your chaperone waits."

"What did I say that frightened them?" I asked, wondering what could strike such fear in sea-hardened men.

"Sirens." He rolled his eyes as he pinched the bridge of his aquiline nose. "There is talk of ships disappearing at the ports and sailors are a superstitious lot."

Just as the old men had whispered of in my father's court. I was so stupid for even bringing it up.

"I'm sorry, I didn't mean to ruin the evening."

"It's fine. We'll be at Whiterok by daybreak, so you should get some rest anyway."

I wasn't ready for the little dream to end. All that waited on the other side of the night was the thing of nightmares. Marriage to a monster. An unknown city on the sea miles away from everything I loved. The end of my life.

"Have you been there before?" I asked. Stalling.

After a long pause the captain finally answered, "Yes."

Too short. I wanted a sentence in that soothing voice.

My face twisted as tears stabbed behind my eyelids.

"What have you heard of the man who created it?" I focused on my trembling hands. Able to feel the captain's gaze lingering on me, while fearing if I looked up at his handsome face and met the stare of those comforting eyes, my own would rain with tears.

"I know ... that he is a good man. Now, goodnight, Lady." Then he left.

It was a silent walk back to my room with the drucia, the black night so clear that the sky dazzled with silver stars. But the beauty of the clear night disappeared the moment she locked the door behind me, leaving only a glimmer visible from the small window of my room as I laid my head down to sleep.

CHAPTER 7

A flash of light illuminated the small cabin. Thunder split the air, followed by a crescendo of rainfall.

Hollering from the crew, muffled by the downpour, made it to my ears in indistinguishable mumbles. On my toes, I craned my neck to witness the angry storm outside through the small window. Then I heard it, in the distance past the drumming of the rain and crashing of the waves. It was faint and distant but there. A small lilt on the sea. A harp? A lute? Who brought an instrument on a ship? Let alone played it amid a storm.

The ethereal sound ebbed in and out of my ears, rising and falling like the tide. My breath slowed to its sound. It was a voice, no, a chorus of voices both haunting and enchanting singing with the music.

Men no longer yelled orders to one another. Only that music, the storm, and the waves were audible.

Suddenly, the ship pitched fast and hard. My feet gave way at the large shift that sent me slamming against the wall. My back panged from striking the unforgiving wooden panels that lined the room.

Something wasn't right.

I gathered myself to my feet and ran for the door, twisting and pulling at the knob desperately, but it did not relent.

"Let me out!" My fists pounded against the only exit. The rain fell fast and my heart raced to its tempo. "Please! Let me out!" But there was no response. The music was loud now, drowning out all thought. It surrounded me. Was I going mad?

Finally, the knob convulsed and the door opened. It was the drucia, her sacred clothing drenched, plastered to her face around her wild, bulging eyes. She pulled down her mask, eyes darting side to side in panic, trying to will the words into my mind, but finally she spat, "The sailors are in some sort of trance!"

"Do you hear that singing?" I asked. Her mask sagged below her chin as she nodded yes. She fell to her knees and traced the prayer beads on her wrist, rocking back and forth. "Allfather, Terragos save us!"

Stepping around her, I went through the doorway and up the steps to the deck. Cold rain crashed all around, blurring my vision as I made my way across the deck, trying to keep upright as the waves rolled beneath the ship.

I saw him, the captain, thank the Guardians. He stood working at something, surely redirecting us.

"Captain," I yelled. But he did not turn around, and only kept working away. "Captain!" I shouted louder through the rain and that ghostly song, but nothing.

Finally, grabbing his broad shoulders, I swung him around and demanded, "Captain, what is happening?" But he didn't reply. His face held only a groggy grin.

Shaking his large body as hard as possible, I screamed in his face, "Answer me!"

But he said nothing and returned to his work.

The other sailors did the same, like they were drunk or dreaming, silently working at ropes and sails manning the ship like there was no storm pounding at their backs, nor a ghostly song shrieking in their ears.

Through the wind and rain I made it to the edge of the deck. Through the haze of the storm, in the distance I spotted a rocky fixture jutting out of the sea.

The rippling of sails pulled my attention. Chumly and others hoisted them just right to catch the wild storm's gust, lunging us straight for the rocks.

A light glimmering beneath the water caught my eye. My hands met the slick railing of the ship as I leaned to get a better look at the sea, dizzy from the height. Another light appeared, then another. They were surrounding us just beneath the sea. Light somehow swimming alongside the hull, like they were guiding us to those jagged outcroppings.

Rocks grew larger as we neared, waves crashing on their jagged teeth. Chumly passed by me, a mound of rope in his hands. "Chumly! Chumly!" I screamed desperately. "Stop the ship! There are rocks ahead. You must stop the ship!" But he only continued past me. They all ignored me. Walking phantoms headed to their deaths.

Unsettling grinding threw us all forward. The ship splintered and cracked as wood met rock, water whooshing into the belly of the ship. Quickly, the nose of the bow pitched down.

The music pierced my body, my mind, wild, sharp, and loud now, wailing in the rain.

Then the sailors all stopped in their tracks like pillars.

A heartbeat passed, and then they marched in unison. What the *fuck* was happening? The captain passed me, still in a trance, heading straight for the nearest guardrail. His gaze was transfixed on the stormy horizon.

I ran before him, digging my heels into the deck and using all my might. I tried desperately to stop him. But it was useless. With ease, he pushed past me, put his hand on the guardrail, and to my horror, jumped into the dark, swirling waters.

One by one his men followed.

And I was helpless, left to watch every man jump off the ship, to their deaths.

The music stopped.

The rain eased to a patter, my ears left ringing from the absence of music, but the waves continued to crash against the boat with relentless force. Each impact threatened to send me tumbling into the frigid, dark waters that pulled the vessel ever closer into the sea's embrace.

Fighting to hold on with a white-knuckled grip, I hauled myself, hand over hand, up the railing of the almost-vertical ship. Wiping water and red ribbons of hair from my eyes, my muscles seared with pain. I willed them to be strong as each surge of waves weakened my hold.

But where was there to go? There was no more climbing, no escaping, only the empty black sky above and the roiling blackness below. This is what I wished for—I guess. Maybe Nymphaea was real and she had heard my plea. Sent a storm to claim me instead of an unwanted man.

A bitter scoff fell from my lips. Guardians be, could she not think of a better fucking way of helping me that didn't include dying?

Vega would wail when she heard the news. Sent away on my first trip without her and I wound up dead. But that was the only person I clung on for. Not me. Not anymore. Vega would find solace eventually and maybe she would understand that this was better. Death was better. This cold, watery grave was better than ten or twenty years trapped in some cold marriage bed. This was freedom, and this could be my choice.

Summoning the courage, I counted, *One*, *two*, and with a final long breath, *three*. Surrendering, I let go.

Chapter 8

My body cleaved through the waves, the impact stealing air from my lungs. Salt singed my eyes as my sodden dress weighed me down, down, down, pulling me into the dark depths.

I fought against the disorienting currents, but in the blackness, up was down and down was up. Death wound around me in the darkness. I would never see Vega again. Or Granger House. Or the mountains. Desperation had me sucking in water, briny and bitter as it burned down my throat.

Then, a dark-blue light glowed before me. No, around me. I could breathe. But how?

A hand penetrated the surrounding light and ensnared me, pulling me in tight against someone's body. At first I fought against whatever it was that held onto me, the feeling of a hand clutching my waist distinct. But a sublime sound danced in and out of my mind.

You're safe. Nymphaea has saved you.

Squinting my eyes, I saw a beautiful being glowing in a rose-colored aura. Perhaps even a Guardian. My muscles relaxed.

Just a little longer. We are almost there. You are safe.

I believed that voice, for whatever reason, and went limp in the water as we dove deeper.

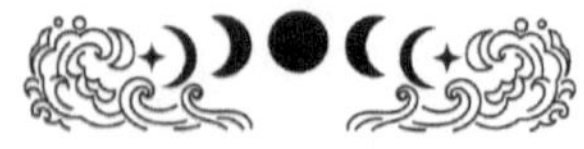

Heaving up bellyfuls of water, I vomited onto stone ground.

Land. I was on sweet, blessed land.

"She's over here." A voice like bells rang. I knew that voice. It was the voice inside my mind just moments ago. No, that was insane.

Tired, I lay on my back, shivering. I was too exhausted to even stand, let alone thank my savior.

"Are you alright?" A small, pale face peered down at me. I blinked away the salt water and brought her into focus. She tilted her head, examining me, sending her short, frizzy curls bouncing. They were a pale ... pink? What? How? I blinked again and again, ensuring my eyes were in fact working correctly.

Behind her, through the glass ceiling, a flock of birds seemed to dart quickly through the night sky, their reflective bellies catching the light escaping the room like they were made of precious metals. They swooped again, shimmering in silver.

Wait. No, that was not a flock of odd birds flying past ... those were ... fish?

I sat up abruptly. Where the fuck was I?

I looked at the pink-haired woman on her knees, looking at me with concern.

"Are you hurt, human?" A deep voice emitted from a muscled man standing behind her, sounding less concerned and more annoyed. His giant arms were crossed. He was dressed obscenely in a small red cloth tied at his hip, which covered next to nothing of his robust body. But his lack of clothing wasn't what shocked me. It was his legs, which varied from the dark brown of his skin to shimmering reds and golds. Was that paint? No. My eyes nearly flew from their sockets. That was his flesh.

And his feet; they were long and slender, drenched in that same red and gold, forming two webbed fins.

Adrenaline flooded my body, and I jolted away from the creatures that stood before me.

"Where ... where am I?" And what in bloody Infernum were they?

"I will give you answers soon, but first you must calm down. Can you stand?" the woman asked, still at my level. Her outstretched hand was a rose hue, each finger bound to the other with a thin, pale-pink membrane.

I turned and vomited, *again*. What on earth were these strange monsters and where was I?

"See, she's fine," the man, beast, whatever, said. Then he pointed to my wrist. "Is that a ventus?"

"Yes, I would have missed her if I hadn't seen its glow," the other answered.

"Clear skin like that, besides the freckles, not a pockmark or scar. She must be someone important."

My heart was in a full canter, my breath ragged.

"Can't you soothe her? A song or happy thought," the man asked.

They continued discussing me as if I was not there.

"She's too stressed for that now. It wouldn't work," the woman said as she stood. "We must tell Hylos."

Where her feet should have been instead stretched slender appendages in gradients of rose and purple, akin to her counterpart's. Like fishes' tails.

I rubbed the sick from my mouth. I needed to get my wits about me and get out of here, wherever here was.

Behind the pair, another creature emerged out of a pool in the center of the large room. She had long hair of pale green falling in wet rivulets down her back. A song emitted from her, sounding softly through the room. But she did not sing it. It just poured from her. And in her grip, she pulled a soaked sailor I recognized from dinner, smiling in that strange daze. Like the look on the captain's face on the ship during the storm.

What possessed them so that they didn't fight back?

"I'll find some guards to help take her to a better location so we can decide how to deal with our ... *guest*," he said.

I did not like the sound of that.

Then he turned to walk away, wide shoulders roped in muscle. He was powerful. But with his back turned, it was my only opportunity.

Shoving past the pink-haired woman, I lunged for the pool.

"Wait, calm down, you're alright!" she shouted.

Like Infernum I was! If I could get into the water, I could swim back to the surface. I reached the pool and jumped in feetfirst. The chill shocked my system. I bobbed to the surface as the water warmed around me. Treading, I realized that the blue glow had returned, haloing me. Just like before.

"Just do something already, Raylik," the woman said, flustered.

He grunted, then stalked in my direction. Dammit.

Panicked, I dove as deep as possible, but my tired body struggled to fight down. I buoyed up, my back scraping a rocky surface now above me.

My eyes adjusted in the briny water as I scuttled underneath the structure, inching my way. Bubbles and pressure filled my ears, then an audible splash rushed through the water. I knew he was after me.

I kicked harder, swimming with all my weary strength, trying to flee. But then a hand clasped my ankle.

I turned to face the fiend, and his entire body was glowing a deep, bright red, like fresh blood. His eyes brimmed with the color. I screamed, sending bubbles streaming through the water. Kicking and fighting, I struggled against him. But he was *so* strong.

He pulled me through the water with ease, despite my kicking and fighting. When we breached the surface, he scooped me up into his large arms.

The pink-haired woman came closer to us. "I know my words mean little," she said, "but I promise you. You are safe."

Exhaustion settled into me rapidly. I was far too weary to fight anymore. My eyelids were heavy. I struggled to fight sleep, let alone the monsters.

"This is why we don't take women off ships, they're relentless," the man said, his dark-brown curls already drying. Water was wicking off his skin.

"Why was she on that ship? Calypstra's intel said it was only for cargo."

I gawked at the glass dome above us as more creatures like this pair swam by, glowing. I realized then: they were the lights surrounding the ship. The song that had called the men to jump into the sea.

The pink-haired woman must have noted my fear, because her face melted into another worried smile. "Do not fear, friend. Nymphaea saved you." She nodded to my wrist resting in my lap. "We will take her to my room."

"*Nixie*, we do not know her."

My vision faded in and out under heavy eyelids, exhaustion settling into my bones.

"The Holy Mother sent her to us. We must welcome her, Raylik," she answered.

We walked and walked before turning down another smaller hall, lined in colorful silks that passed by in vibrant smears. Until a door opened, and in dim glowing light, Raylik placed me down carefully on a comfortable couch. My body liquefied.

"I shall help you change and then you must rest," she, Nixie, said. "You endured much today."

"Guess I get to tell Hylos of your *guest*, then?" he grumbled.

"Thank you," she chirped.

Chapter 9

The room I awoke in was fantastical, as if crafted from pure magic. There was a bed at the center of the room, untouched. Its layers of pearlescent pinks and yellows gleamed in the morning light. Towering white columns encircled the room and reached up toward the soaring glass ceiling. Light filtered through from the dark sky.

No. That was not sky. Hundreds of fish swam by, shimmering in silvers and golds.

I jolted upright, a surge of adrenaline slamming into my sternum. Memories of the ship, the crash, and the strange beings flooded back to me.

That was water outside … *outsea* … that shone hazy blue-green. Because somehow, I was beneath the ocean.

"Good, you're awake," the pink-haired woman, Nixie, said as she peeked in from the entrance. My skin prickled as she breezed through the room and I kept a wary eye on her.

The longest end of her mauve dress kissed the marble floor, while the shortest end exposed her muscular thighs sparkling with opalescent scales. *Scales.* Like a fish. They twinkled past her calves in the light and blended into those long pink fins that she used to propel her in the water just outside these walls, as she did when she saved me.

She disappeared through an archway, a bolt of blush-colored fabric hanging from it. A rush of water. "I'll draw you a hot bath and leave you some clothes," she called over the sound, her voice crystalline, like a note from the treble. "I asked around and found something modest. I know your people dress more than we do." She returned through the archway. "Hylos, our ruler, requests you join him for breakfast."

Her ruler ...? Did sea-dwelling monsters have such things?

She entered the main room and stood before me. Completely and utterly mythical.

"He is kind. So please, don't ... I know it's hard not to but ..." She looked down at her finned feet. "But ... please don't be afraid."

I couldn't help but stare at her.

A wave of embarrassment washed over her features, which she flattened with a smile.

"After you bathe and dress, we'll go to Hylos *together*."

"What are you?" I asked, finally meeting her light, gray-pink eyes.

"I should have started with that," she said coolly. "We're children of Nymphaea." She pointed to mother's prayer beads. "Sirens."

I rushed my hand behind my back. "Sirens are fables for the overly religious," I parroted Vega.

She looked down at herself, evidence I was very wrong.

The words of the old men at the Yule feast about sirens taking ships swam back to my mind.

Vega had dismissed them, but it seemed they weren't wrong in their accusation of who or *what* was taking those ships. Who had also taken the ship I was on.

"And where are we?" I asked.

"Naiadon, the castle under the sea."

The under the sea part was obvious.

"The men on the ship? Where are they?" I pressed.

"They're here too, and safe. But Hylos will give you more details. Is there anything else you may need?"

"A way home for myself and the men you abducted would be lovely. *Thanks.*"

Her smile faltered. Good.

"You can speak with Hylos about that matter. For now, I'll give you some time to freshen up." Her tone was wounded as she started for the door.

"Nixie, that's your name, is it?" I asked.

"Yes."

"If anything happens to those men ..." I started, but the threat rang hollow, even to my own ears. What could I really do? Either way, I let my eyes pierce into hers, a silent promise to fight back whatever way I could.

"You have my word. They will be safe. You as well," she answered.

"What is the word of my jailer?"

"I didn't know jailers kept their prisoners in their personal bedchambers," she snapped back.

I looked around at the shades of rose that decorated the room beautifully. It clearly belonged to her.

"A cage is a cage no matter how lovely," I quipped.

"And fear often forces us to remain behind bars. Even when the cage door swings open. I'll be back within the hour to fetch you for breakfast." Then she dipped her head in farewell and left.

I followed the sound of rushing water, startled to see a ball of liquid swirling and steaming in the air, pouring itself out into a clawfoot bathtub in the middle of the room. Was it safe? Licks of steam unfurled as my muscles begged for relief. Did I care?

Out of my robe, I climbed into the long tub, likely meant to accommodate those long flippers. Fins. Whatever they were that the woman possessed.

I sank into the bath, soaking up to my nose in the exquisite heat as my mind sped. Sirens were real. Not just fables or cautionary tales but living beings in the ocean's depths. I racked my mind for any morsel of information from the sacred prayers about their existence while running a thumb over Mother's prayer beads.

I dunked the bracelet into the water, waiting for that strange blue glow to return. Nothing. I looked up to the glass ceiling, rays of sunlight beaming down, the swaying sea disorienting. Everything around me said land. But out there, it was clear there was nothing but sea.

I needed to find out how the bracelet worked if I wanted to escape back to the surface. I couldn't even see the break of waves above. How deep was I? And what of the captain and his crew? Could they swim to the surface themselves without whatever magic my mother's prayer beads possessed? My mind was working through the puzzle desperately.

But one piece didn't fit anywhere at all. Why did my mother's prayer beads have some sort of magical ability?

I huffed in frustration, bubbles in the steaming bath popping from my lips.

I thought of the captain and those kind honey eyes that he hid behind hard looks and orders. Was he afraid, wherever he was?

I sat up, leaning against the back of the tub. Tendrils of red covered my breasts and floated in the soapy water like rivulets of blood. With a deep breath, I steadied my thoughts. I needed answers, and it appeared those would come with meeting this siren ruler and figuring out what he wanted.

All rulers wanted something.

The water lost its heat as I devised a plan.

Nixie had laid out a dress made of lustrous green material for me. It was shorter than anything I'd worn before, hemmed just above the ankles and tied at the nape of the neck, leaving my arms bare. It was lovely. The material was light and swished as I made my way to the tall gold mirror in the bathing room, a table with brushes laid out beside it.

So human. So normal. Selecting one, I noticed the image of Nymphaea embossed in gold on the handle. Because like us, even they prayed to the Guardians. Or at least to one.

I worked the brush through my wet curls, uncertain who I was trying to impress.

Leaders were an unpredictable lot. I'd learned that firsthand in my father's court. Though I'd encountered few, Vega had taught me that with nobility it was crucial to begin on sure footing. To be palatable at all costs. At which I had failed miserably at Highthorn.

Even so, I would follow these creatures' lead in tone and manner. Patience wasn't my forte, but it was necessary now more than ever.

"Are you ready for breakfast?" Nixie twittered from the doorway of her room, returning as promised.

I nodded a yes.

Ready as I could be.

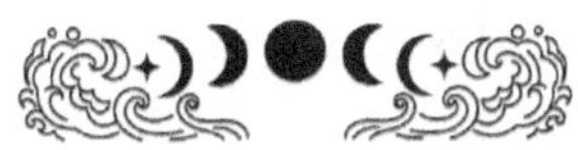

We walked down an expansive hall, illuminated by the surface sun beaming through the latticed windows. I looked out over an entire world of life appearing and disappearing in metallics or splashes of rust-colored fins flicking in the cloudy water.

"Far better than any view on land, but I'm biased," Nixie said, sharing the vista with me. I watched her cautiously as she drew near.

She was right. It was beautiful in its strange, saturnine way. Dark and cold as I read the North Elder Sea to be. But from this level, everything glowed in a soft green light and life shimmered everywhere, making itself known.

Creatures like Nixie swam in the distance, their bodies aglow in different pale shades as their legs, tightly together, propelled them.

We were so far away from everything I knew, in a castle beneath the sea. It was incredible but technically horrifying. Then why was I not absolutely petrified? In fact, something about this place felt oddly calming.

We proceeded through a towering archway marked by a hanging track of blue fabric and entered a room dominated by a long table made of glass. Seated at the center, I recognized Raylik, as Nixie called him, from the night before, with his hulking broad shoulders and muscles that rippled beneath his brown skin. He still wore only that small bit of red fabric around his waist.

The other being was positioned at the head of the table. He was more dressed, but his appearance far more unearthly. He ran a steady, finned hand through a wave of blue hair, long on top and sheared on the sides. His pale skin was imbued with a subtle blue tone and covered in intricate navy tattoos that swirled around his arms, up his chest, and faded into the white tunic that twisted over his shoulder.

The two sirens rose politely.

"Thank you for waiting for us," Nixie said.

"Of course," the blue siren at the head of the table answered with a charming smile. Then he bowed in my direction. "Thank you for being a guest at my table."

So he was their leader. But he seemed so young. Surely, younger than me by a few years. His face was smooth and unlined, the dimples in his cheeks boyish.

I tipped my head in return, determined not to allow his unusual coloring to unsettle me. I needed to be strategic. Diplomatic. Even if my pulse was racing.

"Really, Hylos ... a bow?" mocked another siren so stark-white he glowed like a full moon. He sailed through the room, dressed in a bright-yellow cloth wrapped low around his hips, similar in style to Raylik's.

He sat and began picking fruit off a platter on the table.

"You can't wait for our guest to be seated before you stuff your face?" Nixie sneered, gesturing with her chin to the open seats beside him and ushering me to join the table.

I sat, trying not to stare at the utter lack of color in his flesh and hair. Even his eyes seemed devoid of hue beneath his icy white lashes.

"Nix, darling, I am famished. She had us all waiting for—"

A grape pinged off his cheek from Hylos' direction.

"Manners, Morvyn," Hylos tsked.

The pale siren sighed, placed a heavy elbow on the table, and rested his broad chin in his palm.

"Where's Lumina?" Nixie asked Hylos. Her tone was so *informal*. They were all before him as if they were merely friends sitting around, about to play cards. Not breaking their fast with their leader.

"She's handling the cargo from last night," Hylos answered quickly.

"She won't be joining us then?" Raylik asked.

"No, she's busy," Hylos answered curtly.

I noticed the quick look that passed between Raylik and Nixie.

Through the glass table, I spotted the pale siren's soles, fused together with that translucent membrane between each digit, just as Nixie's and Raylik's were.

He twiddled them like toes.

I looked up to meet his cold stare.

"Wanna touch?" he said with a wink.

I tried to keep my face in check, despite the scowl tugging at my lips.

I clutched the table knife at my place setting. "Sure."

"Oh, I like her!" he said with a ridiculous giggle.

Great, off to a very undiplomatic start.

"Leave her be, Morvyn," Hylos said, then with a mere flick of his wrist, he summoned a resounding beat like a drum that rolled through the room.

Frigid dread settled in my gut. He'd summoned music, just as they had when they hypnotized the captain and his crew. But this song was different. Not eerie or enchantingly beautiful, but demanding, like the sound of a military tabor being struck.

Two sirens holding large platters overflowing with food entered the room. One was violet from head to toe, with a smooth head. The other was a more earthly-looking being with long black hair and skin that twinkled, scales of gold trailing down his legs to his fins. They placed food upon Morvyn's plate.

"Thanks love," Morvyn said flirtatiously.

Then the siren placed a hunk of raw fish on my plate next, with a heaping pile of odd, purplish grain that made my face contort.

My stomach growled.

"It's not that bad," Nixie said quickly, "but this will help." She pushed her palm at the plate, and a tinkling sound rang with the motion. The meat began to darken and cook before my eyes.

A gasp rushed from my lips.

"When will you all learn?" Morvyn said through a mouthful of food. "Terras need to be warned before you invoke stuff around them." He looked to Hylos, then Nixie. "Freaks 'em out." He turned to me. "It's like MA-GIC."

Before I could even tell him to fuck off for speaking to me like a child, even though he was right in some regards, Raylik spoke. "She's tougher than she looks."

Morvyn scoffed and returned to his food.

Raylik continued, "She gave me a run last night *after* nearly drowning to death."

"She's a fighter," Nixie added as she forked up her meal with a pleased smile, like she was proud of that fact.

"A fighter, you say," a raspy voice drawled. A woman appeared. She wore a short, sheer, black dress, and slinked to Hylos's side, perching on the arm of his chair.

His hand found its way around her lower body as she picked off his plate.

"Calypstra, this is the guest Nixie was telling us about," Hylos said, looking up to her as he mindlessly patted her ass.

Her midnight eyes narrowed at me as sharp teeth pierced a bite of food. Her skin was a pale, grayish color, like that of the dead, in contrast to her jet-black hair cropped short to her chin, which sliced through the air as she spoke.

"Why were you on that ship, terra?" she asked.

She was utterly terrifying and fiercely beautiful.

"Now, Cal, let's allow our guest some time to settle before we interrogate her," Hylos said.

Interrogate. I did not like the sound of that.

I looked around the table, noticing only six chairs.

"Are none of the men from the ship joining us?" I asked.

Nixie squirmed uncomfortably at my side.

Hylos cleared his throat. "They are safe, but occupying a different portion of my castle."

The joyless smirk of the death-toned woman told me it was somewhere I wouldn't wish to be.

"You see," the violet siren filled Hylos's chalice as he spoke. "Sirens have been vanishing, taken from the sea in the night. So I've ordered my people to intercept ships traveling between Whiterok and Oakhaven."

The memory of sirens' song came screeching back into my mind, burning my ears as it had the night before. *Intercept.* What he really meant was seize, like they had with the captain's ship.

Hylos met my gaze, then swirled his cup as though carefully considering his next words. "I believe the king of Oakhaven is behind my people's disappearance."

Chapter 10

My spine stiffened. This strange creature before me, the harbinger of Nymphaea's wrath, thought my father was taking his people.

If he thought the sailors were complicit in those crimes, enough to imprison and interrogate them, what would he do to the daughter of his enemy?

Hylos continued, "We believe the sailors may possess some knowledge of the fate of our people."

"Maybe you know something about that, considering you're of nobility," Calypstra said from Hylos's side.

I didn't miss the eyes of the others trained on her with what looked like fear washed with disdain.

"I am *not* nobility," I lied.

"Hair that red is known to be common of Blackthorns, plus those stones on your wrist are worth a fortune. Not to mention invoked. You're either some Duke's wife or a bastard."

"I am no bastard." The words flamed from my lips. Then I realized my error.

"A *legitimate* daughter of someone important. Noted." She smiled, pleased with herself.

Hylos's arm vanished from her side as she sat up and sauntered to the seat beside him.

"You may tell us who you are in good time. But for now, is there a name we may call you?" He asked like he hadn't even heard the accusation from the woman whose ass he was just palming.

"Elowyn," I answered. My name was common enough. It wouldn't raise an eyebrow, yet the black-haired woman's sharp eyes marked me all the same.

I stared back. She wouldn't discompose me. Not again.

"Well Elowyn, you are a guest here in Naiadon," Hylos answered with a tip of his chin and a sip of his drink. "But I would suggest no more late-night dips. You're fathoms below the sea, and if you go out there," he waved a hand to the large round window melded into the stone, which opened to infinite sea, "you will never reach the surface. That bracelet may help you survive the elements of open ocean, but there are monsters in these waters that would devour you in one bite. Or worse."

My stomach soured and I pushed away the plate before me, no longer hungry.

"I'm a prisoner then." I met his ocean-blue eyes, which seemed kind. But I wasn't a fool. He thought he could placate me with civility. I would dance the dance for now, as long as I received answers.

"You are a guest," he said with another polite smile. Niceties were always the easiest mask to don. "Also, Nixie and Morvyn will be your escorts around Naiadon."

Morvyn choked on his wine. "What, why do I have to play nurse-maid?"

Hylos ignored him, keeping his gaze fixed on me. "You are, of course, free to walk my domain as you wish." He raised a blue brow. "But I strongly recommend an escort for the time being. Few sirens here have encountered a human not behind bars or lulled in quite a while, and there's no telling how they might behave."

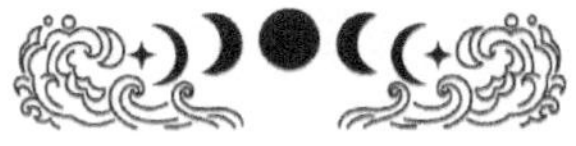

"You'll be staying across from me," Nixie said as we walked the halls together, the latticed glass windows holding back the sea, the ocean landscape just outside. "Elowyn, I want to say … I promise that …" She fumbled with her words but finally settled. "You are safe here."

"What of the men on the ship? Are they safe? What of the holy woman?" I said sharply.

"We didn't know women were aboard that ship," she said, watching me sidelong as we walked.

But *how* did they know who was and wasn't on a ship in the night?

Nixie continued, "We avoid vessels with women aboard, to honor the Holy Mother. But also, it's cruel. We cannot lull women as we do men. So they can only watch as—"

"As every person they dined with that evening jumps into the sea to their death? Yeah, it was *fucking* terrifying."

I balled my hands into fists. Anger warmed my cheeks. Mad because of the agony I went through. Furious for the drucia rocking in prayer to soothe herself. Where did her body rest now?

Nixie winced. "I'm sorry, Elowyn, for what you witnessed."

Sorry wouldn't bring the dead back to life.

Sorry wouldn't erase the image of the captain plunging into the sea.

But maybe sorry would make her feel guilty enough to offer answers.

Nixie turned into the niche where her room was and opened the tall glass doors across the way.

"This is where you will stay," Nixie said.

The room was large but far less pink than hers. Light refracted from the sea outside and danced on the walls in rainbows. It was lovely, even if it was a prison.

"Hylos said the men were being questioned. Are you torturing them?" I asked.

"We do not *need* to torture them," she said, shaking her head.

"They tell you freely what they know?" Impossible. Those prideful men would rather die at the sirens' hands than share any knowledge pertaining to king and country.

"When we lull them, we can step into their minds," she said.

My disgust must have been blatant, because Nixie winced at my expression but continued, "We can see what they see, hear what they hear. Essentially take over their mind's eye. We don't know their thoughts or wants, but we can parse those out through their actions and words. That is enough to know *certain* things."

Like charters, mapped routes, or siren capture.

"What if they know nothing? Have seen nothing? What if they're innocent?" I saw the thought worm its way through her mind as silence sat between us. She knew more, thought more. But Nixie wasn't the person who held the men captive. Nor who held me captive. She was simply following orders.

"Then I am sure Hylos will let them go. He is a just ruler, as his father was before him. He will not let any harm befall prisoners of—" Of war.

"I should go. Let you settle," she said, unwilling to share further, then turned and left, shutting the door behind her.

I let out a shrill, muted yell. Then sank into the comfort of the large, circular bed at the center of the room in defeat. Billowing lengths of white fabric swept down from the high ceiling, cascading in delicate, gossamer bolts. I let out a breath. From one enclosure to the next.

My eyes drifted to a book on the bedside table. Its cover was stained like it was once waterlogged, and I flipped through it. Words like "passion" and "love" leaped off the pages.

I rolled my eyes. Nixie had likely left it for me. She was trying so desperately to make me feel welcome. But why? And then cold sank into my belly. If she knew who I truly was, of my origin, would all kindness stop?

I needed to get out of this place. To do so, I'd need to venture out of the damned room they'd quietly tucked me away in.

Hylos claimed I wasn't a prisoner but a guest in his domain. It clearly wasn't true, but I could at least test the bounds of what I was permitted to do without escorts. If I could explore the castle, at the very least get a feel for its layout, maybe I could figure out where the sailors were.

I watched bubble trails race upward past the window, unable to even see the surface of the water from here. *You're fathoms below sea.* The siren king's words needled through my mind.

One thing at a time. Learn the castle. Find the men. Then figure out the actual getting out alive part.

Clutching the book in hand, I rose from the comfortable bed. There had to be a library here if there were books. That, at least, would be my excuse if anyone were to question me. I swept out of the room, noting that Nixie's door across from mine was still closed.

Stepping out into the hallway, I turned a corner and collided head-on with a wall of blinding white.

"Going somewhere, terra?" Morvyn said, that vexing smile playing on his lips, still indecent with no top part of his clothing in sight.

I held up the book like a shield. "I'm looking for a library. I assume you have one, unless everyone around here is as uncouth as you?"

He let out a chuckle and leaned against the wall, deliberately blocking my path. "Hylos owes me two gold, you know."

Despite being so strange-looking in coloring, he was classically beautiful, with high cheekbones and a chiseled nose, like a marble bust from forgotten times.

"He thought you wouldn't leave this room for the rest of the day. But I knew." He let the words linger as his gaze swept over me. "You're far too curious for your own good."

I stilled my features. How much danger was I in, standing in the presence of this creature? This siren. And why wasn't I more afraid?

"Do you stalk every *guest* around here?" I said.

"Just the pretty ones," he answered, then turned his alabaster back to me. "Come on then, I'll show you around."

Chapter 11

The thin fabric of my dress flitted with each step, light and airy, as we walked down a long hall, turning into an entrance with a sweeping glass staircase.

"So, where are you from then?" Morvyn asked coolly as we ascended the steps shoulder to shoulder.

I eyed him warily.

"Come on, I promise not to bite. Unless you want me to, of course," he added with a devious smile, his sharp upper canines exposed, as white as his flesh.

All the sirens I'd encountered had sharp teeth. Besides Hylos's, which were blunt like mine.

I pointed skyward. "I'm from up there."

Morvyn's smile deepened and his nose crinkled. "Of course, those pathetically small feet gave that away. But what region?"

"What do you know of the regions on lands?" I asked.

"Never heard of a map? Talk about uncouth," he drawled.

"I lived by the mountains in an area called Ashbourne." It wasn't technically a lie. I had spent most of my life at Granger House, which slept at the base of the Ashen Mountains outside of Ashbourne.

"That's quite a way from the ocean," he said.

"Yes, I was sent away."

The corners of our eyes caught as we wound up the glass staircase.

"By who?" he asked.

"My father, to be married," I answered, unsure why I was telling him the truth at all.

"Blah, marriage," Morvyn scoffed. "Repugnant."

"Agreed," I sneered.

"I take it the marriage wasn't your idea then."

I shook my head, a silent no.

"Well, no grotesque husband awaits you here in Naiadon, my dear. Marriage is not a common practice among sirens; our inclinations lean toward a more *liberated* expression of love."

They didn't marry? That wasn't even an option in Oakhaven. Unless you wanted to be a spinster who died alone in a hovel in the woods, or joined a drucia convent.

"But if you're looking for a good time for the night, we can provide that," he added, elbowing me in the side.

I flinched at the unexpected touch.

"Sorry," he apologized with a polite nod, then created space between us. A minuscule but respectful gesture.

I paused, looking past the glass that surrounded the staircase, and stared in wonder at the sprawling castle that stretched beyond. Glass spires of stone and crystal reached heavenward, their edges blurred by the blue-green shimmer of the sea. "How is this place even here?"

"Well, I was never the best pupil, believe it or not."

"I believe it," I quipped.

He smiled, reveling in the remark, then continued, "But, I know King Aegir the Great created it. He is ... well, *was* the king of all three seas. Hylos will tell you he still is, but his father has been missing for years now." The corner of Morvyn's pale mouth dipped into a frown for a heartbeat.

I continued my ascent. "Is his father one of the missing sirens Hylos is looking for?" The sirens he thought my father took.

Morvyn reached my side, no sly smile to be seen. "Aegir was the first to go missing."

My stomach sank. Hylos's revenge on my father wasn't just for his people, but his family.

The staircase gave way to a sizable circular room. Tremendous white marble bookshelves lined the walls, filled with hundreds and hundreds of manuscripts and books of various colors, their spines aligned, with scrolls tucked into honeycomb grids. My heart thrilled. I'd never seen so much literature in all my life.

Morvyn collapsed dramatically onto a white armchair, kicking his finned feet up on its matching ottoman and throwing a lazy hand around the room. "All the wonders of the sea, m'lady."

It would take hundreds of lifetimes to read them all, and that made my very soul sing. So many worlds to uncover. So much truth to be garnered. At Granger House, books were lifelines to the world past my mountains. The only opportunity to be completely free. To wander safely through a thousand lives in the absence of my own.

I walked to one of the colossal bookcases, a ladder leaning against it. It was begging me to climb up and harvest its bounty, to reach the highest fruit. My eyes traced the shelves of books past a mezzanine filled with more volumes, which stretched to the glass ceiling that glittered with life in the hazy blue sea. Spectacular.

My fingers grazed their covers, most aged and worn.

"May I?" I questioned, looking to Morvyn, who watched me curiously.

"By all means," he answered from his seat.

I picked up a red book, its cover making a crisp noise as I cracked it open. The scent of old paper and ink whispered from the pages that cascaded at my fingertips. The words were strange, neither in Oakhaven nor any of the other five languages I knew.

"Lumina's always banging on about these books," Morvyn remarked with a smirk. "I'm surprised she's not around here with her nose stuck in one. She says they're lost to the terra world, but we've plucked them from the depths, hidden away in sunken ships or forgotten cities." He sauntered over to my side and peered over my shoulder. "Usually, I just look at the pictures."

I looked up at him. "I don't know this language."

Morvyn plucked the book from my hands, his ice-blue eyes scanning the pages.

"That's because it's old Praetirum, a language that's about six hundred years older than you."

"Morvyn, I hope you're not bothering her." A voice rang through the room, warm and cantabile.

I turned to see a radiant siren dressed in a yellow silk dress with layers of tendrils that danced as she coasted our way. The color of her gown contrasted with her deep mahogany skin but matched her gilded fins, visible with each step.

"Be wary," she said to me with a knowing smile. "Siren men are shameless rakes who often see humans as conquests." She stopped before Morvyn and me.

"Lumina, *whatever* do you mean?" Morvyn said as he leaned an arm on the bookshelf, flexing his biceps with the motion.

"You Morvyn, of all sirens, know *exactly* what I mean," she said, looking up at him. Golden scales coruscated on the crests of her cheeks as she raised an eyebrow.

"Lumi, love, are you jealous of my conquests? If you wanted to be one of them all you ever had to do was ask." He reached out and tucked a brunet braid behind her ear. She leaned toward him in familiarity, but she still rolled her beautiful brown eyes for show.

"See? Shameless," she said to me. "You must be the human visitor all of Naiadon is speaking of. I'm happy to meet you. I have so many questions."

Anxiety fluttered in my chest. Questions?

Morvyn retreated to the couches. "Careful how you answer, Elowyn, or you will be stuck answering her *questions* for the next millennium while she scribbles them down."

"I'm sure she would prefer that then being flirted to death. Besides, we haven't had a terra woman down here in a while. Much has likely changed on land," Lumina answered.

Did that mean there had been others before me?

"Terra." The new word rolled clumsily off my tongue. "I've never heard that word before."

"Terra, like the Guardian Terragos," she answered. "You and your people are his children, as we are Nymphaea's." Her words were warm but matter-of-fact. "Nixie told me about your prayer beads for the Holy Mother, how they granted you breath under the sea. We call it a ventus, an invoked gift blessed with siren magic to allow you in our domain." I hid the piece behind my back. If it was magic, like they said, it might be my only way out of here.

"Where did you get such an item?" she asked, her eyes quizzical. She looked at me as though I was some strange phenomenon she was trying to figure out. She was so beautiful; it was almost hard to look at her. Like her bright eyes would shine a light on every secret you ever held.

"It is a prayer bracelet, used to recite prayers," I answered. "It belonged to my mother."

"I'm familiar with prayer beads, but I've never known them to be invoked. Interesting. Well, I'm glad you had it. It likely saved your life. Now you're safe here with us."

Safe wasn't exactly how I'd describe being a prisoner among mythical creatures that hated my father.

"Nixie believes Nymphaea herself saved you," Lumina added.

"Some of us are more *spiritual* than others," Morvyn said as he flipped through a book.

"Can you even read, Morvyn?" Lumina said. "Sirens are made in the great Mother's image, after all. How could we not believe in her wonder?" She pointed down to her long, slender, finned feet, scintillant in gold.

I looked at her in awe, struggling to pull my eyes away.

"Have you taken her to the treasury?" Lumina asked Morvyn.

"That's what I was thinking next. Will you join us? You know all about that old stuff."

Lumina shook her head, "Your grandsire found half those relics and gifted them to King Aegir the Great. We get it, you're another ignorant wellborn, but at least pretend like you know something of your dynastic history." She looked back to me. "Thank goodness I'm here to rescue you from pure and utter brain rot," Lumina said with a smile.

"We were having a lovely time before you arrived, for your information." Morvyn sounded insulted.

"Of course we were," I said, then shook my head no at Lumina in jest.

She smiled softly. Despite her otherworldly beauty that told me to be wary, I liked her.

"To the treasury then," Lumina said, and turned for the stairs.

Morvyn followed, as did I.

Then I saw it.

Out of the corner of my eye, on the second level of the mezzanine, hidden in one of the towering bookshelves, a faint blue gleam like a sapphire star twinkling in a dusky sky. Was I imagining it? It seemed like the more I looked at it, the brighter that light became.

Then a sharp clamor rang through the library, like blackbirds calling to one another in a garden.

"What was that?" Lumina said as she looked back at me.

Morvyn turned too.

Heart still, I trained my eyes on them, avoiding what had my true full attention.

I shrugged my shoulders like I'd heard nothing at all.

Morvyn and Lumina passed a look between them. Then they turned back toward the stairs.

With one last glance, I noted the spot above their heads that still glowed, increasing its light as I trailed them out of the library. Something on that level of the library called to me and I needed to know why.

Chapter 12

We descended the winding stairs, then turned down another lengthy hall made entirely of glass. It extended like a bridge over a vast, dipping ocean field. Sirens swam beneath, weaving through a forest of swaying sea grass, toiling in the gold-green strands. It was incredible.

"Many sirens live and work in the castle. Those below are tending to farms or fishing," Lumina explained.

"Do they not need to breathe?" I asked.

"We take breath from the water as you do the air upon land."

"Then why a castle if you can live out there?"

"Great question. Many of our kind do still live in the open sea."

"Ew, just imagine," Morvyn interjected.

"Some have their own homes, modest and grand, that are completely submerged. However, King Aegir built this castle, Naiadon. It was the first of its kind. Mirrored after the castles upon land. Today, the other noble families—we call them Circles—have created structures of their own to emulate this one. But Naiadon is the largest and most grand to date. Here, we are out of the ocean's elements."

"Plus, we can have pretty guests, like you," Morvyn added with a playful wink.

"I suppose there is some truth to that." Lumina put a finger thoughtfully to her chin. "Many say King Aegir created this castle for his lover, Hylos's mother."

I surveyed the castle stretching into the distance, all stone and sparkling glass. Its peaks rising from the depths. All of this for love.

"Lumi, you make pickups sound so *unsexy* when you follow them with facts," Morvyn said as we passed through a stone archway into a large rotunda. Its imposing stone dome looming above was supported by matching columns that divided various halls and chambers.

Sirens hurried in and out of the passages, each adorned in vivid hues. They moved through the other archways carrying large baskets, or wielding spears. All marched purposefully to their destinations. They were spellbinding.

My stomach flipped as extraordinary colored eyes flickered with curiosity in my direction. Their gazes quickly diverted when they recognized Lumina and Morvyn flanking me. Clearly my guides were important and feared.

"Don't mind them," Lumina said at my side. "They rarely see humans. They're all far too busy preparing for the celebrations to be bothered, anyway." *Celebrations?*

The crowd thinned as we turned down a narrow hallway lined with glowing orbs of water lights that cast dancing shadows on the walls. At the end stood a towering, studded door. Lumina waved her hand past it, and with an illustrious hum that radiated from her, water formed and spun out of her fingertips before swirling into a hole in the door, like a key in a lock.

The door clunked open, revealing a room filled with treasure.

My breath caught in my throat at the sight before me.

"Brilliant, isn't it?" Morvyn said as he and Lumina entered.

Following him, I carefully avoided the piles of gold coins scattered about. Magnificent objects of all shapes and sizes topped short pillars that stood at intervals. Glinting crowns, tiaras, a necklace with black sapphires so large they could fill my palm. Riches filled every corner of the space.

"The treasury holds all of Naiadon's greatest jewels," Lumina declared, her voice resounding in the filled chamber.

Morvyn picked up a delicate tiara, its ornate details catching the light, and placed it on his head. "I call it Naiadon's Hubris Hall. I swear Hylos has taken every girl he's ever fancied at least once to show them the *family jewels*." He elbowed Lumina, who didn't laugh.

He snatched up a tarnished metal crown, spun to me, then placed it atop my head with care.

"Fit for a queen," he smiled.

Balancing the weighty crown upon my head, I looked around. There was more opulence in this room than I had ever seen before.

"Did you take it from ships that you forced to crash, like the one I was on?" There was more bite in the accusation than anticipated.

Lumina's forehead crinkled in concern. "Just like the library's books, we've salvaged these items from the ocean floor. We aim to save and restore. Not take."

"Yet here I am." The snap of the statement was purposeful that time.

"You are the only one on that ship who was saved." She looked at me squarely, a scowl carving her gentle mouth. "The rest being taken from the ship goes against everything I stand for."

So she did not agree with her leader, then. Good to know.

Were there others like her who disagreed as well, and so openly?

But then my attention tore across the room when I spotted it. "Is that a virginal?"

I stepped over gold coins and jewels, drawn to it.

"Be careful," Lumina urged me. "These relics are priceless."

My eyes scanned the basic wooden instrument. It wasn't as nice as the one I'd played at Highthorn; it was far more simple, like the one I'd possessed at Granger House. My fingers pressed into its simple wooden keys, awaiting that sweet sound I was craving among all this chaos. A flat, clunky sound clanged instead. I frowned.

Morvyn bounded to my side. "What is it?"

"A virginal," I said.

"A what?" His features twisted in confusion.

"A musical instrument."

"Can you play it?"

"Yes, and well."

He grinned at that. "Then we should have it brought out. It's not doing any good hidden in here." His webbed hands glided across the keys. They didn't sing to his touch either.

"It's broken," I said.

He stuck out his bottom lip in a frown.

"What did you find?" Lumina called from her spot across the room.

"A virgin, quite rare in Naiadon!" Morvyn bellowed back.

"A *virginal,*" I corrected as we waded through the wealth back to Lumina.

"Ah, do you like music?" Lumina brightened a bit with the question.

"Yes, very much."

"Please don't get Lumina started on the topic of music or we'll be here for hours," Morvyn said, walking out the door.

"Music is the world's gift from Nymphaea," she said, following Morvyn.

I looked back longingly at the virginal, yearning to lose myself in its keys, but followed Lumina and Morvyn instead.

"Every siren has their own unique song that manipulates water in a brilliant way. Despite all the studies of siren scholars, there is no clear rhyme or reason why our songs all differ. One day I wish to figure it out. But, the most brilliant part—"

"Told you not to get her started," Morvyn sneered.

"The most *brilliant* part," she repeated, her words measured and deliberate, "is that every living creature, from the depths of the ocean to the heights of the sky, possesses a melody, a song that echoes through space and time. Even long past one's life. Though you may not realize it, humans even hum at their own frequency. Yet, sirens alone possess the ability to channel and refine their songs. We can weave our melodies into the very fabric of existence and manipulate water *through* it."

"We get it. Sirens are awesome. I could have told you that," Morvyn said with a lecherous smile. A clanging tune echoed through the chamber. With a dismissive wave of Lumina's hand, water surged against the heavy door, slamming it shut behind us.

Lumina shot Morvyn a sharp glance. "It's not that we are simply great. Many creatures are great. Look at humans, for example. It's that we are ... well, we're simply magical. We take an element of this world and through sound and beauty, we change it," she finished.

It was astounding, their ability to harness such immense power with sound alone. Water bowed to their commands with a tone and a flick of their wrists. But it was also horrific. Water could be gentle as baths or summer showers. Yet waves could swallow metropolises whole, and rivers could carve through stone with time. Being able to harness the power of water and the minds of men meant sirens were unthinkably powerful.

What damage could they do to Oakhaven? What chance did my father's subjects have against them?

We walked back into the large room, but now the clusters of sirens had paused and the sound of clashing metal crashed.

"That must be Hylos practicing," Morvyn exclaimed. "We've got to see this! He'll put on a show with all these spectators."

We wove through the tightly packed crowd, my stomach churning as sirens surrounded me.

We passed through an archway that opened into a vast, globe-like glass room, a pool shimmering at its center. Arms of all types hung on weapon stands, sharp metal gleaming.

Clang. Hylos intercepted Raylik's relentless blows as his muscles rippled beneath his pale-blue flesh. Each clash echoed with raw power as steel met steel. Blow for blow, Hylos held his ground, but he was struggling to gain an advantage.

They were both skilled fighters, but Raylik was clearly physically stronger.

On the other side of the room, Calypstra sat on a velvet chair, uninterested. Her legs were crossed, exposing her strong-lined hamstrings under her short, sheer black dress. Over her shoulder, in the sea behind the crystal barrier, were three deathly pale creatures, nearly transparent.

Their hair bobbed like black streamers as they gaped blankly, exposing sharp teeth too big for their mouths.

"What are those things?" I asked Lumina at my side. Goose pimples pebbled my arms. They were revolting.

"Deep-sea sirens. They're a breed apart from us. They come from a depth we call the Midnight Realm."

"Why are they here?" I asked.

"To carry out Calypstra's bidding," Lumina replied with a hint of concern. "Calypstra hails from a Circle located there."

My throat tightened.

Raylik unleashed another thunderous blow from above that caused Hylos to lose his footing. A fleeting hint of wounded pride worked in the ruler's jaw. Hylos tossed his sword aside, a cocky grin stretching across his face.

"We *are* meant to work on your swordcraft." Raylik groused.

"If you're afraid of a little challenge, brother, just say so," Hylos said, his grin widening. With a graceful leap, he arced through the air, his body forming a perfect arrow as he plunged into the pool.

Raylik shook his head and followed suit.

A silence fell over the crowd.

"This'll be good," Morvyn remarked, a gleam of excitement in his eyes.

Behind the glass, a blur of glowing blue marked Hylos's swift movement through the water. He was so unthinkably fast.

Raylik's red glow followed in relentless pursuit, a pure predator on Hylos's trail.

Abruptly, Hylos paused, pivoted, and faced Raylik head-on. They both treaded water with their fins keeping them centered. This is what the siren king and his court did for fun, it seemed. Fight.

A mere heartbeat passed, and then they were swimming swiftly toward one another, finned feet bound in muscle, propelling them head-on, closing the distance.

With a powerful, silent crash, they collided in the murky sea, grappling in the water, spinning and entwining blurs of red and blue.

The crowd hushed, their collective breath held as Hylos found himself bound by Raylik's strong arms. With a free hand, Hylos flicked his wrist, conjuring a tide rushing beneath the water, pummeling them both.

The crowd erupted in cheers. Morvyn whooped along with them.

But a frown tugged on Lumina's mouth. "He's cheating," she said softly.

The fighting pair regained their stances, squaring off again. Raylik burned in merciless red and swam full speed back to Hylos, who was waiting for him with a smile.

They crashed into each other in a storm, grappling with their boulders of muscles, vying for grip. But Hylos had the upper hand, finally wrapping his forearms firmly around Raylik's neck.

Raylik thrashed against the hold. Hylos's smile was stark white in the water. He had Raylik right where he wanted him.

Raylik finally tapped on Hylos's arm around his neck and the crowd went wild.

It seemed the sirens didn't just fight for fun; they relished watching it too.

"Incredible!" Morvyn cheered.

The fighters finally broke the surface of the pool and pulled themselves up as water slicked their muscles.

Morvyn, still clapping, strode to meet Hylos.

"Good show, friend." He cupped a hand around Hylos's bare neck and shook him.

"It wasn't easy," Hylos panted, still trying to catch his breath. "Raylik always tries to make me look bad in front of my subjects."

"All I saw was him letting you show off," Morvyn said.

Raylik walked up, breath steady as he shook his hair dry.

"It was entertaining, but you need to be strong on both land and sea."

Hylos ignored the statement and walked instead to meet Lumina and me.

"What did you think, Elowyn? Do they fight like that on land?" Hylos asked.

Lumina flinched at my side. Something in his stance or demeanor unsettled her.

"I've seen nothing like that before," I answered.

Calypstra sauntered to Hylos's side. Her creatures tried to follow her beneath the water, mindlessly bumping into the panes that thankfully kept them out.

"What did you think, Cal?" Hylos said as he swung a heavy arm over her shoulder. She didn't answer. She kept her eyes locked on me.

"Let's celebrate your victory!" Morvyn exclaimed.

"We need to train more," Raylik said.

"Come on, Raylik, don't be such a drag," Calypstra drawled, oily eyes still trained on me. "Besides, we should show our guest how sirens like to have fun." A smile exposed her sharp canines.

"She should return to her quarters," Lumina answered, not looking at the pair.

"No," I interjected. "I'd like to join you." It was crucial for me to learn as much as possible about this place, its layout, and even the sirens themselves if I was to find a way out of here.

Hylos gave me an approving smile. "We'll meet you all in the Grotto then."

Raylik returned his and Hylos's swords to a rack and reluctantly exited the training grounds.

"Tomorrow we train your swordcraft," he grunted, passing Hylos, who was already buried in Calypstra's neck.

"Come on," Lumina said to me, turning to leave.

"Don't tear down the place, you two," Morvyn shouted to the couple as we left.

A song thundered through the air. I turned to take one last look at the pair, only to see Calypstra's eyes still on me. Why was she so enthralled with me? Unease burned in my gut. The others all seemed so eager to make me feel welcome in their own way. But not her.

Hylos flicked a hand, conjuring a wave that crashed against the door, sealing it shut with a resounding slam. Water lapped at my heels.

"They're ridiculous," Lumina scoffed.

"Come now, Lumi, green is not your color," Morvyn chided.

Lumina's eyes flared as she cut a look at Morvyn.

His words had hit her somewhere low.

"If you wish to keep your head, I'd suggest you shut that hole in it," Raylik rumbled.

"Lumi, you know I'm just kidding." Morvyn softened his tone.

"I have some studying to do. Good evening, Elowyn. Enjoy the revelry; it is all we seem to do around here now," Lumina said. Without a second glance, she strode quickly down the hall and out of sight.

Morvyn's lips pinched to one side. "It was just a joke."

"There is always the bitter taste of truth in jest," Raylik said coolly.

Chapter 13

The polished white marble interior relinquished us into the raw mouth of a cave. Before it, a statue of Nymphaea stood. Below her were waves rising around her coiled tail, and soaring above her with unfurling feathered wings was Aeretha, the Guardian of sky. The pair was locked in a reaching, desperate lover's embrace, immaculately carved from one breathtaking piece of marble.

It was a masterpiece against the natural chaos and jagged teeth of the cave opening. The two Guardians clung to one another in imagery I'd never seen before.

"They don't speak of that in terra prayers, do they?" Morvyn remarked as we approached the stunning statue and the dark-amber door behind it.

"Speak of what?" I asked.

"The *scandalous* love affair of Nymphaea and Aeretha. Very sexy and *very* dramatic. Sirens grow up on the heart-wrenching tale of the two most powerful Guardians in the world who found love during their joint effort to flee the cruel world of Terragos," Morvyn answered.

We padded nearer to the entrance, the vibration of song in the distance charging the air. The sound had put my senses on edge since the ship crash. I tried to steady my nerves.

Morvyn pointed to Aeretha. "One Guardian created sky," he said, then pointed to Nymphaea, "and the other created the sea, all to escape Terragos. In his anger, he cursed them to never leave their domains, giving one wings and the other a fish's tail."

As we neared, I could better see the immaculate detail: the intricacy of the waves spraying in a rush, the anguish carved into the lovers' eyes.

Morvyn continued, "Terragos was jealous of their love, so he forced an ocean and a sky to permanently separate the two paramours."

"I've never heard that part before," I said.

My list of unknowns was growing.

"Of course you haven't; terras just recite all the *boring* holy prayers," Morvyn drawled.

Were there other stories of the Guardians I did not know? More things in this world that were a mystery to me?

We passed the stunning statue and entered the mouth of the cave.

"I did not know you were a theologian," Raylik said to Morvyn, hard-faced as he opened the large amber glass door, releasing the strange music held behind it.

"Don't ask me about any of the prayers on sacrifice or restraint; I never listened to those bits," Morvyn said.

"That's obvious," Raylik said as he swung his large, muscled arm and gestured for me to enter.

I forged ahead. The sound hit me fully, a bewildering vibrant noise that rebounded off the rocky cave walls. My ears strained at the soundscape; it was absolutely otherworldly, trilling and quivering with the thrum of some strange percussion that vibrated through me.

Sirens of all shapes and colorings swayed to the melody together under a cold, glowing light seeping from the plants that clung to the rocks in clusters above, throbbing to the swell of music. The light illuminated the colors of the sirens' skin beautifully as they rolled their bodies and reached for one another in sweeping movements.

Morvyn sauntered ahead, dancing to the beat as he worked his long, lean body through the sea of flesh.

"Stay close," Raylik ordered.

I did not argue. The sight was the strangest I'd seen yet, besides the sirens themselves. But even though a part of me feared the music and the sirens' power, another part was mesmerized. They were absolutely divine. Like holy prayers coming to life.

Raylik and I worked through the bodies, following Morvyn, whose brilliant smile said he was absolutely reveling in the scene.

The music was completely overtaking my senses.

I tried to capture it, the sound, the harmonies, the tempo, but it was so wild and incredible. Impossible to comprehend even with my knowledge of music.

Webbed hands glided across my body as if I belonged to the crowd, to the music that begged me to roll my hips and sway as the sirens did. To melt into their barely clothed and glorious bodies that glistened, their scales twinkling, like stars beneath the sea.

We broke free of the pulsating assemblage and passed a large piece of green sea glass jutting out into the space. Sirens clustered around the structure, and behind it a pink siren handed out chalices that sloshed with drink as she placed them into empty hands.

Morvyn led us to a tall table with stools, and we all took a seat.

"They sound marvelous this evening," he said over the music.

I'd heard of taverns; dark, dingy places where men drank from tankards, but this was nothing like that. This was brilliant.

A siren approached our table, her dark-green skin hardly covered by fabric that tied on each side of her expansive hips with a strip across her ample chest. Her hair was like a green river rippling down her back.

"Why *hello*, Bryn," Morvyn said with a wink.

"Good evening," she said, placing two chalices before Morvyn and Raylik.

"And for you, love?" she asked me.

"Water and food. Cooked," Raylik answered.

"I believe she asked me," I said sharply.

Morvyn raised his pale brows. "I believe she did."

Raylik kept his lips in a tight line.

"What are you two having?" I asked.

Morvyn puffed a laugh that made me regret the question.

Nixie appeared from the densely packed crowd. "Oh Elowyn, you're here. What a surprise." Her elevated voice chimed over the thrumming beat as she skimmed a gentle hand over Raylik's broad, bare shoulders in passing.

"She insisted on coming," Raylik answered.

Nixie sat between Raylik and Morvyn and looked at him, a thought seeming to pass between their minds.

"I'll take a cup of firewater, Bryn, please," Nixie said to the green siren.

"I'll have the same," I said.

"I don't know if that's the best id—" Nixie started.

"Let the girl have some fun!" Morvyn interjected.

"I'm not a girl," I snapped.

"You're right! You are no girl, but a woman, who can have a bit of firewater with her new friends." He raised his glass to me and smiled.

"So, a cup of firewater and—" the server asked.

"And some bread, please," I added for good measure.

"And three shots of Dragon's Breath, darling," Morvyn said.

"No," Raylik ground out.

"One Dragon's Breath ... for *now*," Bryn said with a knowing smile, like she had seen this play out before.

"Were you able to see some of Naiadon?" Nixie asked over the music.

"Yes, I saw the library and the treasury," I answered.

"Oh, the treasury is such fun! Rayly and I go down there to try on the jewelry." Her pink eyes grew wide as she spoke.

I looked at the large, lumbering figure to her right and tried to imagine him frolicking through the archives with little Nixie at his side.

He looked me straight in the eyes as he took a deep drink, without an ounce of shame.

"Raylik is more fun than he lets on," she continued. "Don't let all the silence and brooding fool you."

The server set two drinks before us, then disappeared.

"Precisely why he should have a shot of Dragon's Breath with me! Come on, just one itsy-bitsy shot. Please, please, please," Morvyn whinged.

Raylik waved a hand at him to shoo him off.

I took a drink of the firewater. It was bitter and spiced with the familiar burn of alcohol. I'd restrain myself from drinking too much to keep my wits about me, but maybe it would help calm the last remaining nerves clawing at the nape of my neck.

"Oh, one won't hurt," Nixie said with a sly smile, "and it'll get him to stop grumbling." She eyed Raylik over the rim of the cup, his shoulders settling under her gaze as he nodded a yes.

"Four Dragon's Breaths!" she shouted, her voice like a bell's toll cutting through the music in the cave. The sound made it to the siren tending the station at the sea glass structure, who nodded a yes.

"Make that six!" Hylos bellowed, his hand on Calypstra's waist as he guided her through the dancing crowd.

Did he ever stop touching her?

Morvyn drummed his hands on the table, rattling our chalices. "Now we're talking!"

Hylos clapped a heavy palm on Raylik's shoulder.

"We drink to celebrate the good news," Hylos said as he and Calypstra took a seat at the table.

Morvyn sketched a bow. "As your humble servant, I must obey my king regent's command," Morvyn said.

Nixie rolled her eyes.

Regent. I noted the word and Morvyn's comments from earlier. Hylos believed his father was still alive. Captured by humans. Somewhere in my country, held captive by my king and father.

"You haven't even heard the news yet," Hylos laughed, a warm, broad smile radiating across his young face.

"I don't have to, my liege. For you, I will party at your mere command," Morvyn added.

"You'd drink yourself stupid at the command of a crustacean," Raylik responded.

"I resent that, *Rayly*." Morvyn said his friend's name in a high-pitched tone, mocking Nixie.

Nixie whirled her finned hand through the air, thumping him hard in the chest, making him grunt.

"Do not mock me, Morvyn, or I'll kick your scrawny, pallid ass."

I felt like a trespasser, intruding on an intimate moment. Like someone peering in on a family through an open window. They were so comfortable, so at ease. Words flowed effortlessly between them, as if they knew each other's thoughts like the beat of their own hearts.

A family. Friends. Both things I had never had before. Not truly.

"Tell them already," Calypstra hissed, drinking from the chalice that appeared before her from the knowing hand of the dutiful Bryn.

Calypstra didn't seem to fit. It was like she was a piece shoved into their lives. Even her relationship with Hylos seemed strange. She was older by some years. Closer in age to me than him. And I noticed the uneasy eyes from the others trained on her.

"The Great Circles have arrived at Naiadon," Hylos said, smiling at his friends. "Well, all besides Circle Twynox. But that was to be expected. Draveen's likely busy murdering some relative of his or committing some other heinous atrocity," he said casually.

My blood ran cold. Were the sirens truly so brutal? Looking out into the crowd of beautiful dancing bodies, there wasn't a hint of that violence. Only beauty and song.

"An insult to you," Raylik said, his voice like gravel.

"Those from the Midnight Realm have a longer distance to travel. It is no insult to the king," Calypstra remarked smoothly, not calling Hylos regent. Strange. Morvyn had said it was what he preferred to be called.

"And more time to plot," Raylik said, his eyes staunchly on her.

"Morvyn," Hylos interrupted the two, "your Circle just arrived. I invited them here tonight."

Morvyn spit out his drink.

"That got in my fucking mouth." Calypstra grimaced as she wiped at her face.

"I need to get out of here." Morvyn stood abruptly.

"Sit down." Hylos pulled his friend back down into his chair with that boyish grin. "The *good* news is that all the Circle leaders have agreed to come to the deipnon tomorrow night, and afterward the symposium."

Morvyn groaned. "Including my *horrendous* family?"

"Of course Fushdmuir Circle will be in attendance. They possess all the fjords of the North Elder Sea. They are one of our greatest allies," Hylos answered as he sipped his drink.

"Ugh, my horrid aunt has been hounding me all year to mate with that absolutely drab girl from that unheard-of Circle in the Nordhavet Trench, to strengthen ties or *whatever*."

"The one whose father is *extremely* wealthy and manages all trade in your Circle's territory?" Nixie added.

"All the wealth in the world cannot buy a personality, Nix darling." He rolled his pale eyes. "Plus, I already have plans to mate with Thalassa, Nyra, Julian, and Calliope." He counted the names on his pale, webbed fingers.

"However will you have time?" Nixie teased.

"Exactly! There's only so much mating one young, male siren can do in a single evening. Even if the flesh is willing."

Mating? What exactly did they mean? Sex?

As if reading my mind, Calysptra snapped her head toward me. "Have you told the human of Hydroxia yet?"

"No," Nixie answered curtly.

"And why is that, Nixie?" She smiled.

Nixie turned to me.

"Hydroxia is a holiday of sorts, like Yule or Beltane," she said, listing common high holidays. "We feast and celebrate the bounty of Nymphaea."

"And then they all fuck," Calypstra drawled.

I remained composed despite her clear attempt to unsettle me.

"You're so crude," Nixie said, rolling her eyes.

"You *all* have sex?" I looked around at the table. Well-versed in many cultures from across the world, I had never heard of anything like it.

"Hydroxia is the longest full moon of the year. We *usually* pick one siren to mate with, if we choose, to celebrate the fertility of the sea that the great Mother Nymphaea has given us. The holiday coincides with siren mating patterns. The hope is for children."

"For those who can have children," Calypstra said pointedly.

Nixie frowned. The words seemed to wound her, but Raylik's hand found hers under the table.

"Oh, it's the most wonderful time of the year!" Morvyn said zealously. "See all these ravishing sirens?" I looked out with him at the crowd shifting to the music that drummed through my bones. "They're courting. That song you hear, it comes from them, hoping to attract the perfect fit for one blissful night of glorious carnal pleasure. The days before are full of feasting, drinking, games, and of course, debauchery."

"This year we will keep the debauchery to a minimum," Hylos interrupted. "At the symposium I will make the announcement of our planned advance on Oakhaven and request aid from the other Great Circles."

The firewater burned in my gut.

"You plan to attack Oakhaven?" I said over the siren's song.

Hylos's sea-toned eyes met mine from across the table. "Yes. We plan to advance on Oakhaven after Hydroxia."

"Why?" I asked. And why was he telling me this?

His brow furrowed. He wasn't used to being questioned.

The rest of the table fell silent, the hammering of the siren music filling the void of their banter.

"You will start a war." I pushed further.

"As I was saying this morning, sirens have gone missing from the seas. We must swiftly retaliate and find our people." Like his father. "Otherwise the abductions will continue," he answered.

I looked around at the table, hoping one of them could see reason. They all averted their eyes, finding interest in their drinks. Besides Calypstra, of course, who was watching my every breath.

"The ship I was on, did their crew show you that through their memories?" I asked.

Hylos looked around at his table. Nixie squirmed, giving herself away as the person who had explained their techniques.

Hylos said nothing, which was an answer in itself.

I knew the captain didn't believe in such things as sirens; he'd told me. He was more annoyed than concerned by his crew's fears. To his men, they were legends or myths. There was no way any of them had ever seen a siren, let alone captured one.

"So you haven't. Then why are you so certain it's Oakhaven that takes your people? You can control men. It doesn't even make sense. Your people are violent, as you just said. You're likely picking off one another."

"Watch your tongue, terra," Calypstra hissed.

"You know nothing of the situation," Hylos dismissed me with a dry laugh as he leaned back in his chair.

"I know war means the death of your people and mine."

"Your people?" Calypstra raised one of her black eyebrows in my direction.

"It will be an easy siege. We can control most humans, and we are physically stronger. We will invade, find the missing, figure out how Oakhaven is taking our people, and then leave," Hylos said.

He seemed so immature in his ignorance.

"Every leader thinks their war will be easily won." I shook my head in disbelief.

Something leaped in Hylos's jaw and his eyes darkened to tempest blue.

But I continued. "You think women will not fight you while you control their men? Are you ready to kill them in the process?"

Nixie's eyes flitted between us. Had she not thought of that? Had any of them thought this situation through? War would inevitably mean death.

"Some may die, yes, and that's a sacrifice I'm willing to make to ensure Naiadon and my people are safe," Hylos ground out.

All eyes still avoided me, except Hylos's and those of the snake at his side.

"Here you go, seven Dragon's Breaths. Just in case you all would like one," Bryn said as she placed a silver tray in the center of the table with small, smoking cups.

"Enough politics," Hylos answered, grabbing one of the drinks.

Each of the others grabbed one too. So did I.

Hylos smirked. "Cheers." Then he raised his cup to me. "To new alliances."

Then they all knocked back their drinks. And I did the same.

Chapter 14

Nixie and I walked down the dark corridor to our rooms. The sea, held back by the latticed glass, could have been mistaken for a midnight sky. Only the strange, swirling siren light illuminated our path.

War. Hylos wanted war. I'd read and reread history books on the subject throughout my education. I'd always had a strange and morbid fascination with the subject. With learning what horrendous things men of power would do to one another during times of conflict. The lengths they would go to for their proclaimed cause. Some wars were virtuous—at least that was how the victor painted them—but most were senseless. Driven by honor. Valor. Pride. Or the desire for more power. And in exchange for their vanity, influential men sacrificed the blood of innocents, just as Hylos was willing to do.

We turned to the alcove that held our rooms. A potted orchid rested upon the sill of the expansive, sea-filled window above a stone bench that bridged our rooms. Despite being in the ocean's depths, the flower still found filtered sunlight that coaxed the orchid into bloom, even so far from true sky. Its vibrant, purple petals seemed to gaze back at me. I had to do something to stop Hylos.

"Is there anything else you need tonight, Elowyn?" Nixie's voice carried a weariness that matched the heaviness in her mauve eyes, which they'd retained since Hylos spoke of war.

What did she think of this? Of her leader? Of Oakhaven? I thought of asking her, probing how she justified such drastic measures. Why war was on their lips when sirens were mere legends upon land.

But in the pit of my stomach, which still burned from drink, I knew she wouldn't tell me. At least not truthfully. She would instead paint a pastel picture to convince herself and me of the righteousness of her leader's actions, the same way many loyal followers before her had prepared to march into battle for their leader. Even at the expense of the lives of their friends and family.

There was only one course of action left for me to take.

"No, I'm fine, thank you." I smiled, hiding the turning of my thoughts. "Good night."

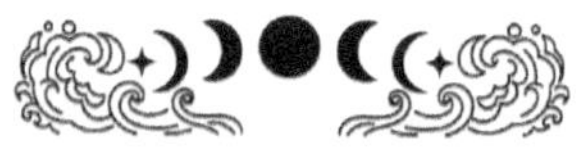

Ear pressed against the bedroom door, I waited until there wasn't the slightest sound before slipping out of the bedchamber.

In the hall, silence greeted me. The siren light had waned to deep citrine and collected in pools on the white marble floors as I crept soundlessly with the smallest semblance of a plan.

First, find one of those pools that led to the ocean.

Then, dive into its depths.

Finally, pray.

Only Nymphaea herself could safely guide me to the surface, the somehow-invoked prayer beads the only thing protecting me from dying in the sea's black belly, gasping for breath.

The armory's pool seemed like my best bet. Hylos and Raylik had easily swum out to what appeared to be open sea. Calypstra's monsters slithered through my mind like eels. They were lurking out there. I looked out to the surrounding sea, past the arching glass ceiling above. Shadows lurked in the folds of the sea's darkness.

My blood ran cold. *There are monsters in these waters that would devour you in one bite. Or worse*, Hylos had warned. But I couldn't remain idle when he was planning an attack against Oakhaven.

I had to warn my father. And I didn't ignore the small hope that wriggled in my chest either, that maybe he would even reward me for warning him and allow Vega to return to my side, or even call off my marriage to Cedric.

Then, a soft shimmering of yellow appeared, lightly bounding to the center of the dark hall.

I stepped closer, straining my eyes to see the source of the light. In the center of the lemon-colored aura was a butterfly. How did it find its way down here?

Princess, many voices woven into one called. *Come to me, little forgotten princess. I will take you home.*

Curiosity and that voice compelled me to step closer to the butterfly bouncing through the air, as if on an unfelt breeze.

Let us go home, the voices called louder, warming in tone with each step I took nearer, the sound intoxicating. *Home for the princess, safe and sound, sweet forgotten princess no longer lost at all.*

Yes. Home. That is what I wanted. What I needed.

When I reached out to touch it, wishing it would land on my finger and grace me with its acceptance, it flitted just out of reach.

I smiled. It was as if we were playing a game. I took a step forward, and then another, until I was walking down a set of steps, not even watching my footing in the pitch black. That little yellow butterfly was all I focused on, just out of reach. All I could see. All I could think of.

Home for the princess, it said again and again, calling me forward, step after step. Deep in the haze of my mind, logic tried to remind me, *You are no princess at all. You have no titles. You are no one.* But that beautiful voice kept on repeating it until I believed it true.

Home for the princess.

Home for me.

The butterfly passed through a craggy wall with effortless grace, plunging me into darkness. My heart tripped. I *had* to follow it. It would take me home. It knew the way. A nipping breeze trailed fingers across my skin, thick with the smell of damp and brine.

Come, princess, the voice demanded, pulling me from any sense. *Let us go home.* The familiar yellow glow illuminated a seam in the stone, like a crack of light under a door.

Desperately, my fingers found the grainy, rough seam. The wall only appeared impassable. With all my strength, I heaved the stone to the side. The rock broke my nails and made my fingertips painfully sore, but that harmonic voice dulled all aches. All questions.

Stone scraping stone echoed through the black. I shifted the impasse enough out of the way so that I could writhe through the gap, rough rock snagging on my skin, clawing my body. It was worth it for home.

I stood on the other side in a cave-like room with a pool in its center, not perfectly circular like the others I'd seen that allowed the sirens to come and go from Naiadon. This pool was uneven, like a natural fixture. An inky pond in the center of a dark cave. I should have been afraid. Should have been wary. But above the center of the pool, that happy little butterfly fluttered and my heart swelled.

Let us leave, little princess. Let us go home. A smile stretched across my face. Home. Mother hugging me, my face hidden in her thick, raven hair. Home. Father picking me up, raising me above his head with ease as I giggled so hard I couldn't breathe. A time long ago when I was the center of their world, all candied in that yellow light. Home. Granger House bloomed in my mind. The warm sun on my skin, Vega bringing me tea and sweets as I read on a blanket in the garden, the mountains surrounding me like an embrace.

The water's black skin gave way to more lambent butterflies that danced out of the water, one after the other, until hundreds fluttered around me, gilded and radiant, blessing me in winged kisses.

A laugh bubbled from my chest as I smiled.

Yes, they would take me home.

Then, a glorious golden stallion cantered out of the water, huffing clouds of hot steam.

Let us ride there, princess. It was the owner of that beautiful voice that sounded as if it came from Nymphaea herself.

Yes. Let us.

Wading into the pool, I found a step beneath my foot; it was slimy and slick but I did not care. I ran a hand over the steed's smooth-coated neck. The creature whinnied, nuzzling its velvet nose into my palm.

I would go home. I would be safe. I would find my mother, and my father, and Vega. And all would be right in the world again. This magnificent steed would take me there.

With a steadying breath, I prepared to mount.

"Get the *fuck* away from that!" a voice demanded, a thunderous rhythm pulsing beneath the words, drowning out the comforting call of the horse.

It was Hylos, an orb of illuminated water bobbing at his shoulder.

Chapter 15

His eyes widened in fear. "Elowyn," he shouted, "run!"

The horse's mouth unhinged like a snake preparing to devour its prey, revealing rows of deadly sharp teeth and wailing out a horrendous, shrill scream that pierced my world, stabbing into my eardrums and shattering the balmy dream its words had coaxed into my mind.

Dread strangled a scream of pure terror swelling in my chest.

Hylos's song filled the room, his orb glowing blindingly bright. With a flick of his wrist, he hurled the sphere of water at the monster. It splashed against its skin, burning the creature, the smell of scorched hair filling the air.

The beast let out another screech, furious at Hylos. He raised his finned hand, rhythm thrumming with the movement, and shoved his palm in the beast's direction. The song charged with the water in a racing stream to the creature.

The monster turned swiftly to flee into the dark pool, showing the dreadful other half of its body. It was like a slimy crab, and one of its long, scuttling legs slammed into me with a hard blow to my diaphragm, hurling me across the space.

My teeth clattered as I landed, my head bouncing off the unforgiving ground.

Hylos's music stopped.

The only audible sound was that of my heart slamming into my sternum and the sloshing center of that oil-black pool.

"Are you all right?" Hylos said, rushing to my side.

"What in Infernum was that thing?" I asked between gasping, painful breaths. I could already feel the bruise across my rib cage, puddling under my skin in black and blue.

"A kelpie." He scowled toward the pool, but held out a finned hand to me.

I took it, and he pulled me to my feet.

"A what?" I asked.

Reality was hitting me hard and fast, spinning me dizzy.

Why had I followed that voice down here?

"They lure humans into the water, take them deep below to drown them, then consume them. Nasty vermin. Thank the Holy Mother I was having trouble sleeping and walked the castle. If I had not heard that strange song ..." Hylos looked at the still-sloshing water. "It's so odd. They're usually found in lochs in the northern country when they're not hibernating in the Midnight Realm. I've never heard of one attacking in Naiadon." His blue brow furrowed. "We have no free roaming humans for them to feed on."

A splitting headache carved through my head, and I rubbed at my temples.

"Yeah, their call has that affect. Dreadful migraines. Come on, let's get you something for the pain."

We walked up slippery, moss-covered steps and wove through winding, worn halls. Did I truly make my way down this path all on my own? I remained close to Hylos and the lambent orb he kept bobbing at his shoulder. It was far more horrifying in Hylos's light, without that voice guiding me.

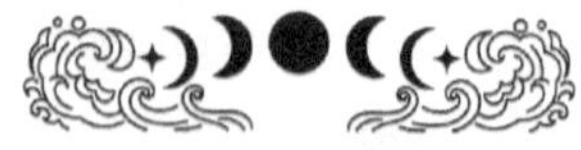

We turned down an impressive corridor that led to towering double doors. Music emanated from Hylos's hand, and with a simple motion, the doors swung open, revealing a comfortable study. The world outside an immense tracery window was graying as morning broke.

Hylos pointed a finger at a hearth-like structure in the center of the room, and a deep, thunderous percussion struck, conjuring a ball of steaming water that whirled inside like a strange fire.

"Have a seat," Hylos said, pointing to two couches facing each other. Needing relief, I did as he said, passing a large map of Oakhaven made from a piece of white coral. I noted the ship-shaped figures littering the top.

Hylos handed me a thick, soft blanket, and I settled into the plush couch, the pulsing in my head persistent. At a counter beneath the hearthside bookshelf, Hylos prepared two mugs of something steaming, like he was fixing a cup of tea for a friend.

"This will help," he said, handing me the steaming mug, his own in hand.

Warily, I scowled at the dark liquid, but didn't take the mug. Could I trust it? Could I trust him?

"It's safe," he said with a scoff, but I didn't relent.

He took a sip. "See? Safe." Then he returned the warm mug to me.

"Well now you've tainted it with your siren-y spittle," I complained, but smirked.

He let out a chuckle and sat in the seat across from me.

Something about Hylos was comforting, despite every logical thought in my mind telling me to flee the strange being before me with his blue, otherworldly features.

But it was like he was safe, or familiar. Like those dark-ocean eyes were a long-forgotten memory.

"Is this your study?" I asked.

"Technically, my father's. But my mother commandeered it when she visited Naiadon. She loved to read and write. Well ... so I've been told. I come here to be close to her." He leaned back into the seat, pulling a blanket across his lap, and a look washed over his boyish features, aging him into the man that circumstance had forced him to become.

I knew that look well.

"She is no longer alive?" I asked gently as I pulled my knees in. I sipped the drink and it unknotted the throbbing in my temples.

"I don't think so," he said, watching the hearth. There seemed to be more to the story, but we both let his words dissipate and be overtaken by the gurgling of the fireplace we both watched.

"My mother died when I was young," I said. "Well, was murdered, really." Saying it out loud gave it the weight of truth. I could never utter those words upon land, not without the threat of a traitor's death.

"It is a strange feeling," Hylos said, "not having the people who brought you into this world there to guide you through it."

I nodded. "A lonely feeling."

"So lonely," he added.

Like you were adrift at sea, never knowing when you would see land again.

"But you find ways to see them in the world," I said. "To hear them. Feel them. You were once a part of her. She's forever a part of you."

He smiled gently. "Among my people, they say that if you listen close-ly, you can hear the song of your ancestors within your own. Maybe every note we sing carries the voices of those who came before us, woven into ours like threads in a tapestry. I can't say how much is truth and how much is hope, but I like to believe my parents still live together, at least in my song." We let the thought settle between us, quiet and warm. It was as if, together, we could feel his mother in that room—reading, writing. Living.

Sadness sank into me. What did my mother love? There was so little I knew of her. Her name was like a curse in my father's country. A memory he had ensured was thoroughly erased from the face of the world. All that remained of her was me.

"I heard what it called you. And I want you to know"—his blue, familiar eyes softened, truly kind—"when you're ready to tell me who you are, no harm will come to you."

I believed him.

"Will you tell me about Oakhaven?" I asked.

"What do you wish to know?"

"When did this all start?" I drained my mug and placed it on the table beside my seat, my head feeling exceptionally better.

"The first siren to disappear was my father." The true king of the sirens. "At first, like you, we assumed it was another rival siren Circle. My father had enemies, but it would have been odd for no ransom or other actions to follow. His inner circle searched all three seas meticulously, from the darkest midnight depths to the tropical shallows. But they found nothing."

He frowned. "But then something *changed.* More and more sirens were taken mysteriously, like they were ripped from the sea to the sky without a trace. No one could figure out how, or why. Until ..." Hylos stood, walking to the large map.

I followed him, the blanket wrapped around my shoulders.

He pointed at an area east of Oakhaven.

"This city formed on the ocean, raised from the sea like magic. It's no coincidence. The missing sirens. My father's disappearance. All of it has to be connected."

"Whiterok," I said, wrapping the blanket tighter around my shoulders. My prior fate.

He offered me a terse nod, not peeling his eyes from the map. "I think it's made with siren magic."

But how was that possible? Cedric was the one who built it. There was no way he knew of sirens, was there?

"Tonight you tried to leave," he said, still not lifting his eyes from the map of my father's country. "But that bracelet you possess, the ventus, it's no mistake that you possess it. No mistake you're here. The sirens have a saying: Nymphaea sends those to be saved. She sends people to us for a second life, one not afforded to them above the waves."

He looked up at me. "Elowyn, I believe there is a reason you are here. The Guardians themselves have ordained it. Nymphaea herself has sent you to us." Sincerity saturated his voice. I wanted to trust him, wanted to believe; he was almost as convincing as the kelpie's entrancing call. "And maybe it's because a 'forgotten princess' needs a place to start over."

But this was not my home. If the Guardians had done this, then it was only so I could leave and tell my father of the fate that brewed in the oceans past Oakhaven's borders. That was the only thing that made sense. What else would the Guardians want from me?

"I wish to leave." My words cut quickly through Hylos's trance.

He frowned, then turned and looked out the large window, his back to me. Dark-blue ink swirled in waves on his skin, images of sea creatures visible between them.

"I'm sorry," he said, watching the light permeating the sea and fishes lazily swimming awake. "But I can't let you."

Anger boiled my blood, heating my cheeks. I wouldn't stop trying to escape. Even if it meant my life would be at risk, because it would be worth that small chance that I could make it back to land, to Vega, to warn my father and his people of what was to come. To do *something* for Oakhaven for once besides being locked away at another fucking ruler's behest.

"The captain of the ship," Hylos said into the void.

My heart went staccato.

"Calypstra reports he seems to know of the instrument you told Morvyn you enjoy, the virginal." He turned to me. "And we just so happen to have one that needs mending." He arched a blue brow at me. "All ordained."

He stepped near and I didn't retreat, instead hanging on to his every word. "I will allow the captain to leave his cell each day after breakfast. You will work with him on repairing the instrument and be with your own kind. Hopefully, you will find comfort in that."

But my mind was already threading through a plan. If I could speak with the captain, spend time with him daily, maybe we could conjure a way out of here, together.

"On one condition," Hylos added.

"What?" I asked.

"Spend time with us. See my people for who they truly are, what we stand for. See past the terra holy tales and learn what isn't told in your prayers."

I thought of the captain's temperate hazel eyes that had undone me with one look. Thought of the wonderful rhythm of his voice that sounded like the gentle rise and fall of sunlit waves, warm and golden, breaking on shore. Crashing over me.

"Fine," I said, trying to hide just how much I yearned to be with him again.

"And ... " he started.

"You ask two things of me when I am offered only one?" I scoffed, knotting my arms across my chest. "That's not how negotiations work."

"It is when you hold all the power." He smirked.

"What is the second demand you *unfairly* ask of me?"

"Stop trying to flee."

Never.

"Not just because you will die if you make it out of the safety of Naiadon, but because I believe our fates are intertwined. That there is more to this story than either of us know. I feel it in my very blood. I hope with time you will see it too. When the time comes for you to decide which side of this war you wish to stand on, if you believe it is truly not mine, then I will allow you to walk out of here without another word."

"Fine." I would bide my time, *then* escape with the captain and his crew. Once on land, I would return to my father's castle and tell him all that I knew about Hylos and the sirens so he could stop them. So Oakhaven would be safe.

Hylos stuck out his webbed hand, and without hesitation, I shook it.

Chapter 16

"Hylos told me what happened last night with the Kelpie," Nixie said, her large, mauve eyes watching me carefully.

Did Hylos also tell her what the monstrosity called me? The voice still lingered, a ghostly echo in my mind. *Lost princess.*

We wound up the library stairs, the glass steps radiant in the morning light that stretched through the green-blue sea. A sunny day likely shined above, the air still touched with cold from the winter sweeping off my father's land, and not a cloud in the sky blocking the sun that beamed so brightly that it had found me, even at these depths.

I could almost feel that sunshine on my skin. Smell the snow in the distance. How I longed for home.

"Nasty creatures," Nixie continued, despite my lack of response. "They come from the Midnight Realm. Born in pure darkness. I think that's what makes them evil. A lack of light and beauty."

We reached the top of the stairs, and I saw the captain standing in the center of the library next to Raylik and the broken virginal. Raylik's webbed hand firmly grasped the captain's shoulder, and the captain's face flashed with recognition steeped in ire. As though I was not his ally but his enemy.

His captain's coat was gone. He wore only a white undershirt stained with salt water and sweat, unbuttoned to reveal the hard lines of his chest. Those honey-gold eyes that had once glowed with warmth over our blissful dinner had now dimmed, tempered and cool.

It was one thing for the sirens to imprison me; I knew cages. But the captain had only ever been bound by the horizon of the sea. It made my blood boil to know they had trapped him below it. The man had no business being confined.

Raylik shoved him in my direction, and I lunged across the room to support him. The weight of his heavy frame was staggering. The captain steadied his balance.

I gathered his restrained hands in my grasp.

His eyes flared at my touch and he ripped away with a scowl.

"Why is he bound?" I demanded. A gash ran along his jawline. My hands longed to trace over it gently, to assess the damage. But this time, I kept them firmly at my sides.

"To protect you," Raylik said.

"Why do I need to be protected from him?"

"You are a guest here," Raylik grumbled.

"I am as much a prisoner as this man. Shall you chain me next?" I snapped.

Nixie frowned. "Sirens are wary of terra men. These restraints were mostly for show as we walked through the castle."

"Calypstra saw in his mind that he locked you away on his ship," Raylik added.

"Who did what to my mind?" Arlo exclaimed.

A shiver ran down my spine at the thought of Calypstra, that snake, even nearby the captain. Sinking her fangs into his thoughts.

"He was told to keep me confined in that manner," I said. "That was not his choice. Unshackle him."

"There is always a choice," Raylik argued.

I turned to Nixie. "*Please.*"

Nixie nodded to Raylik, who grunted disapprovingly but obliged her silent request.

He brushed a hand over the chains, a deep sound pounding rhythmically, and water shimmered from his palm. With a click, they unlocked and clattered to the marble floor.

The captain watched us warily, like a fox cornered by hunting dogs, his chest rising and falling rapidly as he tried to breathe through the fear. My heart panged at that look. The brave, stalwart captain was afraid.

"And may we have some food and drink as well?" I asked Nixie, unwilling to try Raylik again.

"Of course." She nodded and turned to leave, but Raylik stood sternly, arms crossed.

"Raylik, will you *please* assist me?" she called from the staircase.

He was reluctant, scrutinizing the captain, who stared back boldly, ready to fight. They were the same in height but Raylik was broader and I knew his strength was unnatural.

I sent a prayer to all four Guardians that Arlo would remain calm. Otherwise they might not allow him to visit me alone.

"Try anything stupid and I'll drag you to the bottom of the sea and watch as the fish eat your meat, *human*," Raylik said, then shouldered past him, sending the captain stumbling.

Then the pair disappeared down the stairs.

"Are you alright?" I asked.

"Where the fuck am I?" he said, rubbing at his wrists. His breath was slowing, but he scanned every corner of the library, no doubt searching for an exit.

I pointed up at the glass dome that topped the library, to the expanse of sea above, as a large fish swept by.

He looked up with me.

"A castle ... under the sea." It sounded utterly mad.

He grimaced. "But how?" No panic touched a single syllable, even though his eyes remained wide and searching. He was trying with all his might to remain calm.

"I have no Guardians-damned idea how." I'd never even heard of such things, castles at the bottom of the ocean. Yet here we stood.

He narrowed his gaze at me. "Are you one of those monsters?"

"We were both on the same ship together, do you not remember?" Had he been injured in the shipwreck? Hit his head? Had he forgotten the time we spent together? I ignored the fact that the thought wounded my feelings.

"A beautiful maiden who charms a captain and his crew, then sirens are summoned. It sounds like something straight out of a holy prayer. You could have called them to our ship," he said, his brow knitting.

"So, you think I'm beautiful *and* charming?" I said with a smirk, reaching for the banter we'd shared on the ship.

He scoffed and shook his head in disgust. Ouch. Then he turned to inspect the library.

Maybe it wasn't the time for jokes.

He was reaching with his accusations. Which was understandable. How could anyone reason in this situation at all? But how did he conclude that the king's only daughter was a siren?

Then I realized. "You truly do not know who I am, do you?"

"No, I told you before I didn't," he said tersely, still eyeing the room.

"Do you make a habit of trafficking unknown women on your ship, captain?" I crossed my arms before me. Flames sparked in my belly. He had the audacity to hold me captive and bring me across the sea, and he didn't even know why.

"No, I don't. It's bad luck to bring women aboard, but it was a favor to Cedric."

Cedric? He said the name with familiarity, and without the appropriate title. He knew my betrothed. But why did Cedric pay for my passage and not my father? And why did he insist on me being locked away?

"He also paid me ridiculously well. But now we're in this mess." He waved his hands above to the water-crested dome.

"Glad you were *fucking* compensated for my imprisonment," I said back snarkily.

He let out a bitter laugh. "Well, at least I know it's the same supposed *lady* from my ship with that language. That foul mouth of yours will get you into trouble one day, you know."

I cocked an eyebrow at him. "More trouble than being at the bottom of the ocean imprisoned by mythical beasts?"

"Imprisoned? Only one of us is being paraded about in shackles," he said, watching me closely. Those damn strong features sharpened with deadly precision. I tried to ignore what it did to me, even in disdain. "You're dressed pretty in their clothes and throwing orders about. You're no prisoner at all. The question is why?"

"Beautiful, charming, and dressed *prettily*. Careful, Captain, if you keep complimenting me I may just fall in love." I lolled my head to the side and gave a toothy smile.

He rolled his honey-colored eyes. "Well then, who are you?"

How would he react to meeting the king's daughter below the sea? Or, what if this was all a trick? The sirens might have lulled him, or whatever, into compliance to ask me such questions.

Hylos had promised me time to tell him my true identity, but could I really trust him? He was my captor and an enemy to my father, and therefore an enemy to me. What if instead of waiting, he'd used a handsome, familiar face along with the virginal to butter me up, all to learn who I truly was?

I stepped to the virginal and grazed the keys, wishing they would sing back to me.

"What do you know about this instrument?" I asked.

How in Infernum did a captain of a ship have any idea how to repair such an instrument, anyway? It had to be a ploy.

"I asked *you* a question first," the captain said firmly.

"And I'm ignoring your question," I answered, then crossed my arms. "Look, if you can't help me, I can just tell Raylik—you know, the enormous one who's awfully ill-tempered—that there's no need for your assistance after all. He can just send you back to—where were they holding you again?" I leaned on the virginal.

His hazel eyes blazed when Nixie appeared at the top of the stairs, right on time with my threat, a platter of food in her finned, pink hands, its savory scent filling the room.

"I've brought you both some cooked fish and bread." Her cheery, singsong voice belled through the library.

"Well actually, Nixie, I don't think we'll be needing any food after all," I said, watching the captain.

"My father was a luthier," the captain blurted out. "I assisted him as a boy."

Nixie's gaze flitted between us. "Yes, that's what Calypstra saw in your mind ..." Nixie said, confused, not realizing how intrusive the statement sounded.

The captain watched her, half in fear and half in revolt.

Nixie tried a smile to shake his weighty stare. "Okay then, I'll just leave this right here and get out of your way." She placed the platter on a small table.

"Lovely," I replied. "I think we're ready to get to work. Isn't that right, *Captain*?" I needed to see for myself if he really knew how to mend a virginal. I would decipher whether he could be trusted before I attempted to discuss plans of escape with him.

Luthiers were a rarity in the foothills of the Ashen mountains, passing by Granger House only yearly, so I often did the maintenance on my virginal between their visits. I knew enough about the task to decipher if he was telling the truth or not.

"Fine," he said reluctantly. "Call me Arlo. The whole captain thing is a little formal considering our *current* circumstance."

"Yes, siren prisoners don't really have room for that type of formality, do they?" I said.

"My thoughts exactly." He cut a hard glance at Nixie.

She raised both rose-colored eyebrows at me. "Well, you two are clearly cut from the same strange cloth." She let out a breath. "Do you need anything else, Elowyn?"

"No. Thank you, Nixie."

She tipped her head, smiled sweetly, and left us again.

"Elowyn, that's your name?" The captain—*Arlo* looked me up and down.

"Yes," I answered. My stomach tumbled; had he already put together my true identity?

But then the smell of food distracted him, pulling him by the nostrils like a ravenous dog. He grabbed a thick slice of crusty bread and wrapped it around some cooked fish, then scarfed it down in one bite.

"Are they starving you?" I asked.

"Couldn't tell you," he said, inhaling another bite. "I've mostly been in and out of some strange dream. Until I came to here."

Lulled. While they searched his mind for details of missing sirens, they'd kept him in that spellbound state. And all they found out was … he could repair virginals.

"So, you really expect me to mend this thing … at a time like this?" He gave the instrument an accusatory look, then turned that look to me.

I nodded yes. If he could actually fix it and this wasn't a trick, then maybe we could figure out how to get out of here. Ideally with him and his men alive.

"Seems like a tremendous waste of time, but okay. If you insist." He dusted the crumbs from his palms and turned to the virginal, his long, slender fingers fiddling with the keys. "Besides the wood being in poor shape, I'm guessing water damage. Considering where the Infernum we are." He pressed the keys and looked inside the instrument. "The action isn't working here either." He pointed inside the belly of the instrument. "The whole thing needs to be restrung; some strings are broken, most corroded." He returned to the marble table for more food and washed it down with a glug from a pearlescent cup.

That all sounded accurate. The water damage was a given, but the rest surpassed common knowledge of the instrument.

Arlo stood to his full height and scanned the library. Then looked at me abruptly, an idea taking hold. He strode back to the instrument, his boots clacking against the polished marble flooring.

"Here, look at this." He leaned in close to the virginal, waving me in. "Closer, right here," he said again, and I leaned in to look with him.

Then his hand ensnared my upper arm, pulling my ear to his mouth. Cedar and salt wafted off him, driving me mad.

"My turn for questions." His words were sharp. "Why do they trust you?" I tried to pull back, but his grip dug into my skin.

"Let go of me," I hissed.

"Why are you here and I imprisoned? If you're not a beast, then why do they trust you?"

"They don't. I'm as much a prisoner as you." It sounded as absolutely foolish coming out of my mouth as it did swimming through my mind.

They kept him under lock and key, somewhere with the others, and I was free to roam their halls. But why? What did they want from me?

He looked me dead-on, eyes crosshatching my face, thick lashes fluttering, until understanding flushed his features.

He released my forearm, repulsed.

"You are content." Disgust scorched each word.

"Content?" I questioned.

"Unless—" He quickly grabbed my face. He held my chin, moving it with those beautiful hands side to side, our faces so near my heart halted.

"What are you doing?" I said, shaking him off.

"They haven't entranced you, I don't think."

"They can't. Apparently it doesn't work on women."

"So why are you playing house cat?" His gaze seared me, the accusation more painful than when he thought I was aiding the sirens. As if accepting my circumstances was a greater offense than deceiving him.

"I am not content." I scoffed at the assertion like it hadn't injured my pride. "I tried to escape *twice* and nearly died trying, both times."

But Arlo said nothing. Only stared at me as a frown tugged on his lips.

I knew that look well. Pity.

But he did not need to pity me. I fought as hard as I could. But what was the point of resisting blindly, without thought, when I could navigate this situation with strategy? Especially if it meant keeping him and his crew alive.

"Come now, don't be rude," Morvyn drawled from across the library.

Fear flickered in Arlo's eyes, quickly chased by anger.

"Elowyn darling, is this *brute* misbehaving?" Morvyn sailed beside me. His white hair was swept back, showcasing the edges of his sharp cheekbones. In contrast to Arlo's raw humanity, Morvyn appeared absolutely otherworldly.

"No, he is not," I said flatly, stepping to Arlo's side to make it clear who I stood with. "He simply wonders the same as I. Why am I free and he and the others are not?"

"You're free to roam Naiadon because Nymphaea brought you here to be saved." Morvyn's mesmerizing white eyes flitted to Arlo. "And she sent you here to repent, *tiny toes*."

Arlo didn't flinch or falter under Morvyn's icy regard. Instead, jaw clenched, he took a step closer.

I gently grasped Arlo's forearm, giving it a firm squeeze, hoping to calm him. Now was not the time to fight. He flinched at the touch, but didn't pull away this time.

"Why are you here, Morvyn?" I said, trying to distract the siren.

Morvyn turned from the captain, his ability to make the movement an insult impressive.

"My *dear* king regent requests I assist the two of you with your little project."

CHAPTER 17

After more fuming, Arlo finally gave Morvyn a list of tools and materials he would need to fix the virginal: a lengthy list of strings, wood, and other supplies. But the room remained tense.

Relief washed over my nerves when Nixie and Lumina entered the library. I needed reinforcements to keep these two from tearing out one another's jugulars.

"Lumi, why don't you escort the captain to his quarters," Nixie offered, noting my unease.

"What?" Morvyn drawled, "But I was so excited to spend a little time with our new *pet*." Morvyn smiled impishly. "I was going to teach it to fetch."

Arlo cut the siren a deadly look. "I'll *fetch* a blade and show you what an animal I am, you—"

"Enough." A brilliant hum radiated from Lumina with a wave of her gold-finned hand, and Arlo lulled before my eyes, his face relaxing into that peaceful smile he'd borne when his ship was headed to its doom.

My stomach sank.

They could control a man with such ease.

"Thank you, Lumina," Morvyn said.

"If only I could do the same to you, then you would finally stop talking so much," she said, then left the library with Arlo in tow.

"Will he be safe?" I asked Nixie.

"Regrettably," Morvyn said, inspecting his nails.

Nixie elbowed Morvyn, then her eyes softened. "I promise, on my life, that no harm will befall him, Elowyn. Along with the others."

"I'll escort you to your room, if you would like?" she added.

"I'd like to browse the books," I said.

"Of course," Nixie said. "Morvyn can escort you after—"

"I know my way to my room. I do not need an escort." There was something else I needed to inspect in the library. That faint glow from the day prior, pulsating gently like a heartbeat in blue upon the bookshelf, out of reach. I hadn't spotted it on this visit yet, but the captain had distracted me from scanning the shelves for its subtle gleam.

A look passed between Morvyn and Nixie that I knew carried a thought.

"You say I'm a guest here but you worry about me lingering in a library without a chaperone?" I pushed, but kept my features neutral, not letting on just how much I longed to be alone with whatever called to me from the bookshelf atop the mezzanine.

"You are an honored guest here," Nixie said.

"Fine." I glided past them, testing the statement and its bounds. "Then I will head to my room after I find something to read, unless I am not *trusted* to do so."

"It is not you we distrust, Elowyn." Nixie's pink brow furrowed, telling me all that I needed to know.

Ice puddled in my gut.

"Am I in danger?" I asked with false bravado, although fear settled, frigid, in my spine.

"The kelpie, last night—those creatures do not dwell near Naiadon ..." Nixie said reluctantly.

"Nixie, Hylos said—" Morvyn started, but Nixie cut him off.

"She needs to know. Elowyn, someone likely summoned it here."

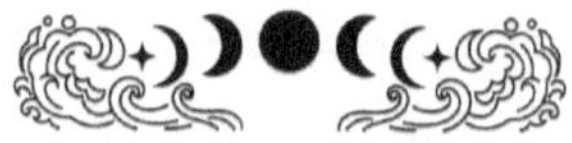

Back in my room, I noted another book at my bedside, likely placed there by Nixie's webbed hands. She was persistent. Did she really believe I would find comfort here? Why give me a false sense of safety when Naiadon was clearly dangerous?

And how could she promise safety for the others when something lurked in the shadows, summoning beasts here? Either she lied or she was a fool. Maybe they all were. Either way, it was clear. Naiadon was not safe for any human.

I settled into the bed and skimmed the pages of the book. The worn book had kept its pungent scent of ink, melded with sea salt. The prose was old, with clunking words spelled differently than what I knew. The story was of a woman who fell in love with a man she didn't know was her betrothed. It reminded me of the fairytales that preached the same morals to little girls. Do as you're told, marry the man your father tells you to, and be a dutiful wife.

Cedric haunted my mind and I shuddered. That loathsome look on his face when I slammed fists into his chest. *I never thought you were foolish enough to not know your worth.*

He was an idiot if he thought I was worth anything. Infernum, I couldn't even convince my father I was worthy of spending more than a single night in his court.

If I returned to land, I'd be forced to wed him. Then Cedric would attempt to use me, as my father had tried to use my mother for an heir and failed. When I disappointed Cedric, I would be at his mercy.

The mere thought made my stomach roll.

Yet I was prepared to return to land, to warn my father of what was to come, all to save the people of Oakhaven.

Standing, I walked across the room, pressing my forehead to the cool glass, my mother's prayer beads glinting in a stray sunbeam. *Nymphaea brought you to Naiadon to be saved.* Morvyn had been sincere when he said it. Hylos seemed to believe it too. What if it was true? What if the Guardians had saved me from my awful fate?

Fish darted in and out of beams of sunlight, snapping in silver, yellow, and orange.

No. That was a ridiculous thought. No Guardians would save me. I was nothing. No one. Title-less. Powerless. Born of a dead woman, her name struck from history. No Guardian had saved her. Such things did not happen.

Then there was the captain and his crew. They needed to be saved. No Guardians would do that either. Sure, the sirens were kind to me, but I could only imagine the nature of the crew's confinement from the manner in which they treated Arlo even in my presence. How maltreated was he when I wasn't there to defend him?

I knew what I had to do. Save Arlo and his crew, and warn my father of what was below the seas. Save my country. Even if it would never save me.

A rap on my door pulled me from thought. I opened it and Lumina's stunning face radiated back. "Hylos wishes for you to attend the deipnon tonight."

"The what?" I asked.

She was dressed in a flowing yellow gown, her hair braided high above her head, with flecks of gold painted on her cheeks into her hairline.

"A deipnon. It is a social gathering where we eat and drink, then afterward all guests come together for what we call a symposion. It is a meeting of minds, accompanied by drinks, music—"

"Got it." I stopped her. "Like a feast."

"Yes, like a feast of sorts. Will you attend?" she questioned.

Hylos had said the night before that he planned to discuss Oakhaven at this very event. If I attended, then I could learn about his plans and tell my father that information as well.

"Yes, I will go."

"Very good." She walked past me into the bedchamber, two sirens trailing behind her. "You will need to be dressed appropriately."

"Sure, come on in," I said under my breath.

I sat on an ottoman across from the large, gold-filigreed mirror in the bathing chambers as the two Sirens pulled and brushed my hair and painted my face. They trilled with a song they passed back and forth over my head.

One siren with long swaths of violet hair painted my eyes jewel-blue with a delicate hand, and with a tacky substance placed small gems across my nose and cheeks over my freckles.

The other siren, her skin, eyes, and hair all a pale yellow, frowned as she attempted to tame my riotous red curls with elaborate plaits that pulled at my scalp. She wove them into a larger braid that swung behind my back.

"It may seem a bit *pompous*," Lumina explained, "but it is fitting in siren culture to dress in this manner. We take pride in colors and show. We believe it honors the great Mother to emulate the variety of colors she paints her people and her ocean."

I thought my hair and makeup at my father's court was extensive, but this was a whole other level.

When they finished, I slipped into the dress Lumina selected for me. The fabric was gorgeous, like liquid-blue sapphires, vivid against my pale skin. The style was revealing, with a large slit in the skirt that revealed my pale legs. But it was stunning. I maneuvered the fabric to hide my curves.

Looking in the mirror, I saw the woman who peered back was completely transcendent.

"Yes." Lumina nodded, looking in the mirror with me. "This will do."

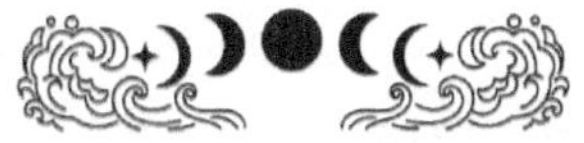

As we made our way to the deipnon, I paused, looking up past the glass arching overhead. Large creatures floated through the midnight waters, their forms glowing with a pale light, ruffling across the black water like hundreds of moons phasing through the night sky.

"The sirens call them jellyfish," Lumina said, noting my wonder. "Incredible creatures, despite being so unusual. They're quite beautiful."

They were beautiful and unusual, as everything appeared to be below the sea.

"Have you enjoyed the books I've asked the servants to leave you?" Lumina asked.

"You're the one leaving them for me?" I questioned, looking at her sidelong.

"Yes. They are not my usual reading material; I prefer nonfiction, but I thought stories from your land would help you adjust better. Books were a comfort to me when I first arrived at Naiadon. They allowed me to make heads and tails of this strange new world."

Her finned hands twined at the front of her waist as we walked. "At first I was afraid, too. Most are. But up there ..." she pointed above.

She meant past the glass ceiling, past the expansive sea, and up on land. "There was only unhappiness for me."

"You lived on land?" I asked.

"Yes, I was once human, born in the city of Guardian's Watch," she answered.

"But how are you a siren now?" I asked, looking at her finned hands and feet that gleamed in gold scales like the flesh of a golden fish.

"I was made. That is what we call it. When a human is turned into a siren."

Humans could become sirens?

"Why?" What would make a person become a creature tied to the bottom of the sea for the rest of their life?

"I will tell you if you wish to know. I think it may help you see our people better, but I wish to warn you. My story is *gruesome*," she said in her soft, tepid tone. "Many of the made sirens' tales are, sadly."

I nodded yes.

"Guardian's Watch is a hard place to live. As I'm sure you know. It is especially hard to live in when you are one of seven children and your family is impoverished, as mine was. There was little work for me. So I, like many others, turned to begging. On one evening, I was only a few coins short for a bowl of hot oats and I stayed out past nightfall. I knew the streets were more dangerous in the dark and had heard stories about the dangers of the city at night, but food was all I could think of. There is little room for logic when you're starving."

Images of the dilapidated shacks leaning against one another, dusted in snow, came to mind as we walked through a stony section of hallway. My eyes never left Lumina's beautiful face as the siren light played tricks on her skin, reflecting in iridescent shades off her scales. I couldn't envision such a beautiful being on land, let alone in the wretched city outside my father's castle.

"Most people ignored us. I wasn't alone in my begging, but sometimes people were cruel. They would spit, curse, or shove. But usually nothing violent. That is, until they found me." She swallowed hard, like she was there again, trying to gulp down the fear. "Two large men who beat me nearly to death."

My stomach soured.

She stopped in the middle of the hall and turned to me. "I do not tell you this for pity or emotion. My story is not rare; many have similar ones here within Naiadon. I tell you so you will see the mercy of the sirens. Their inherent goodness. Those men dumped what little was left of me into the Nettle River and luckily, my body drifted to the sea. There, a Circle of sirens found me and *made* me."

My heart ached for Lumina, but another emotion burned far hotter. Anger. This atrocity happened in Oakhaven, in my father's realm. No food? No law? No one stopping a little girl from being beaten in public?

"That never should have happened to you." It was all I could offer her. Empty apologies. Because my father allowed such reprehensible things to happen in his country. In his great city. One of the wealthiest in the world. All while he hid behind his castle walls and feasted.

"Sirens are not perfect," Lumina added. "We have our prejudices, our wars, our traditions that bind us to rules that are antiquated and illogical. Just as upon land. But here in Naiadon I can learn, I have adequate food, and comfort. Most importantly, I have peace."

"At first, just like you, I was so afraid, angry even. Then I saw and learned and *read* of this world and others beyond it. Places I couldn't even imagine, kindness I couldn't even comprehend." She turned and walked on. "I often mourn my younger self, begging on the street, unable to even conceive of a place this beautiful because only suffering and misery surrounded her. But now, I dream enough for us both."

I reached out to Lumina's finned hand and squeezed it.

"Thank you for sharing your story with me." I said.

A small smile sparked on her lips.

"Thank you for listening," she said. "Now, are you ready, Elowyn, to face the greatest siren Circles of all three seas?"

"Ready as one can be," I answered. And together we walked onward.

Chapter 18

A celestial choir of siren song welcomed Lumina and me in the banquet hall, a harmonious blend of highs and lows that ebbed and flowed through my veins.

The singers, draped in varying shades of purple and blue fabrics, shone as they moved in unison. Their music poured from their souls, spilling out into the space.

Heart fluttering, I drank in that sound. The sirens' song was always exquisite, even when it had hunted the ship I was on and controlled the sailors to the sirens' will. No two melodies sounded the same, but when they came together as one, it was beyond beauty. It was transformative.

"There's Raylik and Nixie," Lumina said, ushering me to the long glass table, the same one I'd first sat at to break my fast with Hylos and his inner circle. Now it was adorned with flowing streams of gauzy blue fabric. Swirling siren orbs bobbed on the tabletops, which shimmered with the rainbow visages of sirens sitting around them, chattering away like they were ordinary dinner guests.

"Good evening," Lumina said to Raylik.

Two young siren girls sat beside him, no older than sixteen and clearly twins, with matching slim, strong chins and mirrored blood-orange eyes. Even the gowns with flame-red ruffles they wore were identical.

"Good evening. Elowyn, these are my cousins, Myra and Lyra, from Mariscal Circle." Clicks and hums transpired between the girls, but Raylik sent them a harsh glance that silenced the pair. "Speak in the common tongue here," he ordered.

"Hello Elowyn," they said in unison. The pair shared Raylik's coloring: rich brown with flecks of fire-colored scales.

I dipped my head in a quick hello to all. "Hello there, lovely to meet you."

Then I sat in a free seat next to Raylik's cousins as Lumina took the other open seat beside me.

Hidden by Raylik's large figure, Nixie leaned forward with a little wave and a smile, her short pink curls pinned to one side and her eyes painted in glossy pinks that faded into her cheekbones. She quickly leaned back in her seat, and I could hear her clear voice chiming to whoever sat beside her.

"Myra and Lyra are here with their father, my uncle Melquin, Leader of Mariscal Circle," Raylik said, then looked across the table to a siren with the same intense eyes as his daughters and long dark braids that draped over his shoulders.

He was speaking to another ancient-looking woman, her coloring ice-white like Morvyn. They shared hushed words, and by the way their eyes darted in my direction, I knew they discussed me. It seemed that no matter the court, I was a spectacle.

I scanned the room for Morvyn and spotted him talking to a siren carrying a tray of chalices, a flirtatious smile painted across his chiseled face that made him look superb. The way he wielded that smile told me he knew it.

His eyes caught on mine, and he raised his glass as a greeting, and winked.

I smiled back. *Ridiculous.* Why was I not surprised that he was conversing with anyone *but* the honored guests?

Eventually, Hylos entered the room dressed in a glorious ocean-blue robe, a crown of aureate shells that cupped gems wreathing his head. There was no announcement, nor a royal address; he didn't need either. Just the fact that he had entered the space immediately made the chamber's attention bend in his direction.

It was the first time I realized just how well Hylos could command a room.

Among his friends in casual settings, he just seemed like a young man. All smiles and jokes. But here, now, he seemed every bit a king. Even if he was merely king regent. But regent or not, tonight Hylos was the true ruler of Naiadon, and that was apparent to all that looked upon him.

The young sirens beside me clicked and trilled in their strange tongue to one another, this time more quietly to avoid Raylik's wrath. Girlish smiles lit their young faces, and then one turned to me. "Do you think him handsome?" Lyra asked, or was it Myra?

"Hylos?" I asked as we all watched him work his way around the great table, greeting each guest.

"Who else is worth speaking of in this room? *Well*, besides you. But it would be rude to speak of you now."

"Thanks for sparing my feelings." A smile flashed across my face at her lack of subtlety. "Unfortunately, my type rarely has fins."

The girls both looked at me flatly, not budging at the joke.

Tough crowd.

"Yes, he is handsome," I answered.

They trilled to one another giddily. Apparently that was the right answer.

I supposed it was true. Hylos was handsome, especially now as he beguiled his guests. But he still looked like a boy to me. I suppose he was. Beneath the robe and crown and bravado, I'd seen the child who missed his parents so much that he spent his free time in their study just to be close to them. The boy who still believed his father was alive, despite him being missing for years.

But my thoughts didn't matter. All that mattered was the way his people looked upon him now, how they basked in his presence with admiration and pride.

Their young, strong, charismatic leader. Taking the helm from his father, who held the epithet "the Great," and doing so wonderfully.

Sadness panged in my chest. His father and mother would be proud to see the man he was in this moment. The king he had become in their absence.

I couldn't help but compare him to my father. The only other king I knew in the flesh. He too had a kingdom thrust upon him unexpectedly. His brother died from the sweating sickness one night and the following day he was king of Oakhaven. My father was the spare to the heir and found himself in a position that he'd never expected. That he was not prepared for.

I always wondered if that was why he was so transfixed by ensuring his line of succession. Maybe he didn't wish to burden someone unready to rule with a crown. Or maybe he was simply a narcissist obsessed with ensuring a part of him lived on after him. I would likely never know.

Hylos laughed heartily at something a siren with a pink complexion said. There was another obvious comparison to be made between Hylos and my father as well. Where the king of Oakhaven sat above all at the Yule feast, looking down at his people, Hylos greeted his subjects at their level, and seemed to truly enjoy them.

"I hope at my first Hydroxia, father arranges for me to mate with him," one twin said, her head tilting as she stared at Hylos longingly.

"Me too," the other added. Would that not be a little awkward? "To have his progeny would be the highest honor."

"But I would have his nasty lover sent away or kill her myself."

My eyes widened at the casual threat.

Calypstra was at the head of the table next to Hylos's place. She was clad in a sheer black dress that showed every inch of her, the nipples of her small, taut breasts on display. Her dress was paired with a dangerous look that spoiled her gorgeous face.

"Do you think he loves her?" one asked the other.

"At times, I sense great love," the sister replied, "but more often, only lust."

Sense love and lust? What did she mean by that?

"A siren of barely twenty years, and they say he's one of the strongest in all of Naiadon. Maybe even all three seas. Power radiates from him and yet he wastes it on a made siren who cannot bear him any children," the nearest twin said to her sister.

Made. Like Lumina. So Calypstra was once human too. I couldn't imagine it; nothing in her held humanity. Was her story as horrendous as Lumina's?

Hylos turned to us, a wide smile warming his face.

The twins sat up straight in their seats at his attention.

"Myra, Lyra, a delight to have you here this evening," Hylos said, taking their hands and kissing their knuckles. "You both look enchanting."

They nearly melted beneath his touch.

"Thank you," the two said as one.

"As always, we are loyal servants to you," one said with a tip of her sharp chin.

"And hopeful to continue *forging* alliances with you and your Circle," the other finished, batting her long lashes.

Forging was one way to put it.

"Circle Mariscal always has a seat at my table," Hylos said, tipping his head graciously to them. Then he turned to me. "Elowyn, you look wonderful. Lumina did a marvelous job dressing you for this evening."

Lumina could hardly lift her eyes to meet his. A strange tension sat between them that both seemed to ignore. But Hylos was far more capable of doing so than Lumina.

"You look every bit a siren," Hylos said.

"Not quite, but I would certainly stand out at home."

"That is a fact. Thank you for joining us," he said. "Please, enjoy the meal and wonderful company. And be sure to stick around for the symposion as well; there will be great conversation."

Yes, about war.

Hylos made his way to his place at the table's head. He raised a blue-imbued hand, flicked his wrist, and a thunderous sound roiled through the banquet hall, cuing a procession of servants dressed in gossamer white fabric to flow into the room. Each carried trays overflowing with red lobsters, colossal and steaming, and meticulously arranged fish, both cooked and raw.

The servants looked like phantoms as they glided around the tables and piled food onto plates, unfamiliar purple and orange vegetables landing in steaming heaps. A small bowl of round beads that looked like black pearls was placed at the corner of every setting with its own small spoon.

When they finished, Hylos clasped his chalice, the polished gold gleaming in the siren light, and spoke. "Esteemed guests, thank you for sharing this meal with me. Each of you here is a gift to myself and my castle from the Holy Mother herself." He bowed his head in thanks, then raised his sharp chin.

I looked around the table and noted that most smiled at this sentiment, but some held clenched jaws and furrowed brows. Interesting. An ember of hope sparked in my chest. Maybe this was a tougher crowd for Hylos to win over than I'd thought. And without the other Circles, would he be able to start a war?

"You each hail from the greatest Circles in the three seas. From the strongest siren families in existence, with your own rich histories, stories, and honors. As do I."

He let the words settle in the silent room, every eye captivated by him, even if in wonder or choler. "And to have us here together, now, sharing a meal, is truly history in the making. Some may even say it is ordained by the blessed mother herself." He looked at me on that note. "So thank you, sincerely, for joining me, and I hope it is the first of many deipnons where we may share in the sea's bounty. Praise be to Nymphaea," he shouted.

"Praise be to Nymphaea," the room echoed in unison.

Then Calypstra stood beside Hylos, smiling.

Hylos's gaze shifted to her, his eyes narrowing, a flicker of confusion rippling through his features, which he quickly steeled.

Calypstra raised her cup.

"And here's to our most honored guest of all," she said, her voice a soft purr.

Her eyes fell onto me.

"Princess Elowyn *Blackthorn*."

CHAPTER 19

My stomach sank.

The sirens all buzzed with whispers.

The nearest twin whipped her head toward me.

"Are you joining Hylos in the war against King Eadric Blackthorn?"

Against my father.

"Is that why you're here? As an ally?" the other said.

My heart lodged in my throat.

Hylos looked nearly as shocked as me as he eyed Calypstra. But her charcoal-lined stare didn't meet his. No. Instead, she watched my every breath.

"Yes," Hylos said loudly, reining in the room, "to Elowyn *Blackthorn*, our most honored guest here in Naiadon. We thank her for her visit. Let us all raise a glass, *again*, to Nymphaea and thank her for all she brings to our table, including those beyond the sea. Praise be to Nymphaea!"

The guests raised their glasses again, eyeing one another with confusion, but still echoing the words, less enthusiastically than before.

"Praise be to Nymphaea."

The room was spinning.

Hylos drank deeply and sent a mere glance to the choir, urging it back to life, their song filling the room again with beauty. But my heart only raced with the speeding tempo.

Everyone in the banquet hall had one thing in common. Besides being violent, powerful creatures.

Oakhaven was their enemy.

Hylos had called them to Naiadon this evening to discuss war against the king and his country, and now they knew who I truly was. His daughter.

Why was the music so loud? The swirling siren lights' spinning made me dizzy. The captain was right; I had grown too content. Complacent. Relaxed. I should have been more careful. More calculated. And now they all knew my true identity. How long had Hylos known?

Raylik's chair skittered back loudly as he abruptly rose from his seat. The sound sent me lurching. My nerves were wound tight.

Muscles strained and fists clenched, he marched toward Hylos.

Nixie nodded to him once, as if she understood his destination. Then looked at me. I avoided her soft, rose-colored gaze.

"Move over," Nixie demanded to the twins.

Each scowled in her direction.

"We do not take orders from made sirens," one snapped.

"Our cousin's mate or not," the other added.

"I said, move over."

Orange eyes rolling, they relented.

"Spoiled girls," Nixie hissed as she sat in the chair beside me.

Lumina's eyes were on me now too. "We can leave after this course," she said gently.

Nixie added, "Absolutely, we can leave as soon as the excitement calms down and—"

"No." I cut her off.

Calypstra had established the stakes, and now I needed to adjust. I mastered my looks and steadied my breath. I raised my eyes to meet

Calypstra's. She still had that stupid grin on her face. Coolly, I took a drink from my chalice and raised my chin. *They will not see us falter.* Vega's words, which she had offered me when I was walking to my doom, echoed in my mind. I would not forget them now as I drowned in despair.

"I am fine." There was no going back now. "And refer to me as *Lady* Elowyn. That is the appropriate title." I ate a bite of my meal despite being sick to my stomach. Nixie quirked her head in question as she looked to Lumina.

"Not Princess Elowyn?" Lumina asked.

"No. Just Lady."

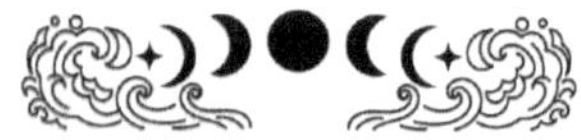

After all three courses, the plates vanished and the room's lively chatter faded into a murmur. Although I didn't hear the conversations, my father's name likely still lingered on the lips of every bloody siren in attendance that evening. Heavy on the tongues of his unknown enemy surrounding me.

Hylos rose to his feet and addressed the guests. "Let us all walk through into the symposion."

The party rose from their chairs, chalices in hand, and flowed through the archway that connected the rooms.

Hylos stood at the exit and smiled warmly at each departing guest while Calypstra slunk to his side like a shadow and Hylos's friends encircled me.

"Are you okay?" Morvyn asked, his marbled features softening in concern.

I shot him a piercing look. "Do you care how I feel?" I glanced around at the circle, each of them sent by Hylos to watch my every move. To keep me prisoner. To keep Arlo's men prisoner. Each of them readying to go to war against my father. "You're ordered to spy on me, not care about me. Drop the charade. All of you."

Morvyn shrank as hurt settled in his pale eyes.

"Calypstra should not have done that," Raylik said in his low timbre, standing behind Nixie, who looked on in silence. A look of worry and maybe anger. But was that false too? What was true here?

Hylos said he would allow me time to share my identity, but that had clearly been a lie. I was a fool for letting them dress me up and parade me about. This was clearly a trap I fell straight into, just as I had in my father's court before.

Lumina watched me, her lip twitching downward. Did she regret telling me her story? Regret sharing her past maltreatment on my father's own soil with the daughter of her leader's greatest enemy? But was it even a true story at all? If my father's castle was a place of illusions and lies, as Cedric had said, then this place must be a nexus of deception.

Hylos stalked to us, smile rapidly fading. "Morvyn and Lumina, ensure the guests are comfortable. This evening needs to go perfectly. There can be no more errors—"

"Did you approve that ridiculous display?" Lumina snapped. She hadn't spared Hylos a glance, let alone a word, in the time I'd observed them together until now.

Hylos's face flashed with surprise at this too.

"Shouldn't you watch your tone when speaking to your king?" Calypstra said, still behind Hylos.

My hand ached to slap her.

"Leave us," Raylik ground out in her direction, like he was waiting to descend on her at any moment.

But Calypstra remained unfazed, all smiles despite his growl.

"Is that your wish, Hylos?" she purred.

"Yes. I'll meet you in my bedchamber after the symposion," Hylos replied curtly, not sparing her a glance.

"Of course, my king." She slipped between Lumina and Hylos. Lumina watched, unable to look away from the lingering kiss Calypstra left on his cheek, even though it looked like a knife plunged into her gut.

Then Calypstra, ass on full display under the sheer black dress, sauntered away.

"King. Should we all call you *King* now? Have you given up on your father too?" Lumina said sharply, boldly.

Everyone tensed.

"You know I prefer to be called King Regent, *Lumi*," Hylos said, his tone softening.

She winced at the nickname, like that was the worst thing he had ever said to her, but she shook it off. "Do you understand the danger this puts Elowyn in? You wish to go to war with her father, yet declare her identity to all here. Nymphaea sends those to the ocean to be saved, Hylos. You have failed the Holy Mother and Elowyn with these actions."

My stomach sank. She was right; I was in danger, more so now than before. Caught wounded, bleeding in the center of swarming sharks.

Lumina's warm eyes locked with Hylos's ocean stare until he could no longer hold her gaze, his eyes retreating instead to the banquet table littered with half-drunk wine glasses.

"Yes, I understand." he responded softly, passing a nervous hand through his blue hair.

"And will Calypstra face any punishment for putting Elowyn in danger? Or did you direct her to do so?"

"I would never have done that," he said, hurt, as if he could not believe Lumina would think such a thought. But he hadn't answered Lumina's other question.

"She will face no consequences then," Lumina said, shaking her head, "because bedding some immoral *bitch* is more important than honor. Once again." She brushed past Hylos to the connecting room to carry out his orders.

Morvyn's eyes went wide as he trilled a whistle. "Oh shit."

"Shut up, Morvyn," Hylos said, stepping forward, only a flutter in his jaw showing how much Lumina's words had hit their mark. "You go too. Help her," Hylos repeated.

Morvyn looked between myself and Hylos like he had more to say to me.

"Now," Hylos growled, his demand final.

Morvyn complied and followed in Lumina's wake.

"Nixie, you and Raylik will escort Elowyn to her chambers. Raylik, remain outside her door for safety and—"

"No," I said.

His eyes flared, blue lashes fluttering. "This is not up for debate."

"You invited me this evening. Why?"

"We are not having this discussion right now—"

"Why, Hylos?" I repeated.

"To have you hear of the situation in Oakhaven. I was hoping you would—" He looked down to the marble floor, searching for the right phrasing.

"Hoping I would join you," I said. If he couldn't put it plainly, I would. "The daughter of your enemy would be a phenomenal pawn in your war. Is that right?"

"Not a pawn. I would only want your help if you agreed."

"Is this how you form alliances then? Start with entrapment, hold them against their will, then reveal their identity in front of a crowd of their enemies, hoping to twist their arms to bend to your will?" I challenged, meeting his gaze.

"I did not order Calypstra to do that, and we are not your enemy," he insisted, disbelief coloring his tone.

"You plan to attack my country. You are my father's enemy." The words settled in the air, red-hot and charged. The only way I would be safe in a situation like this on land would be to bow and swear fealty to the leader that held me hostage. That was what I should have done. I clenched my teeth. My vain, prideful heart pounded at the thought. "But I will join your symposion."

"Elowyn, now that they know who you are, it will be harder to protect you," Nixie said, her mauve eyes softening as she looked up at me.

"You just said they are not my enemy." I laughed bitterly, ignoring Nixie's plea. "Which is it, Hylos?"

"Sirens are unpredictable. Brutal. Especially those not from Naiadon. Here, we are more accepting of humans, but the deeper sea sirens are not," Hylos added.

"You have invited me this evening, knowing damn well who I was all along, and now I wish to hear what you have to say. Just like every other royal guest here."

Even if I was about as royal as a blade of grass, gaining more knowledge was imperative. My plans for escape would need to be expedited, and the more I knew of the sirens, their plans, and their minds, the easier it would be for my father to stop them. If I could even get out of here alive.

"Fine." Hylos relented. "Raylik, do not let her out of your sight." He looked back to me. "I assume you have experience meeting with the elite?"

"Of course," I scoffed. A lie.

"Good. Keep your wits about you and stay with Raylik. He will ensure your safety," Hylos advised, searching my eyes for any sign of hesitation. But there was nothing more to say.

Chapter 20

Although strange-colored stares followed me, I walked calmly across the room filled with low-lying couches clustered in semicircles. Sirens lounged casually on them, audience to a lone siren woman who stood upon a bright-blue marble stage framed by two towering columns.

Her deep-violet curls cascading around her olive complexion, she sang exquisitely, eyes closed. The melody hung in the air, forming a vision above the sirens' heads in dreamy pastels. I drew in a sharp breath at the shock of it. But the other guests did not look up or gawk. They merely refilled their chalices and continued with their conversations.

It was so beautiful and casual. Not at all where I'd envisioned the discussion of war to take place.

"Where would you recommend I sit?" I asked Raylik in a murmur, slowing my steps, waiting for his answer.

"Starwyrt Circle," he rumbled over my shoulder, and nodded to a cluster of four fantastical creatures with bright-yellow hair and long, slender limbs that stretched under layers of prismatic fabric.

I looked up at him flatly. *Seriously?*

"Colorful sirens usually dwell closer to the surface. Starwyrt Circle has experience with humans, as they live so near to shore. They are kind, but talk too much," he explained.

Fine.

I continued across the room. "Why did Lumina speak to Hylos in that manner?" I asked pointedly as we neared my targets. I looked back at him quickly to show that I wanted a true answer.

Raylik cut me a hard look, telling me this question was bold, but still he answered. "Because she cares for him deeply. That binds her to honesty."

The pain in her eyes when Calypstra kissed him told me it was far more than care. She loved him.

We stood before the colorful females. "May I join you?" I asked, mustering all my polite sensibility.

Their violently cherry-colored eyes inspected me.

"Princess Elowyn Blackthorn, yes, please sit with us," the nearest answered, her voice deep and relaxing with a slow, steady cadence. "We were discussing you after that *interesting* show at the deipnon," she continued.

"I'm sure," I responded as I took a seat.

The ethereal being smiled knowingly as I sat beside her. "My name is Serenous, Leader of Starwyrt Circle. Although I am sure that kind Raylik of Mariscal Circle has already told you my origin." She craned her lithe neck, encrusted in berry-colored twinkling scales. "Hello, Raylik," she said to the watchdog standing a few steps behind me.

"I am Raylik of Aquin Circle now," he grunted.

"That is right. You have joined Hylos's inner circle. Did you know Raylik's father was a great warrior?" she said, leaning into me. I tried not to flinch at just how unnatural she looked. "But he lost all spirit when King Aegir defeated him. The last Circle to fall. That is what they call Mariscal Circle in whispers behind their backs." She smirked. "But Raylik is a greater warrior than his sire. He thrives within the Circle his father on his deathbed claimed to be his nemesis. The hard-headed brute never understood that your adversary should always be your closest acquaintance."

I swallowed the dryness in my throat. This was my safest bet?

"Oh, interesting." I lunged for the wine at the center, grabbing up a cup. I was going to need a drink.

"Together we are stronger," Raylik grunted, looking straight ahead, unbothered by the forward conversation, his hands clasped behind his back.

"Indeed," Serenous agreed. "Princess, this is my sister, Serfie." She pointed to the siren who shared her couch, propped up on a satin pillow. "And my daughter, Siggy." She nodded to the other, much younger and with a thick, yellow braid. She was pouting. Or perhaps that was just the look of her round face and full lips.

"It is lovely to meet you all. And please, call me Elowyn."

"Because your father considers you a bastard?" Serenous asked plainly.

"Because that is what I prefer," I answered promptly, impressed with myself for keeping up. "But it's reassuring to know even at the bottom of the ocean they debate my legitimacy."

"Terras are abhorrent gossips and my realm is filled with them." Serfie scowled. "In the sea, we do not believe in such things as bastards, and titles are not easily given then taken."

Serenous nodded in agreement. "I hardly knew Siggy's father. We mated only once, a night filled with such fierce and all-enveloping passion. The man could do wonders with his tongue. I surely orgasmed at least four times."

I coughed, nearly choking on the wine.

"Mother!" Siggy cried.

Serenous continued, "Siggy is no bastard. She is clearly of my blood. Her coloring tells of her origin. Starwyrt Circle, audacious and true."

Audacious and true were definitely accurate descriptors for Serenous.

"A lovely sentiment." I cleared my throat. "I wish my father felt the same way."

Raylik grunted a bit of warning. Oh, now I was the one oversharing in this conversation?

"Seek nothing from men who murder their wives and abandon their children." The words hit hard. The truth of it all. But Serenous held my stare firmly, even though the blow had me gasping for air. "But I suppose it matters far more what you think of your father than I."

Because she believed that would determine what side I would stand on in this looming war. But it didn't matter how I felt for my father. It was my country I would stand beside.

"Anyway, we like to tell riddles at the symposion; would you care to join us?" Serenous said.

"Sure," I answered.

"Siggy, you go first," Serenous said to her daughter, who snapped an annoyed look at her mother.

"Do I have to?"

Her mother just looked on and smiled, not giving her a choice.

"Fine." She looked at the chalice within her hand then started, "I loosen tongues and warm souls. I make the brave cry, and the fearful bold." She paused, bringing a thoughtful finger to her pink lips. "I'm present at both the start and end of life. But in excess, I'll ruin a good time. What am I?"

"Drink," Raylik answered.

Siggy frowned with a huff that fluttered her heavy yellow fringe. "Yes, that is correct."

"That was a good one, darling." Serenous patronized her.

"Now you go, Serfie and Raylik." She gave him a bold smile. "You may only answer if you sit with us and have a drink."

Raylik didn't budge.

"Fine," Serfie said, as if she had played this game far too many times before. "I'm a symphony of sighs."

Serenous's smile smoldered. "Oh, this one shall be good."

Serfie continued, "In the darkest of night, I'm clear as daylight, a dance as old as time, and if *good*," she lingered on the word, forcing a diabolical smile from her sister, "too much of me can lead to a sleepless night. What am I?"

"Well, Siggy won't know this one," Serenous jeered.

"*Mother*," Siggy whined again.

"Well, do you, dear?" she asked.

"You're so *embarrassing*!" Siggy rose to her feet and marched off.

"She's always been a sensitive child." Serenous rolled her large eyes. "I know Raylik unquestionably knows the answer, isn't that right?" She looked up at Raylik, who only nodded a terse yes.

"Of course you do. I see the way you look at that feisty little made female." Then in a hushed tone she said to me, "His father would roll in his tomb if he knew." Then she let out a little laugh. "But do you know it, Princess?"

My mind skimmed over the riddle. "I'm not sure I do."

"You'll feel *quite* foolish once I tell you, because I think you're familiar with this step, although I'm unsure anyone has danced it with you well."

"If you know the answer, come out with it, sister," Serfie added dryly.

"Ah, I know the answer all *too* well," Serenous responded.

"Then say it. You play the game too slow and turn riddles into other riddles," Serfie said, irritated.

"That is the fun in it," she trilled loud enough that guests glanced at her. "You see, Princess, if someone knows the answer or thinks it's another, that indicates one's heart." Then she took a deep, dramatic drink from her chalice and looked at me. "And the answer in this case is sex."

This would be an interesting night.

"Correct," Serfie answered, unfazed.

Serenous beamed with pride. "I just love this game! Now you go, Princess."

"I have one," I started, unsure where I was headed until the words slammed into my mind. "I am paid a fated debt before it is due. Yet I have no pockets to fill, only coffers."

A thrill worked through Serenous, still smiling. "Go on ..."

"Men fear me but are my makers. Mothers warn of me, yet their sons are my takers. In the end, both will know the cost of my path. What am I?"

I looked at Raylik to see if he knew the answer, but he still looked forward.

Maybe Serenous was right about this game; it showed the truth of one's heart.

"That's not a very good one." Serfie shook her head. "Are you sure you understand the game?" she asked.

Then Serenous's face darkened and she swallowed. "She understands the game completely."

"Then what is it?" Serfie asked, annoyed. But Serenous didn't answer, only looked at her sister. "Well, then?" Serfie looked at me with her dark, nearly-red eyes.

Meeting her gaze, I answered, "I am war."

Chapter 21

The lone siren's song halted and the vision above the stage disappeared.

Hylos stood at the front of the room, no longer wearing his crown, only his blue robe, as he looked out at his people. The noise of the party waned so the sirens could hear their leader speak.

"Thank you for spending this evening with me and for gracing Naiadon with your attendance for Holy Hydroxia."

A swell of cheers came from the crowd. I noted that even those who'd scowled before seemed pliant in Hylos's presence now, likely from good drink and a decadent feast.

"As you all know, the symposion is a time for entertainment of course, but also for philosophizing, strategizing, and even unifying. Many profound conversations that have been shared over wine among the bravest sirens of history have prevented famine, ended generational feuds, and inspired brighter futures for us all."

"And tonight, there is much to discuss." Hylos paused. The room was enraptured. "Our way of life is in danger." Whispers were swarming. "First it started with my father, who went missing. Then with a strange, unnatural city upon our ocean."

Cedric's Whiterok, which was at the center of it all.

"And now, as you all know, more sirens have gone missing in the body of *our* mother." He ground out the words, emphasizing the impact of the insult. "And we know exactly who is at fault for these crimes."

The crowd murmured in hisses that prickled my skin.

"The king of Oakhaven," Hylos said.

More condemnation filled the room at the mention of my father. My skin tingled at the feeling of eyes stabbing holes in my back.

"There is only one response to this affront to the Holy Mother!" Hylos boomed.

Serenous side-eyed me through pink lashes.

"Retaliation."

War.

"We have gathered information on where the king's men assemble, his naval ships, his greatest ports and trade routes."

Bile rose in my throat. Not gathered, but plundered from the minds of sailors. From men like Arlo and his crew.

"Naiadon, under my orders, will make our first attack to remind the king that Nymphaea's children have inherited our mother's sea. That these are our waters, not theirs. And the only creature who should be afraid within its depths are terras." This elicited more cheers.

This was not good.

"As the greatest Circles in *my* three seas, given to me to wield by the Mother herself," he continued, "join me in defending our waters. Lend me your armies. Fight by my side. Protect our mother's holy body. Protect our people!"

The room erupted in approval. Hylos, his strong chin held high, basked in the applause.

Did any of them know what this meant? What the sacrifice was? *Who* the sacrifice was? No war could be won without death.

"What of the terra princess?" A cold, metallic voice cut through the room.

The crowd silenced in an instant as their eyes fell upon the stark-white figure, an ancient-looking woman set in gypsum. The same woman who'd spoken in whispers and eyed me with Raylik's uncle.

"What of her, Elspeth, Leader of Circle Fushdmuir?" Hylos said sternly.

So, she was Morvyn's aunt.

The woman rose to her feet slowly; she was unthinkably thin and old, with long wisps of white hair swaying past her knees, blending with the white layers of fabric she was drowning in. I understood why Morvyn avoided her. She was frightening.

"Will the terra princess stand by you in this attack you speak of?"

My pulse became thready. No way would I ever do that. I looked at Hylos, who kept his eyes on Elspeth.

"That is for her to decide." He raised his hands, addressing the crowd. "As it is for each of you to decide."

Whispers rushed from each cluster of sirens, sounding like doubt.

"But," Hylos continued, "I believe it speaks of her intention that she sits with us this evening."

I had absolutely no intention of agreeing to join this foolish, one-sided war.

The entire room snapped its scrutinizing gaze to me. Fuck. A fist clenched my heart. Hylos locked his eyes on me, willing some type of answer. If I told him no now, it would make him a laughingstock among these other leaders. Which was not my concern. This was clearly an intimidation tactic. But angering him would put me in more danger.

I swallowed the dry lump of fear lodged in my throat and rose to my feet. "I—" Words felt thick, but I forced them out, determined to be clear and concise. "I am here to *learn* of the situation between your people and *mine*." It was the truth.

More whispers bristled through the room, and Hylos let out a breath, a small smile thanking me. But the tactful answer wasn't for him. It was for me. For survival, for the captain and his crew. I was Infernum-bent on getting us all out of here alive.

"Now that we have discussed the necessities of our duty ..." Hylos turned back to the crowd, addressing them as I found my seat again.

Serenous's and Serfie's searing-pink gazes both sized me up.

"Please enjoy the rest of the evening, drink my wine, discuss with one another. But hold in your mind your role in the fate of our people's future." Then Hylos walked off the dais and headed straight toward me.

"Serenous," he drawled as he took her slender, webbed hand and kissed the top.

"My liege," she said, cocking her head, sending her scales twinkling in the light. "Interesting discussion is to be had this evening."

"Indeed," Hylos agreed, not faltering under her watchful gaze. "And what do you think of Elowyn?" he asked, settling into the couch where Siggy had sat, filling a chalice of wine for himself.

"She is a delight. Far more interesting than most humans I've encountered. Many fear us, but she does not. She looks at us more like *riddles* she's intent on solving." She looked at me again with a devious smile, then continued, "A curious mind, and I suspect a loyal heart. Whoever's side she sits on in this impending war, I sense she will be a great asset."

I nearly laughed. I was no asset at all.

"Although I'm uncertain her mind is made up," Serenous added.

But it was. I would stand with the innocents of Oakhaven. Forever.

"What of the great minds of Circle Starwyrt?" Hylos asked Serenous and her sister Serfie. "Are they made up?"

The pair did not even glance at one another when Serenous answered. "Not quite. We will need a stronger alliance before I'll go to battle for you, young king," she purred.

"I am bound this Hydroxia." He cut her short, sipping his chalice and searching the crowd.

Serenous's strange eyes inspected Hylos. "You still waste yourself on that miserable made siren? It would be one thing if it were for love. But your heart does not belong to *her*—no matter how hard you try to convince us otherwise—and my daughter Siggy is quite beautiful. She hardly smiles, like your paramour, if that suits you best," she offered.

"The leader of my Circle would be the one to arrange a mating between two great Circles. When my father returns, he will decree which it shall be with."

"*If* he returns," Serenous added.

Hylos's face hardened. "When." Then that charming smile returned to smooth any bite away and he leaned into Serenous. "Besides, we all know you're the true beauty of Starwyrt Circle and the only one worthy of my *full* attention during Hydroxia."

His compliment hit its mark and Serenous's bright-yellow eyebrows rose as she let out a peal of laughter. "Well played," she said. "Serfie and I shall speak on the matter."

Then the pair rose, towering above Hylos and me in their lissome height. "Good evening, Hylos, and to you, *Princess* Elowyn. May you never forget who welcomed you to their table and who cast you aside," Serenous said.

I blinked the words away, not letting them penetrate my skin or my heart.

Then the pair glided away.

Hylos sipped from his drink and let his mask down for a second before me. That look of a ruler, regent or not, faded into the tired and worried soul he was below the surface.

"Did any agree to join you this evening?" I asked, my tone gentler than expected. Despite being my enemy, I felt for Hylos. He carried a world upon his shoulders in the absence of his father.

"No," he sighed. "Lots of half answers and enough witty repartee for a lifetime, but no formal agreements. Plenty of offers to mate with daughters and sisters though." He rolled his blue eyes.

"Ah, so your sex life is up for discussion around here too, I see. In that, our worlds are alike."

Hylos half-smiled and raised an eyebrow at me, reveling in the bold statement. "At least it is different here; it's only a night and must be agreed upon by the two respective parties. I'm sure it'd be fine ... great, even but—"

"But it's not as *appealing* when you're asked to do it," I finished. Something was so miserable about the whole concept. It felt sterile. Contractual.

He let out a breath. "Something like that. You know," he turned to me, "you're not what I'd expect a terra princess to be like. You're very straightforward."

"Well, that's because I'm not a princess. Serenous knows of my story; I'm surprised you do not."

"Ah, yes. Calypstra told me when you arrived who she assumed you were, and your circumstances."

That was a polite way to put my father disowning me.

"I'm sure she reveled in just how miserable my existence is," I said.

"I'm sure she didn't at all. Calypstra is ... " He searched his cup for answers. "She's misunderstood. Like many of the made sirens here, her path to the sea was rough."

Like that was any excuse for her being absolutely horrendous. Could anything that happened to her be any worse than Lumina's story? Yet Lumina remained kind. A bit reserved, sure, but not cruel. She even defended me, a complete stranger, to her leader. Because she knew what Calypstra did tonight was wrong.

Struggle or not, Lumina had a truly good heart. So did Nixie. Calypstra did not. That was clear. Hylos' judgment was so wrong on multiple levels. Like he was wrong about Oakhaven's role in the missing sirens altogether.

Hylos drank to the dregs of his cup, then stood. "Well, off to more begging and bartering I suppose."

"Hylos, wait."

"Yes?"

"Do you have regular meetings with your war council?" I questioned.

He looked up at Raylik, who still stood above us. "Yes, I do," he offered cautiously. "Raylik and I meet each evening."

"Just you and Raylik, that's it?" I asked in disbelief.

"Yes, he's my head commander."

That wasn't much of a war council, and how much *talking* did Raylik really do?

"If you'd like me to consider joining your cause against my father, then I wish to be there. I'd like to see what truth there is to your claims." If others were bargaining, so would I.

"A terra princess on my war council." A cheeky smile marked his features, making him look again like the boy I still knew him to be.

"Not a princess," I rebuffed the title. "I'm serious. I'd like to sit in on the meetings going forward."

"I think that's a fine idea; we could use your insight," he answered.

No insight would be imparted. At least not from me.

"Raylik and I meet each evening for dinner. You are welcome to join us starting tomorrow evening."

Chapter 22

The next morning, Morvyn was all smiles, carrying the tools and parts Arlo had requested as we walked to the library. No trace of the night before was on his pale lips.

"Let's see if that human is good for anything besides eye sweets for you," he said with a pestering smile.

I cut him a hard look. "What are you talking about?"

"Oh, so we're pretending you don't constantly look at him yearningly every time you're near him? Got it," Morvyn said as we turned to the stairs that led to the library.

He was insufferable. But I was thankful he was avoiding the topic of the deipnon the night before. As we walked through the halls in the portion of Naiadon that Hylos and his friends occupied, it was more empty than when I first arrived, as though they were restricting the number of sirens allowed in that section of the castle. Since Calypstra had revealed who I truly was, the unsettling shift was enough to unnerve me. It was for my protection. Morvyn, however bothersome, was a welcome reprieve from the seriousness of the fact that my life was in danger.

When we settled into the library, Arlo was silent, uncomfortable in Morvyn's presence and still uncertain of mine as he unstrung the virginal. I tried my best not to stare at him to avoid any more of Morvyn's pestiferous taunting, and set out to get my hands on whatever it was that glowed on the second floor of the library.

I took my time, fingertips grazing the leather-bound spines on the first level, appearing to search for books to take back to my room.

"Find anything good, Elowyn?" Morvyn said. "More smut, perhaps?"

I scowled in his direction. "I need something to pass my *imprisonment* with."

"Aren't you the luckiest prisoner in the world, to have such beautiful jailers?"

I rolled my eyes.

"How do I access the second floor?" I asked, heart thrumming but my expression steeled as that strange glow glimmered in the corner of my eye. Whatever glowed was just above where Morvyn lounged, pale fins kicked up as he picked off the platter of fruit laid out for Arlo and me.

"The stairs are just over there," he said carelessly as he threw his chin at the back corner of the library.

Perfect.

Red silken skirt in hand, I curled up the spiral mezzanine stairs and made my way to the bookshelf that held the glowing light. With each step closer, that strange light shone brighter and brighter. What could it possibly be?

With each careful step, I watched for any movement from Morvyn, having no clue what I would do even if he caught me. Then, Arlo looked up, his eyes wide in fear.

Shit.

I shook my head no at him, willing him to understand.

Do not say anything.

Please, do not say anything!

I felt it in my bones. This, whatever it was, would help us get out of here.

"Aren't you meant to be toiling away at that instrument, Tiny Toes?" Morvyn sneered at Arlo.

I froze. I couldn't see where Morvyn was from my angle. If he walked toward Arlo to bother him, he would see the light reacting to me.

Arlo quickly turned back around to the instrument, pretending to work at it.

"Good little human."

Arlo bit his bottom lip, holding back whatever slew of curses he had running through his mind to ensure Morvyn stayed put.

Perfect. Then Arlo looked at me briefly and gave me a small, affirmative nod.

I was in the clear.

Heart lodged in my throat, I took one steady step at a time. The spine of a book was coming into view at the center of that light, almost too bright to look at. I lifted a hand to shield my eyes and stretched out to reach it.

I just barely touched the grainy, worn, sky-blue canvas that bound the text when a song like a birdcall tolled through the library in a cheery twittering. Then the light vanished.

Arlo coughed loudly to cover the noise.

"What's wrong with you? Do you have the plague or whatever you puny humans get?" Morvyn said.

"Just something caught in my throat," he said, hitting his chest hard.

"Humans are so bizarre," Morvyn muttered.

Arlo looked back up at me, raising his eyebrows. I gave him a smile and a nod. I had whatever *it* was in my clutches. He turned back to the instrument.

My heart steadied as I peeled back the hard cover, the pages stuck together, unopened for some time. I flitted through the pages, greeted by rows of neat handwriting in precise lines, in my language. But the pages weren't water-stained like the other texts Lumina had left at my bedside, just well used.

The first page, in a different handwriting from the rest, read, *To my one and only. May this journal hold your mind as you hold my heart.*

A journal? But whose was it? I turned to the next page. It was dated in the top right corner: *Spring 5339 AT.* That was only twenty-seven years ago. How did it end up here?

"Elowyn," Morvyn said.

I shut the book quickly.

"Yes?" I looked over the marble half-wall, down to Morvyn, who was standing and staring up at me, hands on his bony hips.

"What are you doing up there?" he asked, pale brow raised.

"Are you going to watch my every breath? I wasn't aware I was even in danger here among all of this ferocious ..." I looked around. "Literature."

Morvyn nervously rubbed at the nape of his neck. "Sorry, you were just being so *quiet* and—"

"It's a library, Morvyn, you're meant to be quiet."

Arlo let out a laugh.

"Quiet, terra."

"I am not the one yelling," Arlo said in a low, steady voice.

Morvyn shook off whatever his instincts were telling him.

"Arlo, are you content?" I asked, repeating his accusation against me from the first time we were in this library.

Arlo's head hit the open lid of the virginal with a thud, drawing a hiss of pain from him.

"What?" he said, rubbing at the top of his short-sheared scalp.

"Are you content ... with the *food*?"

He looked up, scanning my face for meaning until it clicked.

"No. I am not content."

"What's wrong with the food?" Morvyn said, genuinely offended.

"For starters, it's stolen cargo from *my* ship." Arlo scowled.

Morvyn smirked. "True."

"Morvyn, we need something more satiating. Maybe cooked fish and bread?"

He let out a melodramatic sigh.

"Fine, come down here and we'll go together," he answered.

"No," Arlo said quickly. "I need someone to test the keys while I tighten the strings."

Morvyn eyed us both curiously, but relented. "I will be quick." He turned to Arlo. "And if you do anything stupid, I *will* know, Tiny Toes."

Arlo huffed back in response.

Morvyn left, and I rushed down the winding stairs, the book against my chest as I made it to Arlo's side.

"What the fuck was that—"

Quickly, I slapped my hand over his mouth. His eyes flared in surprise. His soft lips brushed the palm of my hand. He smelled like sea and pine planking and perfection. Warmth curled in my lower belly.

Infernum, it was going to be next to impossible to think logically if he had me in a heady high every time he was near me.

"In that lulled state, they can hear everything you hear. See everything you see. We might already be found out from what you just witnessed, but don't make it worse."

He nodded in understanding and I removed my hand.

"Do they know my thoughts?" he asked.

"No, those are safe, at least so they say," I answered. "We need to think of a—" How could I word it so that the sirens wouldn't know what I was getting at?

But Arlo seemed to already understand my meaning, nodding along. He propped a hip against the instrument and crossed his strong arms, processing.

"The sirens are very *kind*," I started. "They take me all over this place to show me around." I willed the thought into his mind. I could find a way out for us while they continued to parade me around this place.

He nodded. "I see. Well, if the sirens are so *kind* to you, then I should really get to work on this instrument. You know, to return the favor. After all, your comfort seems important to them." Then he began loosening the strings quickly, unstringing the instrument. He was slowing his repair.

A heart-faltering smile sliced across his face as he looked back at me.

He was so handsome. *Too* handsome. And bloody smart. Thank the Guardians. He would earn us more time together and I would look for a way out for all of us.

But there was something I needed to do first. I owed it to Arlo to tell him the truth.

"There is something else I should tell you that the sirens already know," I said, swallowing my fear. "The reason I was on your ship."

He turned back to me, waiting.

"My name is Elowyn *Blackthorn*. I am the king's daughter."

Arlo searched my face for meaning. "But why would the king allow his only daughter to be transported on a cargo ship?"

"Because he doesn't care about me and—" Nothing in me wanted to claim the truth, but I had to. "I was on my way to marry my betrothed, Sir Cedric Gyldford, at Whiterok."

Arlo took a step back, like the words were a physical blow.

"It was against my will," I answered quickly.

He remained tense, thoughts lingering in his honey-soaked eyes.

"And I was an accomplice in this forced betrothal." His voice dipped into a lethally low octave.

"There was no way for you to know," I said softly, taking a step closer. It was not his fault.

"No one should be forced to be with or without someone against their will."

"Unfortunately, that is *exactly* the fate of a king's daughter, legitimate or not," I said with a weak smile, looking down.

Softly, Arlo brushed a curl behind my ear, sending sparks of pleasure across my skin. His hand lingered there for a moment. I looked up at him.

"It shouldn't be anyone's fate. You only have one life. You should be with who you choose."

Our eyes met, and it felt like he'd poured sunlight into my soul. Then his gaze shifted from my eyes to my mouth.

Did he feel it too? This strange attraction?

I leaned in closer.

"Elowyn, I … I can't." He pulled away, taking all his warmth with him. "There's someone else—they're waiting for me." The sentence was like an arrow stuck in my chest.

"Oh." I took a step back too, shoving down every feeling this man that I hardly knew made me feel. "Of course." I smiled cheerily, despite wanting to die of sheer embarrassment. "My apologies for being so forward."

Dumb. I was so fucking dumb.

He reached for my wrist, but I maneuvered out of his reach. "Elowyn, please don't be ... It's not like that, it's—" he started, making the situation all the more mortifying.

"Okay, you land-loving lot," Morvyn said from the top of the staircase, a platter of food in hand.

Thank the Guardians above. A distraction. For the first time, I was thankful for that annoying, pale buffoon. "Terra grub is served." He glanced between us. "Oh, great ... more sexual tension. *Brilliant.*"

Arlo huffed, then returned to his work at the virginal.

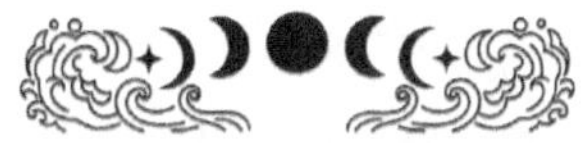

Morvyn escorted me back to my room soon after, thankfully. The time after that horrendous situation was unbearable. I tried my best to pretend like I didn't wish every window in Naiadon would shatter so I could drown to death to avoid sharing the same space as Arlo after I'd completely misread his feelings for me.

At least the blue journal was in my grasp, safely nestled between two other books as Morvyn and I walked the empty halls of Naiadon.

I thought Arlo wanted to kiss *me*? I was such an *idiot*. Of course a man like Arlo had someone else. A beauty waiting for him in a port somewhere. He was handsome and kind. Men like him had women waiting for him. But me? I had no one. Maybe a spare cook's son to screw behind an oak tree in secret. But not passion. Not romance.

I would only ever have secrets or betrothals.

"Nixie and Lumi mentioned going to a picnic in a little while. You should join them," Morvyn said, pulling me from my thoughts.

"Are picnics not meant to take place outside?" I asked.

"When you see the glade, you'll get it. Who knows, maybe you'll even have a little fun, *princess*." He winked.

I rolled my eyes. "*Not* a princess."

We paused at my door. Morvyn lingered in the hallway, bathed in the soft glow spilling from the sea through the glass windows.

"I believe the qualification is to be the daughter of a king." He booped me on the nose. "Check. And to of course have a royal air about oneself, and occasionally I *suppose* you meet that requirement. When you aren't scowling or cursing wickedly."

"Once my father had my mother executed and me delegitimized, I was no longer considered a princess. The only reason you and the others insist I'm his heir is because your leader seeks a strong ally in his war. Unfortunately for him, all he got was a waterlogged, *illegitimate* daughter who was in the process of being banished on a damned cargo ship."

"Well," his lips quirked to one side, "who doesn't love a *wet* princess?"

My eyes widened at the crass comment. "You're *absolutely* repugnant," I sneered.

"I heard you were positively sopping when they found you," he continued, earning a smack on his arm from me.

"All thanks to Tiny Toes and his terrible *steering*," he chuckled.

A smile swept across my lips, betraying my attempt to maintain composure. "You're abhorrent!"

Morvyn had an irritating talent for cracking through my defenses and making me grin despite everything.

Our laughter settled.

Morvyn leaned against the wall across my door, his figure blending into it as he folded his long limbs before him. "Just so you know, I do care."

"What?" I asked.

"Last night, after Calypstra outed you, you asked if I care. I do. When she did that, despite you holding it together wonderfully, I realized how afraid you might truly be here. How strange this all must be for you. I just kept thinking that I don't want you to feel more uncomfortable because of us."

"But why?" I asked, genuinely wanting to know, even if it was just a lovely lie told to keep me complacent.

"Besides you seem like a decent person, *despite* your terrible taste in men," Morvyn started.

My face contorted in an attempt at offense.

"Because I think you need someone to care about you. Someone who believes in you for being you, not just some rich asshole's daughter."

For a second I let myself believe Morvyn cared. That the others maybe cared too.

"Thank you."

"Anytime, *Princess*."

Chapter 23

In my bedchamber, I sank onto the plush bed, the softness enveloping me as fish glided past the large tracery window overlooking the open sea. I turned my attention to the sky-blue journal in my hands, running a fingertip over the well-worn cover. I opened it and read.

I will love him for the rest of my existence and beyond. Even if that love existed for only a single breath, I would love him again and again, no matter how short-lived or how much the circumstances changed. Because the nights beneath the sea in Naiadon are when I feel truly at home. Each morning I curse the sun for its betrayal, for shedding its light on my reality, and damn the Guardians for making me human and he siren. The world seems bent against us, forcing me to leave Aegir each night.

Aegir. Hylos's father. This journal belonged to his lover. Was it Hylos's mother? Was she ... human? Was that even possible?

A knock rapped on my door. Quickly, I jammed the journal under my pillow and stepped across the room.

I opened the door to Nixie and Lumina.

"Morvyn said you were up for a picnic, still care to join us?" Nixie asked, a white woven bag slung over her bare shoulder like we weren't hundreds of feet below the sea. Like I wasn't the daughter of a king they called enemy, and they weren't creatures I'd only heard of in holy prayers.

Lumina stood beside her in a filmy yellow gown.

It was another opportunity to explore this place and maybe find an escape. I nodded in agreement. "Sure."

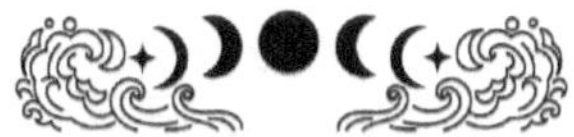

As we walked through the castle, it was apparent that the news of the human royal in Naiadon had broken. Eyes followed me intently as we walked through the halls, more so than when I was merely the human woman wandering freely among the sirens. Whispers followed in our wake, pricking my skin. A human *royal* in their midst was clearly more interesting. Especially one they believed could aid their regent in a war against her father.

We turned into a section of the castle I hadn't seen yet and ascended a grand staircase, the stone steps broad but shallow. How far was I from Arlo and his men here?

The air felt warmer with each step upward, and then a familiar sound warbled in the distance. My heart faltered and my eyes grew wide; the birdsong I'd heard in the library. Did something else glow and sing for my touch? Lumina and Nixie looked at me knowingly. So they heard it too.

"Is that—?" As if answering my question, the birdsong rang true.

Nixie smiled at me brightly. Even Lumina's lips drew upward.

I hurried up the stairs two at a time until they flowed to rolling, clover-covered hills, skyward glass bowed above, and the blue-green sea beyond it. The room brimmed with sunlight and was teeming with life. The sun made the space warm, like a giant greenhouse, as birds trilled and dove through oak trees.

"We thought you might miss home, and this is as close as we've got here in Naiadon," Nixie said beside me. Lumina stood on my other side.

"How are there birds here?" I asked in awe.

"Hylos's mother cherished the sound of birds in spring," Lumina said as we walked out into the glade. "Aegir created this place and brought them here for her."

The clover-covered ground, lush and soft, pressed against the bare arches of my feet.

"Love brought them here," Nixie said.

"But how did he get them down here?" If all this life could get here, surely there was a way for me to leave this place with a crew of men in tow.

Nixie stopped and spread the blanket on the ground under an oak tree.

I craned my neck to admire its reaching limbs against the sea-sky. It was purely magical that it stood rooted here at all.

"It isn't clear. But I'm sure he invoked something similar to your bracelet. He was a very powerful siren," Lumina answered as we gathered on the blanket.

"Is that—" A hum buzzed by my ear as a fat, happy bumblebee zipped by. "Are those bees?"

"Yes," Lumina said. "The glade is a fully functioning garden. We have an apiary, two dozen fruit trees, and of course, many florals. We crafted an ecosystem and each living creature plays its part in maintaining the grounds. The bees pollinate the flowers, the flowers grow then perish, fertilizing the ground, the birds eat other bugs found here, and on some days water will collect and it will even rain. Those are my favorite days." The sound of life was music to my ears.

"After Aegir *left*," Lumina continued, "it went by the wayside, but I've been working on getting it back into shape, along with some others. Made sirens, like us"—Lumina nodded to Nixie—"especially cherish this space. A parcel of land but on our terms."

They were both made. How many other sirens here were like them?

Nixie pulled out a bundle of silk, untied it, and revealed red gems of jellied sweets coated in powdery white. She offered me one. "Love created the glade, and now love keeps it alive," she said.

Lumina's proud smile waned with a touch of mourning. Something in this space was bittersweet for her, and I wondered if it was because of how close it likely was to Hylos's own heart. How close he himself was to her heart.

"This place is amazing," I said, stuffing the treat in my mouth, the sugar powder sticking to my fingers.

"It is," Lumina admitted, her eyes closed and head lolling back, savoring the sun's blessing.

All of this, the castle, this glade, for Hylos's mother. The woman whose journal I may have found in the library.

"Hylos's mother enjoyed birdsong, and Aegir created this very castle for her; is that because she was human?" I asked.

Lumina and Nixie exchanged sidelong glances.

"Why do you ask?" Lumina asked.

"I'm curious, mostly. What kind of remarkable woman meets then convinces a siren king to build all of this for her?" But more importantly, how did she get here, and did she leave here alive?

The pair remained silent as around us, sirens enjoyed the glade, their strange coloring more vibrant here as they walked or lounged on blankets in clusters, relishing the sun.

A pair of red siren children, one a tall, gangly boy and the other a slender girl, both with matching glossy black hair, ran past our blanket in fits of giggles.

"Little is known of his mother," Lumina said in a dismissive tone.

"Was she made as you were?" I asked.

"No, she was human, and remained human from what we know."

"Let's start with some siren basics. The birds and the bees as they say," Nixie said, splaying a finned hand in Lumina's direction.

"What?" Lumina asked.

"Well, tell her."

"Why do I have to explain everything?" Lumina scoffed.

"Because you know *everything*, Lumi," Nixie said as she stuffed another sweet in her mouth, a bit of powder left on her rose-colored lips.

"That is absurd, I do not know everything. That would be impossible." Lumina rolled her big brown eyes. "But I will, as long as you do not interrupt me. I *hate* when you and Morvyn interrupt me when I speak."

"Of course. If you keep it short and sweet. No rambling on about too many particulars."

"*Fine*." She let out a huff that shook her long brunet braids. "But the complexities of siren genetics and mating especially in relation to other species isn't exactly a simple topic to cover, considering—"

"You're already doing it," Nixie interrupted.

Lumina looked at her flatly, then continued, "I'll start with those like Nixie and me, the made sirens, created by siren invocation or magic as you know it. When you're made, you may no longer have children. Sirens call this the sacrifice. We are *essentially* sterile."

Nixie fidgeted at the statement. The topic of children seemed to make her uncomfortable, as it had when Calypstra brought it up in the grotto as a sort of dig at Nixie.

Lumina realized her unease too, and placed a gentle hand on her knee. "Sorry," she said softly.

"It's fine, keep going," Nixie said, and tried to smile.

"We relinquish the creation of life to Nymphaea for our new life below the sea." Lumina continued, "Then there are the sirens who are born, like Raylik and Morvyn, their parents both sirens. They're believed to be the most pure of our kind, often Circle leaders or influential members of inner circles." But not Hylos's inner circle, I noted; they were a mixture of made and born sirens. "And on exceedingly rare occasions, our kind come from the love of humans and sirens." Lumina looked at the children with me.

"The children of human and siren relations often perish before they quicken in the womb, especially if the mother is human, as Hylos's was. We don't know her name; it's not written anywhere, and Aegir was careful to keep it a secret. He referred to her as the queen of Naiadon. The first human to *ever* be given a title below the sea in written history."

Lumina paused and looked up. The scales on her cheeks shone in the sunbeams as she lifted a finned hand to block out the rays. "Which upset many. Aegir had already united the sea, which was a new thought in itself, and then he essentially crowned a human, refusing to be with a *pure* siren, or forge a worthy match with someone of his status like a Circle leader's daughter or sister. It was very contentious. Many assumed unfruitful. Until of course one day, Hylos appeared here as a baby."

Lumina let out a breath and Nixie sat up, crossing her legs before her and pulling them in as if for protection.

This story made them uneasy.

"But only Hylos appeared here in Naiadon, out of thin air, and his mother was never seen again."

"Aegir was devastated," Nixie added.

"There is no written account of his feelings," Lumina stated factually, "but some state he searched for her on land for years."

Nixie interjected, "Hylos grew up without a mother, and with a father who was absent for most of his life."

"Records of that time period also showed taxes went uncollected, and rebellions broke out." Lumina stated the hard facts rounded in sadness. "It was chaos. Then one day Aegir vanished."

"Vanished?" I asked.

"Gone, without a trace. Hylos was only fifteen, and after months of the king's absence, Aegir's trusted inner circle named Hylos the regent in his father's stead," Nixie said.

"We weren't here then." Lumina shook her head, hurt settling in her eyes. Like it was a crime she was guilty of. When she was likely too busy going through her own hardships in Oakhaven.

"But Hylos had Raylik and Morvyn at least," Nixie said. "Can you imagine?" She elbowed Lumina playfully, trying to shake the sadness brimming in her eyes. "This place must have been a disaster! Hylos as regent of all three great seas, with Morvyn at his side."

Lumina let a smile slip.

Nixie giggled, twinkling in pinks in the sunshine. "Sacred Mother, this place probably smelled like a brothel and those three had to be drunk off their asses every night."

"At least Raylik was around to keep them in order," Lumina added.

"He was probably so relieved when we arrived." They both laughed now, light reflecting off their skin and dancing around us on the spread blanket as they leaned into one another.

The little siren girl in front of me stuck her tongue out at her brother. A melodic chime followed, and water whipped through the air, splashing his face.

He scowled, wiping a wet black lock from his forehead.

"They match in coloring, like Raylik and his cousins," I said, pointing my chin at the two.

"Very observant," Lumina praised. "Sirens usually inherit their coloring from their mothers, originally for camouflage. For example, those from the ancient Twynox lineage, who stay in the deep sea and don't mingle with other Circles often, have kept their original gray and black hues."

"They don't get out much," Nixie joked.

"But here in Naiadon you will see sirens of all coloring. But relatives often have correlating coloring. As you likely share your mother's eyes or father's hair."

I was all my father. I knew that. From my red hair to my amber eyes.

The two children ran around in circles, giggling. How different my life would have been with a sibling, with a family, especially with a brother.

Then maybe my mother would still be alive.

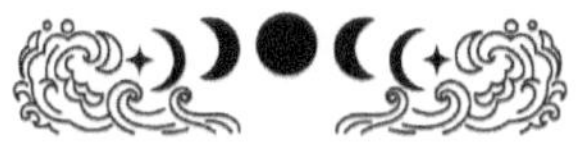

Summer 5339 AT

45 days away from Naiadon. Away from Aegir. Each night marked with innumerable tears. The grave look on Aegir's face when I finally appeared at our meeting spot, a cove on the Nettle River beside Guardian's Watch, was horrendous. I never want him to feel that agony again. I know in my soul that he came for me each night. I knew he waited for me. He would for eternity.

Tonight, he pleaded with me to stay in Naiadon for good. He spoke of marriage, a wild thought considering his people do not even believe in such things, but he said he would marry me if it meant I would stay, and he would make me a siren, like the other sirens here. But his unwelcoming court already looks at me like a scourge. If Aegir married a made siren it would topple all he has worked for, surely. But I know him, he wouldn't care. He spent his life building this powerful kingdom below the sea and he would give it all up in a heartbeat for me. A love like that is dangerous.

I cannot stay. His purpose is to rule his people, and mine is to elevate my family. I am young and, many say, beautiful. With the proper match, my family will rise in ranking. I cannot stay in Naiadon past dawn, even if it is where my heart dwells.

Aegir sleeps soundly now, in his bed, and I lie next to him, writing in this little journal, listening to his breathing. How can one man be so perfect?

How will I ever tell him I'm to be married? A match too great for my father to reject. That if I don't marry him, if I were to disappear and never return to shore, my family would surely be in grave danger.

Chapter 24

With a sweep of Hylos's palm, he conjured a deep-timbre sound that rang through the air, buzzing in my chest and lighting the massive cartography table, which was carved from a large piece of coral. The light bathed the books that lined the dimly lit shelves of his study.

"Let's start with what we know. All the sailors we've captured have followed these routes." Another song drummed from him with a wave of his hand, and water in strings traced paths upon the map like twine-wide rivers.

"Our current location?" I asked over the dissipating hum of his song.

"Here." Hylos pointed far off the coast, to the northeast of Oakhaven.

I'd had my suspicions that we were far from land, and he confirmed it. It would be impossible to swim from here if I ever managed to get through one of those entry pools.

"Here is where the disappearances have been reported." He moved his hand again as red-illuminated spears of water ticked the mapped seas surrounding Oakhaven, all falling outside of the ship routes.

"So, *none* coincide with the routes?" I asked.

"As of now, no," he answered.

"Doesn't that mean that the ships are not part of the disappearances then?"

Hylos's blue brow furrowed.

"The sailors have limited knowledge of sirens as well. Aside from folktales or religious prayers," Raylik said. "We haven't collected a single person with memories of true sirens."

"So you essentially have … *nothing*," I said, knitting my arms across my chest.

"Tell her, Raylik," Hylos said.

"We have the account of a young siren, named Orlan of Fallon Circle, who claims that while headed to warmer waters with his family, a strange sound overtook him and his Circle. A song he'd never heard before. He described it as wild and terrifying, like a broken heart. He passed out and awoke to his entire Circle gone. We assume they were taken."

Hylos shook his head in disgust.

"But strange noises at sea sounds like something your people would have a hand in." It was a sad story, sure, but what did it have to do with Oakhaven?

From the folds of his tunic, Hylos pulled out a small coin. "When the child awoke, he was at the bottom of the sea, and beside him was this."

"A coin?" I asked, taking the copper piece from him. On the front was the shape of a bear with a fish's tail.

My stomach sank.

"You know that creature, then?" Hylos raised an eyebrow at me.

I did. Unfortunately. It was my betrothed's familial heraldic beast. The same one on the hull of Arlo's cargo ship. But what did the Gyldfords have to do with this?

"Flip it over," Hylos said.

On the other side of the coin, embossed in its metal, was the word *Whiterok.*

I met Hylos's ocean gaze. "When you told me the name of the city on the sea, it all came together."

Was Cedric somehow a part of all of this?

"And when you look at the abductions and use that *unnatural* struc-ture as a point of reference, it all comes together."

With a movement of his hand, new paths formed. Slicing lines that traveled back and forth from Gyldmare to Whiterok.

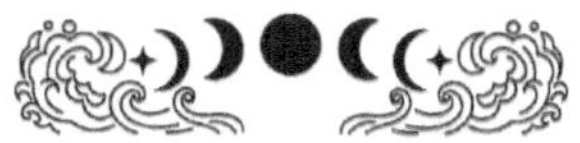

In silence, Raylik escorted me to my room. The wine from dinner had soured my gut and the thought of war was bitter in my mind. What if it was true? What if Oakhaven had something to do with the disappearance of sirens? Did that mean that war was inevitable? But what did Whiterok and Cedric have to do with any of this? Maybe it was all him behind this. He was a terrible person. But why?

"Have you seen battle?" I asked Raylik.

"Long ago, as a boy, I fought by my father's side to defend our Circle against Aegir and his conquest to unify all the great Circles. We fell. I was taken by Ageir as his ward." So it was true; Hylos was Raylik's family's greatest enemy. "My father died shortly after."

"Serenous said your father was a great warrior."

The siren light spilled down the hallway, glowing against the black void beyond.

"He lived and breathed war," Raylik answered. "My first steps were with a spear in hand. He assumed it was the only answer. But war can be for many reasons. Aegir fought to unite us. My father fought to keep us apart," he said steadily.

"Life will be lost if Hylos attacks Oakhaven. There will be bloodshed. Even if you take the humans' with ease."

"Hylos is *determined*," he answered, not looking at me as we continued down the hall.

"Determined to send people to their deaths."

Raylik sent a warning look in my direction. He was a soldier and commander. Steady and loyal. "Hylos is a good leader. He will do what is best for us all."

The measured statement wasn't a disagreement. That was something.

"But you hope that 'what is best' is not war?" I pushed further.

Raylik only looked ahead, not answering my question, which again was an answer in itself.

Because he didn't want war.

But he would follow his leader's orders. No matter what.

"Are you good with a sword?" Raylik asked, changing the subject.

I let out a snort. "Me? Good with a sword."

He didn't laugh, only kept that slow pace. It wasn't a joke.

"No, I'm not good with a sword."

"What about hand to hand?"

"Like dancing?" I asked.

"Hand to hand *combat*," he clarified.

"The only combat I'm familiar with is what I've read in books. I have no skill in fighting. It is not ..." The words tasted disgusting on my tongue. "It's not becoming of a lady."

"Nonsense. Everyone should learn to hold a sword and defend themselves."

He was right. If I had been a son, surely I'd have learned to fight and hold a sword. Every boy from the age of five did.

"Could you teach someone like me?" I asked. Half-waiting for him to laugh in my face.

"Of course," he answered curtly.

If he trained me a little, maybe I could learn the sirens' strengths and understand their weaknesses. It could also help us escape when the time was right. Also, I could pass the information along to my father.

"Would you teach me?" I asked.

"I will speak with Nixie. We both should train you. She is the second-best fighter I know."

Petite Nixie was the second-best fighter Raylik knew? When he was raised by warriors and had the muscle mass to show for it?

"And who is the first?" I asked.

"Me."

CHAPTER 25

Nixie appeared at my door disgustingly early the next morning.

"What time is it?" I groaned, squinting at the unforgiving white daybreak shining behind her.

"Early as Infernum. Now, get dressed. Today we start your training." She shoved a wad of emerald silk into my hands.

"At this hour?" I questioned, eyeing the small amount of fabric.

When I asked Raylik to teach me to fight, I didn't think it would mean waking up at this obscene hour.

"You'll thank me later for the early start."

I put on the billowing silk pants and matching top. It was revealing, but covered more skin than Nixie's attire, her pink silken bottoms so short that her lean thighs were bare, along with her toned midriff.

We arrived at the armory, where Hylos and Raylik had grappled for the siren crowd. The large room was now empty, the gentle lapping of the water in the center pool, once my potential escape route, punctuating the silence with sloshing licks against the stone.

"To fight well, you must first be strong." She walked to a shelf of various round balls made of polished black stone. Picking up the smallest of them, she handed it to me with ease. Under its weight, I huffed. It was heavy for such a small thing, only the size of a melon.

Nixie grabbed a larger one and stood before me. She raised it above her head, lifting it up toward the sky, all while keeping her balance. Then, letting out a steady breath, she lowered the weight behind her head.

"We'll start with three repetitions of five for a warm-up," she said, continuing to pump the stone into the air repeatedly.

I copied her movement, but after the third push my shoulders burned.

All morning we lifted or squatted in place with the weighted stones. My legs shook as sweat beaded my brow. But it felt oddly good to concentrate on the movements so I didn't drop the damn thing on my head. It forced my mind to be present and not drift away to war, betrotheds, fathers, or duty.

"You're naturally strong," Nixie said through a proud smile.

Not half as strong as she, especially for someone so small.

"Are all sirens as strong as you?" I asked. Despite enjoying this strange form of torture, I was here for reconnaissance.

She let out a laugh. "Most are stronger. I'm small for a siren, likely because I am made. Natural-born sirens are the strongest of us, though. In both magic and physical strength."

I nodded in understanding. That was a good bit of information that I tucked away. Although, from the look of them, it was hard to tell the made sirens apart from the born.

With time, heat intensified in the training room, turning it into a furnace. The salted sea in the pool at the center of the armory steamed the space with briny, pungent curls that burned my eyes. The reason behind Nixie's choice of an early start was clear. The rising temperature made the room almost unbearable. Drenched in sweat, I glistened in the daylight cascading through the glass dome above our heads, and my clothes clung to my exhausted frame.

"I wasn't aware *princesses* did such unbecoming acts such as train," Calypstra's unmistakable voice sibilated as she walked into the armory.

When I turned to see the awful bitch, my jaw almost dropped in shock at the giant beside her, a siren built from layers of rippling muscles that hid behind sickly pale skin.

Nixie kept a careful eye on the pair, which had me on guard immediately too.

"What do you want, Calypstra?" she said, completing another repetition of her weight.

"I was just showing Draveen where the Jawro will take place in a few days. Then we're headed to greet our king."

"Your king *regent*," Nixie corrected, "will be glad to see you, Draveen. We missed you at the deipnon the other night."

"I was busy," he said in a strange, thick accent as he looked at his nails with a nasty grin.

"Ah, busy killing your mother? Or was it one of your brothers this time?" Nixie asked, forcing the male's inky eyes to flare in anger.

Calypstra let out a nasty laugh. "It's always fun when you come out to play, Nixie; that innocent act is so boring. You should save it for trying to trick Raylik into your bed."

Nixie rested the polished stone on her narrow hip and cocked her head to one side. "Is that what you do? Trick males into your bed? I've never needed to do so, *personally*."

I bit down on a smile that threatened to show just how good it was to hear someone tell Calypstra off.

Her black-lined eyes pounced on me.

"Speaking of bedding. I've heard you've found another human to mingle with. That's good. You should really stick to your own kind."

Draveen scowled. "There are more of them wandering about here? I thought Hylos had the sense to keep them in cages."

"Unfortunately, there are more," Calypstra drawled. "How is that human male? To your liking, *Princess*?"

"He's imprisoned, thanks for asking. And he doesn't exactly like your kind either. I don't think he could stomach looking at a siren without being sick. I'd hate to see his face if he saw you lot."

I wasn't playing nice anymore with Calypstra. She'd exposed me for whatever reason and put me in danger. Maybe even the captain and his crew. Fuck her. But then, Calypstra's lip twitched downward for a heart-beat. Did I actually hit a nerve? Just as quickly, it was gone, buttoned back up behind her evil, joyless smile.

"Nixie, are you practicing for the Jawro competition? Draveen and I were just discussing who we would challenge this year." Calypstra looked at me with a smirk, exposing her sharp canine teeth. "He was saying a human would be a fine opponent, someone he could tear apart limb from limb."

Apparently she wasn't holding back anymore either, because that sounded like a threat.

"I'm surprised you aren't challenging Hylos for the third year in a row to take his throne," Nixie said to Draveen, who crossed his ridiculously strong arms over his lethally toned, muscly chest. "And you know I train daily, Calypstra. Or is that your formal challenge for me? Because I'd gladly kick your ass. Someone needs to silence that foul mouth of yours."

Calypstra faked a frown. "Oh Nixie, are you really still mad at me for the other night when I outed your little princess friend? I was just trying to help."

"More like wondering why you'd go against direct orders and endanger an ally of Hylos."

"My *king's* guest needed a little push in the right direction, to own up to her identity, instead of us all dancing around the facts."

"I'm right here," I said.

"That you are, *Princess*. For now."

Yeah, that one was absolutely a threat.

"Ah wait, sorry, should I just call you Elowyn? You don't have any titles, after all. Isn't that right? Which makes sense. What king would send his *real* daughter on a cargo ship out to sea?"

My cheeks burned like the anger growing in my chest.

Calypstra leaned in. "But I wouldn't let the other Circle leaders find out you're really a nobody on land. Then they'll have no use for you."

Autumn 5339 AT

If wrath was a man, his name would be Aegir, Siren King of the Three Seas. He roared and cursed each Guardian above when I told him of my marriage, which will take place in one month's time. The ocean churned with him in anguish and the sky was in torrents, as was he.

Aegir offered, again, for me to become siren. To leave the world ashore behind. To truly be his queen. He knew my answer long before he asked, but he will never stop asking. I know that and love him for it.

That was a fortnight ago, but the wounded look in his gray eyes tells me he will never heal from this. Nor shall I. Our hearts will remain forever chained together, no matter what marriage vows to the Guardians I make.

This evening he gave me a gift. He calls it an Opening and explained that the enchantment behind it creates a direct doorway between our two worlds. That way there is no need for him to swim each night to meet me and wait. With this, I can walk directly through and be in Naiadon. It is like a doorway. It looks like a painting, a beautiful portrait of my likeness, its mirror the image of the sea.

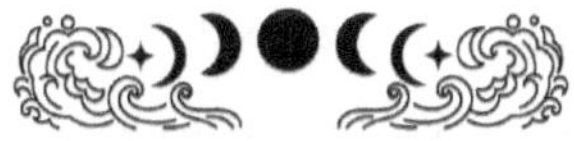

I'd practically run to the library, slowed only by Nixie at my side, trying not to let on how eager I was to tell Arlo about what I'd read in the journal over breakfast in my bedchamber.

Morvyn let out a dramatic sigh of relief when I rushed up the stairs. "Finally! I'm so bored. He won't even banter with me." Morvyn rose to his colorless, finned feet.

Arlo continued to work on the instrument and didn't even bother to look at me as I entered. Which was fine by me. Preferred, actually. Because he had *someone* waiting for him. So, if he could just keep working on that damned thing while I talked, then maybe we could actually get out of here without me getting distracted by this dumb, handsome lug.

"See? Boring! He won't even pine after you, even when you're wearing that absolutely risqué dress."

I glared at Morvyn while trying to hide my legs, exposed by the high slit in my skirt. I was running out of modest dress, but what was the point of dressing modestly if everyone else was mostly naked anyway?

"Ah, now you're fun! So easy to torment and actually entertaining to repartee with. But, unfortunately, Hylos *insists* I kiss up to my dreadful aunt and cousin, so you're on your own today."

Perfect.

"I'll be back in the hour, but if you need anything, there will be two guards at the bottom of the library stairs."

"To spy on us," Arlo said from the virginal.

"For Elowyn's safety, Tiny Toes. Just in case you show your true colors." Morvyn rolled his pale eyes to me. "If you need anything, the guards will assist you." Swiftly, he kissed me on the cheek. "There, that'll help get him going," Morvyn whispered.

I turned and Arlo was staring, arms crossed.

"They're kissing you now?" he asked.

"Apparently, but I'm not sure why you care." I slowly lowered myself onto the white velvet couch, my legs screaming in protest from the beating they'd taken during my training with Nixie.

His eyes blazed, and he walked to me. "Are you hurt?"

"No, no." I waved him off. "I was just lifting weights with Nixie and ... Never mind."

He eyed the stairs at first, then me, and then sat beside me. Which I wasn't prepared for after the other day. Even worse, my heart skipped in my chest.

No. I couldn't fall into this trap again. He had someone else. I moved over, giving him room on the couch.

"I think I have an answer to ..." I looked around the room, searching for the phrasing that wouldn't tip off the sirens when they swam through his mind, then spotted the virginal. "Fixing the *action* of the instrument."

He slowly nodded a yes in understanding.

"Yes, the *action*, and what is your solution?" he questioned.

"Instead of the other way of *fixing* it ..." I puffed out my cheeks and plugged my nose, pretending to hold my breath underwater and swim to the surface.

He cocked his head to the side in confusion and gave me that perfect, taunting smile that made my heart falter. "What are you doing?"

I rolled my eyes. "Never mind. It seems there is a shortcut I've learned of from a book in this library." He looked around the room.

"They just left the answer, lying around this place? It has to be a trap." He pursed his lips.

That was actually an incredible point. "I hadn't thought of that."

But maybe they didn't know it was here. There were hundreds of books in this library. It clearly took generations to amass such a collection. What were the odds I would find this one? That when I was near it, for whatever reason, it would glow?

"Well, I guess tell me what this shortcut is. We can weigh our options from there," he said.

"The thing is, I know what it is." It was some magical portal, painting, thing. But I couldn't tell him that. "But I'm not sure exactly where it is and—"

He stood on his feet, taking his warmth with him.

"So, you have nothing."

"It's not nothing. It sounds like a very important *something*."

He returned to the virginal with a huff, loosening the strings.

"How many days have we been down here?"

I went quickly to his side, drawn to him despite the scorching pain in my thighs and ass.

"It will be a week today," I answered. Had it really been so long already?

He shook his head to himself. "It feels like years."

I leaned a hip against the virginal and watched him. "What do you mean?"

"That state they put me in." He shuddered. "It's just reliving my memories again and again. It's *maddening*."

"That can't be all that bad, can it?" I asked.

"There are some things I'd rather forget, and those seem to be the ones that repeat the most often." He fell silent, golden eyes losing their luster as they narrowed on the work before him.

I reached out and touched his shoulder, momentarily pulling him from whatever haunted his memories. "We'll find a way," I reassured him, "to fix the action."

He smiled, then turned to me.

I held my breath, attempting to prevent myself from indulging in his inebriating scent that was seeping into my thoughts.

"You said you don't love the man you're betrothed to," he said, heavy brow furrowing.

"I don't," I answered. In fact, I hated him. The only thought I spared for that bastard was to wonder why he created Whiterok, and how it was tied to Hylos's missing people.

"Will you not have to ..." Marry him if I returned to land.

"I likely will," I answered.

"Why not flee instead?"

He said it so easily. As if it was an obvious answer. But it wasn't.

"I will need to tell my father." About the sirens. "I have a duty to—"

His eyes widened as he understood my meaning. Then he clasped my hand unexpectedly.

"What are you—" My hand seemed so small in his warm, rough palm.

"Elowyn, what has Oakhaven ever done for you?"

It was another good point. This man was full of them today. What *had* Oakhaven done for me? Besides turn its back on me. Or was that only my father's crime?

But had no one wondered where the only child of the king had disappeared to? Did no one beseech him to spare my mother's life?

I wanted to be angry. Bitter, even. But another thought bent my wrathful mind: what about the children in the dilapidated shacks? What about the little girls like Lumina waiting for an unimaginable life? What would that life look like if sirens attacked their home? If their fathers and brothers died in another senseless war.

I pulled my hand from his, despite wanting to keep it there desperately.

"Oakhaven doesn't have to do anything for me to protect it. That is not how responsibility works."

His honey-colored eyes searched my face as his jaw set.

"The person waiting for me—"

"It's fine," I interrupted. "You don't owe me an explanation."

"It's my daughter." He grimaced with the words.

Daughter?

"I am not a good man." He shook his head, looking at his hands as if they had committed unthinkable crimes.

"Why on earth would you ever say that?" I asked. Arlo was a good man. What he did for his men, what he did for Alistar. He was kind and noble. Maybe morose at times, but he had a fine heart.

"I *had* a wife."

"You monster," I said with a little laugh.

"No, you don't understand." He looked down at me, pain settling in his features. "I took her as my wife because I was a selfish young fool who thought with his prick instead of his head. As soon she fell pregnant, we wed."

"And that makes you immoral how?" I asked.

"I forgot my place in this world. My mother ... she had plans for me. I knew that. She was always very strict and when she found out I had married, she had my wife murdered."

The look of devastation on his face made me want to collect him in my arms and save him from that fate. Even though it had already come to pass.

"Your mother murdered your wife?" My stomach soured. What kind of villain would do such a thing?

"Yes. When she died, I couldn't care for my daughter. I was young and didn't know the first thing about being a father. I left her with my brother. He loaned me money for my ship, I fled my mother, and became a captain. Like the disgrace I am."

I took his large face in my hands, lifting his strong chin up. "The only monster in your story is your mother, Arlo."

"You don't even know the extent of truth in that statement. But that's why I must get back to land. However much I *really* wish to," he looked me up and down, "I cannot get distracted by this alchemy between us. I visit Cate only twice a year. She has no mother because of me, and I'll be damned if she has no father, however useless I am, because I got swept up in *this*."

Gently, I dropped my hands.

"I see." That was all I would allow myself to say, hoping to fend off the feelings that were burning through me.

Arlo felt this pull between us. He wanted it. He wanted me. But he wouldn't let it stand between him and getting back to his daughter.

And that made me want him all the more.

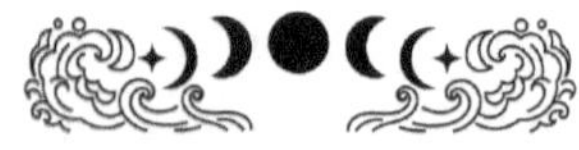

A tempest raged in Aegir's eyes upon discovering the bruise inflicted on my arm by my husband. He begged me to stay in Naiadon again. But he's

oblivious to the danger my family would face above if I were to disappear. My proud husband, capable of unthinkable fury, would release his wrath upon them if I disappeared without a trace.

I can endure a few blows. The safety of those relying on me takes precedence. But there is another matter that I'm afraid Ageir may never understand. One that I'm not sure I have the heart to tell him. But I must find a way. Because I am with child.

<h1 style="text-align:center">CHAPTER 26</h1>

The ocean floor loomed into view outside the castle, each step immersing me deeper into the dark sea as Nixie guided me down a sloping hall into the belly of the castle. Rolling my shoulders, I tried to shake the anxiety scuttling up my spine.

Another strange siren event. Another situation where I was entering the lions' den.

This also meant there would be no war council with Hylos and Raylik. Even though I had so many questions for them both. Like, what would someone even want with sirens? What could Cedric's city on the sea possibly have to do with their disappearance? How does one even take a siren?

"I'm surprised you agreed to come," Nixie said, her glossy red dress swishing with each graceful step, the translucent lace of the drop waist revealing the hard lines of her stomach. She offered a gentle smile, colored with apology. "Especially after the last event you attended." When Calypstra revealed my identity.

The gauzy dress I wore was a lovely shade of green and felt light, its tendrils flitting with each step.

"I'm curious." I shrugged in response. It wasn't a lie. I was curious about the location of the strange, magical painting of a woman, which was an actual passage out of Naiadon. I was also curious about what I could learn of these creatures. About what I could tell my father to stop them and ultimately protect Oakhaven.

The hall poured us out into a large space, its walls stretching for seemingly endless miles above. A cool air wafted from the wet, cavernous walls that smelled of saturated stone. At the center of the expansive room was a giant, black, swirling pool that made my blood run cold. Onyx-colored water vortexed down, down, down, begging me to plunge into its depths and succumb to its blackness. Around the pool, the Circle leaders stood leisurely, their faces familiar from the dinner we shared the other night. All apparently too busy measuring one another to bother with me now.

"You said this is an offering ceremony, right?" I asked Nixie. We had similar traditions on land. The Guardians were greedy, so we'd leave an orange on a doorstep for Terragos or coal beside the hearth for Helionyx. All to keep them content and ward off ill intentions for us mere mortals. It all seemed like rubbish. But I once thought the same of sirens.

"Yes, we offer things we cherish to Nymphaea to seek her blessing for a bountiful year and the hopes of a fertile mating during Hydroxia," Nixie said coolly as we neared the endless black pit. "We call this a swallow. There are multiple across the sea floor. They say they are sacred portals to the Mother herself." Portals. Like the paintings from the journal. Was this another way out of Naiadon?

"Do people ever go through it or come out of it?" I asked.

"Some have offered themselves to it, or *others*, but they never return," Nixie said as she pinched her pink eyebrows, telling me it wasn't recommended.

Hylos walked out onto a platform that protruded over the swallow, making me uneasy. One wrong step and he would vanish into the black, roiling water. He was dressed plainly, with white fabric wrapped around his lower body. I could make out the dark-blue lines that marked his body from here. "I sincerely thank you, once again, for celebrating Hydroxia here with me. We will begin the ceremony shortly," he called loudly, his voice amplified by the swell of siren song.

"Did we have a choice in the matter?" a voice in the crowd muttered. It was Raylik's uncle, dressed in layers of blood orange.

Nixie cleared her throat.

He turned and looked down at her, his murder-red gaze filled with hatred. "A disgrace for you wear those colors. *Made*." He said the word like a curse.

"I merely wear the color of my mate's scales for Hydroxia. As is tradition. Melquin, *Leader* of Mariscal Circle." Red, for Raylik.

"Another disgrace to my Circle. My brother's only son wastes his seed on a barren made siren." He spat at her webbed feet.

Nixie scowled angrily, but I could see the hurt there too.

"The only disgrace is your ill manners," I said, too quickly for my own good.

The siren towering above me, who could likely break me in half, glowered.

"Hylos keeps such poor company. But what else would one expect from a mongrel?" Melquin said with precision.

I knew discontent when I heard it. Well, I had read enough about it to spot it. Hylos did not have a grip on his vassals.

"Hylos is your king regent," Nixie said quickly. "And I suggest you remember you are in *his* domain before a member of his inner circle. Made or not. Raylik is also a member of that inner circle, in case you forgot. I don't believe he has challenged anyone to the Jawro competition, *yet*."

She narrowed her pink eyes at him. "I have a feeling if he heard you speak in such a manner about both his leader and mate in the same breath, he would likely challenge you in a heartbeat. And lest you forget,

Melquin of Mariscal Circle, the only reason you sit on the throne of Raylik's birthright is because Aegir cut down his father for you. We all know you are no great warrior."

Her words were swift, sharp, and out for blood.

The fear quivering Melquin's lower lip told me he didn't want to be on the receiving end of Raylik's rage. Nor would I.

Nixie's sugary-sweet smile returned in a flash. "Oh, and happy Hydroxia to you!" She tipped her head politely, looped her arm into mine, and we moved onward through the crowd.

"That was bloody amazing," I said.

"He just about shit himself," Nixie said with a wry smile.

What a strange contrast she was. Kind yet fierce. Small but mighty.

"The Jawro competition. Calypstra spoke of it the other day as well, what is it?" I asked as we made our way closer to the swallow, still arm in arm.

"Essentially, two sirens fight. It's brutal. Also, it's an opportunity to challenge another for their spot in a Circle or to have the hand of a mate for Hydroxia. Really, it could be a challenge for anything. Even just for honor."

"Ah, so you have pissing matches here too, then?"

"Hey, sometimes you just need to bash someone's head in to prove a point."

"Melquin fears Raylik would challenge him and take his throne?"

Nixie nodded. "I wish he would, to silence that damned fool. But if he did, he would have to go there to lead, and he would never leave Naiadon."

"He'd never leave you," I said.

Nixie looked at me sidelong. "Yes. Or Hylos. Especially not with all that's going on with Oakhaven."

War against my country.

I slipped out of Nixie's grip, realizing that I was walking literally arm in arm with my enemy. What a strong contrast that was too. Because she felt so much like a friend.

Hylos's voice boomed over our heads. "Today we offer what we may to the Mother herself, hopeful she will continue to bless us with fertility and bounty for another year. For my offering I give to the great Mother three gifts. First ..." He took a large woven basket from a servant behind him and emptied it into the black water. "Gold, from my treasury." The coins splattered into the pit and disappeared into the void.

"Second, my song." He raised his arms. From the tips of his fingers, water formed and an intense low-pitched sound thundered forward, a baritone voice riding throughout that sang, *Mother of sea, I give to you as you give to me.*

"Finally," he said, picking up a knife. He held his hand over the swallow and sliced into the heart of his palm. "A blood oath." He squeezed his hand and his blood dripped into the water. "To defend these seas and my people. Now and forever."

The crowd cheered loudly, the sirens' song roaring with it in trills or booms. I wondered just how ardently Melquin cheered. Or others like him who were displeased with their leader. Hylos had his work cut out for him. Before he could convince these people to join in his battle, he would need to gain their respect, which he apparently didn't have.

Hylos continued, "Please come and make your offerings. Praise be to Nymphaea!" he boomed, and the crowd echoed his words.

"Have you thought of what you will offer?" Nixie asked me as we shuffled with the gathering, making our way to the stone steps up to the overhang. I'd given it some thought, but I had little to offer. Lumina explained the gifts were all mostly symbolic, so I would give the only thing I had arrived with.

"I asked Lumina to bring the dress I was found in." The fine wool petticoat of the ornate gown my father gifted me. I wouldn't miss it.

"Why did you select that?" Nixie asked.

"Eh, it's a terrible color on me," I answered.

Nixie snickered. "Maybe keep that part to yourself. You're meant to offer something of value to you."

Sirens dressed in long white tunics, eyes swiped with black from temple to temple, wove through the crowd with trays of slender, long-stemmed chalices. Nixie declined, but I took the last drink from the tray of a lavender-colored siren.

"What about you?" I returned the question as I took a sip of the drink. The bubbles sizzled on my tongue like champagne, but with a faint bitter taste.

"Before you arrived, my hair was very long. Down past my waist. I cut it to be my offering."

The line shifted forward as the sirens stood atop the perch above the swallow and dropped their offerings into the pit, each declaring the gift and its meaning.

"Why?" The question flew from my mouth unexpectedly, like the drink had bubbled it out.

"Well, it was bothersome when I would train." She shook her head, her pink curls coiling. "But also to show the great Mother that I understand it is not what makes me feminine. It is my heart. My soul. My feminine strength gifted to me by the Nymphaea herself that does so. With or without my hair, or my beauty, or my *fertility*." A rose-colored smile blossomed on her face. "I am as strong as she is."

For some strange reason, my hand clasped around hers. "I hope to be as strong as you one day." The words suddenly popped from my lips again.

"Thank you, Elowyn," Nixie answered, a bit bewildered but also genuinely grateful for the compliment.

We were next in line when another thought shadowed my mind. "Hylos should not start a war against Oakhaven." The words flew from my lips entirely against my will.

"Elowyn, I know that's how you feel, but now is not really the time for that conversation. Not here," Nixie said under her breath, her mauve eyes searching me.

"You may die and I don't want you to die at my dreadful father's hands. I don't want anyone to."

"What did the terra girl say?" a dark-green siren said with a scowl.

I tried to keep my lips sealed, but my mind could only focus on the truth, swirling round and round like the swallow itself.

"You all would be fools to go against Oakhaven," I said loudly. "Even if you are all strong, the war would not be won without a fight." I clasped a hand over my mouth, desperate to stop the words from flying out.

"Elowyn, be quiet," Nixie said in a tight-lipped whisper.

"Today is a time of offering," I heard Calypstra say at Hylos's side. They stood atop the platform watching the offerings of his people. "Why not offer the truth, terra?"

Something was wrong.

Despite how hard I tried, I could not stop the words in my mind from brimming over, the truth from spilling out. It was there, on the edge of my thoughts. But I couldn't touch it. No, I could not say—"I will never agree to fight with Hylos, no matter how much he tries to persuade me. No matter how beautiful this place and you people are." The words belted from me.

Hylos appeared wounded. "Elowyn, please make your offering and leave. We can discuss this at another time."

"Your eyes are like a memory," I said to him, because every thought became words instantly. "They are sad and empty, but proud. The only thing about you I trust."

"What are you talking about?" Hylos asked, this time concerned. Then I realized, before my mind could trace the words, where they headed next. My hand slammed over my mouth again. My lips moved with the thoughts in my mind. That no, I was not okay. I wanted to leave Naiadon desperately and plotted to do so with Arlo. I would find a way out of here. And I would never stop. Never be content.

My hand was shaking. It seemed to have a mind of its own too, and fought to pry from my lips, threatening to expose the truth behind it that would not stop rushing out of me.

I prodded at a familiar wound, right when my palm flew back to my side. "I am nothing to my father, and no use to you in a war. I have no power. No title. I am a terrible ally to you in this foolish war that will end in only bloodshed and death."

Hylos's finned blue hand covered my mouth now. He sniffed at me. "You smell of eelgrass." He cut a hard look at Nixie. "Did she ingest anything strange?"

"Only a glass of champagne given to her by a servant."

The deep void below swirled and swirled below, pulling me, calling me, swallowing my soul.

"Elowyn, someone has poisoned you," Hylos said carefully. A gasp shuddered through the crowd as murmurs spread like a brushfire. "The effects start with truth telling."

Calypstra watched beside him, her black eyes swirling like the dark pool below.

"Then hallucinations."

My eyes flared and my pulse quickened. Hallucinations?

"You *should* be okay."

Should be?

"Elowyn, listen. You must not think of anything you do not wish to say. You have control over this. Over your thoughts. But you *will* share anything that comes to mind." His words washed over me like the tide on a beach. "Avoid what you are not ready to say."

The room spun around at a dizzying speed, blood whooshing in my ears with thoughts that threatened to tell all. There is a journal under the pillow in my chambers. His mother's journal. In it is the secret of how to escape Naiadon. Which I plan to do. Escape. With Arlo. With his men. My lips moved with the thoughts against my will under Hylos's blue hand, the only thing keeping my secrets concealed.

"The captain," Nixie said at my side, her voice clamoring like a thousand church bells. But with the captain only came thoughts of escape, of plotting. How we worked together each day in the library.

My lips ran with betraying words.

"I've seen how you look at him, you think he's handsome. Think of that," Nixie declared. My thoughts wound around Arlo, the sweet warmth in his eyes. Of his body. And instead of shoving them down, like I often did, I allowed them to unfold.

Nixie was right, that was a truth I could tell. How his sea-sharpened body made mine feel hot and alive. How his perfect, slender fingers would play the virginal so well, and I longed for them inside me, curling just right with his beautiful mouth doing the rest of the job. How I knew it when they first touched me. Even if it was to force me in that damned room, the bastard. The domineering, glorious bastard.

"Will that work? Do you have him in your mind?" Hylos asked.

When he spoke, his eyes morphed into something else. Someone else. Truth. He was the truth.

I nodded yes.

"Good. Nixie, take her to her room immediately. This will only get worse. Stay by her side. I'll send Lumina to help, maybe she knows of a cure."

Hylos finally removed his hand, and the words were like a deluge: "Captain Arlo Fynn is so bloody handsome, it is absurd. Even if he is an overbearing asshole. He is exquisite. *Resplendent.*"

"Come on, let's get you out of here," Nixie said as she ushered me through the sea of words spinning around me, the world tilted on a bizarre axis.

"And when that handsome, annoying man looks at me, for the first time in all of my life, I feel seen. I believe he sees me. For once someone sees me."

Chapter 27

In my bedchamber, the hallucinations gripped me. Nixie and Lumina were near, but felt lifespans away, only visible as rose and gold smears that bled into one another.

The truth still dribbled out of me in broken sentences.

"I need to get out of here," I choked out, my body thrashing but heavy from the world's distortion.

Or did someone hold me to the bed? Did someone chain me to this bed?

"Set me free!" I yelled, and the words shimmered before me in the room. "I need to find Arlo. We need to leave."

"Who could have done this to her?" Words like blush peonies, shuddering in a meadow, fluttered across the room like butterflies.

"You know who did this." Candlelight flickering in a dark room said, "*Calypstra*." The name caught flame and burned to black ashes before my eyes.

Then, at the base of the bed, my mother appeared.

Stark and clear as day. Sound and color and time cascading around her, like she was a stone in a roaring river.

"You are a princess, Elowyn." Her voice rippled, finding me in this strange place that felt like it was between life and death itself. "You are a queen!" Her voice boomed as she watched me writhing under the weight of the words.

"No," I yelled. "I am nothing. No one."

"*Queens* do not cry." But a torrent poured from her dark-blue eyes, like the angry sea, gushing and gushing, dark-blue waves washing over me. Lapping over me. Drowning me.

"Did you cry when I left?" I asked, desperate to know the truth. "Did you love me, did anyone love me?"

"Guardians save the queen!" Mother chanted as swells of tears streamed out of her eyes, down her cheeks. Filling the room with an ocean of her tears. She didn't answer me, only repeated, "Guardians save the queen!"

"Did you love me, mother?" I begged. "Did you cry when I left?"

She shut her eyes, stopping the flood of her tears.

"Queen Elowyn Blackthorn, the first of her name!"

I didn't want to hear it. I didn't want those words. I wanted only her love. Someone's love.

She opened her eyes again, but this time, they were the same as they had been long before all my pain and agony started. At least before I knew it. Before they were red from crying often. But were they not always red? Were they not always sad?

She stepped forward in her cerulean evening dress, her long, sleek black hair braided over her shoulder. Not a day touching her perfect young skin. No longer pregnant, with a thin, tapered waist that I knew from before she was with child. Before I left. Before my world flipped upside down.

Then a loud *thwack* shattered the room, resounding through my body.

To my horror, her head was severed from her shoulders and rolled onto the bed, sopping with her tears, into my lap. Frozen, I could not move, not even to flinch. Her eyes looked up at me, two clear blue sapphires of pure honesty.

Burning, sacred truth.

"Did you ever love me?" I asked. I needed to know the truth.

"Love dies," she answered. "Glory lives forever."

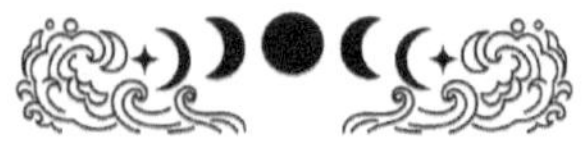

Daylight pierced the sea and dispelled my night of torments, as if none of it happened at all.

The room was empty, my body aching. Anxiety seized me, relentless. I reached under my pillow and felt the hard cover of the journal. Thank the Guardians, it was still there, just where I'd left it.

I was alone, but the presence of Nixie, Lumina, my mother, and my demons lingered. When had they left me?

I sat up in bed.

You know who did this. Lumina's words still burned in my mind, as they had in the depths of my agony.

Calypstra.

But why? On Hylos's orders? But he had prevented me from divulging my secrets right at his feet, before all.

If he didn't order it, then who did?

Everything felt strange, as if hallucinations and truths still lurked in the shadows, even in broad daylight. I needed to leave, to let the past dissipate and haunt someone else for a change.

Surging from bed, I changed into the silken emerald training outfit I'd worn the day before and rushed out the door of the empty room that was overcrowded with my past.

I knocked on Nixie's door across the way from mine.

"You're awake," she said as she rubbed at the dark-crimson circles under her eyes. It had been a long night for us both, then.

"I'm ready for training," I said curtly.

"But last night, you hardly slept—"

"Nixie. I need to."

And with a nod, she agreed.

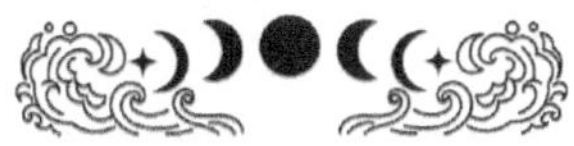

A bead of sweat traced a path down my spine as Nixie guided me through the stances of my next lesson in the armory. The scent of salt from the sea and my sweat melded. She explained how to plant my feet and hold positions steadfastly. But I was weak and shook under the weight of my body.

"I could never win a fight with a siren," I said. If I needed to, I would be defenseless. The helpless thought made me sick.

"With a bit of wit and determination, I think you could stand a chance," Nixie said as she circled me, analyzing my pose. "Plus, sirens are cocky. You can always use that against them."

"Speak for yourself," Morvyn retorted from across the room beside Raylik, who watched too. Both pretended to find interest in my progress, but something told me they were given orders to keep an eye on me.

No one spoke of my strange outburst, or the calling out to my dead mother I surely did in my torments. Thank the Guardians. I wanted to forget it all for as long as I could.

"Keep your feet flat, and drive that big toe into the ground," Nixie ordered. "You may even be better than some of the finned folk because your feet have more dexterity," she encouraged me, then gave my shoulder a firm shove, the connection feeling good as I stood my ground.

"Fantastic! Now, step toward me and lock back into that position."

I did as she instructed. But her next shove sent me off-kilter.

Raylik walked the distance between us.

"The best way to remain standing in a fight is to avoid getting hit at all," he said, even-toned. "Avoid her blows."

I reset the pose, and Nixie prepared to strike, but I stepped backward, avoiding her.

"Good!" Nixie praised.

Raylik nodded his approval.

Nixie lunged at me again, and I sidestepped her shove. As she increased her speed, I dodged again, a triumphant smile stretching my lips.

"*Very* good!" she exclaimed, then reached for me once more. I stepped back as I had before, but this time I collided with something at my calves, sprawling onto the unforgiving stone floor which bit into my ass.

Morvyn let out a hearty laugh, his finned foot protruding. He had tripped me.

"You bastard!" I hissed, but I couldn't even feign anger. I laughed too, despite everything.

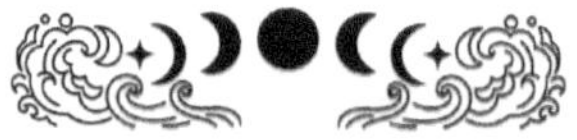

"You're late. I've been here at least thirty minutes alone," Arlo said, hunched over the virginal, heavy eyebrows knitted and wearing a grimace to match. He turned to face me. Instantly, his features smoothed and softened.

I collapsed onto the couch.

The restless night plus the hard training I had forced Nixie to push me through had me exhausted. But my mind still raced. Thoughts of who was after me spun, chased by my mother's words of pure and utter treason.

"Any luck finding the *fix*?" Arlo asked, meaning the portal out of this damned place.

"No."

I was further from answers than ever before. Morvyn had left my side only long enough for me to spend *some* time alone in the library with Arlo, but I knew he loitered protectively at the base of the stairs.

They were all on guard after last night. I hoped by now I'd garnered enough trust to wander Naiadon freely to look for the portal, but it seemed I was back at the start. All because someone here plotted against me.

Arlo crossed the room, boots clacking on the marble. He stood before me, his eyes cross-hatching my face.

"Stop that," I said.

"Stop what?"

"Looking at me like *that*." Like he could read me like a damned book.

And when that handsome, annoying bastard looks at me, for the first time in all of my life, I feel seen.

Infernum. This was all such a disaster.

Arlo kneeled before me. Those eyes of pure sunshine landed on my skin, trying to burn off the storm clouds rolling through my soul.

"What happened?" I tried hating him for the gentle way he asked. Because it made me want to reach out to him, touch him. Maybe even tell him what I'd shouted in front of everyone. *He is exquisite. Resplendent.*

I was such a fool.

We had no time for feelings.

We needed to find the portal.

We needed to get out of Naiadon.

We needed to save Oakhaven.

"Tell me," he said, trying his stern captain's voice. Fuck, why did I like that voice?

"I'm not your subordinate," I said, crossing my arms.

"Oh, I am well aware. If you were my sailor, I'd have you flogged daily for defiance," he said with a sly smile.

"*Stop.*"

He put a callused hand on my bare knee. "Come, tell me what's the matter."

"I had a night terror. That's it."

That's what I'd call it. So he wouldn't worry that someone was attempting to … well, I wasn't sure what they were trying to do, really. But whoever poisoned me had ill intentions, clearly.

His finger drew figure eights on my knee, igniting a wildfire up my thigh and between my legs. That was all it took. My heart leaped in my chest. Little traitor.

"What was the night terror about?" he asked.

I pushed his hand off my knee and stood up. "Nothing of importance." I walked to the virginal. "Will you be able to fix it?"

I ran my fingers over the keys, but frowned when no sound rang out at my touch. I longed to lose myself in its music and quiet all these senseless thoughts.

"Elowyn," he said, following me, "if you keep secrets from me, I cannot help you."

"There are things you can never help me with."

Like my dead mother and hateful father. The world and how it sees me. Or how it doesn't see me at all.

He grabbed my wrist and pulled me toward him.

"*Arlo,*" I said weakly.

He lifted his large hand and delicately traced a thumb over my cheek. His other hand fell on my waist. I shuddered. What was he doing? Why couldn't I tell him to stop? Remind him not to be distracted, nor to distract me. So I could appropriately wall myself off further from him. Instead, my hands, with minds of their own, traveled up the muscles of his broad back to rest on the lower curve of his ribcage, where strength and vulnerability met. He was so solid. So steady. So real. When everything else felt fleeting and false.

"When I heard a noblewoman would be on my ship, I thought you would be snobbish, cold, removed. Then I saw you there, in your wool under-frock," he growled in a low voice that filled me. "And I knew you were different. Then you sat with my men." He smiled that perfect, damnable smile, crinkling lines into his nose. "You dined with us. Laughed with us. Like you were meant to be there all along at my table."

I wanted to bathe in the pool of contentment that was Arlo. Bask in him. My personal sun below the sea.

"That world you were born into, you do not fit its confines," he said.

"Yes, I know that I don't exactly fit in among the elite—"

"No. That isn't what I mean." His hold tightened around my waist and heat radiated from him, seeping into my soul. "Elowyn, your life is worth more than dressing ridiculously for feasts and stamping out that fire in you. You're meant to be free. Wild and unbridled. I had a hand in locking you away once. I can't bear to do it again. I will not. That's why we should—"

I put a hand over his mouth to stop the words from spilling forth, so the sirens would not hear them when they searched his mind. But also, so I would not hear them, because I wasn't sure I'd be strong enough to refute them.

Our faces were so close. I yearned to know what he tasted like. Felt like.

But I took a step back instead.

"I need to help my people." That meant warning my father of the sirens waiting in the sea, forming their attack. Returning to my fate. Possibly marrying Cedric.

"Why? Why help any of them at all?" There was an edge to his voice.

"Why help Alistar? You could have left him to starve on the streets. He wasn't your problem."

"That's different—"

"No, it's not. You helped him because you know it's not right to turn your back on those put in your path in need of saving. That is Oakhaven for me. They are my people."

"They are your father's people."

I took another step back, running into the virginal. It hurt, but I couldn't decipher why.

"Elowyn." Morvyn was there at the top of the stairs, right on time. "Are you okay?"

"I'm fine."

But Morvyn didn't accept it, scowling at Arlo. "Hylos is waiting for you. Are you ready to go?"

"Yes." I turned from Arlo, leaving him. Angry at him for stating the simple truth. They weren't technically my people. Oakhaven wasn't mine. But my mother's words still haunted my mind, repudiating what Arlo said.

"Elowyn, wait." Arlo stepped forward, reaching for me, but Morvyn threw a hand and sang, and in a heartbeat Arlo was lulled and we left.

Chapter 28

"A bsurd, isn't it?" Morvyn said with a smirk as we stood at the entrance of Hylos's bedchamber. "A ruler should have the finest bedchamber, I suppose. But this seems a bit overkill to me."

The room was made of navy marble, so dark it was nearly black. It looked like if I set foot in the space, I would vanish into a void of night sky or sea. Its arched door stood three men tall, left carelessly open. Not a guard in sight. The most powerful siren in all three seas didn't need bodyguards.

"Go on, have a seat, he'll be here shortly," Morvyn said, ushering me into the room and toward a seating area of plush, cerulean velvet chairs framed in—"That can't be," I exclaimed.

"Oh, but it is, my dear," Morvyn answered, still smiling. "Pure gold."

I looked around the room. Every flagrant decorative piece, crown molding, and ornate pillar was gilded.

I carefully sat on the overstuffed, opulent furniture, but strained my neck to see the main bedchamber through another grand entrance framed in swaths of dark-blue fabric. Likely they were used for privacy for Hylos and whoever joined him under that luscious, cobalt-blue counterpane that spilled off the massive bed.

"Does one person really need such a lavish room?" I asked.

"Like I said. *Absurd.*"

"Oh please," Hylos scoffed from the threshold. "If you were king regent, your bedchambers would be a hundredfold more ostentatious, Morvyn." Hylos clapped his friend's pale, bare shoulder with a smile. "And the bed would be three times as big."

"That is absolutely"—Morvyn feigned insult, then gave in—"correct."

Hylos grinned. "I'd invite you to join us, but I believe you have dinner plans with your aunt and cousins."

Morvyn rolled his pale eyes. "You mean you're forcing me to dine with Elspeth against my will."

"Exactly. You are my ambassador, Morvyn. I believe meeting with other High Circle leaders is in the official job description."

"See, I just *assumed* that title was more of a formality. You know, to keep me around for my wonderful wit and good looks."

"I fear not."

"Fine, fine. But I *will* request an increase in my wages come year's end," Morvyn said, then left the room.

"Now that he's gone," Hylos began, padding across the expansive room to where I sat. "We can break out the wine. Otherwise he'd never leave."

"Will Raylik not be joining us for the war council?" I asked, noting Raylik's absence.

"Not tonight. There's no new information, and he wished to spend the evening with Nixie. She was very ... *upset* about last night."

About me losing my absolute mind in front of her. I would thank her when I saw her again. I should have this morning when she trained with me despite being exhausted herself. But I was too raw then.

"What about Lumina?" She had been there too. "Is *she* alright?" I asked. Who would stay the evening with her to ensure she was okay? Likely she only had herself and her books.

"She'll be fine," he said, turning toward a small drink table beside the seating arrangement, where matching chalices sat beside a flagon. "Lumina is strong."

That she was. Strong enough to watch the man she loved be with another, all while helping him achieve his ambitions. Even when it clearly broke her heart.

"How are you feeling?" he asked as he poured wine into his cup.

Confined. Confused. And for some Guardians-damned reason, utterly unafraid. Despite the very real fact that someone was out to expose me, or worse, harm me.

"I'm fine."

Hylos raised the other chalice to me in question.

I nodded a yes. Why not drink? I'd been running from the shadows of my past all day. I tried beating it out of me with Nixie, tried hiding from it with Arlo. Neither worked. Why not try to drink it away?

Hylos handed me the filled cup, and I drank it down in two gulps.

Hylos raised a blue eyebrow at me. "Ah, about as fine as me then, I see. Another?"

"Please. What is there for a siren king to fret about?"

"Besides my people being taken in droves by—" He paused, shaking his head. "Besides that situation. I was worried for you." He filled my cup. "I feel foolish that someone attacked you, *again*, on my watch." He handed me the cup and met my eyes. "I'm sorry, Elowyn, I truly am. I want you to know that I had no part in what happened."

"Then who did?" I pressed. Apologies were fine. But they didn't hold answers.

"Truthfully, I'm not sure. There are many new faces in the castle and—"

"Was it Calypstra?" I asked pointedly.

I'd seen the way she looked at me when the poison started working through my veins. It was like she knew my fate before anyone else.

Hylos hesitated, uncertainty flickering in his eyes. "She wouldn't."

But it wasn't a no.

"Who are you trying to convince? Me, or you?"

Hope twinkled in his gem-blue eyes, but then it faded and died. He didn't have an answer. At least not for that question.

"Why stop me from revealing my secrets? Wouldn't it have served your interests to know my thoughts, as your enemy?"

He met my gaze squarely. "We are not enemies. The war I wage is against your father."

"Which makes it my war."

Hylos let out a breath. "I'm not at all surprised to hear you say that." He shook his head and smiled as he sat beside me in the matching chair. "I know you feel strongly about protecting Oakhaven. It's in your blood to do so."

"What is that supposed to mean?"

"Elowyn, you are his heir," he said softly, like I would flee at the very statement. Which is exactly what I wanted to do.

"I've told you, I am not his heir. I am not in line for the throne. I am a illeg—"

"Tell me your heart does not argue otherwise." He cut me off. "I know it does because mine does. We are the same, destined to take from our fathers. Born with a natural inclination to do so. Ready to seize the moment we rise and meet our destiny."

"That is not the truth for me. Unfortunately for you," I said, grabbing the chalice to busy my hands. But doubt slithered up my spine. Did I long for my father's crown? The vision of my mother, was that truly her, or was that me wailing my own selfish desires?

"I stopped you from sharing your thoughts because I believe you'll help me with this war when you're ready to. You're no fool. The missing sirens aside, your father's rule has been a contentious one. Your people suffer at his hands. You know that. You yourself have suffered at his hands," Hylos added.

I'd never thought of it as suffering. If anything, I always felt my circumstances were punishment or penitence. For not being a man in this cruel world.

But did my mother die for the same crime?

Were we both truly guilty? Or was my father simply wielding the blade of justice incorrectly?

Cedric's voice scraped over my mind. *He doesn't hate you. He fears you. They all do.* He was so bloody certain that I had some untapped power. Just as Hylos was now.

"I could put you on his throne," Hylos said, pulling me from my thoughts. "If we rise from the sea, march into Guardian's Watch, we could take the city with ease, just as we do the king's ships."

My heart thrummed in my chest. Was he truly offering me my father's throne? Offering me Oakhaven?

"Oakhaven is not a ship, Hylos. It is a country with armies and navies."

"We can brandish water and control people."

"You can control a *portion* of the population."

"The more powerful part," he countered.

"And you plan to put the *weaker* part of humanity on the throne? A feeble woman such as myself?" I scoffed. "You doubt the strength of women at your peril. They will fight for their men. For their children. They'll rip you apart with their teeth for their Guardians-damned country."

"You're right. As would you. So save it. From him." He said it so easily. "You have the heart of a fucking king, Elowyn. He only possesses the withered, black, dying organ of a leech."

"You don't even know me." I had no king's heart. I was a lover of art, history, and stories. I possessed the heart of a reader, a musician, a poet. Not the heart of a fighter, a ruler. "You also do not know Oakhaven. I'd be challenged *immediately*. A woman has never ruled."

"The sea would defend you. I would defend you."

"Why? Why would *you* ever do that for me?" I asked.

"Because you would never harm my people."

Understanding dawned on me. "You think I'd be a good puppet."

Hylos didn't believe in me, he sought to control me. Just as Cedric did. Just as everyone did.

"No. I think you would be my ally. Land and sea would be united for the first time. We would be unstoppable."

It was an absurd, juvenile hope. One that would be cut down and battered, just like every person before him who'd dared to go against my father.

Heavy silence settled between us. There was nothing more to say. Nothing left to do. It was a foolish plan by a foolish boy-king, and I needed to get the fuck out of Naiadon before I was forced to comply with his childish whims.

"I'll think on it," I lied.

His smile fell, like he could hear the doubt in my voice. He took another sip of his drink. His jaw set. "We have another event tonight, with the royal sirens. Will you join?" His tone had changed. It was heavier, more guarded.

I eyed him warily. "Are you sure it's safe?"

"Yes, security will be increased and only royal guests were invited."

"Will Calypstra be there?" I asked.

"No. She is unaware of the event." Wrinkles formed on his brow, the truth etched in them. He didn't trust her to be aware of the event.

"Yes. Sure, I will attend."

I couldn't stop looking for an escape now, not after this conversation.

"Good. The guards will come for you tonight."

Hylos poured the remnants of the wine into his chalice.

"Want more?" he asked.

I would need it to keep me sane at this point. It felt like Naiadon's walls were closing in around me and soon I would drown below in these depths. "Yes, please."

"I'll grab another bottle," he said, walking to the other end of the room and pulling a bolt of dark-blue fabric onto a hook. It exposed a small wine cellar that Hylos stepped down into.

Then I saw it, just briefly. An object as tall as him leaning against the back of the cellar wall, shrouded in a cloth.

My heart raced.

It couldn't be, could it?

"What is that?" I asked, trying to keep my voice from quivering.

"What?" Hylos asked. Bottles clinked as he selected the one he wanted.

I rose to my feet and walked toward him, trying to get a better look. "That thing, covered and leaning up against the wall?"

Hylos reappeared. "Oh, that." He glanced at it as he walked past, a wine bottle in hand. He untucked the fabric and it flowed back into place, hiding the small room and the object inside.

"It's a painting." A frown dragged on the corner of his lips.

"A painting of what?" I was holding my breath.

He winced like the thought pained him. With a wave of his hand and siren song, the wine bottle's cork popped. He caught it smoothly in the air.

"Of my mother."

My heart sank. It was the portal out of Naiadon.

Winter 5339 AT

Aegir has warmed to the idea of me becoming a mother. Even if it is not his child. At first, he was furious. Distraught even. But one night, amid the quiet of his bedchamber, the sea twinkling in silver moonlight, he confessed his love for the child growing within me. Because the babe is mine, and I am his.

Aegir fusses over me incessantly, showering me with attention and care like a doting parent-to-be. From rubbing my sore, flattened feet to bringing me jelly sweets. He can't resist the urge to caress my growing belly. His love for the unborn child is evident in every touch.

He's convinced it's a boy. He claims to sense a strong energy from the small flutter in my womb, that the child's inner song is brave and wise. I hope he's right. Every powerful man wishes for a son. Maybe that would quell my husband's callous nature.

Chapter 29

A suffocating darkness wrapped around my senses as someone forced thick fabric over my head. Hands pulled me from sleep.

"What is the meaning of this?" I shouted, fighting their hold.

No response.

When had I even fallen asleep? I was reading seconds before, eager to learn more about the portal and how it functioned while trying to stay awake for whatever event Hylos had planned.

Fuck. The journal.

I reached for the bed, desperate to ensure the book was safe under my pillow. But I couldn't see a damned thing through the material impeding my vision. Touch was all that I had to guide me.

Then, *thud. Damn it.* The book fell to the floor.

Hands dragged me up and walking against my will.

"Let me go!" My heart was a battering ram in my chest.

The night pricked at my skin through the flimsy nightgown that offered little protection from the cool air as the faceless hands dragged me into the hall.

This could not be good.

Whoever was guiding me was strong. Based on their footfalls, it was three sirens. One on each arm, gripping me hard. One trailing behind. I was surrounded.

Where in Infernum were they taking me?

A left, then a right, another right, then down a long stretch of hall. I tried to form a map of Naiadon in my mind, but I had never traveled this route before.

Smooth marble turned to coarse stone, pressing into the soles of my feet.

Then I heard the crunch of granite. We moved forward through a passage. There were others I could sense around me.

Unease slithered through my stomach. I tried to steady my breathing. A cool head would help far more than fear pumping through my veins urging me to run. Finally, the hands removed the blind.

In a black, cavernous room drenched in pale siren light, I recognized Morvyn's aunt scowling in layers of stark white to my left. To my right stood Raylik's uncle, dressed in fiery robes. Both had guards of their own. Surrounding us were clusters of sentries around other Circle leaders.

At the forefront of the room stood Hylos, clad in white, crustacean-like armor layered over a pleated, royal-blue tunic. He peered at us over a jagged pool, its dark waters sloshing relentlessly.

"Why have you brought us here, Hylos?" demanded a male voice somewhere out of sight.

"I've summoned you this evening to be escorted to the most sacred of places within Naiadon. Tonight we ride to the Great Womb of Nymphaea."

Whispers rushed in waves from the royal sirens.

What did that even mean?

He cleared his throat, commanding the room to silence in an instant.

"As the leaders for each of your Circles, I present you with this gift of knowledge as an offering of trust. I will show you the location of my realm's greatest source of power and, consequently, my greatest weakness." He fixed his gaze upon me. "Do you accept this invitation?"

If this place was important, and truly his source of power, why would he offer it so easily to these outsiders? Behind his back, they spoke in a way that most rulers would deem treasonous. He could hardly trust them. He could hardly trust me.

"At what price?" barked Draveen.

"No cost at all. It is a show of good faith to my guests."

"And we can make the holy sacrament?" Elspeth asked, her metallic voice sharp and swift.

"Of course," Hylos answered.

"I accept," Melquin said swiftly.

Hylos nodded in acknowledgment.

"I accept," added Elspeth.

"I too accept," Serenous called.

Draveen coughed out his acceptance. Another deep but weary voice agreed too.

This place truly had to be important if they were all ready to follow Hylos to it after being dragged from their beds by guards against their will.

Hylos's eyes settled upon me.

"You dare take a human to the Holy Mother's womb?" Draveen demanded.

The others muttered their disapproval as well.

"It is an affront to Nymphaea," Melquin grumbled under his breath.

"Elowyn Blackthorn is our *ally*. As I am hers."

The room fell deathly silent.

It would have been a nice sentiment if it didn't feel like a manipulation tactic. *Allies*. Officially. Against my father, and against Oakhaven. By naming me so, he implied that everyone who took this leap of faith with him was making a similar declaration. Which was the first step for him assembling an army against Oakhaven.

It was a well-played move, especially accompanied by the show of force. Dragging us all here in the night yet allowing us to make the ultimate choice, so he said, to follow him wherever this holy site was. Then surely to follow him into battle. It was a trust fall into the night in the name of war.

To stop Hylos, I would need to know his plans.

"I accept," I said.

A smile quirked the corner of Hylos's mouth.

"You *all* will be safe in my charge," he said to the room, but I knew the words were meant for me because I wasn't safe at all. Which made my heart drum.

Hylos raised his hands over the pool. Deep percussive tones thundered from him and vibrated through the water, sending it churning.

Then, eight beasts surged from the depths.

I stumbled back, the memory of the kelpie snapping into my mind as horse-like chuffs escaped from the creatures' snouts, steam tumbling in their wake. Their heads resembled white horses, but instead of velvety pelts and silky manes, they had hard, sleek skin, with spines where ears should have been.

Hylos, with practiced ease, swung his leg over the back of one of the beasts, aligning perfectly with the hard ridges. He gripped the two spines on its neck and shouted, "Onward!" The creature bucked, turned, and its hard-shelled tail cracked against the water's surface as it plunged beneath the water.

The guards nudged me forward. With cautious steps and a trembling hand, I reached out, brushing my fingers over the creature's hard, plated side. It whinnied at my touch, just like the horses I loved to ride at home.

Summoning my courage, I hoisted myself onto the creature's back, mirroring Hylos's seat. My hands tightened around the makeshift reins and with a flick of its tail, it propelled itself around, cutting through the water with an effortless plunge as we dove into the black sea.

Chapter 30

Naiadon faded behind me, swallowed by black sea. The blue light of my mother's prayer beads cradled me. Ears popping at the depth, I inhaled, only to choke on salt water.

Panic clutched my heart. What if the bracelet didn't work anymore?

I gasped again; the briny water burned in my chest, but was somehow breathable. Like sawing breaths after running hard—scorching, inadequate, but necessary.

My mount surged upward fast. I held on tightly, its speed forcing me back into the seat. Breaking through the water's skin, we emerged from the surface, and above hung a never-ending plane of twinkling silver stars. The glass-flat water surrounded me like a mirror of liquid night. I had not seen the sky in weeks and it was glorious.

My beast caught up to Hylos's, racing atop the water, both our creatures gliding effortlessly through the waves.

Hylos, smiling broadly, shouted, "The sky welcomes us!"

A laugh flew from my chest at our speed and the sight of the stars. Despite everything, this tasted like freedom, even if it was only for a fleeting moment.

Our beasts dove into the water again, Hylos's azure glow at my side as we went deeper and deeper into the sea. He was the only thing that felt even remotely familiar here. A blue light at the other end of a strange, ever-stretching tunnel.

Until the others showed. Halos of light surrounded us in winking flashes of pastels that raced beside us, then faded. High-pitched bursts of melody zinged through the water. Sirens.

Welcome, King Hylos.

Welcome, our great king.

Their words clicked on the ridge of song.

In a flash of blinding gold, one appeared at my side. Her hair flowed in golden rivulets, rippling in the water as she swam hard. Her body was barely covered in a clinging siren dress that matched the glow of her skin as she moved. Her lean muscles rippled with her undulating motion.

She cocked her head at me inquisitively, golden light overflowing from her eyes as she scrutinized me.

What is a human doing here? She shrieked in song, loud and achingly beautiful. Then she reached out a glowing, finned hand toward me.

Swiftly, I dug my heels into my mount's sides. The creature bucked, then surged forward, swimming unthinkably fast, outpacing the siren. Her golden light dimmed and was swallowed by the abyss.

My stomach twisted into knots.

How many more sirens were out there in the sea?

How many of them wanted a piece of human flesh?

In the distance, the dark water unveiled a strange structure rising from the ocean floor. The entrance came into focus, framed by onyx pillars. Our steeds slowed. Hylos and I drifted onward, side by side, through the entrance.

Then, as if stirred by our arrival, symbols carved into the pillars flick-ered to life, illuminating a long, sandy path that stretched ahead. At its end stood jet-black monoliths arranged in a circle around one pillar at the center.

When we stopped before it, Hylos dismounted gracefully and swam before the towering obelisk.

He kneeled as if in prayer, and song barreled from him. Then the surrounding pillars shook, taking Hylos's unique song in all its somber pride, and echoed it.

My eyes widened as I watched the monolith's glow intensify until the sound faded. But it did not stop, instead rebounding infinitely off the pillars, blending into a hum that persisted.

"This is a reserve of Nymphaea's power," Hylos said on siren song. "My father tapped into it to create Naiadon years ago. It alone keeps his castle in place." Hylos's glowing stare met mine meaningfully. This was his greatest vulnerability. What kept the home he loved upright. The sanctuary for those like Nixie, Lumina, the other made sirens, and even his mother.

"They say Nymphaea created it herself, but I'm not sure I believe all that," he continued. "For hundreds of years, sirens have passed through here, giving small pieces of themselves. As we will tonight." He smiled, looking at me. "Lumina once told me sirens started this practice because of its effect of echoing song. But I think she just believes we're a vain bunch." He laughed to himself as if savoring a memory, then continued.

"Over the centuries, siren magic seeped into the stone, infusing it with power. There are a handful of these structures scattered across the sea. Hard to find, unless you know where to look. We see it as a privilege to sacrifice a piece of our power, as so many before us have done. To build on something that will outlast any one lifetime."

The sirens were always giving pieces of themselves away. As they did with the swallow.

On land, men often took without second thought.

Hylos nodded to the still-shimmering pillar. "Your turn."

But I had nothing to offer. Not even my voice while submerged. I narrowed my gaze at him, willing the thought to him.

"Allow it to hear your heart," Hylos said. "At the very least you can *try*."

It sounded like a slight.

I rolled my eyes, then dismounted. My nightgown shifted up around my body. Ribbons of red curls coiled skyward too. Buoyancy was pulling me to the surface, to where I belonged. But another force, some strange siren magic, kept my feet flattened into the silty sea floor as I walked to the pillar.

Copying Hylos, I kneeled before the monolith. But what would my song even sound like? I *tried* to listen for it myself. Whatever that meant. But I only sank deeper into deafening silence. Because I had no song. Not of my own. But I could create them.

So, I thought of playing the virginal. Of the lively tune I liked to play on a warm summer's day, when the doors stood open to the rose garden at Granger House. Vega sitting nearby, embroidering and tapping her foot as my music intertwined with birdsong rolling off the foothills of the Ashen Mountains. Sunlight, casting bolts of warmth over my sweet home, nestled in the heart of my country. A place I loved fiercely because it was something to behold. Gorgeous. Glorious. Mine.

The markings on the pillar flared. Then the stones stirred, groaning like bowing branches in a gust of wind. Then, a chorus of birdsong rang out, their melodies twisting and diving through the water like a song carried on the sound of the wind woven with the quick, bright notes of a virginal.

Hylos turned to me, his eyes wide.

"Elowyn, that is your song." He shook his head as if in disbelief. "I think I ... know it."

What did he mean?

Before I could look to him for an answer, Hylos's head whipped to the entrance, his wonder fading, replaced by the hard, steady gaze of a leader with a plan.

It was the other Circle leaders.

One by one, each siren paid homage to the great stones, offering their gift of song to Nymphaea as we had, forcing the monoliths brighter, until they vibrated with power.

Then Hylos spoke. "There is a great threat to our ways. That is why I call you here today. Why I share with you Naiadon's greatest source of power. My power. Nymphaea's power. The womb of the great Mother now holds a small piece of you. A mere drop of your strength that you offer back to her. To the sea." His song was growing, and I realized the others were adding to it. Amplifying it. Like a war chant. "With the rest of your power, defend our people." The pulsating song dove into an unthinkable bass that rattled my bones. "Defend our way!"

Their song was hungry for blood.

"Join me and stop the king of Oakhaven! Stop him from ever harming another siren in our great seas!" Hylos's chest heaved as he raked a hard look over us. "Who here offers their arms and allegiance to me against Oakhaven?"

I was going to be sick.

"I do," Draveen belted loudly, his song strong and coarse behind his words.

Hylos nodded in acceptance. "Thank you, Draveen of Circle Twynox."

Circle Fushdmuir, Starwyrt, Orman, and Mariscal each offered their allegiance to Hylos.

Then his eyes fell to me. The music halted. "What of Circle Blackthorn?" Hylos asked. Circle Blackthorn. But I was not the leader of my people, of my *Circle*. I was no one.

I wanted to plead with the others, explain that this meant death. Like the totals accounted for in history books and the forgotten gravestones clustered in valleys shrouded in moss. Death of humans and sirens. When Hylos didn't even know who the true culprit was in the taking of his people. What if it wasn't Oakhaven attacking the sirens? What if this was all for naught? Hylos hardly had any evidence besides one measly coin, found at the bottom of the sea by a scared young siren. A boy. Just like him.

I couldn't be a part of this war.

I couldn't harm my people.

I shook my head in a slow, steady no.

Chapter 31

Hylos couldn't even look me in the eye as we all mounted our horses and left. Now he was a whisper on the sea, glowing ahead of me. A reminder that he was still out there. He always would be. Waiting in the ocean. Readying his attack.

I needed to return home. I needed to warn my father.

War was coming.

Then, a horrendous screech shattered all my thoughts. My steed thrashed madly. Was it more sirens? It didn't sound like them. The sound screamed through the water like a hawk's cry.

I looked around for siren lights, but only saw Hylos's, which waned in the distance and headed toward the surface.

Something was wrong. Without a second thought, I dug my heels into the plated sides of my mount and sped after Hylos.

That strange, vile sound blared again, devastating my senses. I was closer now to whatever was looming above.

My stomach sank when I saw Hylos ensnared just below the water's surface in a large net.

He was limp and his mount was nowhere to be found as the ropes pulled him toward the surface.

I pushed my mount closer and began tugging at the thick netting, all while striving to maintain my position atop the beast that continued to buck under me.

My fingers seared with pain as I desperately attempted to unravel the knots. The thick, braided rope was as wide as my wrist. I begged the Guardians to grant me the strength to free Hylos. But my pleas went unanswered and the net dragged upward toward the surface. Where were the other Circle leaders? Were they stunned too?

If I could see what had him, maybe I could stop whatever created the terrible sound that was beating down on us.

I raced toward the surface, breaking through the crashing waves.

"Oy, there's anotha one!" a man's voice boomed in a thick Oakhaven accent.

No. It couldn't be.

The ship was large and unmistakably royal. Its sails heaved against the night's winds, buckled in black and red. The colors of my father's kingdom. Tensing my core and kicking my steed, I maneuvered back below the water. Back to Hylos.

I had to get him out of here. I needed to save him.

They would hurt him. Or worse.

Hylos's position was more shallow now, as the ship's men hauled him in. I grappled with the stubborn netting, trying again, but I was too weak. But Hylos was strong. If he was awake, he could easily break free.

That small song the monoliths showed me warbled through my mind. My song. It was how the sirens communicated. How they carried their voices. I reached for it. Tried wielding it. I tried to sing-speak as he did.

Hylos, you must wake up, you are in danger.

Nothing.

Focus. I had to focus.

I chased the words over the ridges of mountain peaks that framed my world and jutted through my mind. My song, hasty, happy, and beautiful like a woman playing the virginal too well for the comfort of others.

And from my very soul that song swelled.

Hylos, wake up!

His eyes flew open. He heard me. Thank the Holy Mother herself, he heard me! Together, we tugged at the netting, but it was useless.

He met my gaze. "Back up!"

Hylos pushed his finned palms towards the netting that separated us. Quickly I turned my mount to follow Hylos's demand, but I wasn't fast enough.

A deep, rumbling note ripped through the water. Hylos's glow intensified until it blazed like a beacon. Then everything erupted.

The force hurled me far from Hylos. I clung desperately to my mount, barely keeping my seat.

Another hideous shriek tore through the depths. How were they doing it? I scanned the water, searching for Hylos's light. At last, I spotted him. That faint, familiar blue flickering in an ocean of black.

Gripping the reins, I kicked my mount hard, slicing through the currents with desperate speed. Hylos's glow dimmed with every heartbeat, and I knew if it vanished, he'd be lost forever.

At last, I reached him and pulled his limp body into my arms. His light was faint, his form motionless. He was completely unconscious.

With another swift kick, my steed surged forward.

Away from the ship. Away from that dreadful noise. And away from my father's grip.

Chapter 32

We broke through the pool's surface into Naiadon. My lungs expanded for the first time in hours as I hacked up salt water.

Hylos and I poured off my mount. My hands shook and my palms burned from pulling at that thick netting that had entangled him.

The truth was slamming into me.

Hylos was right all along.

My father knew of sirens. He could take them straight from the sea. He *was* capturing them.

Hylos shot into consciousness. His storm-blue eyes opened wide and ready. He staggered to his feet, raised his palms into the air, and let out a deep sonorous note that clattered my teeth.

Exhausted, he hunched over, his hands on his knees as he panted. "Do you believe me now?" he spat between breaths. "Or do you need more proof?"

Excuses caught in my throat. I saw it with my own two eyes: a ship in my father's colors capable of incapacitating sirens.

"Now you see why I must act. Terras are against us. They are coming after us. After my people, Elowyn!" He was working himself up into a fury. "We need your help. To stop him from hurting our people and his own."

"Hylos ... I ... I can't do that."

Hylos grabbed my shoulders. "Try!"

Anger wasn't the only tempest that brewed in his eyes. Desperation swelled there too.

"Hylos," Lumina ran into the room dressed in a thin silk nightgown. Thoughtlessly, she reached out to him, her fingertips tracing the angry indentations of red crisscrossing his flesh the netting had left.

For a second, he looked at her. I could have sworn the love that reflected in her eyes was mirrored in his. Then it faded as he looked up and past her to Calypstra, who was pacing into the room.

Hylos brushed passed Lumina, and I tried to ignore the hurt in her eyes.

"Oakhaven attacked us," he said, racing to his lover, who looked over his shoulder at ... me? Anger was slick in her oily black eyes. This was getting ridiculous. I had nothing to do with any of this. What the fuck was her problem? What did I ever do to her?

"Hylos," Raylik shouted as he ran toward his ruler, short sword in hand, ready to fight. "You sent a battle call? Are we under attack?" Nixie was not far behind him, two daggers clutched tightly in her fists.

"Tonight, after showing the High Circle leaders The Womb of Nymphaea—"

"You did what?" Raylik exclaimed.

"Oh shit," Nixie cursed, pink eyes wide.

"On the way back, an Oakhaven ship attacked us."

The group straightened up at Hylos's words.

"How did they attack you?" Lumina asked as she walked back into Hylos's view.

"It was like siren magic, similar to lulling, but it worked on me. I was completely stunned, but Elowyn was not."

Lumina took in what he said, thumbing through that endless library of knowledge she held. "How is that even possible?"

"How did you get away?" Nixie asked, shock marking her features.

My eyes remained trained on Calypstra. She didn't show an ounce of emotion at the fact that Hylos was almost taken. No fear showed on her features, no sadness. She did not care. She just stared at me with tight-lipped resentment.

"Elowyn saved me..." Hylos said, realizing it for the first time himself.

Lumina, Nixie, and Raylik all turned to me, staring with a mixture of disbelief and awe.

Calypstra stepped forward. "We *must* retaliate."

Hylos nodded a terse yes, agreeing.

"We need answers," Lumina said, "before we charge blindly in. We have no idea what we're up against."

"You dare make orders of your liege?" Calypstra hissed, baring her sharp teeth.

Lumina ignored her, turning to Hylos. "You were almost lost tonight."

She almost lost him tonight.

"Nonsense," Calypstra scoffed. "The king of all three seas does not fear humans. We will retaliate against them. We will fight them. We will make them pay."

"If we charge into battle without strategy, we risk losing too much. We already lack numbers," Raylik said, desperate to slow this madness too.

"A risk worth taking," Calypstra said to Raylik, fury in her eyes. "And we will cut down anyone who stands in our way." *She* would cut down anyone who stood in her way.

"We have the numbers now, my friend," Hylos said with a wild-eyed grin at Raylik. "Tonight, every Circle leader pledged their arms to our cause."

Everyone but me.

"So ready our forces and those of the other Circle leaders," Hylos ordered.

Nixie retreated to Raylik's side. A look transpired between them. She was afraid.

Raylik said nothing. He only looked at his leader and friend, baffled.

"What of the Hydroxia feast? It would be disrespectful to Nymphaea if we waged a war on her most holy of days," Nixie said.

She was buying them more time. She didn't want this war either. None of them did. Besides Calypstra and Hylos, desperately. Blindly.

"Who cares about some foolish religious bullshit?" Calypstra hissed.

Lumina stood there, her large brown eyes softening as she said definitively, "Hylos cares."

"Hylos," Morvyn called from the entrance. His body was rigid and tense as he stalked in.

"What took you so long, you know you must respond to the war summons call immediately Morvy—"

"*Hylos*," Morvyn repeated, sadness sinking into his eyes. Something was wrong.

"What is it?" Hylos asked.

"The prisoners ..." he started, like he couldn't even bear to finish the sentence. "I'm so sorry, Elowyn."

My heart sank like a stone.

"They're all dead," Morvyn said.

No. No. *No.*

Lumina rushed to my side.

Arlo. Please, not Arlo.

Nixie was beside me in an instant as well. Both her and Lumina supported me as my knees gave out.

"*Arlo*, he is alive. Whatever killed the others spared him."

Arlo was safe. Thank the Guardians above. That bloody brooding fool was safe. A sick, twisted sense of relief worked through me, hand in hand with grief. But every member of his crew was dead.

Then anger screamed through me like a banshee.

"Did you order this?" I rose to my feet and ran to Hylos, ready to pound fists into his chest, but Morvyn swiftly scooped me up in his long, pale arms.

I fought against his hold. "Were you behind this?" I shouted.

"No, I would never—" He started, but I cut him off.

"Did you fucking do this?" I shrieked, the words shredding through the room.

"I would never order something like this." He looked me squarely in the eyes, compelling me to believe him. But how could I? How could I ever trust him. How could I fucking trust any of them? They promised the crew would not be harmed. They swore.

It was as if this whole time, I had been floating in this dream, and now I was slammed into cold, hard, reality.

I was at the bottom of the sea. Surrounded by my father's enemy, and they had just killed every man I arrived with.

"You cannot control anyone or anything in this damned place!" I screamed, so loud I tasted blood, my throat raw from the force. "You want me to take over my kingdom? You can't even control your own!" Tears were streaming down my face, hot and angry. "You Guardians-damned fool. You fucking child! Their blood is on your hands!" I did not breathe, I only yelled. It was hitting me repeatedly like waves of reality, surging. "I couldn't help them!"

I crumpled in on myself.

Morvyn kneeled with me as he held me tightly.

Tears streamed down my face.

"I couldn't save them."

CHAPTER 33

Arlo would never smile again. Not on his own. Maybe if the sirens lulled him, or if he forced himself to for others, but never from true happiness. I knew it in my bones. He was too strong. Too proud. Too righteous. Too Guardians-damned perfect to ever allow himself to feel anything but at fault for this atrocity. When it wasn't his fault at all. It was Hylos's.

My heart broke for Arlo and the loss of those already-rare smiles. This would be the death blow to his happiness. He had already lost so much. A wife. A child. Now his crew.

But the ache in my heart was twisting and gnarling into something more potent. When the tears stopped and ire replaced sorrow, I demanded to be taken to the prisons. Hylos didn't argue. Likely because he was so desperate for my support. The idiot. I would never support him.

Nixie led me to a distant, disfigured tower in Naiadon. I would never have found the prisons on my own. Not even if I had one hundred years to wander Naiadon freely.

This part of the castle wasn't sparkling white, like a lie. It was all nightmare. Black, bleak, and best forgotten. The cells, carved out of existing sea caves, were damp and dribbling. Reeking of brine, sweat, and blood.

I wanted to weep with joy when I saw Arlo, standing there at the center of the cell among a sea of murderous bloodshed, lulled by one of the two sirens standing guard.

"Did you kill them?" I snapped at the guards, who were unshaken.

"They were just ordered here to protect Arlo," Nixie said.

"So, you left them here unguarded before?" My blood was boiling.

"There shouldn't have been a need to protect them. Hylos's orders were—"

"Obviously there was a fucking need!" I turned on the guard nearest me. "Get him out of there. Now," I demanded.

Nixie nodded at my side, approving the order. The guard clunked the barred door open.

I hardly remembered the march back to my chambers, drowning in thought. Why kill Arlo's crew? What good did that do for anyone? And why spare Arlo?

I'd be the one to tell him. I owed him the truth, because this was my fault. I'd failed them.

The sirens were fascinating, and kind. Hylos even believed I could rule. An offer I fought, but it was tantalizing nonetheless. Naively, I thought that there was a way for everyone to win. To help Hylos discover the true cause of the sirens' disappearances and end all talk of war against Oakhaven. What a tremendous waste of time. I had my answer. The one I had all along. My father was taking Hylos's people.

The thought sank like a stone in my gut. But did it even matter? Maybe my father had his reasons? Maybe he knew how cruel and violent the sirens could be. A lesson that had taken the carnage of Arlo's men for me to learn.

I remembered their faces, glittering in candlelight as they laughed over mugs of warm ale, enjoying the comfortable companionship of one another. Were they gathered around a table in death now? The head of the table set, yet empty, waiting for their captain.

Nixie lead Arlo into my bedchamber and shut the door gently, looking me over in concern. Fuck her and her concern.

The morning light was beaming through Naiadon's glass walls, forcing everything stark white and too bright, burning my tired eyes.

I needed sleep, but my mind would never let me rest. Not even if I drank three bottles of bourbon dry. Not with this on my conscience.

"When you're ready, I will lift the lull," she said.

I could hear the tinkling of her song like thousands of crystalline chimes behind the bedchamber door, wrapping around Arlo's mind.

"Are you sure you don't want me to be there with you?" she asked.

"No." I would do it alone.

I turned to enter my room, but Nixie stopped me. "Elowyn." She reached out, taking my hand in hers and squeezing it softly. "Your anger is entirely just." She looked me over, worry furrowing her pink brow. "And I *will* find out who did this. I promise."

"And what if you find out it was on Hylos's orders? What then, Nixie? What will you do? Blindly follow his whims as you do now? Make excuses? It's all fine if it leads to saving your people, right?" I let out a bitter laugh. Fire licked my heart. "But my people died today. Do you understand that? Thirty Oakhaven men who swore to see me safely across the sea until *you* took their ship!" The words shattered down the hall.

I rubbed at my eyes and lowered my voice. "You took them and now they're all fucking dead. So stop pretending to care about me or them or any human. You have chosen your side. As have I."

Hurt welled in her sharp, pretty features, at odds with one another, just like her soul. Both warrior and nurturer. Fighter and lover. But she would have to pick who she would become in this rapidly approaching war.

I turned from her again, not wanting to see the hurt I'd inflicted. Nixie was kind to me, but there was only so much that kindness could excuse.

"Whoever killed those men," she whispered, "will be punished. I swear it."

I wanted to believe her, but she had assured me once that the men were safe here. So instead, I slammed the door in her face, unable to hear any more empty promises.

Nixie's song faded, and with it, so did Arlo's listless smile. His face flattened and those gold-hazel eyes flickered into focus.

"Elowyn?" He scanned the room. "Where are we?" he asked.

"We're in my bedchamber."

"Why?" He hadn't noticed the pain in my voice, not yet. He was too busy eyeing the room. Gaining his bearings. "This is where you've been staying?" He let out a small, breathy laugh that I wanted to cling to. "I don't know what our prisons look like, but based on the stench that lingers on me when I'm awake, I could only imagi—"

"Arlo."

His gaze snapped to meet mine.

"What is it?" In two swift steps he was before me, searching my eyes, his hands ready to reach out to me, but hesitating. Guardians, how I wanted them on me.

"*Arlo*," I repeated, voice cracking as I tried to gather the courage to tell him. "Your crew ... The others ..." The words splintered, catching on the jagged edges of the break in my voice. I wasn't ready for the pain I was about to inflict at the other end of my sentence.

"What about them?"

Brown, dense facial hair crawled across his hard jaw and cheeks, almost a proper beard now. We'd been here for so long. Too long. Because I'd failed him.

"I'm so sorry, Arlo."

"What do you mean?" His features hardened. "Where are they? What happened?" he demanded, retreating into the comfort of authority to calm his captain's mind.

I swallowed my sadness. It was cruel to let his mind wander to hopeful answers when only the worst was true.

"They are all dead."

"They can't be." He shook his head. "We were going to get them out of here. No. *No.* They can't all be de—" He stopped himself, then shoved past me and stormed to the door, shaking its handle.

"It's locked," I said, trying to hold back the tears that were welling in my eyes.

"Let me out of here!" His fist slammed into the door, the sound jolting me. "Let me the fuck out of here!" he roared.

"Arlo." I walked across the room to him, reaching for his broad shoulders, his shirt spattered in ruby-red droplets. My stomach churned. He wore the blood of his men.

He whirled on me. "They did this! They fucking did this, those monsters! I'll kill them all! Every one of them."

"I'm so sorry you lost your men, Arlo—"

"Those were not just my men!" he spat, tears rapidly filling his eyes, spilling down his cheeks. "Those were my brothers. My family. Just like Catarina and Cate. All under my fucking protection. I failed! They trusted me and I led them to their deaths!" He screamed with everything he had left. Then collapsed to his knees, looking at his palms. "They didn't deserve this," he said through sobs. It was setting in. Panic coursed through his features as his breath ran ragged. "This is all my fault. I agreed to go to Whiterok. So desperate to repay Ced that I ignored the rumors. I let this happen." He choked on words and tears.

I wanted to fall into his arms and sob with him. But I kept my emotions at bay. There was only room for one of us to crumble today. Instead, I kneeled to his level and placed a hand on his chest. He flinched at first, ready to fight.

"Breathe, Arlo. Come on, in." His strong, good heart pounded fiercely under my palm. "Now out."

He was unraveling beneath my touch, fraying at the edges. He didn't deserve this amount of agony; he'd already endured far too much before. He deserved happiness.

"Breathe in ..." I repeated, inhaling too. He tried to do the same through tremors that coursed through his body. "Good, *good*. Now out."

I would get us out of Naiadon. Alive. Then I would go straight to Highthorn and warn my father of the sirens. They would be stopped.

"Come on." I hoisted Arlo to his feet and to my bed. As he sat on the edge, I peeled off his leather boots. His skin was chapped and dirty under his yellowed stockings. It had been weeks since he'd last bathed. I worked off the other boot and walked to the bathroom, taking a basin of rose-scented water and a washcloth.

He stared out the window as I washed his face, his chest, and worked him out of his bloodstained shirt. He was lost at sea with his men, trying his best to guide their ship home. But he never would.

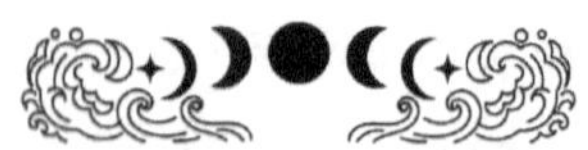

Autumn 5343 AT

When Aegir dusted off this little journal and brought it to me, it transported me to another time, to when my biggest fear was simply being apart from Aegir during the day. How I would long for such trivial worries now.

Looking back at the pages, I've realized just how much has changed in these three years that have raced past me. How ironic my last entry about motherhood was. Its beauty. I needed to read those words today. Because I'm sick with nerves about being with child once again.

We assumed it couldn't happen, that something went wrong in the last birth that made me infertile. My husband had all but given up on the subject and wandered to other beds. For that I was thankful. He spent his nights with whomever he chose and so did I. But that's exactly what places me in such a precarious situation.

I am past the quickening, and my stomach has rounded. My husband's dark eye lingers too long on me. He has come to the same conclusion as I.

I'm pregnant and the child is not his.

Chapter 34

Arlo and I slept through the day, and then the night, needing all the rest in the world to summon the strength to survive.

The next morning, I stepped numbly into the routine I'd grown accustomed to. I needed to keep up appearances if I wanted to escape. I knew where the portal was. I had Arlo with me. Now I just needed a plan.

Training at least meant punching something hard and lifting my body's weight in stones. I hoped it would stop the thoughts of Arlo, his bloodstained shirt, and his agony spiraling through my mind so I could focus on our escape. Arlo remained in my room, still asleep when I left. Not lulled. Not caged. He would never set foot in another cell. Not if I could help it.

Surprisingly, it was Raylik in the armory waiting for me. Arms crossed, his tight-coiled curls piled atop his head in a bun.

"Where's Nixie?" I asked.

"She's not ready to see you after your argument yesterday."

I felt guilty, but maybe that was for the best.

"I'll be training you."

Perfect. Raylik was a muscle-laden warrior. He would train me hard enough to dull all thought.

"We'll be stretching."

After much complaining on my part, Raylik walked me through a flow of movements, stretching and reaching. Rolling our spines up slowly to the glass ceiling above as he spoke.

"When the world is hard and fast, you can always be slow and calculated," he said as we both stood, our palms planted on the ground. My hamstrings burned. He was surprisingly limber for someone so large.

"Feel your body from the swirls on your fingertips to the soles of your fins. Be present."

But I didn't want to be present. Not here, not now. I wanted to be home at Granger House. I wanted the past. Tears pricked my eyes.

We sat on the ground and turned our legs into butterflies, fluttering in place.

I spent my whole life preparing to leave that sleepy country house, and now I desperately wanted to be banished back to it. Back to a place and time with no sirens, no war, and no broken Arlo. Even if that meant no Arlo for me at all.

"How is he?" Raylik asked, as if reading my mind.

"I'm not sure," I answered.

"In battle, when a person faces a great loss of life, they often retreat into their mind."

"For how long?" I needed Arlo now more than ever.

"Some for the rest of their lives. But it helps if they have something to return to," Raylik said gently.

Arlo had little in Naiadon to return to. Not with his men dead.

"Was Lumina able to convince Hylos to halt his attack?" I asked, changing the subject. How much time did I have left?

"Hylos agreed to wait until after Hydroxia, which is in a few days." His lips formed a tight line.

"Lumina and Hylos, have they ever?" I asked, wishing for an alternative world in which Hylos listened to Lumina instead of Calypstra, who had even more bloodlust than he did.

"When Lumi first arrived in Naiadon, Hylos was very *protective* of her, because of her story. He showed her the libraries. Taught her to read."

"Lumina couldn't read?" She was a walking chronicle now.

"They do not teach poor unfortunates to read if they do not have coin in your father's realm," Raylik said bitterly.

I knew it to be true.

Raylik continued, "There was a time when I thought Hylos and Lumina would be together. That any moment they would embrace what was clearly between them. But then Calypstra arrived and changed everything," he said, frowning. "Hylos always had an eye for pretty women, wanting to get lost in the shoal so he could stand and wade back to his search for Aegir. I think Lumina is too deep for him. That he fears he'd get lost within her depths and lose sight of what he thinks is important."

"Being happy is important," I said.

"It is. When happiness is there, you need to seize it. Before it vanishes."

"As you do with Nixie. You love her," I said.

"Unquestionably," he answered, without hesitation. "You should know, Nixie's heart teeters between land and sea. She chose this life to be with me. But you and Nixie have more in common than you know." He stood and offered me a finned hand.

I took it and rose.

"When you accuse her of choosing a side, know that she does not see sirens versus humans. We are equal in her eyes. And for that she suffers the most. No matter who wins, she will mourn."

"Do you mourn the lives of Arlo's men?" I asked, hard-faced.

"I do. As does Hylos, Morvyn, Lumi, and Nixie. We all do."

"Then why did it happen?" I asked, with more cut in my voice than expected.

"I don't have an answer for that. But I know it cannot be undone. That it has changed everything."

"How has it altered anything for the sirens?" I asked.

"Because now we have made an enemy of you."

Chapter 35

Arlo sat looking out to the sea, despondent. Lost in his mind, as Raylik had said.

The rage had come and thundered through him, followed by soul-swallowing sadness. Now nothing. He needed to feel. Needed something to return for. I couldn't drag him through this bloody castle and into Hylos's private chambers to the portal if he was completely unresponsive. I needed his help.

"Sit and eat with me," I said, walking to the small table set with a loaf of bread, cheese, and some cooked fish laid out for our midday meal.

"I'm not hungry," he said, dismissing my offer.

He hadn't eaten since the news of his men.

"I didn't ask if you were hungry," I bit back at him as I sat and unfolded my napkin on my lap. "I told you to sit and eat."

He stood quickly, irritated, but sat at the table. I poured us both brimming glasses of wine. Arlo took a sip. I did the same.

Then there was a long, deep silence. The absence of his arrogant remarks or quick quips was a new form of torture. Especially when there was so much to say. He only sat rigid, looking out that damned window, his true cell bars, as I served us both our meal.

"Eat," I demanded again.

He let out a huff but obliged.

"Do you want to know the plan?" I asked.

He forked at his food and took a large bite. Good.

"We'll need to get into Hylos's bedchamber. That's where the portal is."

He continued stabbing at his food.

"Did you hear me?"

He was taking in another large bite but stopped and drank the wine to the dregs.

"I thought you weren't hungry?" I said, trying the sarcasm that was so easy before.

"Didn't say I wasn't thirsty," he snapped.

He was still in there. If he needed to be angry with me, that was fine. I could work with that.

"The sirens have a holy holiday at the end of the week. It's the perfect time for us to follow through with my plan and make it out of here."

"What's the fucking point?" He poured another glass of wine for himself. "I'm captain of a dead crew, a complete and utter disgrace." He leaned back in his chair, avoiding my gaze. "*Once again.*"

"It's not your fault—"

"Not my fault? A captain's duty is to ensure the safety of his ship and crew. Or die trying. Instead, I'm here on my ass, drinking wine and eating off fancy plates with a fucking princess." He shoved the meal away.

"Arlo. It is *not* your fault."

"I was too complacent." He crossed his arms and scowled. "I sat back and let this happen. I could have fought them. Stopped them. But I didn't. I did nothing. Just worked on a fucking instrument instead."

"Is that what your men would have wanted? For you to give up?" I snapped. Delicate cooing was not working. "What of your daughter. Does she not need her father?"

He said nothing. I was losing him. He was walling himself off, brick by self-loathing brick. He needed to fight. Fight to leave here. Fight to save himself. Fight to live. We both did.

I slapped my plate off the table, sending it shattering on the floor and exploding into shards.

He looked at me, dark brows knitting.

Good. I had his attention.

He let out a controlled breath, then got up and stalked toward the bathing chambers.

"Where are you going?" I demanded, following him.

He walked faster, reaching for the door, trying to shut it in my face, but I wedged my body in the way.

His eyes widened, then settled into a glower. "Leave me alone."

"Is that what you want? For me to leave you alone so you can give up entirely? If it is, say it again. But this time, mean it." I pushed in further and he relented. "Say it and I'll leave you alone so you can rot here. I'll try to figure a way out without you. But I'm telling you now, I don't know if I *can*. Not alone. But just say the word, Arlo, and I'll fucking leave. *Or* I can be here. You can throw whatever you have at me. But then we need to pick up the pieces and get out." It was true. It wasn't just that I needed his help. I needed him. Needed to know he was still in there. That he would still be there after this.

His eyes fell to my hips, reminding me of the tight, red silken shorts and matching top I wore to training. My thick thighs on full display, exposed like my midriff. Arlo's hungry look reminded me of what had simmered between us from the start. What he had been avoiding so we didn't lose sight of saving his men.

Now that they were gone, fuck it.

His jaw flexed, eyes darkened, and he didn't ask me to leave.

This. I could work with this.

Devouring the space between us, I marched forward. He inhaled sharply at the advance, eyes closing for one brief second.

"You can be angry. You can be furious, even, but you cannot give up. I won't let you." This could be the way to bring him back. To keep him anchored to reality and not lost in hopelessness.

Inches away from my face, he let loose a breath.

"I don't know if I can, Elowyn," he said in a whisper.

I shoved him hard into the wall.

"*We* can."

He needed it. The force. The pain. The anger. He needed to be shaken from the sad daze and slammed into earth.

Slammed into *me*.

His eyes met mine, crosshatching my face.

"You don't want to give up and you sure as Infernum do not want me to leav—"

He grabbed my waist and pulled me into a bruising kiss, deep and greedy. Straining on tiptoe, I pushed into him and parted my lips as he sent in a sweeping tongue. His taste of salt and wine was intoxicating as I angled my mouth wider.

Together we would feel.

His grip clamped onto me, persistent, driving my body into the hard lines of his.

I felt him grow hard as his searching hands explored me. Breasts, waist, hips, ass, again and again as he claimed every part of me.

I pulled away from the kiss, pressing my forehead into his. "We will get out of here, Arlo," I said, stroking him long and slow, admiring his length and that blessed hardness.

"*Fuck*," he moaned.

"Say it," I demanded, slowing my touch.

"We will get out of here," he repeated.

Urgently, I tore at his buttoned shirt, exposing his strong chest. I continued down in kisses past his chiseled stomach, hips, and the glorious, deep V of his muscles that led me straight to all of him.

I fell to my knees, working at the lacing separating us. With one pull his length was freed, exposing him completely. Smooth, hard perfection.

Captain Arlo Fynn was naked before me, in all his glory, looking down at *me*, completely and utterly transfixed. We both needed this.

I took him in both hands and licked him shaft to head, fiendishly slow. His mouth parted open and wanting as his hands tangled in my curls. Our eyes locked, watching one another. That look alone rushed between my legs, making me hot and wet for him.

Rising, I met his gaze and found my hand around his jaw, forcing his head to one side. Forcing him to be here and now. I licked the strong column of his neck slowly, just as I had his cock.

He released a throaty moan from deep within his chest that vibrated through my body. "Tonight we do this," I whispered into his ear. "Tomorrow we fight." He nodded slowly, those long lashes fluttering. Then, forcing his chin back to me, I kissed him again. Deeper. Hungrier. He kissed me back, desperate for more. His strong hands gripped around my thighs, lifting me up and guiding my legs around his waist with ease. His rough, sea-worn hands cupped my ass as he carried me to the bed.

Collapsing on the bed, our limbs tangled as we centered ourselves without sacrificing a breath apart. He slipped off the minimal fabric that still separated us with ease. His lips were on me, sopping kisses over my neck, chest, breasts. Gorging on me.

We flipped, and I was on top, straddling him naked. Rising from our kiss as I watched his heavy stare trace my body.

"You are unreal, Elowyn." My name on his tongue was symphonic.

I lifted myself, his cock in my hand, and rubbed the head of him slowly, diabolically, against the entrance of my drenched core. Showing him exactly what he did to me. How wet he made me.

"Do you want this?" I asked.

"*Absolutely*," he breathed.

"I do too," I said.

He shuddered, then pushed into me, his chin raised to the ceiling, that glorious, smart mouth gaping as he filled me. Stretching me beautifully.

My inner walls fluttered at the feeling of him.

He sat up quickly, eyes aflare.

"*Please*," he begged, "do that again." I clenched my core around him and he let out another moan into my ear.

"That?" I asked.

He nodded into my collarbone. I clenched around him again and again, riding him mouth-wateringly slow, the clenching and moving sending me over the edge. Drenched for him. For the captain. For Arlo. For the man who was here, below the sea, with me. For me. Who saw me, not my dead mother or king father. But me. Just Elowyn. Although he was not mine to keep, in that moment, he was mine to have.

My core flexed and grasped him with every rise and fall of my body. His eyes stayed on me as I leaned back, one hand seizing my breast, the other on him for stability. My head lolled back in pure paradise as he thrust to meet my apex and held my hips in place, speeding us to a sinister tempo that had me tumbling toward climax.

"*Unreal*." His voice broke through another brilliant moan.

I leaned into him. His strong arms wrapped around me, understanding that I needed more of him, closer. Grasping that strong neck for balance, my body moved frantically as he paced into me. Until it was inevitable. I spilled over again and again onto him as he spilled into me. We moaned in unison into the void, back at destiny, at circumstance, at all that tried desperately to destroy us both.

We roared back at it. In its face. Because here and now, we were together. Despite everything, we found pleasure in a sea of misery.

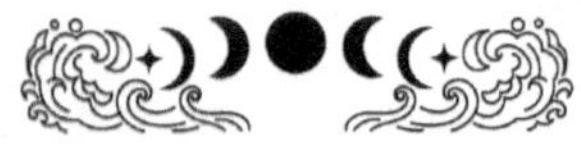

Winter 5343 AT

The news has officially broken that I am with child, no longer able to hide the growing swell of my belly. Reluctantly, I accepted the whispers and a physician visit confirmed it. Many are excited. My father is happy to make good on his debt to my husband on more children, and my husband seems to accept the pregnancy. But something in his demeanor tells me he knows the child is not his, and instead he schemes against me. A delicate nature, bastards are. If the babe is his, by some miracle, he would be the happiest man in the entire world if it was a male. An heir. But if it is not, and he waits too long, then it would be his burden.

Aegir begs me to flee, his voice weighted with urgency as he claims that every day closer to the birth, I place the child and myself in danger. He's right. Who's to even say what the babe will look like. Aegir is plain-featured, with dark-gray tresses and human-colored flesh, but sirens can be an array of utterly inhuman colors. There's no telling what this child will look like.

Yet leaving my daughter seems unthinkable, and taking her with me? What life is there for a young girl below the waves? And what future does she give up here on land? Her father is powerful, affluent, and she is his only child. Women do not inherit property or title from men but maybe that could change. Perhaps her very existence could herald a new world. I am uncertain what I should do, but I know for certain that I am running out of time.

Chapter 36

I awoke in Arlo's arms. We had fallen asleep naked and spent. But supper was nearing, and I needed to attend Hylos's war council to evaluate his next moves.

I got up, brushed and braided my hair, and changed into a luscious evergreen dress that reminded me of spring. Tenderness between my thighs forced me to look back to the bed, where Arlo still slept perfectly, his back turned to me, the striations of muscle in his strong, magnificent body visible.

The urge to wake him throbbed through me. To kiss him and ensure that before wasn't a dream. But he needed rest. Maybe there would be time to share beds and soft whispers when we escaped. If we escaped.

I walked out the door, and Nixie was there.

"Oh, Elowyn. Hello," she said, still clearly hurt from my words the other day.

I thought of what Raylik said. That Nixie truly didn't want anyone to be harmed. It was true. I knew that. None of them wanted this war besides their leader and his lover.

"I'm sorry for what I said the other day. It wasn't fair for me to blame you for what happened," I said.

"It's fine. I know you were deeply hurt. I understand," she said, offering me a small smile.

"Are you headed to Hylos's study for the council? He called us all to attend. I'm heading that way too. Want to walk together?" I asked, lifting up my arm to loop into hers as we had many times before, like friends.

She smiled, taking it. "I'd like that."

We took a few steps, then she scrunched her nose as if she smelled something foul.

"Oh my Guardians, you didn't?" she practically squealed, pink eyebrows raised.

"Didn't what?" I asked, confused.

"*Nothing*. Nothing at all!" she answered too quickly, trying to continue walking.

I planted my feet. "No, tell me."

"I haven't told you this yet because I didn't want to make you uncomfortable, but sirens, we can—well, we can scent certain things."

"Scent things? Like what? Does my breath smell or something?" I breathed into my palm and sniffed to check.

"Well, we can scent just one thing. Love, in all its forms. Lust, emotion, but especially ..." She sheepishly averted her eyes.

"I don't understand."

"Elowyn, you absolutely reek of sex and if you do not bathe, we'll be stuck listening to Morvyn make a slew of crass jokes all evening."

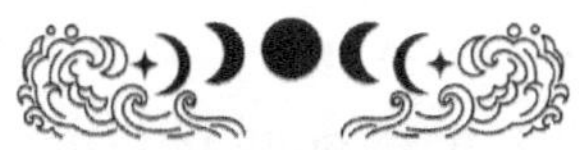

After scrubbing every inch of my body and passing a sniff test from Nixie, we walked to Hylos's study. I couldn't believe she didn't tell me they could smell arousal and sex. She explained that it was a part of their mating habits and the sense heightened more with every day that neared the full moon.

Mortified, I thought back to every interaction and wondered if Morvyn's hunches about my feelings for Arlo were more than just that. I could feel my cheeks burn red when we turned into the study.

In the study, amid stacks of books, half-eaten meals, and the buzz of siren magic holding small figures in swirls upon the map, were Lumina and Hylos. Nixie and I shuffled in. Raylik and Morvyn were behind us.

"Good, you're here. Lumina has found a portion of Oakhaven that's essentially uninhabited, and apparently underdeveloped." Hylos looked up at me as he brushed a tendril of blue hair out of his face. Dark-blue crescent moons hung under his eyes. He looked like he hadn't slept since we last spoke.

I tried to ignore the fact that he didn't even ask how I or Arlo were doing, but it stung.

"Elowyn, what do you know of Thornley?" he asked, not looking up to speak to me.

Thornley Forest, craft archers' bow, forever a strong wooded home for the Guardian of all, Terragos, grant us your gifts, father of all land. The nursery rhyme rambled through my mind.

"I've heard of it," I answered.

"And?" Hylos asked.

Lumina held her breath as she looked at her leader, frustration pursing her lips.

"It's heavily wooded. Few people. And it's freezing fucking cold." Thornley was the northernmost point of Oakhaven and likely snowed in at this time of year. What did Hylos want with that area?

Calypstra lurked in, dressed in a black silk dress that rippled against her pallid skin, the neckline plunging deep toward her navel. Her head snapped toward me, eyes wide and unblinking. A mixture of anger and pure disgust boiled on her face.

"Cal, good, you're here. I was explaining the plan we discussed last night," Hylos said, not noticing the visceral reaction she was having at my mere presence.

But Nixie marked it immediately. She stepped to my side swiftly, as if to protect me. Raylik, not far from her, was watching, on edge himself.

I only stared back defiantly at Calypstra.

The room fell silent, everyone feeling the tension.

"What's the matter? Why are you all so quiet?" Hylos said, looking up from the map.

Morvyn swirled his chalice nonchalantly. "I'm *assuming* everyone is just now smelling the sex Elowyn reeks of."

"That is *disgusting*." Hylos shook his head. "We have far more important things to discuss. Like war strategy."

Calypstra's coal-lined eyes continued to stare daggers at me, as though she wanted to reach across the table and rip out my throat. What the fuck was her problem?

"So, is Thornley a good launching point then?" Hylos asked me.

"For what?" I asked.

"To take Oakhaven?"

Lumina huffed. "I said it was underpopulated. Never that it was a good route for a siege."

My face contorted. "That would be a death sentence." His forces would be cut off long before doing any damage. "Guardian's Watch, the capital, is here." I pointed to the city in the center of the map. Where my father's castle stood. "This is the only way to take all of Oakhaven. You would be miles away from it. Not to mention this route would have you all landlocked. Which, I don't know if you're aware, but water is kind of your whole *thing*. It would be a mistake," I said, holding back that the far better route would be through Gyldmare. But even that path would be a death sentence.

"That's exactly what a foreign adversary would say," Calypstra drawled, still scowling and suffering under the weight of whatever my presence was doing to her.

"What would you have us do, Elowyn?" he said, clenching his jaw.

I looked to Lumina, desperate for a reprieve. She was out of answers too. Morvyn only sipped his drink while Nixie and Raylik eyed one another.

"Well? We don't have all day, tell us, oh wise one," Hylos urged. He wasn't thinking straight, far too upset after the last attack that nearly took him.

"I'd suggest you slow down. Maybe listen to your council." I looked around the table at his inner circle of friends.

"Slow down?" He laughed mirthlessly, then took the chalice from Morvyn's hand and finished it.

"Sure, we can share ..." Morvyn said, blinking.

That wouldn't help either.

"I am no child; you do not need to lecture me like one," Hylos snapped.

"You're acting like one. You need to think clearly if you truly wish to attack Oakhaven," I said. Even though it was the last thing I wanted, and I would do everything in my power to stop him, it was the truth.

"I *am* thinking clearly," Hylos answered while pouring another drink.

"Is that what the drink is for? All that clear thinking you're doing?" I rolled my eyes, then leaned over the map.

Hylos leaned in with me, filled drink in hand.

"Oakhaven has withstood *hundreds* of attacks. It's an island, its ruler at its heart, surrounded by land and militias buffering it from outside assaults. The only way I've heard of it being taken was Byllard the Suppressor, who simply had the sheer numbers to overtake the castle." I met his storm-blue eyes, "How many men do you have?"

"You dare ask him that? What, so you can run and tell your father the second you have a chance? Disloyal *bitch*," Calypstra hissed.

"Shut the fuck up," I sneered back at her. "I'm here because Hylos wants my counsel, and whatever issue you have with me you should leave at the door when you enter a royal meeting."

Hylos rubbed a nervous thumb over the rim of the cup.

I continued, "I'll *assume* the number is far less than the thousands of local militias Oakhaven has. Not to mention its great navy. You don't know what you're getting yourself into. Are you ready to send your people straight to their deaths?"

"I am ready to do what is *necessary*," he said through gritted teeth. There was no reasoning with him. He was determined to do whatever it took to find his father. Even rushing into a war and sacrificing hundreds of sirens. That's why I needed to take Arlo and get out of here.

"Thornley is a bad idea, Hylos," was all I offered, then looked at his friends. "If you go there, you *all* will die."

The room fell mortally silent as I kept to myself how Oakhaven had been taken repeatedly throughout history. How my forebears seized it and how those before them did so as well.

The best way to take down any kingdom was from within.

CHAPTER 37

The war council went late into the night as we all tried to reason with Hylos. But he was insistent. After their holy holiday, he would attack Oakhaven through Thornely. It was final. Raylik and Nixie insisted on walking me back to my chambers, seemingly uneasy from the way Calypstra was acting toward me. It was clear: she despised me. But would she really hurt me? I had my suspicions that she'd drugged me, but Hylos said she wouldn't have. But was she so cruel as to kill every single one of Hylos's prisoners? And why would she of all people spare Arlo? None of it made sense.

I said my goodbyes to the couple at my door and found Arlo still asleep in my bed. I curled in next to him and faded back to sleep. I would need my rest. War was coming.

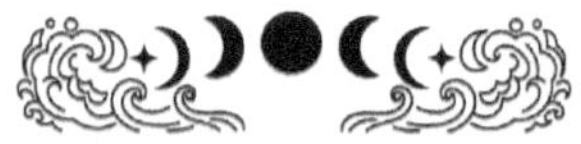

One last siren ceremony separated Arlo and me from freedom. After this, there would be their Hydroxia, starting at midnight, when the longest full moon would be the brightest. While the sirens drank, feasted, and mated, we would make our escape.

But first was the Jawro competition. A part of me didn't wish to attend. I'd rather stay with Arlo and rest. Maybe run through our plan for escaping again. But I needed to get a feel for the atmosphere within Naiadon. Were guards walking about and on edge? Or were people at ease?

I walked with Morvyn through the halls to the armory. All of Naiadon's people seemed present, pouring out into the halls and dressed in bright colors. We turned into the armory, which was filled with vivid sirens in every shade of every color, crackling with anticipation as they filed into the stands that curved against the back wall of the space.

One last ceremony. One more day. I could do this. The cheers and excitement were splendid, though. Reminding me of what people said jousts were like on land, especially the ones my father would hold that I never had the opportunity to attend.

Nixie stood by Raylik both dressed in outfits fit to fight in, red sparring fabric that was thin and tight so no one could get a good hold on them. Their hair both braided in small tight lines against their head, for the same reason. Ready for who ever dared challenge them.

We found Lumina in the stands, a stylus in hand and wax tablet on her lap.

"Lumi, why don't you just watch for once." Morvyn chided as we sat on each side of her.

"Someone needs to scribe what happens, or else it will all be forgotten," Lumina said, looking up at Morvyn. Her golden dress was dazzling against her dark skin.

"I can tell you what will happen. The same thing as every year," Morvyn scoffed, looking out at the center circle. "Raylik will beat whoever is dumb enough to challenge him, gently but well, as per usual. Someone will foolishly challenge Hylos and be defeated miserably. We all cheer. The end."

"And I'll write it all down to ensure it is remembered for years to come."

"Suit yourself. Elowyn and I will do this thing called enjoying ourselves. You should try it sometime," he joked, shouldering into her, earning a smile.

I snickered too.

A deep sound blared through the room, siren song booming through the space, echoing off the glass dome that capped the armory. The crowd cheered with it, sending parts of their own music to blend and bind with the sound.

"Here we go," Morvyn thrilled and whooped with the crowd. Then, his face fell. "And here she comes, my *miserable* aunt. She wouldn't shut up about this *honor* bestowed upon her over dinner the other night," Morvyn said, rolling his pale eyes.

Elspeth walked before the armory pool. The crowd hushed to hear her speak.

"As the longest living Circle leader in these three great seas," she said, her voice loud, siren magic sending it cracking on the song.

"Couldn't get me to admit *that* with a spear to my head," Morvyn murmured.

"*Shhhh,*" Lumina hushed.

Elspeth's voice cracked through the room. "I will judge the sacred Jawro competition. First, the rules. The aim is simple. Whoever removes the bangle from the other contestant's ankle is the victor. Step out of the circle and you will be forced to forfeit."

"That's not a whole lot of rules," I whispered to Morvyn.

"Exactly. Leaves lots of room for *interpretation.* One year, a winner gnawed off the other contestant's leg to remove the bracelet."

My stomach churned at the thought.

"Who here wishes to compete first?" Elspeth looked to the crowd, her frozen eyes scanning for takers.

"I do." Draveen's voice commanded the regard of the crowd.

"This will be good. I can't wait to watch Hylos kick his ass," Morvyn snickered, rubbing his finned hands together.

"Granted. Draveen of Twynox Circle. Tell us who you wish to challenge." I looked down at Hylos, regal as ever. By the tick in his blue jaw, I saw he was readying to stand and fight Draveen.

"I call a human from the very ship of our rivals."

The crowd gasped.

My heart dove through the ground. No. Not Arlo. Anyone in the world besides him.

Blood beat through my body. Through my ears. I stood to my feet to get a better look. Praying to the Guardians themselves it would not be Arlo. But he was the only remaining human left.

I scanned the crowd and found Calypstra, who smiled at me. She was behind this.

The doors of the armory opened and a gasp fell from my lips as a child in worn clothes made his way to the center of the Jawro circle, called by Draveen's lull. A lazy smile was on his face.

Alistar. He was alive. The urge to run out and gather him in my arms was unbearable.

"What is the meaning of this?" Hylos demanded.

"I found this human whelp rummaging about the castle, likely a spy, and I wish to punish him for the crimes of his king," Draveen answered through a foul smile.

"Who is the boy?" Lumina asked at my side.

"He's from Arlo's crew," I said. Alistar's face was dirty, his once-bouncing curls plastered to his head with oil and sweat.

Why would Calypstra arrange this?

"There is no honor in fighting a mere child," Hylos said, baffled.

I was up and stepping through the crowd.

"Elowyn, wait," Morvyn pleaded, but I ignored him. I had to stop this.

"There is honor in showing all of your loyal subjects how easy it will be for us to destroy the humans upon land. This child is a symbol, great *leader*," said Draveen.

"You can't let him hurt him. He's just a boy," I demanded at Hylos's side. He hardly looked down at me.

I cut Calypstra a hard look. "You did this," I spat, but she didn't move, just remained in cool disregard, arms crossed.

"I still say there is no honor in this. You can take the bracelet from him with ease," Hylos said calmly.

Would Hylos really allow this to happen?

"I plan on taking him apart limb by limb first, with my eyes closed. Tear him to shreds until I find the bangle," Draveen said.

"No!" The word scorched from my lips.

Hylos cut me a hard look. "Stand down, Elowyn," he said under his breath.

"Great leader," Draveen said in a mocking tone, "how can we expect you to fight a war against the human king when you allow his daughter to give orders to you? But I suppose ..." Draveen looked to the now-silent crowd. With a smile showing rows of sharp teeth, he said, "That's what we should expect from a half-breed."

"If you wish to fight a child because that is all you can manage, then go ahead. Fight. I thought you would at least attempt to call upon me, since you question my rule so blatantly. But it seems you're too afraid," Hylos said with ease.

A laugh boomed from Draveen. "I would *never* wish to fight you, my great liege."

"Fight me," I yelled, stepping forward toward the monster, looking up at his ghoulish figure, realizing again just how large he truly was.

"I suppose you would be a better example, the daughter of our enemy," Draveen drawled, a finger tapping his cheek contemplatively.

"I said *stand down*, Elowyn," Hylos demanded, alarm sharpening his tone.

"Yes, I suppose I accept your offer to compete," Draveen said, a smile slicing across his ghastly face and sending a chill down my spine. "After all, you're a much better adversary than a mere child, isn't that right, my liege?"

Nixie rushed to my side. "Elowyn, please tell me you have a plan," she said, fear darkening her usually bright tone.

I fought, fiercely, to steady my ragged breath. This space had belonged to Nixie and me before daybreak, now all these eyes were on me. I pushed down the nausea churning in my gut.

"Plan is," I swallowed down the fear, "don't fucking die."

My eyes fell to Alistar, still sweetly smiling. If I died, at least he would live.

I turned to Nixie. "Take him out of here, ensure he's safe."

She shook her head no at me. "I can't leave you now. I need to be here in case—"

"*Please.* He has no one in this world, he's an orphan. Get him out of here and somewhere safe."

She relented, nodding a yes, then scooped up the small boy in her arms, leaving the armory.

"Enough theatrics," Elspeth snapped. "Take your places on each side of the pool."

I nodded in agreement, then walked slowly to the opposite side of the circle, drawing a rush of whispers from the onlookers.

This was not good. There was no way I would win. I was wearing a bloody dress, for Guardians' sake. At least Draveen was unarmed. Only strength and skill would be our weapons, but I lacked both.

Draveen laughed, then called to the crowd, "Who is ready to watch me *destroy* the enemy as our king shall destroy her father?"

The crowd only offered a few stray cheers.

His eyes narrowed at me, sharp teeth bared in a repugnant smile.

Elspeth walked with a young female siren who held a glass box in her wake. She went first to Draveen, whose confident smile never faded. She kneeled before him and placed the onyx bangle around his ankle.

She glided around the circle to me and clasped the matching bangle on my ankle too.

I'd endured so much here in Naiadon. Yet lived so much as well. I left Oakhaven for the first time in my life. I found these strange people in the sea. A good man cared for me well.

I found Lumina and Morvyn in the crowd, watching me in horror.

I made friends.

And I tried my best to save Oakhaven.

If I died, I knew it would be with few regrets.

Elspeth returned to the front of the crowd. "Remember, stepping beyond the confines of the Jawro circle shall cause immediate forfeiture and thus banishment from Naiadon's walls in shame."

I could step out now and it would be over. But that would mean leaving Arlo behind. I needed to survive this, somehow. Or die trying.

"Do you both understand and accept these rules?" Elspeth first looked at me, and I nodded. Then at Draveen, who did the same.

"Good. Now let the Jawro competition begin!"

The stadium roared in applause.

Elspeth raised her moon-pale hands skyward, and a loud song chimed from her fingertips. The room shook with song as the pool in the center of the armory vibrated, then filled in with a giant stone plate. It rose past the floor, creating a raised, circular platform. The circle we must remain in.

"Enter the Jawro ring," Elspeth commanded.

I took a large step into the still-wet ring. Draveen traversed the lip with ease. My thoughts were frenzied. He was so damn big. His oily, grayish skin alone was enough to cause bile to rise in my throat.

This was it.

"Begin!" Elspeth shouted. Loud music blasted from her, pulsating in rhythmic surges that vibrated my body and mind.

Draveen circled me as I kept out of reach, and we danced around one another in lazy half circles.

I wished Nixie was there to tell me what to do, like she did when we trained. To dodge, roll, or punch when I needed to.

Only Raylik stood there, arms crossed.

When the world is hard and fast, you can be slow and calculated. I took in a deep, cleansing breath, feeling my body and calming my mind. I set my stance, holding my arms up firmly, digging a big toe into the hard stone for balance. I thought of the large oak tree I climbed as a girl in front of Granger House. Rooted and sturdy.

Draveen lunged in my direction. I gasped, stepping back, my foot nearly slipping from the ring. This drew a putrid laugh from the beast.

"Puny girl, I'm going to eat you for dinner." Draveen picked at his teeth disinterestedly. This was all a game to him.

My eyes flickered to Morvyn in the stands, who now stood tall above the crowd. His eyes softened for me as our eyes met above the spectators' heads. Lumina stood beside him, pressed into his arm for comfort and unable to tear her eyes away from the impending disaster.

"Or maybe I'll have you for dessert," Draveen cackled.

Disgusting. His confidence was overbearing.

In fact ... *Too overbearing.*

The thought slammed into me. Arrogant men littered history and fairy tales alike. The loudest and most self-assured always seemed to hide something. Their certitude always masked an insecurity.

That was it. At least, it bloody well had to be.

"What did you say, fish breath?" I spat, trying to hide the shaking in my voice.

A nervous chuckle slipped from someone in the crowed.

Draveen turned around to mark whoever dared laugh at him. Then returned his soulless black eyes upon me.

"What did you call me, little *girl*?" he seethed, the words rattling my bones. But I mastered myself.

"Fish. Breath," I enunciated. "And I'm twenty-fucking-five years old, clearly a woman. Not sure if you've ever been this close to one before though."

Another laugh flew from the crowd, unmistakably Morvyn's.

"Or are your eyes just *fucked* from that dark hole you slithered up from?"

More laughter clanged, cutting deeper into Draveen's pride.

I kept at it. "Is every disgusting beast from the depths you dwell in as ugly as you? Or are you just particularly hideous? Because you look like the bottom of the ocean shit you out."

More laughter ensued. Draveen darted his head around, greasy black hair whipping with the movement, each one of his muscles tensed under his oleaginous skin as he growled again, deeper and more guttural.

Keeping my stance firm and my eyes locked onto his, I inched back as close as I could to the rim of the circle, readying for my impending doom.

"What's the matter, you don't like when they laugh at you?"

He bared his teeth and shook with anger. It was working.

"Stupid human, this is why your people die so young."

"Better than walking around looking already dead."

I let out the best laugh I could muster.

My heart faltered. That was it.

"You. Shall. *Die*!" he roared, charging at me full speed, his large legs slamming into the ground with each step, Elspeth's music speeding in tempo as Draveen's hard footfalls shook through the ground.

I held fast, despite every nerve in my body screaming to run. Silence fell over the crowd as vile noises gurgled out of Draveen as he charged me. Closer and closer he came, eyes wild. Pure predator. I the prey. Nearly in his grip.

Then, just like Raylik told me in this very armory, I followed his advice.

The best way to remain standing in a fight is to avoid getting hit at all.

In the blink of an eye, I sidestepped from Draveen's path of destruction, causing him to tumble off the Jawro circle, hurling himself into the crowd.

I let out the breath I'd been holding.

I did it. I *fucking* did it!

I turned to Draveen, on the ground and rubbing his head in pure disbelief.

Elspeth's music came to a halt. "Forfeit!" she yelled.

The sirens laughed wildly at Draveen's disgrace. Simmering, his eyes, black as death, whipped up to me. Black claws extended from his finned hand. Oh *shit*. He shook with anger, then lunged in a flash. He clutched a finned hand around my neck, the claws biting into my flesh. The ground gave way as he lifted me by the throat.

I struggled to fight against his grip, but he was too strong.

"Forfeit! Forfeit!" Eslepth's voice sounded far away, muted by the blood pooling in my ears.

Draveen didn't let go.

"Stupid little girl. It will be as easy as Calypstra said to kill you. Disgusting pest." He shook me about with ease like a plaything. He was going to kill me. I had won, but that didn't matter. Because it wasn't about the competition at all. It was about murdering me at Calypstra's command.

Then, a large mass of force slammed into us, throwing me from Draveen's grip. I thwacked into the hard ground.

It was Raylik who was on Draveen in a red blur.

Elspeth walked to the center of the Jawro circle. "Draveen of Twynox Circle has forfeited the Jawro competition. Elowyn of Blackthorn Circle is champion!" she belted.

The room resurged with applause. My hands reached the tendons of my damaged throat. A small price to pay to live another day.

I searched the room for Calypstra, who had vanished amid the chaos. Draveen clawed and thrashed like a wild animal until Raylik sent an earth-shattering blow to his jaw that knocked him unconscious. The now-raucous crowd cheered on. I stepped out of the circle, somehow, with my life.

Morvyn cut through the crowd and breezed up to meet me. He clasped his alabaster finned hands around my face, pulling me from the prayers I was sending to the Guardians, thanking each above. He gave me a big dramatic kiss on the cheek.

"You fucking genius idiot!" he shouted.

I smiled, wiping the wetness away with a still-quivering hand.

"Not exactly the way the tomes say to do it, but *effective*," Lumina said beside Morvyn.

"Draveen—did you hear him? He said Calypstra told him it would be easy to kill me," I asked, scanning the room for her.

"Yes, everyone did. He practically screamed it."

"She has to be behind everything that has happened to me then, right?"

She was nowhere to be found in the rushing crowd that was still cheering in celebration and watching as Raylik wrangled Draveen.

"She has to be," Lumina agreed.

"Well, looks like she's not here anymore," Morvyn said, scanning the room too.

Hylos walked up to us. "Are you okay?" He grimaced at my neck, telling me it was already bruising.

"I will be fine. What are your plans for Calypstra?" I asked pointedly.

"I've sent my guards to find her, I heard what Draveen said and she'll be questioned."

"She likely poisoned me and possibly killed all of your prisoners ... Infernum, she might even have been behind the kelpie attacking me. Now she has directly worked with someone to murder me in front of you and your entire court and you'll question her. That is it?" I argued.

"Sirens believe in innocence until proven guilty," he said carefully. "But Draveen will be questioned as well before he is banished from Naiadon."

Raylik was dragging Draveen's motionless body out of the armory.

"I need to make sure Raylik doesn't beat the life out of him. Good job, Elowyn. I'm happy you didn't die."

Hylos followed Raylik, dismissing me. That was it.

I looked to Morvyn and Lumina, who just held sorry, sympathetic looks. They saw it too. Hylos would never hold Calypstra accountable.

Summer 5344 AT

The contractions began early this morning. I have gone the day with the pains growing and growing but show not an ounce of pain. Tonight, the babe will come. A funny thought crossed my mind. Maybe it is the pain that is making me mad, or this entire situation, but today I realized the purpose of this silly journal that I've kept for so long.

Aegir gave it to me to allow a place to pour out my soul, an escape, a haven for my truth. I wonder if he always knew that even under the sea, behind closed doors, I hid parts of myself to never pain him. This journal has held my true heart for so long, and now I know why. It is for you, little babe. So you may know me when I am gone.

Because after you are born, sweet child, I shall send it with you to the other side of the portrait, in Naiadon. Then I will face my husband, with you no longer a swell in my stomach. He will be angry. Furious, even, but I will never let him put eyes on you.

In my absence, you may have the absolute truth of my heart.

Please, do not be sad for me. Not for a single moment. The many lives I've lived, even in the worst of times, have been the greatest any one person could wish for. They led to your sister. They led to you.

Your father will tell you of me, and when he speaks of me, if even one tear wells in his eye, remind him not to be sad either. Because this life was beautiful. Messy at times, but entirely mine. I have loved it. As I loved him. As I love you.

Please remember, I will always be with you when I am not with your sister. I will need to divide my time equally between you two as any good mother should. But one day, please find her. That will make my work of being with you both all the easier.

When you find her, tell her of the freedom below the waves. Tell her of Naiadon and your great people. Tell her that there are worlds where women are leaders. Where they are safe to love who they choose. Tell her of me and the life I truly lived, not the lie she witnessed.

See you again, my love.

Chapter 38

"She must have been a noble," Arlo called to me from the bed-chamber. He was on his second read of the journal, hoping a clearer answer on how the portal worked might be hidden in the faded, handwritten words.

I finished the final touches on the braid I had woven. Rose oil that I worked through my curls to tame them lingered on my fingertips. The scent calmed the turmoil in my mind.

My hands still trembled as fear threaded through me from the Jawro competition and Draveen. Hylos hardly cared that Calypstra was behind every terrible thing that had happened to me in Naiadon. It hurt, which was more surprising than his lack of action.

I walked across the room, the marble cool under my feet. I wanted to fall apart in Arlo's arms, but forced a smile instead. After this, there would be time for falling apart. I hadn't told Arlo the full truth about what had happened. I gave him pieces, and let him know Alistar was still alive. Safe with Nixie somewhere. But I left out the part about just how near death I came. He would need a clear head for us to escape, and if he knew someone in the castle was trying to kill me, he'd never be calm enough to do what needed to be done.

Arlo continued, "It would only make sense she was noble because—" he lifted his eyes to me and silenced. The warmth in his gaze blazed to something hotter. "What in Infernum are you wearing?"

"Nixie picked it out for me for Hydroxia tonight." It was a red silk dress that clung to me, dramatizing the curves of my hips and thighs. A thin chain of silver clasped it around my neck.

He looked like a man possessed.

I smiled devilishly.

"You haven't even seen the back yet."

I turned, showing how it plunged dangerously low toward my ass. It was gorgeous, and I looked like a Guardian myself in the sanguineous fabric.

Arlo put the book down carelessly and buried his face in his hands. I walked closer, working in between his thighs.

"What is it?" I whispered.

"I don't know if I can handle it." His words were a low snarl that vibrated through my body.

"What?"

"Knowing anyone can even look at you dressed this way."

I let out a little laugh.

I leaned into him and he pressed his chin into my sternum between my breasts as his arms wrapped around my thighs.

He sniffed. "*Mmmm* ... You even *smell* amazing."

He stood to his full height, towering above me, looking down through those long lashes. "One last day in this place, in *these* clothes." He trailed a finger down my spine. My nipples hardened under the gown, aching for more of his touch. "Then we leave this strange place behind."

His hands found greedy palmfuls of my ass as he gathered me in his arms and flipped me onto the bed with shocking speed. His lips were on me in an instant. Our bodies collided into one, sending the journal toppling to the ground. Arlo plastered his hard body against mine, spreading my legs, grinding into me, the skirt of my dress lifting past my thighs, exposing me fully as our tongues swirled.

I craved his weight. It held me in place, and without it I'd float away.

"On second thought," he said, chasing kisses down my neck, "maybe keep this dress."

I laughed. "Glad you're feeling open-minded, just in time for me to show you what Nixie picked out for you."

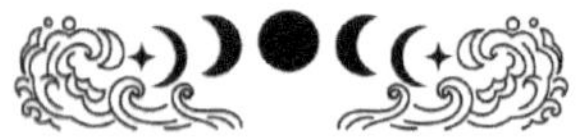

Arlo adjusted himself in his short outfit, pulling as much of the black fabric down over his muscle-toned thighs as he could. Damn, I could get used to him in siren clothing. That glorious, strong chest and muscle-toned abdomen to match, all on display, was fantastic.

"Come on, it can't be that bad," I snickered, bumping into his large frame as his dark eyebrows furrowed.

"You have twice the amount of clothing on. Speak for yourself."

"Well, at least I'm enjoying the *view*."

"Don't get used to it ..." he murmured.

"Tiny Toes!" Morvyn laughed from behind us.

Arlo's eyes rolled at the mere sound of Morvyn's voice.

"You have truly assimilated, my friend." Morvyn wore bright pinks that popped on his white flesh, his hair half-knotted, a large pearl necklace draped around his collarbones, and of course, his favorite accessories of all, two drinks in hand.

"One for the lady," he said as he slipped the cup into my grip. "And there's plenty more over there." He pointed to a fountain in the shape of a fish, from whose mouth poured a continuous stream of red wine. I sipped the wine and it tasted like sweet cherries.

There were multiple fountains that lined the halls in this section of the castle, all running freely with drink. Morvyn looked over Arlo again and gave a shake of his head with a laugh. "A true joy to see you dressed as one of us, Tiny Toes. Quite *resplendent*, wouldn't you say, Elowyn?"

I nearly choked on the wine at the ridiculous word I'd embarrassingly called the captain at the mercy of the truth poison. Maybe one day, safe on land, I'd tell him what truly helped conceal our plans of escape from the sirens.

"Well, cheers to you both and a happy Hydroxia!"

"Hy, *Hy*-what?" Arlo's tongue stumbled over the foreign phrase.

"Hydroxia! A true shame terras don't celebrate Nymphaea's day of honor," Morvyn said cheerily.

"Hmmm, maybe we're busy doing more important things than thinking of another reason to drink and gorge ourselves on stolen plunder, as your people seem to do so often," Arlo said in a gruff voice as he eyed the crowd.

"Oh, I love when you banter, Tiny Toes," Morvyn beamed. "Another, do another!"

Arlo simply crossed his arms in front of his bare chest.

"Here, let me do it for you." We continued down the halls, following the walking crowd. Morvyn flattened his expression and furrowed his brow. "I need some pants to steer this ship!" he said in a deep, pensive voice.

My hand flew to my mouth, trying to hold back the laugh bubbling up.

"Oh, I know, I know." Morvyn crossed his arms, mimicking Arlo. "How will I ever brood without boots on?" A laugh flew from my lips.

"Fine, I'll stop, but you *do* look exquisite, and you can thank Nixie later when Elowyn here jumps your bones tonight." Morvyn kissed me on the cheek. "Oh, and if any pale women ask you where I am, please tell them I am at the bottom of the sea, dead. Thanks!" Then he disappeared into the crowd.

Arlo and I entered through the large archways that towered above us, draped in red, yellow, and blue silks that marked the entrance. A siren chorus lilted in the night and my heart sang with it. My fingers were longing to tap the place where ivory virginal keys were in my mind.

Hundreds of sirens filled the banquet hall as they drank and laughed. The people of Naiadon. Hylos's people. All beautiful and unique. Completely unaware of the war their leader planned for them just tomorrow. Tremendous change was about to come and upend their lives.

Tonight they were careless and free. A calm before the storm. Another reason to leave this place behind.

If I could stop Hylos's attack, then maybe only a few of his people would be harmed. He would see how foolish this all was and give up on the idea altogether.

Arlo stumbled back, startled by a large sweeping form made of water in the shape of Nymphaea. She swam above a table filled with food that sirens picked off of jubilantly as the Holy Mother did backflips and waved to the crowd.

My hand found his, and I gave him a reassuring squeeze. "It's not real, don't worry," I consoled. "You've got this."

He wasn't used to the oddities here, as he had always been lulled from one place to the next. I hadn't truly realized just how accustomed I'd grown to it all myself.

We made our way to a trio of oversized couches where Raylik and Nixie sat. Nixie's pale pink legs draped over her lover's lap. I smiled as

Raylik ran a hand down her shins. He was the one who chose her, every day. Especially today.

"Elowyn!" she exclaimed when she saw me.

She jumped up and leaped into my arms.

"Raylik told me all about what you did. How you tricked that big ugly bastard!" She shook my shoulders, her smile beaming. "He said your defensive stance needs work, but we can practice tomorrow."

Raylik grumbled.

"Oh yes, that's right," Nixie said.

Raylik stood up beside her.

"We would like to ask you both something," he started.

Nixie continued, "The little boy, Alistar. We wanted to know …" Nixie and Raylik looked between one another. "If we could raise him as our own. I know you said he was an orphan."

"And I know you are like a father to him," Raylik said to Arlo, who looked warily between the pair. "If you do not agree, I understand and he will be returned to you."

Arlo looked to me for answers.

We couldn't take Alistar with us. Not now. Before sunrise, we would be gone.

"They are truly good people," I said to Arlo, trying to ease his mind.

Slowly, Arlo nodded a yes.

Nixie jumped into our arms, hugging us.

Arlo froze at first as Nixie bounced in his arms. "Thank you! Thank you!" she shrilled. "We both have always wanted to be parents. We swear he will be the most loved little boy in all of Naiadon."

Nixie broke away from Arlo.

Raylik shoved his hand into Arlo's grip. A respectful look passed between them.

"Thank you," Raylik said.

"Take care of him," Arlo said sternly.

"You have my word."

"Come now, Hylos is waiting for you both," Nixie said, still smiling cheek to cheek. She would make a wonderful mother; I knew that in my heart. Alistar would be lucky to have her in his life.

Hylos's eyes lit at our approach. I dipped my head in his direction as Arlo loomed at my side.

"Have you seen what your captain has completed for you?" I followed Hylos's hand to the virginal beside him on a dais, in perfect splendor. I knew Arlo had spent all day working on it, but to see it in its glory, I'd realized just how much work it really took. My fingers longed for its keys. My soul begged to hear its sound. It was a lovely instrument.

I turned to Arlo and kissed him on the cheek.

"It's beautiful," I said.

"I am glad you like it. Hopefully it will do the job." Arlo said, with a nod.

"Are you ready for its debut?" Hylos asked, sipping from his chalice. His jaw was clenched; something agitated him.

Calypstra was nowhere to be found.

"Where is she?" I asked pointedly.

Hylos cut me a glance, lips tight, knowing exactly who I meant. "She is not in Naiadon."

She'd fled. Was it an admission of guilt? Hylos would figure it out one day. That he'd let a snake into his bed. But soon it wouldn't be my problem anymore.

"I'd like to play for you all, to give thanks to Nymphaea, for bringing me here," I said, steeling my features.

A glint of true happiness glimmered in Hylos's eyes.

"If that is fine with *Your Majesty*," I added, smiling at the siren king regent.

"Oh, please call me Great Ruler, Your Majesty is my father," Hylos joked with a genuine smile.

Perhaps in another life Hylos and I would have been friends and not enemies. But it seemed fate had other plans.

Hylos continued, "Come on, let's hear it, Princess."

CHAPTER 39

I sat at the polished and gleaming virginal bench and rested my hands on the mended keys, the white velvet underneath them also clean and new.

Arlo was a magician himself with how well he'd revitalized the once-waterlogged and deteriorated instrument I'd found in the treasury only weeks ago. I searched for him in the crowd to will him a thank you for repairing the instrument. He'd breathed life into it. As he did me. But he was gone, already executing the first step of our plan.

So, with a deep, calming breath, I played to distract the sirens.

The first wave of melody was slow and careful as I savored every note plucked from the strings. How I missed this. Closing my eyes, I felt the music. It steadied my racing heart and matched the tepid tempo I kept.

I wasn't lying when I told Hylos I wanted to give thanks to Nymphaea. I did. Despite everything I'd endured in her domain, she'd given me so much to be thankful for.

My music swelled like the ocean upon which she'd delivered me to Naiadon, instead of into Cedric's grasp. Although Hylos was flawed, I was happy to know the sirens. To witness their beauty and wonder. Maybe if such strange and fantastical creatures could exist in this ruthless world, I could too.

My pace quickened, as I also bid a thank you to the woman in the journal. Hylos's mother. Who, against all odds and without her knowledge, had shared her story with me. She hadn't just shown me the way out of this place; she'd shown me her heart. Thank you, thank you, *thank you*—for showing me through handwritten words what it was to love fearlessly while carrying the burden of duty.

I returned to mellower tenor notes, reminiscent of Oakhaven. Clear notes, like hymns echoing in churches worshipping the Guardians. Certain like the sun that rose and fell with or without me. Like the country that waited for me on land. I'd return to it. Warn my father. Save my people. Then face whatever fate awaited me without fear.

Traveling down the keys, I found notes reminiscent of Arlo. Deep like his voice in the night as he held me. Slow like our life if I'd done as he suggested: never returned to Oakhaven and ran away with him. Soft, quiet, and simple. Like summer days filled with laughter, and winter nights spent tangled in each other's arms. They would never be. But they still sounded sweet to dream.

The music flowed from my fingers, lingering at the right moments, quickening at others. The speeding notes blended into a culmination of everything: land, sea, hope, joy, love, and loss. Playing all that my heart could offer until my fingers stilled, and I followed that very last lingering note as it stretched across the room and ended somewhere below the sea.

I opened my eyes to the sirens all watching me in awe. My heart stuttered, recalling how my father's court reacted to my playing too. Forced to clap by their liege.

But they did not need forcing.

The sirens erupted into applause.

"Wonderful! Wonderful!" Hylos cheered, clapping loudly too.

I stood slowly, taking in the sight of their beaming faces, and gave a small bow.

A tear slipped down my cheek, which I quickly wiped away. To share my music with these beings, who were themselves made of song, and to receive their praise, was an honor beyond words.

The applause faded like that single sweet note, and I walked to meet Hylos and his inner circle one last time.

"Elowyn, that was outstanding!" Morvyn exclaimed.

"That was amazing!" Nixie chirped at Raylik's side.

"Yes, you are talented," Raylik said.

"Thank you, the instrument is perfect. So well made," I answered, still in disbelief at its repair. It was a shame to leave it behind.

"I guess we can thank Tiny Toes for something," Morvyn sneered.

"You played wonderfully," Lumina said with tears in her eyes.

"My liege, you're needed in your study," An out-of-breath guard said to Hylos, eyes wide.

"I'm coming." He looked back at me, softening for one moment. "It truly was wonderful, Elowyn. Thank you for sharing your song with us." Then he stormed off and Raylik followed.

"Has anyone seen Arlo?" I exclaimed, our plan racing back to me.

"No, I haven't," Nixie said as Lumina still watched me in wonder.

"I saw him draining a few cups." Morvyn smirked. "He's getting into the Hydroxia spirit at last."

"Oh no, I should go look for him," I said.

"Do you need help?" Nixie asked.

"No, no. It's fine," I said, looking at her face, tracing her sharp features, trying to remember them. This would be the last time I'd ever see her.

"Let her go, Nix, I'm sure she just wants to make boring human love with Tiny Toes. Unless you're trying to join them," Morvyn joked.

"You're so obnoxious." She swatted him and let out a laugh that warmed my soul.

"I should find him and get to bed," I said.

"So early?" Lumina asked. I would miss those deep brown eyes. So thoughtful and intelligent. I wanted to convince her to tell Hylos how she really felt. That she might be afraid of what would happen, but it would be better to know his heart than not.

"Yes, I'm exhausted from the day and I'm sure Arlo is too drunk to even stand. Plus, we don't need to end the night with him finally punching Morvyn in the face."

Lumina gave a little grin. "I wouldn't mind seeing that."

"If I'm going to be verbally abused, I'll need another drink." Morvyn walked off. I wanted to grab him, hug him goodbye. But he vanished into the crowd.

My heart ached as I looked back to Lumina and Nixie. Quickly, I wrapped my arms around them both, pulling them in before they slipped away too.

"Thank you," I whispered.

"What for?" Nixie asked.

"For being my friends." My first true friends.

They both squeezed back.

"Of course, Elowyn, you were brought to us," Nixie said.

"Nymphaea brings lost souls here to be saved," Lumina added.

Tears pricked my eyes, but I blinked them away behind their backs.

"You *saved* me," I answered in a whisper.

Then I pulled away from them and went to find Arlo.

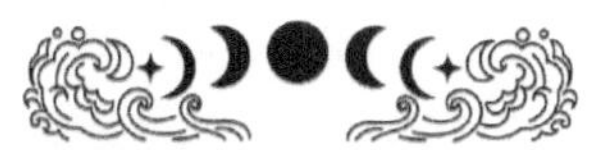

I circled the party twice, appearing to search for Arlo. But I knew exactly where he was. After my third rotation, I made my way into the connected hall. Just past Hylos's study, where he and Raylik had gone, it was a clear shot to Hylos's bedchambers. Where Arlo waited for me.

Quickly, I moved through the hallway. No Arlo in sight. Perfect. We agreed if the path was clear, he would go forward; if not, he would wait for me at the mouth of the hall.

Passing small, laughing crowds heavy with drink, I continued until they thinned out to lovers kissing in corners, too occupied to notice the direction I headed.

Hylos's voice boomed in anger. "Another fucking attack." The door to his study was ajar.

"Directly outside of Naiadon," Raylik said.

"They're closing in."

Did my father also know of Naiadon?

"Good thing our next step is an offensive maneuver," Hylos growled. "No, do not give me that look, Raylik. We attack as planned, *tomorrow*. I've told you, it is final."

"If tomorrow my mate and I face death, then I will spend it with her, not arguing with you," Raylik ground out. I had never heard Raylik speak to Hylos in such a manner.

"Go then, leave," Hylos spat. "Fuck yourself silly. Just be ready to fight tomorrow, *commander*."

"And you will remain here, with your plans?"

"What else would I do?" Hylos scoffed.

"Maybe be with the woman you love instead of hiding from the truth and chasing the past," Raylik said. Did he mean Calypstra? Or did he see what was between Hylos and Lumina too? "But you only listen to those who whisper what you wish to hear, so I shall no longer waste my breath. Good night, my *liege*," Raylik said.

Quickly, I dove behind a nearby pillar. Peeking past the marble, I saw Raylik's tense back come into view, his hands balled into fists at his sides as he walked toward the ongoing festivities.

Hylos backhanded a platter of chalices onto the ground, sending them clattering.

I wanted to beg him to reconsider. Try one last time. But it was pointless. He would hear no reason. Not from Raylik, not from me.

"Psst ..." A whisper cut through the hall. "Psst ... *Elowyn*," Arlo whispered from behind a corner.

I quickly stepped to him.

"Are you alright?" Arlo asked, his strong hand gripping my shoulder. "You look angry."

I wasn't angry; I was sad. Sad for Hylos. He was so lost. And I couldn't help him.

"I'm fine, come on, we better hurry."

Together, with purpose, we strode down the hall, the soaring doors to Hylos's room at the end left open.

"It's almost too easy," Arlo said.

We were so close. I smiled. "Or our luck is finally changing."

We entered the room that was as big as I remembered, set in tones of blue and gold. The room of the greatest siren king of all three seas. Not just Hylos, but his father before him. The room of a man who'd loved a human woman so profoundly that he created a portal between their two worlds so that she could step through and be with him every night.

"This is it," I said, ripping open the wine cellar's curtain and marching back toward the painting of Hylos's mother.

My ears strained at a small lilting that called me to the shrouded painting. Siren song, meaning magic was in its wake.

Arlo marched to my side. "Are you ready?"

"Yes," I answered, even though a part of me wasn't. This place was, in so many ways, a dream that I wanted to linger within. But I couldn't. Oakhaven needed me.

Arlo grasped a fistful of fabric and pulled it off the painting. We stepped back and looked at the woman who'd poured her heart and soul into the journal, the woman who'd loved a siren under the sea. Hylos's mother, who loved him so much she sacrificed herself for his safety.

She was beautiful, poised and waiting. She had dark black hair and was dressed in a blue gown lined with umber fur. She had two piercing blue eyes.

My heart tripped.

I *knew* those eyes.

I cocked my head to the side, waiting for my eyes to adjust or for the portrait to change. But it didn't. I stumbled back, and Arlo caught me. "What is it?"

I knew that face, from a long-distant memory frozen in ice and death.

Looking back at me, smiling softly, was my mother.

But how? There were no remaining paintings of my mother. Every mention of her was cleansed from this earth, struck out in her own blood.

Footsteps resonated through the halls. Someone was headed in our direction. Likely Hylos.

"Elowyn, we have to go, *now*," Arlo demanded. "Do you know how it works?"

I shook my head no, still stunned by the painting.

Why was my mother's portrait here? This had to be a mistake.

Arlo reached out a hand to the painting, but the textured surface of the canvas didn't yield.

"Elowyn, think. What did the journal say?"

But I couldn't think. I could only reach up to touch her. My mother. Could only reach for those eyes that looked back at me as a child the last day I saw her. Before her death. Before the world and my father discarded me.

The prayer beads glowed on my wrist, and a sound hummed in the air. Arlo clasped my hand, and in a heartbeat we were pulled into the painting.

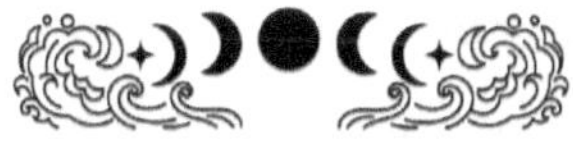

Summer 5344 AT

With Nymphaea's help, I have done it. Aegir said if you were a male, he wished to name you Hylos. It fits well with your sister's name. How gorgeous you are, dazzling with blue hair and your mama's eyes to match. The future king of the three great seas. I've spent all evening holding you, unable to look away, but soon the sun will rise and shed light on my truth, as it always has. So, I must return you to where you belong.

Be good, Hylos. Be strong. Be happy. Find your sister one day. The Guardians ordain her for greatness. I know it. As they do you, my son.

Chapter 40

Cold, black stone replaced the sleek marble of Hylos's bedroom. The whiplash of the transportation made waves of nausea churn through me. Replacing Hylos's fine wine cellar was a damp space occupied only by spiders that hung in webs in the dusty corners.

Spinning on my heel, I returned to the painting, searching for another glimpse of my mother's face, only to see a worn painting of the sea coated in dust.

"It worked!" Arlo exclaimed. "Blessed be the Guardians! It worked!" He gathered me in his arms, but I didn't embrace him back.

I was going to be sick.

"Elowyn, what's wrong?"

I'd left the last remaining family I had on this earth. The last remaining member of my family who may have actually wanted me. I left behind my *brother*. The room continued to spin. My heart was drumming in my ears. Hylos ... *Hylos* was my brother. Right there in front of me this whole time. My brother. The baby. The baby in mother's stomach. It was not just her. It was her and him. They said he died, like all the other babies before.

I was going to be sick.

"Elowyn, are you okay?"

My stomach plummeted. How? How was this possible? It hit me in waves, crashing and crashing into me. The journal. Written by my mother's own hands. I left it. I left Hylos. I left the last pieces of my mother that still sang through this world below the sea.

Hard stone cut my bare skin as I fell to my knees.

"Are you hurt?" Arlo kneeled beside me.

"That painting, it was of my ... my ... mo—"

A heavy wooden door groaned open. I was too numb to act, and Arlo grabbed me under my arms, swiftly pulling us under a nearby desk made of burled wood.

"The final attack will push the siren princeling over the edge for sure," A female's voice hissed.

"Wonderful, now go back through that damned painting, grope the little fish-man, and keep things on track. Once he has attacked, I'll finally be able to convince the king to take the threats of the sea *seriously*," another woman's voice replied. "Then we'll be free to take as many of those damned monsters as we please."

"Yes, Your Majesty."

I recognized that sickening hiss. It was Calypstra.

Arlo looked at me, fear swelling in his eyes too. Recklessly, he glanced over the desk. He needed to see whoever it was for himself, even if it meant putting us in danger. When his eyes locked onto the speakers, he rose to his feet. "Catarina?"

"Arlo," Calypstra responded, her voice softened.

"How ...? What are you doing here?" he asked, his voice cracking.

She didn't respond.

"Well, well, well. How are you, my lovely boy?" the other voice cooed in an overly motherly tone.

"I thought you ..." Arlo stammered.

"What, killed your whore lover?" the other woman said. "Well, I sure tried to. But she is just relentless. Although I hate to admit it, I've grown quite fond of her now. She's delightfully *ruthless*. Ironically enough, she would have made a lovely daughter-in-law. If only your mother listened to your pleading. Oh well, with hindsight comes clarity, I suppose."

"Arlo, I—" Calypstra started.

"Oh, you two lovebirds save it for some other time. What I want to know is how you got into the castle, my child," she continued.

Castle? We were in a castle?

Arlo didn't answer.

"Come on now, son, go ahead and answer," said the woman.

Son? That couldn't be Arlo's vile mother, could it? How was she here?

"Fine, have it your way. Cat, dear, take him to the dungeon, the deepest cellar you can find, then we'll ship him off to Whiterok tomorrow. Your brother will be so happy to see you."

Whiterok? As in Cedric's Whiterok? What the fuck was going on.

The grating sound of mismatched discordant tones chimed through the air, forcing water in a wave around Arlo, who thrashed against its grip.

"You're one of them?" Arlo yelled in fear.

Another sound clamored and Arlo flew toward the voices. The desk I hid under was dragged with him across the room, exposing me.

"Huh, this evening is just full of surprises," said the queen of Oakhaven, my father's wife. She walked until she was standing before me, her heeled shoes clicking against the hard stone. She wore an ornate traveling dress lined with gold thread and jewels. She was no longer pregnant.

"Stay away from her!" Arlo roared, still thrashing in Calypstra's watery grip.

The queen looked between Arlo and me knowingly. "Catarina said you were below the sea, Elowyn, held prisoner by that little fish prince. She was working on your demise. She did *not* tell me, however, of Arlo being with you ... But I see now you two must have formed some sort of bond below. Now for lying ..." The queen smiled back at Calypstra, wagging a finger at her and tsking. "For that she will be punished."

She looked back down at me with a false, saccharine smile, drawing a pointed thumb over my cheek. "Yes, well, I suppose we can find some use for you instead."

"Get the fuck away from her!" Arlo screamed in a guttural, pained yell.

She met his eyes and cocked her head, tossing her flaxen curls, her painted red lips cutting into a vicious smile.

"My long-lost son, I will not leave the Lady Elowyn Blackthorn alone. Finally, you've picked a suitable match. We should celebrate!" She looked back at Calypstra, who held onto her power with fear and pain welling in her eyes. "No offense, Cat."

"You're the queen's son?" I asked.

Arlo went rigid in the watery grip that burbled in the silence.

The queen was Arlo's mother.

He was not just a captain.

He was a noble.

"Oh." The queen reveled. She looked down at me, still on the ground. "He didn't tell you. How interesting. Probably because he's been running from me ever since the *incident* with his wife. He's always been like that. Avoidant. But enough chit-chat. I look forward to hearing the full story at Whiterok." The queen snapped her fingers and pointed to me.

In a breath, frigid water wrapped around me, squeezing hard.

Shoving back at the water, I screamed, "Let me go! Let me bloody go!"

"Cat, dear, a little peace and quiet, please. We don't need any looky-loos."

Calypstra nodded, and water snapped in front of my mouth, splashing up my nose. A matching form was spinning across Arlo's face too.

"Ah, much better. Well, now that we have both the lady *and* my son, we need to expedite things a bit. Catarina, I'll have a carriage for you out front in five minutes. My guards will escort these two to Whiterok, where we can deal with family matters a little more *privately*. Then, Cat, go back to that siren nest, fuck him until he can't think straight, and lead him by his emptied balls into battle."

"Yes, Your Majesty," Calypstra answered, resolute.

"And Catarina ..." The queen paused. Her yellow eyes seared. "Remember, if these two don't make it to Whiterok, if they escape by some strange coincidence, my little granddaughter will be in *grave* danger."

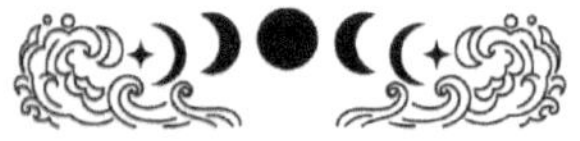

Calypstra dragged us in watered shackles to a dark alley. A horse-drawn carriage pulled up. It was made of metal with bars over its windows. Behind me rose Blackthorn Castle in shadowy stone.

Calypstra removed the water-gag from Arlo's mouth.

"Why are you doing this?" he gasped.

"Cate." She paused, her eyes searching him. "To keep her safe, I have to do as she says. Otherwise I would never do this, I love—" She looked at me, agony and jealousy burning in her black eyes.

It all made sense.

She watched us fall for one another. That look of disgust on her face whenever I neared wasn't hatred. It was jealousy.

"Ced is caring for Cate though," Arlo said.

Then it fully hit me, like the cold, hard sea that night I nearly drowned.

The queen. Cedric. Arlo. Why the sirens' disappearances seemed to point back to Whiterok, to Cedric. Cedric was behind everything, along with his mother.

"He is as much your mother's slave as I." Calypstra's tone was different now with Arlo. Softer. Sadder.

"No. He promised to keep her safe," Arlo said.

"He does, we both do. As long as we do as *she* says. This is what I was trying to avoid, because now that will include you." Calypstra, Catarina, whoever she was, stood so near Arlo it made me want to vomit.

She tried to kill me.

She killed his entire crew.

She was a monster.

But now she looked like a woman, broken before a man she ferociously loved.

Calypstra tore off a piece of fabric from the hem of the black dress she wore and brought it to Arlo's mouth.

"I watched her kill you," Arlo stammered.

"The sirens brought me back to life. But nothing could keep me from our daughter." Her voice caught painfully on the word *our*. "It wasn't long until the queen caught me visiting her. She held Cate over my head. She made me use my newfound powers to help her manipulate the young siren leader into starting a war with King Eadric. Now her trap is set."

Hylos would attack Oakhaven and fall into the queen's trap. He would give them reason to take more sirens. But for what?

They gave her another chance at life, another chance to see her daughter. Nymphaea saved her! She betrayed them all to do the queen's bidding instead of trying to stop her. Instead of fighting.

I struggled against the water over my mouth, wanting to call her every nasty word I knew. The sirens saved her.

She turned on me, hatred burning in her eyes. With a movement of her hand and a sickening clamor of song, the water around my mouth swallowed my skull. I floundered under the weight. The water forced its way into my nose and mouth, swirling in my ears.

Arlo's voice was distant and rounded. "Catarina, stop, please."

The water fell from engulfing my head and splashed around me. The cold Oakhaven wind nipped at my cheeks.

She turned back to Arlo, "I didn't know you were the captain of that ship, Arlo. Ced's kept you a secret since the day you left. If I'd known, I never would have sent the sirens to it. Even if the queen told me to." She hardened. "When I read the crew's minds, I realized they knew your true identity. The queen's son in hiding. I kept it a secret for as long as I could. Kept the other sirens away from their minds as well as yours. But Hylos, he was getting impatient, and it was only a matter of time before he sent someone else to wade through their thoughts if I kept coming up empty-handed. They would have learned who you really were. I had to—I had to kill them. To keep your identity safe."

I almost felt sorry for her.

But the look on Arlo's face was pure hatred. "You're a fucking monster."

Calypstra's mask of misery returned. She nodded affirmatively, agreeing, and worked the fabric over his mouth.

He didn't fight her, just glared as she tied it over his head.

She turned to me. "Stand up, *Princess*."

I caught my breath and spat at her black-finned feet. "I am not a *fucking* princess." She turned and slapped me hard across the face.

"You don't know how long I've wanted to do that."

My cheek burned and I gasped while staggering to my feet, but her water seized me instead, pulling me inches from her face.

Calypstra smiled, exposing her sharp canines.

"That's right. You're not a princess. You. Are. Nothing."

Through the pain and blood trickling from the corner of my mouth, I forced a smile. "Yeah well, at least I'm not a jealous fucking bitch."

Hard-faced, Calypstra tied the gag around my face tightly.

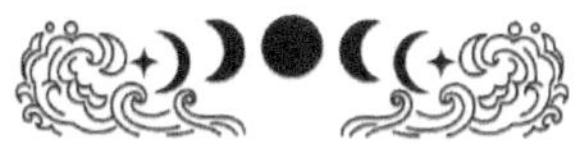

Arlo and I rattled in the carriage at a repetitive tempo that drove me mad. Both gagged and bound, we couldn't speak. But all I wanted to do was ask him question after question. An off-timed bump in the road shattered the percussive pace, slamming me into Arlo, who didn't even look at me. As if I was the liar.

But he was. I'd told him exactly who I was. I was honest, and he still deceived me. I re-thought every interaction, searching for missed signs. Each time I'd known unsaid words lingered on his lips. How he flinched at learning Cedric was my betrothed. Maybe I was a fool for not piecing it together sooner, but he was in the wrong for not telling me. The most mind-bending piece was that I, of all people, would have understood wanting to be someone else.

It wasn't long until the night's ocean breeze found us. This was the same journey I had taken what felt like a lifetime ago. Highthorn to Gyldmare, then to Whiterok. Part would be by land, the other by sea. A small hope sang through me. When we crossed the ocean, maybe the sirens would find me. Return me to what I'd abandoned. Take me back to my brother.

My gut knotted. Nymphaea brought those to the sea to be saved, and I had rejected that salvation. Fate, the Guardians, whoever, had hand-delivered me to my brother, and I left him.

The carriage stopped. Instead of a boat across the Holy Mother's body, the sight that greeted us was a burly man throwing open the carriage doors. A glow of red-orange light radiated high in the black night sky, flickering off a metal surface toward the crashing waves. It was a lighthouse. Without a word, the man hauled us out, slapped shackles on our wrists, and dragged us inside.

Chapter 41

The wind whipped the washing tides. We were so close to the sea, but bars and stone separated me from it. Hylos was out there, and he didn't even know my true identity. His sister. I should have known who he was, felt it tugging in my blood. Those eyes were so clearly my mother's. Now, he headed to slaughter. Calypstra, the viper, had laid a trap that he was about to fall right into. While I remained imprisoned.

I heard a bump in the distance, a rattling of keys. Shards of ice sank in my stomach. How many children of kings had died in towers such as this? Bothersome loose ends neatly and easily trimmed up.

A figure shifted in the shadows, and I readied myself for the worst. I would kick, and scratch, and fight like Infernum. Just like Nixie taught me. Whoever it was would have to kill me, their flesh gushing blood between my teeth. I would not submit.

Metal creaked through the night, and two figures shuffled to the barred cell door, one carrying a lighted torch.

A familiar face came into view. Cedric.

"Are you alright?" Arlo said, pushing past him.

"No, I'm not alright. I'm in a bloody prison cell," I snapped, relieved in part to see him, but miserable at his betrayal all at once.

Cedric's eyes bored into me, disgust gnarling his mouth into a frown, as if he held back bile at the mere sight of me. What treachery did he have planned for me next? Would he drag me to Whiterok? Force me to wed him?

"You know who she is, then?" Cedric asked Arlo.

"I do now," Arlo sneered, eyeing his brother. "Not some unknown wealthy woman needing safe passage to Whiterok, like you said, but the king's fucking daughter."

It stung, for some reason, the bitter way he said it.

"And you know what comes with her care," Cedric said, his dark-green eyes glowing in the flickering torchlight.

My care?

Arlo was silent.

Cedric continued, "Everything you renounced the day you sailed away on the ship I secured for you."

"What is that supposed to mean?" I said, standing.

Cedric did not look at me as he spoke. "That he has spent the last ten years fleeing from nobility, and now he wishes to be tied to it for the rest of his life."

To be tied to me.

"We will simply both flee now," Arlo said, looking at me, hope shining in his eyes.

"Is that what you *both* want?" Cedric asked.

"Just let her out already."

Cedric began working a key into the lock.

"You're letting us go?" I asked.

The lock clicked, and Cedric opened the cell door.

"Yes." He didn't even give me a second glance. Just threw the word in my direction.

"Why my ship, Ced?" Arlo asked.

"Do you love her?" Cedric said in a low, severe murmur, ignoring Arlo's question.

My heart tripped. Love? Sure, we had sex. Which was fantastic. Incredible even. We clearly enjoyed one another's company. But love? I cared for Arlo greatly, admired him fiercely. At least I did, before his deceit. But I only knew a fraction of him. Which was so abundantly clear now, in the face of learning his true identity.

"What?" Arlo stammered.

"Do. You. Love. Her?" Cedric repeated.

"I asked you a question first. Why my damned ship? Why send her to yourself on my ship?" Arlo demanded.

Cedric whirled on him quickly, clutching him by the arm and slamming him hard into the stone wall.

Arlo was taller, larger even, but Cedric was clearly much stronger.

"Why do you think?" he hissed.

Arlo stood stunned, eyes racing across his brother's face. Understanding that I lacked washed over him.

"Exactly. So you better be sure that *this* is what you want. Once you take on this responsibility, there's no forsaking it. Because if you do, I swear, brother, I will hunt you down and kill you myself."

A chill ran down my spine. Cedric meant every word of whatever nonsense he was spewing.

I marched out of the cell and wedged myself between him and Arlo; he was so needlessly barbarous.

"It does not matter if he loves me or not. We care for one another. That is enough."

Cedric looked down at me. His visage was prettier than Arlo's; pale and smooth from years spent lurking in the shadows of court. But a slew of feelings twisted his pretty features. Was it disgust? Or was hatred tightening his strong, rounded jaw?

Finally, he ripped his emerald gaze from me as Arlo spoke.

"Did you know?" His voice cracked. "That Catarina was alive? That my *wife*—"

It hurt. Hearing him say it. The pain he must be in. Angry with him or not, I felt for him. His world had been flipped upside down. As had mine.

Cedric's lip twitched in a grimace. "I knew, but she's not the same girl I watched you marry in the forest in secret. She's a—"

"Monster," Arlo said for him.

A single tear traced a path down Arlo's cheek, navigating past the rugged whiskers cultivated in Naiadon. He'd spent the past few weeks in the same castle as her.

Arlo cuffed that sadness away.

"The queen made her into the monster she is now. As she will make both of you, if you do not flee this instant," Cedric said swiftly.

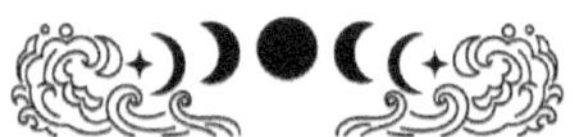

"I have a skiff waiting for you," Cedric called ahead of us, his voice hardly audible over the crushing waves roaring louder as we descended stone step after stone step. "From there, if you hug the coast south, you will find my men. They will collect you, and by tomorrow evening, you'll be out of the country."

But then what? Anonymity? There was so much left to fix. The sirens, the war, protecting the people of Oakhaven and my brother. We were winding down the steps too fast, whirling toward an uncertain future. Then I heard it. Siren song.

Arlo and Cedric continued ahead, but I stopped and turned to the sound, drawn to it like a moth to flame.

The song was a vision calling to me. The vision and song I already knew. I was a part of it once. Each note inscribed upon my heart.

The song of a woman with eyes like the ocean who loved the king of the sea.

"Don't go in there," Cedric cautioned, but he sounded lifetimes away and my hand was already on the sea-sprayed door, pushing it open.

I stepped into the dimly lit, damp room. At its center was a large vessel filled with water, its blown glass warped and rippled, distorting the view, but inside I could make out a figure suspended.

Slowly, I approached it. The song grew. The vision became clearer. I leaned closer, pressing my forehead against the cool glass, needing to discern the person within.

But deep down, I already knew who was inside.

"Clare? My love, Clare, is that you?"

A siren man with a long, scraggly, gray beard and suspended gray locks rushed into view, and his song slammed into my soul.

I could feel my heart crushing under the weight of his words.

He called for my mother.

"No, I am not Clare," I said out loud, my voice breaking.

His song flooded my senses in fast and frantic drumbeats that felt flat and dull. As if aged and worn from time and suffering.

"Little princess," he said through his ancient, tired song.

Tears were blurring him. I nodded my head.

"Yes, it's *me*," I whispered.

"She told me so much of you, sweet little Elowyn. I begged her to take you to Naiadon to save you both. But she knew your destiny, your greatness. She knew that one day you would be queen."

His music painted gossamer colors in my mind, the story in the journal coming to life, but this time through Aegir's eyes. My mother, a young woman with raven hair dancing in a tavern. Her laughter unrestrained. Her warm smile aglow in the tavern's candlelight.

They walked the beach, and the ocean echoed in her eyes. Aegir knew a queen stood before him. A low, bitter note intertwined with the imagery. Because destiny ensured she did in fact become a queen, but never his.

Bruises blued her pale flesh. Her smile dimmed, but the crashing sea never faded from her eyes as she met Aegir each night, even as her belly grew. Aegir's hand pressed to her stomach, pure joy flooding through him as he felt a baby kick. The powerful sound of nature radiating from within. My song. The one I heard under the sea with Hylos.

Naiadon projected into my mind. They walked in the glade, smiling at the birds. They sat by the hearth in the study, reading books and drinking from warm mugs, as Hylos and I had once. They swam through the sea on the backs of the sea horses, and the smile of the young woman in the tavern persisted across my mother's face when she was with Aegir. A smile I never knew. Not until now.

Then a discordant harmony shivered down my spine. Mother was older. The same as I remembered her last, again with child. Every dawn Aegir watched the two beings he loved most in this world pass through the opening, into danger. Until one day, only Hylos arrived below her portrait, the ocean echoing in his eyes.

I knew her fate. Executed on Highthorn's steps for betraying the king. But now I knew her crime. Loving another man and giving birth to his child. Tears streamed down my face in rivers of bittersweet pain. Aegir gave her life purpose, and for that, my father sentenced her to death. Executed for daring to find joy.

Aegir searched for her. Even though he knew in his heart that she was gone. Even when he heard it from the foul mouth of a peasant, a rotten-toothed smile gleefully declaring the death of the Highthorn Whore. But he didn't give up. He needed to return her body to where it belonged. To allow her to finally rest in the sea.

After years of searching, he went desperately into the lion's den; Highthorn Castle. Where he was captured, but not by my father. No, it was a courtier who stumbled upon him, keen enough to know his power. A woman with eyes like a hawk's. *Jessal.* She tricked him with promises of being united with my mother. Foolishly, he believed her. Then she captured him. With time, the courtier became the new queen of Oakhaven, taking my mother's place, all while using Aegir's power.

Black shapes passed through the warped glass, the figures bending over a massive object beside him. Then torturous pain clawed at his skin, but I felt as if his skin was my own. The pain twisted the threads of his song, inverting his lulling notes into something darker. I felt the split as fragments of him were pulled away, siphoned into the waiting vessel.

When they left him, he was weak and hollow, abandoned in the dark until the full moon swelled and restored his strength again. Then they returned, and the ritual repeated: carve into his song, rip it from him, and feed it to the object that Aegir showed me. It looked like a pipe organ, but with markings like those on the obelisks in the Womb of Nymphaea. Did it work like the structure? Taking song and echoing it somehow?

Five long years of this—five years of his song being turned against his people. Because they used it to capture them. Agony sank Aegir to unfathomable depths of despair. He watched sirens arrive with songs strong and defiant, only to hear them falter, fade, and fall silent over time before they vanished, replaced by others. He knew their magic was being drained, but the method was unclear to him from his prison. What was the point of it all? Why were they doing this? It remained an unanswered question that gnawed at what remained of his mind.

Nymphaea take my power, please. Aegir's prayer surfed on his song. A prayer he made every minute of every hour. Repeatedly driving him mad. But the Holy Mother did not answer his prayers. He kept his power. He charged the mysterious object against his will. And they captured his people.

The song's vision ripped from my mind, slamming me back to the present. Back to the prison I stood before now. "*I hear your mother,*" Ageir's song flooded into my mind. "*I hear her song blended into your own. The song of my queen.*"

"Get away from there!" Cedric shouted, and pulled me back hard, breaking the spell. Aegir looked at him, anger marking his worn features. "*Do not trust him, Princess. He helped her. Never trust him. Defend your land with Hylos by sea. Take the crown. That is what your mother wanted.*"

"What have you done to him?" I looked up at Cedric, tears streaming down my face. He dragged me, his hand gripping my arm hard as a vise. I slammed my fist into his back. Hard as Nixie taught me, muscle memory centering me in the stance she made me repeat. Cedric stopped, stunned.

He turned to me, letting go.

"It's the only way to help our people."

"He *is* a person, Cedric." My voice shattered.

Cedric's heavy gaze searched me, something skulking in the thickets of his eyes.

Then we heard it, boots clacking down the steps. Guards were coming.

"Elowyn," Arlo called from the hall, "we have to go. Now."

My stomach sank and twisted. How was I to leave? To allow this to continue? To allow the people who showed me love and beauty and respect to suffer at the hands of the crown.

To allow my father to continue to inflict suffering on so many. I was leaving them all behind to fend for themselves.

"*Go, little princess. Find your brother*," Aegir sang on the end of a single note, weak and fading.

And from my heart, with my song, I sang back to Aegir, "*I already have*."

CHAPTER 42

On the silent sea, in the boat only big enough for two, Arlo paddled along the coast as Cedric had directed us to. North. Toward Thornley. The stars were shrouded behind cloud cover. How much longer until daybreak shined down and Hylos attacked?

If I could talk to him, send him a message or something. Anything. Maybe I could stop this.

"Find your brother." Aegir's words swam through my soul, to my heart, as my fingertips traced my mother's prayer beads on my wrist.

If Hylos knew I was his sister, that he was right all along, that our paths had been intertwined since birth, then maybe the tides of destiny could change. We could save Aegir now that I knew where he was. I could warn him of the trap Calypstra had set, ready to ensnare him. This war could be stopped.

"I need to get back to Naiadon," I said, my heart frenzied in my chest.

Arlo only rowed on, and on, and on. He said nothing.

"Arlo?" I pushed. But still nothing.

The bastard. He thought he could avoid me for the rest of my life?

"Fucking talk to me!" I screamed.

"And say what?" he snapped. "That I didn't have the stomach to be like Ced? For courtier life, like the pathetic weakling I am? That I abandoned my duty to hide at sea? Trading everything to captain a fucking cargo ship? That I abandoned my daughter for—" His voice broke, then faded to a bitter whisper. "All because I was too spineless. I gave up everything ... only to go fuck the king's daughter."

The last sentence was a sword crunching past my sternum straight into my heart, leaving a gash gaping and vulnerable.

That was all I was?

Not a friend.

Not a partner.

But a fuck.

"You could have trusted me," I stammered, staggering from the blow. "As I trusted you."

"I cannot trust anyone!" he shouted.

Tears burned, threatening to fall, but I wouldn't let them. Not now. Not for him.

"I can't do this," I said, realizing it. "I cannot leave everything behind." I stood, rocking the boat with the movement, the sea stretching infinitely before me. Land, a distant dream, behind.

"Elowyn. Don't be a fool. Sit down," he said, stern but fear-laced. His honey eyes no longer beamed at me, obscured by this endless night. But that allowed me to see everything clearly.

I could not leave my birthright behind. Could not hide away and pretend like nothing was happening. All for what? What truly waited on the other side of this boat ride? A relationship with Arlo? Maybe it would have been enough if I was the woman I was before. But I knew the truth now. It was whistling through my bones.

I had to help the sirens. To help Oakhaven. Not flee.

"Elowyn, *please*."

But I ignored Arlo's plea and jumped into the sea.

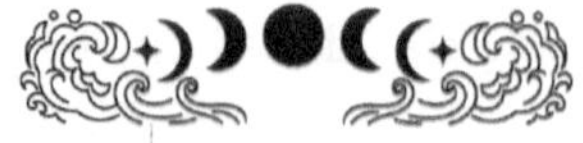

Deeper I swam, with everything in me. The world above was muted and distant. The familiar glow of my bracelet haloed me, warming the water. The strange feeling of being able to breathe the harsh salt water set in uncomfortably.

I would swim to Naiadon if I had to.

A prayer passed through my mind, for Hylos, Nixie, Raylik, Lumina. Guardians, I would even take Morvyn right now. Any of my friends to help me. Infernum, I'd try my luck with a random siren if I had to, and explain who my brother was, invoking the fear of Hylos's name.

My muscles fought against the buoying of my body, the ocean rejecting me, trying to return me to where I belonged. But I would not accept it. I wouldn't go back, not without my family. Nor without knowing my brother was safe.

Nymphaea brings those to the sea to be saved. How many times had they told me that in Naiadon? And I needed saving. But perhaps it wasn't clear enough.

Maybe mortal turmoil was needed to be saved by the sirens. By Nymphaea's children. It was a dark thought, but I was desperate.

The prayer bracelet, the only token of my mother remaining, embraced me. Protecting me from this foreign environment's effects on my body.

The siren saved those near death. As they saved Lumina.

Unclasping the bracelet that still glowed with its sanctuary around me, I dropped it into the void.

Slowly it sank, taking its aura with it.

The cold hit me first. Then the need for air. I trudged deeper, swimming hard into the depths of the sea. That way there was no chance to return. I would die trying to get back to Naiadon.

Panic set in, but I ignored it. My heart raced in my chest, but I only listened to its beat. Its tempo. It slowed and slowed. The burn in my body, desperate for air. To the beat of my heart's slowing cadence, I tried to find my music on the wingspan of wild-crafted song, to call any siren in the sea nearby.

Find me. Save me.

Right as my vision faded, I heard it, a myriad of voices formed into a singular musical composition, resonating on rays of white light that rang proudly.

Oh child, how many times must I save you? The light engulfed me in a sphere of warmth. The ability to breathe returned, just as it had with the prayer beads.

A giant forefinger reached for the orb I was in, as if I was within a marble, and plucked me, bringing me up to its owner's face. I stared up in utter reverence, frozen in unthinkable fear and joy. Guardian of the ocean. Holy Mother of the sea. Nymphaea herself stared back at me. Holy shit, she was real.

Tendrils of white-gold hair danced above her head as she stared back at me through blinding white eyes like beams of starlight. It was as if she was made from starlight. She was glorious, and I could have looked upon her in awe for centuries.

But I was running out of time.

So, I thought in song—a minor mode with a slow, measured tempo. The notes played, and my fingers moved as I envisioned the music as it would fly from a virginal, like birds through the trees.

I need to stop Hylos. Please help me.

You wish to save your brother, she proclaimed, hearing me.

Thank the bloody Guard—well, thank her!

You also wish to save your people too. Her words echoed through her rhapsodic melody. *But the only thing I may offer you, my child, is the gift of the sea. But with it comes sacrifice.*

Her music blared as a dream unfolded before me, revealing a man with dark hair—it must have been Arlo—and myself walking through the countryside, hand in hand. A small red-headed child toddled in front of us.

The vision glittered in gold and green. The sun was setting, lighting that easy life ablaze, like Arlo's warm eyes when they were on me below the sea. Resplendent and heart-shatteringly beautiful.

But it would be a life built on lies.

I was almost shocked at how easy it was to say, *I forsake it all.*

It was a beautiful dream. A lovely thought. But it was never meant for me.

As you wish, child. I shall make you in my image.

My body exploded into song, tearing me apart at the seams, eclipsing the sweet, simple melody of what the future could hold, a song of deep glory and strength replacing it.

Nymphaea's song shifted, the tempo lifting and racing toward me, a war cry edged on the crown of her music.

No, I would never be a mother, nor a wife, nor no one at all. That was not my fate. My people awaited a ruler. It was as clear and bright as Nymphaea staring back at me in the sea. That was my destiny. That was my birthright. I would lift them past rags and cold, give them a brighter future in place of mine. I would sacrifice the love of any man, even Arlo. Even my father. For Oakhaven.

Nymphaea's sound charged louder, faster, toward me.

I answer not only your prayer, child, but that of Aegir, to take his power and gift it to you, daughter of Queen Clare, his soul-tied.

Drums warred, no longer flat but strong and proud as they barreled into me, the power of all the sea's might with them.

I was not a forgotten, title-less princess. No. I was Elowyn Blackthorn. Destined to save my people and protect all that my father abandoned, including myself.

The incessant blows of song pushed me deeper and deeper into the sea until my back pressed against the silty sea floor. The music blared at its pinnacle, remaking my heart and soul, blaring for my destiny, for that little girl abandoned by her father who had killed her mother. Trumpeting for all the people left in the cold by that same man who swore to protect them. Clamoring for the sirens in the sea, taken.

My eyes flew open. The surrounding water was mine to control, made of pure music, so I played it like the virginal—hard, fast, and with un-shackled passion. The only way I knew how.

I propelled through the water, faster, faster, faster. The salt rushing past me shredded away my flesh, filing away the old and honing me anew.

In the distance, deep from within the earth's soil, something stirred. Angrily rumbling like a bear's growl. But I did not care. Whatever it was would wait.

Finally, I broke the water's surface, reborn a siren.

Chapter 43

The sun blazed, the sky pink and orange, breaking through the clouded night, a reminder of time slipping by, time that could not be spared.

Oakhaven glittered to life across the water as the people on the coast of Gyldmare awoke to daybreak. I needed to make it to Thornley, which was far by boat, but not for me. Focusing my mind, I willed the water with music. It was challenging at first, like when I was learning to play the virginal and my fingers felt fat and clumsy. But power was there, right at my fingertips, singing through my veins. The water became an extension of my body, a conduit moving me toward Thornley, where Hylos planned to strike.

In a bay, anchored in the water, I waited. The world was nearly overwhelming. Countless compositions vibrated through the sea, swirling around and through me. The ocean and its song were part of me. The small birdsong I'd once heard echoing back under the sea now emanated from within me, as much my own as the sound of my voice.

But somewhere, nearing, an unmistakable melody boomed loudly, heading my way. That same deep rumbling I'd often heard in Naiadon I now felt in my bones. Powerful. Brave. *Impatient.* Hylos.

He and his army were barreling toward Oakhaven, the crash impending, and I was the only thing standing in the way. I steeled myself, ready to speak with Hylos. Not sure what I would do if he didn't agree to put down his arms. Unsure if I was ready, or capable of fighting him.

One by one, sea steeds emerged, each carrying an armed siren rider. There were hundreds of them. Some in pale moon-white, others in Mariscal Circle red, many even in black. The other leaders made good on their word. Hylos had his army.

Finally, he emerged at the forefront, donning the blue of his Circle and standing in a white-shelled chariot guided by two slick white sea beasts. Anticipation vibrated at my fingertips. I concentrated that feeling and turned it to song, to power that radiated from my heart and mind into water that lifted me across the sea's surface.

Stop! I called, desperation wielding the siren song, forcing it to blast the word from my chest on intense galloping notes to Hylos. The army came to a halting stop. Hundreds upon hundreds of steeds reared and huffed in the water, eager to move forward. Their riders brandished swords and spears, ready to fight at their leader's command.

Hylos propelled himself from his chariot through the water, closing the space between us with astounding speed.

But when he finally laid eyes on me, confusion flashed across his face.

"Elowyn?" Realization washed over him. "Your hair? Your skin?"

I didn't even think about it. What I looked like in my new form.

I didn't care.

"It's blue," he whispered.

I grabbed a lock of hair; it was deep navy, like his, with red strands intertwined with the blue. A combination of fire and sea.

I looked down to my hands, washed in pale blue, just as Hylos's skin was, all the way to the sapphire fins, long and slender, that had replaced my feet.

"All ordained, just as you said, *brother*."

The army below murmured and shifted uncomfortably at my words.

Hylos shook his head, a concise no. "That's impossible."

"Your mother is Clare Adele. She was my mother too," I answered, wanting to wrap him in a hug. "And I found Aegir."

His eyes lit with questions. I wanted to sit with him and answer every single one over a drink in his study. Away from the armies and mistakes that edged the air.

"Where is he?" he demanded.

"I'll tell you everything, I promise. We just need to leave here and—"

"Tell me now!" he roared, the sound of thunder crackling with his words. A strange power emanated from him, making my knees wobble. The power of a siren king. His eyes fell atop my head.

"That crown, where did you get that?" My hand followed his gaze to be poked by a small metal crown. Had it been there this whole time?

"That is my father's crown. It is the source of his power." Choler flared in his eyes.

"Nymphaea said Aegir offered me his power. I wasn't sure what it meant."

The words caught like wildfire across the army.

Nymphaea.

Aegir.

Power.

"No, he wouldn't give you his powers. The only way for a siren to give their power is ... is to give their life. My father, he ... he would never do that. He would never leave me ... not without saying goodbye." His voice broke and tears welled in his eyes, but he still held that same look of wrath.

I hadn't known the weight of Aegir's sacrifice.

My chest tightened.

His prayers were finally answered. Hopefully Aegir was at peace now.

"Hylos, I will tell you everything, I swear it. But we must take the army and leave. This is a trap. Calypstra has betrayed you. She's working with Queen Jessal and they know you're attacking here. It's all a trap to capture you and use you—"

"Get out of my way," he growled, and underneath those words that strange power emitted again from him. It threatened to bend my will, urging my body to obey and bow to Hylos, King of the Three Great Seas. Now officially, with the death of his father.

He turned his back to me, the water propelling him to his armies, to his war.

"*No!*" I yelled with a song that thundered against that strange force he was pushing against me.

He whipped his head around, fear flooding his eyes. He pushed another stronger surge of that commanding power toward me, but I only pushed back against it.

Gritting my teeth, I strained, saying, "If you continue forward, I will stop you!" I warned.

The great force stilled, and Hylos's lips curved into a vicious smile.

"Elowyn, there is only one of you." His hand directed my attention to the army behind him. "And thousands of us."

"You will not harm my people," I answered through clenched teeth.

"Ha! Go to your *people* looking like that and see how long you live. Humans are not kind to what they do not know, Elowyn. And they take as they please. That is exactly why we must retaliate against them. So they will stop, once and for all." That power radiated from him again, but not at me. I could feel it race toward his forces, marching them forward without a single word passing his lips.

Behind me, on shore, a clamor of human voices murmured, noticing the approaching figures on the sea's horizon. They were so astoundingly far away, small specks collecting on the beach, and yet I could hear them. Dull tones and songs that rattled to us. Humble and small. But there were many of them.

"Hylos," I called urgently. "Remember what I told you of Thornley. What Lumina told you of it too. It is mostly uninhabited. But do you hear that?"

He paused, listening.

"Those are people, many of them. Far more than there should be. That is an army, Hylos, waiting. Because they knew all along exactly where you would strike. Because Calypstra told them. Please, don't do this."

He looked back at me.

With bated breath, I waited.

"If there is an army, we will cut it down," he seethed. Then Hylos continued. His army marched onward, toward the shore.

My nails cut into my palms. Power, I could feel it hammering in my soul, slamming into my bones. I reached inside for that force Hylos had, because it radiated from me now too, on the beat of regal drums. The power of a ruler. The power of a king. The power of Aegir.

Reaching out like a steady hand, I pushed on Hylos's forces. They halted under my power. Somehow, I was stopping them. Controlling them.

Hylos whirled to me. "How are you doing that?"

"Would you just bloody listen to me. Plea—"

With a flick of Hylos's wrist and a single percussive beat, a wave slammed into me, sending me flailing across the expanse of sea and slapping hard into the water.

My bones clacked from my impact on the plane of ocean, as hard as stone. My legs tumbled over my head. Deep, I was so unthinkably deep in the ocean. Every bare ounce of my flesh burned from the smack of the impact.

Guardians, Hylos was so unthinkably strong.

But I had to stop him.

Trudging through the water, I swam back to the surface. In the distance, Hylos's army was now progressing toward the city. The siege was fully underway.

Then I saw them, turning a corner across the bay. Large naval ships raced out to meet the incoming forces. Ready for them. Just as I warned Hylos they would be.

None of this needed to happen. No blood needed to be shed. Not today.

Ships and sirens clashed as hard shards of water pierced sails and cannons exploded, sending projectiles smashing into the sea.

The battle began.

Closer, I had to get closer. Hylos had sent me so far from the carnage that the ships and arms of catapults atop them looked like playthings in the distance as they sent deadly projectiles arching through the air, colliding with siren bodies.

Focusing my mind, I willed the water with music, moving me forward. The water rushed past me as I played it, commanded it, far faster than before.

Soon, the shouts of fierce siren warriors harmonized with my melody.

Dodging arrows and firepots that sizzled when they collided with the sea, I waded through the chaotic army for my brother.

Thwack. A siren, handsome with dark-red skin, locked wide eyes with me. An arrow protruded from his crimson chest. His death stare was hopeless and gaping. Blood the color of his flesh dribbled down from the wound and encircled him in the water.

His sea-mount reared, throwing him off its back with a shrill cry. The siren sank, motionless, disappearing into the sea, his song fading with him. Gone before his time.

"Elowyn?" Raylik's familiar voice boomed. With one hand, he wrangled the fallen soldier's mount. "What are you doing here?"

"This is a trap," I said, breath ragged. "I found Aegir, and those behind the sirens' disappearance." There was so much to tell him but no time.

His eyes traced the blue of my hair and skin. Understanding altered his expression. "They shouldn't have been this prepared to fight us. Not yet." He pulled the sea beast toward me. "You need to speak with Hylos. Get on."

In one swift movement, I mounted.

He pointed east, toward the sun rising over the carnage. "Hylos is there."

"It was Calypstra, she arranged all of this," I said over the roar of battle.

Raylik shook his head in a disbelieving no, but said, "We should have known."

A cannonball whistled between us, slamming into another siren, unnaturally indenting her chest in blood and gore. Her body was propelled into three others behind her.

"Hurry, Elowyn," Raylik shouted, then raced toward the impact we had both just witnessed.

Which way, my rider? the creature sang.

It startled me, but quickly I sang back, *To the siren king.*

The sea beast chuffed and raced through the water. I leaned left, then right, weaving through sirens fighting and dying.

Then a familiar ship caught my eye. Black and blood-red sails in the distance. The ship that had stunned Hylos. The ship that could lull sirens.

No. No. *No.*

They all would be rendered incapacitated in mere moments.

Faster please, we must get to him. The beast let out a nicker and doubled its speed, my hair whipping around me in tendrils of red and blue.

Men and women fell around me from the ships above as sirens threw spears through the salted air that shattered armor and crunched bones. The air was heavy with the scent of iron from the blood that tinted the sea.

Then I saw Hylos, still in his chariot. He waved his hands, guiding orbs of water that raced above his army and shot into the sails. Ships were engulfed in his wake.

He turned his head to me as if he'd heard me coming, those hard, sapphire-blue eyes cutting into me.

His song roared on drumrolls, *What are you doing here?*

That ship headed toward us, it's the same that almost took you. Hylos, they are coming for you. Your army will be lulled and taken, I sang back.

His eyes scanned the horizon until he spotted the sails.

With a steady hand and his power, he willed a large swell to rise. It grew and grew and rushed toward the ships. Then with another push, it toppled over, swallowing three ships whole before us.

Move onward! Hylos commanded his army. It obeyed, progressing toward land. An arrow whizzed past my head.

The steed below me reared, crying, *Careful, rider.*

But there was no time for care.

I watched Hylos, his face stern and without mercy, eyeing his target. Land.

There had to be something I could do. Some way to stop this. I had all this power coursing through me, yet knew so little about how it truly worked beyond natural inclination.

"Holy Mother, please help me," I prayed to Nymphaea, who had taken me this far. "*Please*. I cannot do this alone," I begged.

The battle raged on all around me. It was too big. Too great. I could not stop it. Not alone.

But then a song grew inside me, unfurling in my chest. No. From my chest. I listened to it carefully and soon it grew. *Elowyn Blackthorn.* The voice bellowed through me, *You are a queen!*

It was unmistakably my mother's voice, but sharpened within my own. But how?

Then, another woman's voice joined her. I'd never heard it before, but the very marrow in my bones knew it to be my mother's mother, a woman lost to history altogether, whose name I shared.

Another woman shouted on with her, and it was her mother, who also bore the name Elowyn. Then her mother, and her mother, and hers rang true. A chorus of Elowyns wailed and cried and sang across time and space, demanding to be heard. To be known. To be recognized.

How? I asked the calling song. *How can I hear you, Mother?*

Music carries through centuries. Sung into the ears of babes. Hummed as one passes you in the street. It surrounds you. It is you. We are always singing to you, my love, but in this form, you can finally hear us clearly, and we sing to give you strength for what is to come.

Alongside them, I led our battle cry. The power of their hearts and minds saturated me. And Nymphaea, the great Mother of all, cried with us too. Cried for her children discarded, damaged, and forgotten in the sea. For the women whispering prayers promising brighter tomorrows.

The women who sacrificed blood, sweat, and tears for the future. Silently suffering, as my mother did, to ensure their children were safe.

You are not alone, Elowyn, Mother said. *For you carry us all within your heart.*

Another cannonball blazed through the sky, sizzling toward me in flaming red, but a shield of blinding white and water surrounded me. That song. I knew it. It was pestering and playful. Protecting me.

Thank you. I sent the song like a prayer to my moon-white friend.

Here to please, Princess. Down below was Morvyn, conjuring the structure protecting me as it clamored in a tricky falsetto.

Now stop this, he said.

I would.

Higher, higher, higher I rose on a jet of water as around me, song and vision took over, hand over hand, replacing Morvyn's protection. The careful palms of the women who made me stood, encircling me hand in hand, in protection.

Together they raised their voices to the sky, and it burst into a swell of red around me, filled with their power, my power. Our power.

Louder. Louder. Louder. Our chorus sang, audible to all who touched our lives. But it also sang back at all who tried to erase us, discredit us. All who dared forget us. They could no longer ignore our voices, our existence. For together, it was so strong.

The dome of song and love that shielded me exploded, throwing Hylos and his soldiers behind me. Hylos's power, like a fist, beat against it, but my song held true. *Our* song held true.

He needs to be farther away, child. My mother's voice, clear as a crisp spring day, spoke. It was the most beautiful sound in all the world. I pushed back on that angry fist of Hylos's strength, forcing him and his army farther and farther away until he was a whisper on the ocean's salty breath.

Safe. I saved my brother. Just as my mother wanted.

Hylos, she wants me to tell you ... and her song and mine intertwined like jasmine spiraling up an arbor as we both said, *You may be happy.*

Although Hylos was far away, a speck on the infinite sea, I felt his thrashing stop.

His pain stop.

Because he could hear our mother's song. He could feel her there, with me.

So he sang back, *I will try.*

A piercing sound overwhelmed my senses with a scorching, wild tone. Panic set in. My mother's song shattered, choked by that deathly toll.

The queen's ship was directly below me. I hadn't even noticed, too preoccupied with trying to get Hylos to safety.

I tried to fight against it, thrashing in the air, but I couldn't; it was too powerful, too loud. The surrounding swell that was protecting me dissipated, dropping me from the sky. The sea was racing into view.

That horrible noise shrieked again, bursting my eardrums.

Then my world turned black.

Chapter 44

Arlo

Witnessing Elowyn dive into the ocean was painful, but seeing my brother cradle her, gaze at her in a way he had never looked at anyone, was *excruciating*.

She looked far paler than her usual blushing tone. Even her freckles had faded. She was limp and unresponsive. Sunlight streamed through the rocky, narrow slits of windows, casting shifting patterns of light and shadow on the rough stone walls as I hastened to Cedric. For one moment, his eyes met mine, then he darted around a corner and disappeared behind it, taking Elowyn with him.

I followed him into the sunlit chamber. I would have been relieved that he'd found her, praising his name to all four Guardians, if it wasn't for the worried look my brother was trying to conceal.

"What's wrong with her?" I demanded. But he was silent. The ocean waves lapped at the shoreline in the distance, the smell of seawater on the breeze that blew in through the open window, making the sun-leached shutters knock.

He tried to *marry* her.

He put her on *my* ship.

Then the sirens took us.

And I fell for her. Elowyn Blackthorn. The king's only daughter.

Fate is a cruel cunt.

Cedric was always power-hungry, thinking if he obtained enough, he could outrank Jessal and change the trajectory of her path. Help people. He was good-hearted like that, in a deranged way. He wanted to help poor souls out of poverty and starvation. Even if it meant doing terrible things. But it was a fool's errand. People would always starve. Always freeze. Always die. And from atop a damned ivory tower, you couldn't do shit for them.

But on the sea, I helped my men. Gave them work and purpose. Yet once again, the games of rulers took the lives of the ordinary.

This time though, it was done by the woman I loved. No, the woman I once loved. Long ago. When she was all woman and no beast. Catarina. But now the sirens called her Calypstra.

I shook her from my mind. Dark circles hung under Cedric's eyes. His black hair was disheveled. When did he last sleep? What kept him up each night? I wondered only for a second, my question answered by who he trained his gaze upon. Elowyn.

He cared for her. No, he loved her. I knew it.

How ironic it was that despite his hard exterior, my brother was ridiculously tenderhearted. He kept that hidden, like many things, deep in his chest behind a black iron ribcage. I always worried that burying that blossom of compassion so deep inside himself meant suffocating it. I feared that one day it would finally cease to exist at all.

What part of his soul had already died in this mad quest for power? He was smothering his own humanity by slithering through court, all while being trampled on by aristocracy. Destroying himself in search of brighter days that did not exist.

He looked up at me, absolutely ruined.

She would be his undoing.

"How long has she been asleep?" I asked.

"They found her floating in the middle of a bay," Cedric said in his terse, direct way. Tempered so as not to allow a single hint of emotion seep into a syllable unless he put it there. But I knew him all too well. He was hiding more from me.

"How long?" I ground out through clenched teeth.

"She's been like this for three days," he said, eyes never leaving her.

I took her from his arms. The sight of him holding her so carefully was making my stomach churn. She was not a delicate, fragile thing; she was strong. Resilient. Tall. Proud. Her expansive hips and long legs poured out of my arms.

The legs that had been my salvation when they wrapped around me under the sea, bringing me back to life when I had lost everything. My crew, my men, my sanity. All taken by those damned sirens.

I would make them pay, those beasts. For a moment, all those thoughts vanished when she was safe in my arms. And I hated myself for that relief.

Fuck. She might be my undoing, too.

Her skin, warm against mine, sent waves of pleasure through me, her familiar scent of rosewater slamming into my senses. I never thought I'd see her again. When she leaped into the sea, I wanted to dive in after her. Follow her into the abyss. But when the strange lights came and sank out of sight, I knew the sirens had found her. So I turned around and went to the one man relentless enough to find her. Cedric.

Having her back felt like a gift from the Guardians, a blessing I would be grateful for the rest of my life. And a curse. All the same, my shoulders dipped in relief as I held her. Her breath against my neck, the faint whisper of her heartbeat against my chest, all proof that she was safe, in my arms again. I cared so deeply for her. She had saved me. Kept me sane. Showed me I was capable of cracking open my chest and allowing another to witness my scarred heart.

"How did she survive jumping into the ocean?" Cedric asked, too calmly, as he latched his now vacant hands behind his back.

"Her prayer beads, they hold some type of power—"

"How?" he asked concisely, not giving me a breath to spare. "We found her miles away from where you said she jumped. How, Arlo?" He countered like we were playing fucking chess.

"I don't know, and I don't care. I'm just happy she's alive."

The look in my brother's eyes told me he was too, and that turned my stomach. We had both fallen for the same woman, like the idiots we were.

"These are not the clothes she left in," I said, laying her carefully on the cot in the light-house's room beside the sea. Below, in the cells, we were once prisoners. Not anymore. Jessal was scheming again, so Elowyn and I would remain physically free as long as we followed her commands.

Elowyn's red hair tumbled in fiery runnels around her. Wild, wicked, fool.

With a forefinger, I moved an insubordinate curl from her face and tucked it behind her ear, but the curl sprang back into place. The very embodiment of Elowyn. Rebellious. Unpredictable. Fucking stubborn. Just like those breathtaking curls. Like the day I was tasked with transporting her to my brother's island and she cursed like a sailor at the thought of being locked behind a door.

A stupid smile tugged on my lips. Guardians above, I fell for her then. Wanted to keep her there, locked forever. To be behind that door with her. To get lost in her curls, her hips, her legs. To be burned by the blaze that emitted from her amber eyes, her scalding temper and ferocious wit.

But I'd loved a woman before with that same fire in her soul. My *mother* had killed her for it. And loving another woman was something I had resolved to never do again after Cat.

"Lady's maids changed her into something more suitable," he said, pulling me from my thoughts. "What she wore before was unbecoming," he added, knowing the jealous bitter thoughts that circled my mind. Jealous of my brother. Because I knew just how deeply the man loved. Once you were in his heart, you were never free.

"Good." I met his green-eyed stare laden with his own envy. Because Elowyn hated him and cared for me. Just one more thing I'd taken from my brother.

My whole life, I'd fallen under that green gaze that resented my freedom, my ability to evade Jessal's clutches and resist falling into her schemes. Yet it was he who shielded me, he who allowed me that freedom, protecting me from Jessal's schemes by taking them on himself.

He who helped me marry Cat when we were still baby-faced. He who gave me my ship and allowed me to flee when Jessal had Cat killed before my eyes. He who cared for the daughter I could not bear to look at because she looked too much like the woman I loved and lost.

And it would be he who let me have Elowyn, all while loving us both endlessly and resenting us in the same heartbeat.

"Tell me everything you know," Cedric said tightly.

"I've told you all I know. It's your turn to talk, you fucking bastard." Because that's what we truly were. Children Jessal found to keep her husband at bay. Babes of whores who looked enough like the man. Possibly his own bastards even.

That's what we suspected Cedric was, at least, when we were boys and realized the truth of our parentage. But I knew my father. He was the luthier, Giuseppe. He told me once, when I asked about his wife, that she had died in childbirth and had eyes like the sun.

The way he had looked at me as he paused in fixing the duke's virginals that the duke never even looked at, let alone played, told me all I needed to know. That she was my mother, he my father, and that they loved me very much.

"Fine, what are your questions? Speak plainly," Ced asked.

"Why my ship?"

"You know why your ship," he said, emotionless.

Because he wanted Elowyn safe from Jessal and my ship was a secret. My routes a secret. To protect her. Because he wanted to use her. Because he loved her.

"Why did you not tell me who she was?" I asked.

"It wasn't important."

I scoffed, tonguing the inside of my cheek.

"And why not warn me of the sirens?"

"They do not concern you," Cedric answered, shaking his head like it was the most ridiculous thing I could ever ask.

"They held me and the king's fucking daughter captive for weeks. That was a little *concerning*, Cedric."

Elowyn stirred, and for a moment I hoped my yelling would wake her. That she would say something annoyingly clever in that languid voice, like, "Could you please keep it down, I'm trying to get my beauty rest."

But she didn't.

I kneeled beside her. Three days. Asleep for three whole days. What happened when she jumped into the ocean?

"You will marry her in a few months," Cedric said.

Shock surged through me as I meet his envious eyes.

"What?"

"The king has agreed. Well, if she awakes, I suppose," Cedric said callously as he watched me watch her. Like he didn't even care. Like he wasn't holding his breath, hoping the same as I, that she would awake.

"I have a wife." The words came out thick. For so long, I didn't have a wife. Or at least, so I thought.

"Catarina is dead," Cedric said.

"I know she's one of those monsters but by law—"

"No. Not because she is one of those creatures. Because of the things she has done. Arlo, they kill a person's soul."

The same things he'd done. Because I wasn't there to stop him from doing them. Because I left once before. Selfishly. And now I was back, at the king's daughter's bedside, in rapture as she slept.

But how could I not be? She'd been through so much and had somehow become a wonderful woman, not a petulant princess but a humble, kind soul who sat with my men like they were her equals.

She was the opposite of her greedy father, who'd spent the country's money like it was his own. On tournaments, gorging on food and drink at decadent feasts, bundled in fur and fabrics that could clothe hundreds, all while his people starved and froze.

I wanted to guard her kind heart. Take her away from it all. From Mother. From the king. Especially from Cedric, who looked at her in a way that made me want to cut him down where he stood. Was it truly love that made him look at her that way, or was his soul too twisted? Did he only love her for what she could offer him? How he could wield her?

He put her on my ship to ensure she made it to him.

So he could put her on the throne and be king himself.

I wanted to steal Elowyn away from every single prying eye. Because this world broke so many through suffering. Like Catarina. Like Cedric. Like me. But not Elowyn, not yet.

"Mother forced Catarina to do horrible things." Bitterness flooded my mouth as I rose. "Same as you."

"Now so will you both," he answered flatly, stowing away his emotions, although hate burned deep in his eyes, simmering his words. "Because you didn't take Elowyn away."

"Have you tried forcing her to do anything?" I jeered.

"Yes," he answered, lips pursing, allowing me to see that emotion. That rancor. Cedric tried forcing her to marry him and he failed. Now I would.

The smile on my face was absolutely joyless. "And how did that go, Ced?"

"Why did she jump into the ocean, *Arlo*? I need to know if we're going to figure out why she's in this state."

Back to his scheming and plotting.

"The sirens, she cared for them deeply. Thought they were her friends. She sees them as people. That siren king—Hylos, he's called—planned an attack. Elowyn has a good heart." I let that part settle. A good, uncorrupted heart. Not like Cedric's or Catarina's. Not poisoned. Not yet. "She wanted to stop him so that innocent people wouldn't get hurt."

Cedric's head ticked to the side, his tell that the machinations within his mind were turning.

"What now?" I asked, narrowing my eyes at him, but he buttoned up the look.

"Nothing," he answered.

I didn't believe him.

Behind us, wood creaked, drawing my attention to the open window, which revealed a tall, slender man crouched in the frame, perfectly balanced.

"Make your intent known." Cedric said swiftly, his hand falling to the hilt of his sword at his waist.

The man quirked his head as he looked between me and my brother, his features obscured by brown fabric that enveloped him from head to toe, leaving only a strip of stark-white skin and piercing, ice-blue eyes visible.

Fantastic. Could things not get any fucking worse?

"Do you know who she is?" Morvyn asked Cedric, that ridiculous, puckish hint in his voice.

"What do you want?" I demanded.

"Do you care for her too, then?" Morvyn's words were directed at Cedric, who watched him cautiously as the siren casually perched on the windowsill as if it were a bench, crossing his arms.

"Who the *fuck* are you?" Cedric spat in a voice I knew to be the last sound many men had heard just before their deaths.

"Her ridiculously handsome siren lover, with a far bigger cock than either of you."

I just knew that idiot had a shit-eating grin under his disguise.

He reached for the leather satchel slung across his chest. Cedric lunged forward, unsheathing his blade in an instant, standing protectively between Morvyn and Elowyn.

Maybe he did love her, because my brother was never one for rash movements. And this showing his hand was exactly that.

Morvyn cocked his head again, then continued. From the satchel, he withdrew a crimson silk bag.

"What is it?" I asked.

Morvyn's pale eyes flickered between us. "It fell off her head after the skirmish. Can you be trusted with her secret?"

Yes. Undoubtedly. But I remained silent, because the glint in my brother's eyes and the sword clutched in his hand told me his answer was the same as mine.

"I'll take that as a yes. From *both* of you," Morvyn remarked as he extended the bag, which Cedric snatched up. "Good luck with that, Tiny Toes. He's far more handsome than you."

Infuriating prick.

I rolled my eyes, then turned to Cedric as he held up the bag.

"What is it?" I asked Morvyn again, but he was gone. Vanished like a phantom.

"Where did he go?" Cedric questioned, looking around the room. "And why did he call you Tiny Toes?"

"He's one of the siren king's men ... sirens? And he's annoying as Infernum," I answered.

Cedric looked up at me, searching for answers, but I had none. I didn't know what Morvyn brought either, or why.

Cedric reached into the bag and pulled out a crown, a large blue gem at its center. I looked at it, then at Elowyn, still unmoving in slumber.

"Why would he want her to have this?" Cedric asked. He stepped to Elowyn's side.

"What are you doing?" I asked.

"There has to be a reason they would want her to have it. It must do something." Cedric hesitated, his hands hovering over her head. The weight of the crown seemed to pull at him, compelling him.

"Don't!" I yelled.

But Cedric placed the crown atop Elowyn's head.

She jolted upright, her eyes wide and filled with storm-blue light, flaring in bolts of fury. A humming sound filled the room, buzzing from her, then she let out a scream that seemed to echo not from her mouth, but from her soul.

Her gaze darted between Cedric and me. The light intensified as she cried out, "Gloriana! Gloriana! Gloriana!" Her voice multiplied, joining with hundreds of others in an eerie chorus of female voices. "GLORIANA IS KING!" she proclaimed, the words ringing with force.

The urge to recoil in fear or disgust surged within me, but I couldn't tear my eyes away. Her red curls were ablaze, swirling around her, and then from the crown down, every other lock was drenched in ocean blue. Her skin took on a sky blue tone too.

Elowyn extended her hands as the blue tint washed down the rest of her body like water pouring over her, down her limbs. Before my eyes, webbing connected her fingers. Her feet elongated, transforming into sleek, fin-like appendages that shimmered with blue scales, resembling the creatures that sank my ship, held us prisoner, murdered my men, and even took my wife.

Before me, Elowyn changed into the very beings I despised, that had taken everything from me. She changed into a siren.

"You shall pay for this!" the voices shouted in unison, the words roaring like a storm gathering strength.

A ewer beside her shattered, its contents suspended midair, swirling angrily. "You will pay! The queen will pay! The king will pay!" Her voice, joined by the chorus of others, echoed through the chamber. "You all will pay for this in blood."

I knew it was the truth.

A prophecy.

Elowyn Blackthorn would make the world atone for ever forgetting her, and now I knew exactly how.

Chapter 45

Elowyn

I awoke to firelight dancing on decorated crimson walls, the scent of leather, lavender, and clean linens embracing me. Through stained glass, Guardian's Watch slumbered in the early dawn amid a world thawing under sparse spring snow.

"Elowyn, you're awake." The pure relief that flooded me at the sound of that familiar voice brought instant tears to my eyes. Vega.

She rushed to my bedside, her cold hands on my cheeks, pulling me from the darkness I'd been lost in. Tears welled in both our eyes.

"You're awake, thank the Guardians, you are awake!"

Through an uncontainable smile I asked, "Where am I?"

"Safe, back at Highthorn Castle," she said, perched on my bed as I sat up. My head rushed and body complained with the movement.

"But ... how?"

"The queen." My blood ran cold. "Her ships found you at sea, with a captain. Apparently it was her son, Arlo Gyldford." Hearing his full name made my heart stumble. "He was the captain of your ship bound for Whiterok that crashed. Well, you know that, of course." I searched her face for any sign of jest. "He's here too. They rescued both of you from the deserted island you've been trapped on. The captain said you fell ill. Thank the Guardians above they found you in time." Her smile confirmed it was no joke. "As soon as you arrived, your father summoned me."

My father called for Vega? In what strange world had I awakened?

"Elowyn, we've all been so worried. Your father has been tormented."

"*My* father?" I questioned.

Vega smiled and nodded knowingly. "Yes, *your* father. He thought your disappearance punishment from the Guardians. His only child taken from him for sending her away in the manner he did. He now sees it as a miracle that you live."

The thought rushed through me then. I grabbed a lock of my hair. But it was solid red, as it had been my whole life. My hands were not webbed. I was no longer a siren. But how? "They found me on an island?"

"How many questions are you going to ask me, you silly little thing?" Vega said with mock annoyance and a sly smile as she rose from my bed and pulled a green wool dress from an armoire.

I rubbed at my hazy head. My body felt as though I had tumbled down a flight of stairs.

"*Yes*. A ship found you safe, with the captain. Who is very handsome, by the way." She playfully poked at me, loosening another smile from me the same way she had since childhood. "So let's get you dressed. Your father asked to see you the moment you awoke. I think you'll want to hear what he has to say."

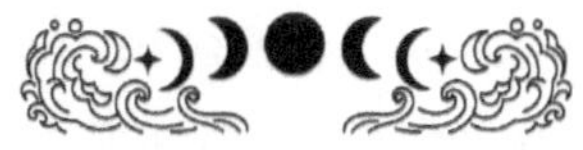

I stood before the same large oak doors of my father's private room, as rigid and foreboding as the day he banished me to Whiterok. But fear was absent. That anxious unrest writhing in my stomach was gone. There was nothing my father could do that would shatter me. Nothing anyone could do, besides kill me where I stood. But even then, I would be okay. I wasn't alone. I never was.

But how did I get here? And the battle, what happened with the battle? My mind probed at the gaps.

The guards on each side opened the doors in unison, the same way they had right before the king sentenced me to wed Cedric.

And I was prepared for him to do so again. Prepared to tell him no. I would not marry Cedric. Or any man. Unless I chose to.

"Elowyn." My father's voice broke as he raced toward me, engulfing me in a large hug. "Sweet, *sweet* daughter," he said as he rocked me like a small child. "I thought you were dead, oh my love, I am so sorry."

I didn't expect it. The hug. The words.

My father, King of Oakhaven, Eadric the Great, took my hands. Purple circles under his eyes above the ruddy cheeks. He looked as though he had aged years in the few weeks I was away.

"Forgive me. Please, forgive me," he pleaded as tears glossed his amber eyes. "I never should have sent you away."

Behind him prowled the queen, dressed in a gold gown that brought out the yellow of her eyes. She smiled that too-pleasant smile and tipped her head in my direction. A recognition. "You've missed much in your absence, Elowyn. But we're so happy to have you back," Queen Jessal said.

I needed to tell my father about the sirens, about the queen's plotting. I needed to warn him. I opened my mouth, but then Jessal said, "Wet nurse," summoning a woman with a bundle of luxurious black fabric swathing a cooing babe. She took the infant from the nurse, rocking it as she stepped nearer for me to see the little face adorned with faint red wisps of hair.

"Elowyn, meet Edward Blackthorn," she said, bobbing him up and down. "The heir of Oakhaven."

Father smiled at the pair as the queen basked in his gaze, the picture of motherhood.

"Jessal has urged me to right a wrong as well," Father said, pulling me under his arm in a sidelong embrace as we looked at the new little prince. "I am to reinstate your titles." Shock worked through me. "You are a true princess of Oakhaven, and it shall be known to all." My heart sprang into my throat, tasting metallic and sweet. "And you are here to stay in court with your family from now on."

It was everything I had ever wanted.

My father's love. A place at court. My titles. I stood dumbstruck.

"And the other news," The queen said, still rocking the babe in her arms. It felt wrong that a baby was in her arms at all. Her child or not. The things she had done to Arlo, to Calypstra. She was pure evil.

"Yes, the captain. As I'm sure you learned, he is of royal blood. He told us of your harrowing tale. Both the only survivors after the sinking of his ship, and then trapped on a small island alone for days." Father smiled, truly, kindly. Filled with love and adoration for me. The way I'd always wished my father would look at me. Almost losing me seemed to truly make him see I had worth. That I was, after all, his flesh and blood.

"The captain explained that through your hardship, you both have fallen in love."

I almost choked on the accusation, ready to deny it with every breath until my last, to protect him. "It seems the Guardians fated all this. A lesson for me that I'll surely never forget. Therefore, if you wish, *only* if you wish," the king clarified, "I will agree to your union of love."

He would allow me to marry Arlo, if I chose to. Astonishment rattled through me. "I am not sure that—" I started, but the queen cut me off.

"Eadric, at least let him come in and see her. He's been waiting for her to wake for days now."

Days?

"Who?" I questioned.

"Guards, let him in," Father ordered.

The doors slowly opened and there stood Arlo. Tall and strong and stable Arlo. Clean-shaven, head sheared, and well dressed. The way he looked the first day I met him. The most annoyingly handsome man I'd ever had the misfortune of being imprisoned on a ship by.

"*Elowyn*." His voice broke. He charged into the room and scooped me up into his arms, lifting me from my feet. I never thought I would be safe in his arms again. "I'm so sorry." He pressed a kiss onto the top of my head. "I'm *so* sorry," he repeated, lifting my feet from the ground. That warm, hard body that had held me in place below the sea.

"Okay, okay. Enough, Arlo," the queen scolded playfully. "After all, she is a princess."

"Oh, let them be," Father said. "They're in love."

Arlo released me and took my face into his calloused hands. "Elowyn, if you want to be married, then we shall be," he said softly. "Because I love you and I never wish to lose you again."

He wished to marry me? But what of Calypstra? What of his daughter?

"Give her time." Father said, clasping Arlo's shoulder. "She's tired, I'm sure."

Then my father took my hand in his large paw and gave it a squeeze, looking first to me, then to little Edward. His heir.

Vega and I walked arm in arm back to my room. There was a strange peace in Highthorn Castle. Spring was soaring to life within its tall walls, the scent of flowers on the crisp air stirring my soul as crickets sang their songs in the distance and the sun set on the somehow-perfect day.

"That captain, he's something, huh?" Vega snickered. "When can we look at wedding gowns? Also, how do you feel about ice swans?"

"Oh great, let me guess. You have the whole event planned?"

"Just need to send out the invitations," Vega teased, bumping into me as we walked leisurely through an ivy-covered archway that led up the stairs to the Onyx Chambers.

Father offered to move me to his wing of the castle over dinner, but I had insisted on staying where it was familiar. I also needed distance to comb through the whirlwind of thoughts in my mind.

Vega paused at the door of my bedchambers, waiting to go in.

I turned to her.

"Would you mind if I slept alone tonight?" I asked.

Her soft face twisted to hold back a frown.

"Of course," she answered. "You've spent so many nights without me, I'm sure there's no need for a governess to be close anymore. Or, I suppose, a governess at all." She offered me a weak smile.

I gathered her into a hug.

"There is always a need for a friend," I whispered into her ear.

She squeezed back.

"And you'll always have one in me." She pulled away, stroking a caring thumb over my cheek. "I'll be in the servants' quarters if you need me." She curtsied. "Good evening, *Princess* Elowyn."

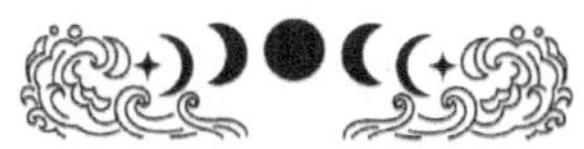

A fire kept the last bit of winter chill away in my bedchamber. Closing the door, a strange feeling washed over me. Somehow, as I slept, the world had gone from tipping seaward to righting itself. But what did it mean? And why did it feel wrong?

Then I spotted an ornate papier-mâché box waiting on my bed. Was it a gift from my father? Carefully, I removed the delicate lid and reached within to find a small red silk bag and a piece of paper. Un-cinching the bag, I pulled out a crown, its white-gold metal catching the warm glow from the hearth.

At its heart was an impressive blue sapphire.

That crown, it belonged to him. Hylos's words flew to me, and the battle slammed in unbearable swells of blood and carnage into my mind. Siren songs wailing as they sank dead into the sea. Into the body of their mother. Back to Nymphaea. Then, my ears rang with that awful, horrendous sound that turned my world to black. I threw the crown on the bed, ridding myself of the memories and the power it radiated.

With trembling hands, I reached for the note nestled at the bottom of the box, heart pounding in my chest.

I unfolded the parchment.

My eyes widened in disbelief at the single sentence, which I read again and again.

Long live the queen.

NOTE FROM THE AUTHOR

I can hardly believe we are here! I wrote *Song of the Forgotten* over countless late nights, weekends, lunch breaks, even frantically on my phone when inspiration struck. Along the way, I shared pieces of Elowyn's journey with the BookTok and Booksta communities, and their encouragement pushed me to keep going.

Thank you so much for reading my debut novel. By picking up this book, you've made my wildest dreams come true. If you enjoyed it, I'd love for you to leave a review and share your thoughts—it means the world to an indie author and helps us to continue creating.

I'm so lucky to share Elowyn's story with you, and I cannot wait for you to dive into the next book in the series. The sky is the limit ;)

XX,

SAL

ACKNOWLEDGEMENTS

Thank you to the following people who make up my own inner circle:

Mom: you inspired this work more than you could ever imagine. When I first learned of Elizabeth Tudor's life, I couldn't fathom growing up without a mother at my side, all because of you. At one point I came close to knowing that reality, and I'm grateful every single day we have together. You've always been my confidant, my friend, my cheerleader, and just a phone call away. Thank you for reading this book not once but twice, for telling me it needed "way more spice" (I'll make you proud in book two!), and most of all for being my mom.

Clay: Thank you for enduring endless hours of writing, for listening to my monologues about siren magic, and for convincing me to name Hylos anything but Hydros (you were right). Thank you for journeying through boundless fantasy worlds with me from the comfort of our couch. Thank you for embracing me exactly as I am, and for showing me what true love looks like. I love you from the sea to the sky and back, forever and always, my other half.

Rose: What sister-in-law reads, out loud, every single chapter of an aspiring author's book? Mine! Thank you for believing in me, for your enthusiasm, and for being the best friend and sister a girl could ask for.

Ashley: You opened the door to fantasy for me. I couldn't finish writing a book, despite always aspiring to be an author, then you shared a little-known fae novel and everything clicked. Thank you for listening to my wild ideas, encouraging me to keep writing, and talking books with me for hours on end.

Thank you to all the people I've cultivated beautiful friendships with through the years, where laughter rolls, stories flow, and you walk away feeling light as a feather despite a heart full to the brim. You inspired the unique friendships in this book.

Thank you to all those who liked my silly TikToks, pushed me to keep writing, and not to worry about what others thought.

And finally—thank you, dear reader. Without you, this dream would not be possible.

STAY CONNECTED

Thank you for reading! I'd love to share more stories, behind-the-scenes details, and updates with you.

WEBSITE
SARAALATIMER.COM

INSTAGRAM
@SARA.WRITES.READS

TIKTOK
@SALECRIVAN

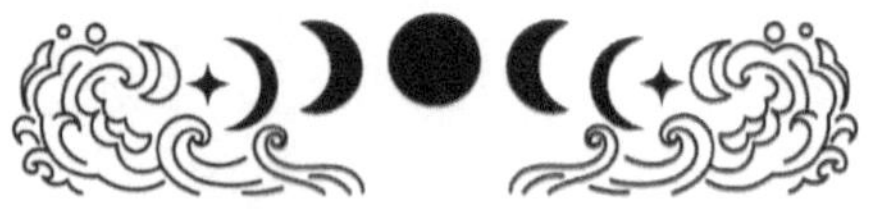